a few short notes on tropical butterflies

a few short notes on tropical butterflies

Stories

JOHN MURRAY

VIKING
an imprint of
PENGUIN BOOKS

VIKING

Published by the Penguin Group
Penguin Books Ltd, 80 Strand, London WC2R 0RL, England
Penguin Putnam Inc., 375 Hudson Street, New York, New York 10014, USA
Penguin Books Australia Ltd, 250 Camberwell Road,
Camberwell, Victoria 3124, Australia
Penguin Books Canada Ltd, 10 Alcorn Avenue, Toronto, Ontario, Canada M4V 3B2
Penguin Books India (P) Ltd, 11 Community Centre,
Panchsheel Park, New Delhi - 110 017, India
Penguin Books (NZ) Ltd, Cnr Rosedale and Airborne Roads,
Albany, Auckland, New Zealand
Penguin Books (South Africa) (Pty) Ltd, 24 Sturdee Avenue,
Rosebank 2196, South Africa

Penguin Books Ltd, Registered Offices: 80 Strand, London WC2R 0RL, England

www.penguin.com

First published in the United States of America by HarperCollins Publishers Inc. 2003
First published in Great Britain by Viking 2003
1

Printed in Great Britain by Clays Ltd, St Ives plc

A CIP catalogue record for this book is available from the British Library

Hardback ISBN 0-670-91347-2
Paperback ISBN 0-670-91348-0

For Valerie

ACKNOWLEDGMENTS

I would like to thank Connie Brothers, Ethan Canin, Paul Cirone, Molly Friedrich, Rae Galloway, John Kulka, Nandini Oomman, Wendy Osborne, Ron Waldman, and Gail Winston for helping to make this book possible.

CONTENTS

a few short notes on tropical butterflies

1

THE HILL STATION

On the first morning of the training in Bombay, just minutes before she collapsed, Elizabeth Dinakar stood in front of two hundred people in the conference hall, pointed up at the cholera bacteria magnified on the wall in front of her, and said "This is your enemy. " The room was long and stuffy, with peeling walls and rattling air conditioners. People coughed and shuffled papers. The bacteria were the size of cars. Elizabeth Dinakar was tall and thin with thick black eyebrows. Her hair was pulled away from her face and held in a bun at the back of her head. She wore a silk shirt and khaki skirt, flat-soled shoes, and no makeup.

She talked slowly and illustrated everything she said with graphs and photographs. "Every child has five to seven episodes of diarrhea a year," she said, "and that is a great ocean of diarrhea. People are floating on it." She spoke as if she were reading, had a familiarity with the organisms that cause infectious diarrhea that was precise and detailed. She saw a beauty in the microscopic world that she knew others could not understand. She took it personally. As she spoke she tapped a wooden pointer against the floor. Beads of perspiration ran down her back. At the other end of the room, two stainless-steel tea urns sat on tables covered with white

1

tablecloths. During breaks, the tea was poured into thick British Civil Service cups on saucers, and that morning she had looked over the rim of her teacup out into modern India, framed by the doors, noisy and glaring in the sun.

Blood drained from Elizabeth Dinakar's face and she felt light-headed. She had begun with a discussion of cholera, a disease with its origins along the Bay of Bengal that had ravaged white-limbed British soldiers in Calcutta. Cholera is one of India's great legacies to the world, she said, something that has struck fear into the hearts of men. She flashed a slide of a nineteenth-century lithograph depicting the specter of cholera hanging over New York City like the Grim Reaper. People at the back of the room laughed a little at this image, and Elizabeth said that it was astonishing how far they had come in just a few years; now cholera could be pinned down in the laboratory with culture, biochemistry, and antibodies. All the mystery has gone, she said, and as she spoke her voice seemed to become fainter to her, muffled, as if it were speaking from a distance. It is a conquest, she said, a conquest orchestrated by microbiologists working systematically, using solid bench science. She wondered if she sounded melodramatic, although she believed that it *was* dramatic; the triumph over cholera represented a triumph of the scientific method over chaos.

She stopped talking and let the pointer slip from her fingers. She turned her back to the audience. It crossed her mind that she was going to die. On the wall above her was a large Bakelite clock with a round white face and huge hands that had the appearance of sharpened harpoons. She stared up at the clock. As she lost consciousness, she saw herself as a little girl watching her father shoveling snow. She felt ice crystals on her cheeks, smelled cigarette smoke, and for an instant heard her father speaking to her. Then she fell to the floor.

A private American foundation was paying Elizabeth Dinakar to train local doctors in the principles of microbiology. She was forty years old. She had made a modest name for herself in the infectious diarrheas, studying enteric organisms that ravaged the gut. At the Centers for Disease Control and Prevention, she had taken charge of the enteric laboratory and now ran it as an international reference center. On her fortieth birthday she wrote "Your shit is my bread and butter" in large letters on a piece of computer paper and stuck it to her door. Her birthday made her feel unaccountably optimistic — as if she were weightless. Nothing seemed solid. Others saw her as serious and rational, she knew. Forty years old and unmarried. Cold. She felt so different from the way she appeared that it was inexplicable to her.

A photograph of the *Eschericia coli*, many times life size, grainy and oval shaped, transmitted in apple cider from New England and the cause of many hundreds of cases of bloody diarrhea, sat above her desk in a thin wooden frame. She did detailed work alone at cool laboratory benches. The specimens came to her from all over the world, although before this trip to Bombay, she had never been to Asia or Africa. When she saw the cholera *Vibrio*, she imagined herself on the island of Celebes in Indonesia, the origin of the seventh pandemic, floating on a colorful reef, smelling sea salt and green bananas. Her thesis, on the *Shigella* strains causing dysentery in Africa, made her think of salty goat butter in tiny cups of acrid Ethiopian coffee, the bottomless waters of Lakes Victoria and Tanganyika, humming with Nile perch, and tall lean men walking in low scrub with hardwood staves.

She opened her eyes and for a few seconds did not know where she was. A group of men from the front row had her by the shoulders and ankles and were carrying her out of the conference hall. The men wore cotton suits and monogrammed ties, smelled like fruity aftershave, and were all talking at once. They had shiny faces. They carried her outside and laid her on a wooden bench under a row of mango trees. It was cooler under the trees and dappled sunlight came through the leaves. She blinked and tried to sit up, but they held her by the shoulders.

Raj Singh, who worked for the NGO in Bombay that was organizing the training, knelt on the ground beside her and put two fingers on her wrist. He was a small man with fat cheeks who wore spectacles that made his eyes swim like fish in a tank. She saw her own face reflected in the lenses of his spectacles.

"Thank goodness. Thank goodness," he said. "Her heart, it is beating quite vigorously. This is surely a good thing." Beads of perspiration clung to his forehead. He had a thin black mustache running horizontally across his top lip.

"I'm sorry," Elizabeth whispered.

"Please. It is I who should apologize. It is too hot." Someone handed him a wet handkerchief and he pressed it to her forehead. Drops of cold water ran into her ears and down onto her neck.

"This never happens to me," Elizabeth said. "I don't get sick."

"Your coloring is getting better. I am thinking that you fainted."

"We should go back inside," Elizabeth said.

"Please." Raj Singh wiped his forehead with the back of his hand. "People are having tea break. There is no urgency."

"I'm wasting time," she said.

"Please. This is no time for heroics. Look up at the mangos and think pleasant thoughts. Please."

The men stood under the trees with their hands behind their backs like benevolent uncles, periodically bending over to look at her face. Elizabeth felt awkward and self-conscious. She would rather have been alone under the trees. She did not think herself worthy of the attention, was already feeling guilty, planning what she would have to do to catch up in the conference hall.

One of the conference attendees came outside to see her. He was carrying a Samsonite attaché case. He put the case on the ground, snapped it open, and pulled a stethoscope into the air, like a conjurer. The tubing of the stethoscope was black and shiny. He listened carefully to her heart and neck, and then pulled a blood-pressure cuff from the attaché case with a flourish and wrapped it around her arm. He had fleshy hands. His breath smelled like tea and there were tiny splashes of milk on the front of his shirt. When he had taken her blood pressure lying down, he got her to sit up and then took it again. He said, "Splendid."

"She will live I think," Raj Singh said quietly.

"She will outlive us all," the doctor said. "She has the blood pressure of a child. She is in super health."

"This is very good news," Raj Singh said.

"Common syncope, I think," the doctor said, putting his instruments back into his case. "Common syncope. In short, you fainted, my dear lady, you fainted."

"I'm sorry for the trouble," Elizabeth said.

"If this is trouble, then I welcome it," the doctor said. "I am not being troubled. Now cholera, for example, now that is trouble."

"Magnificent news," Raj Singh said.

She got to her feet carefully and took a deep breath of air that tasted like dust and rubber. She was taller than the men under the trees and smiled as she stood in front of them. "I'm all right," she said to Raj Singh and walked away by herself. Cool air blew under the trees and felt like water on her forehead. She felt flushed and awkward in the heat.

The mango trees stood on the edge of a gravel car park and were heavy with bulbous green fruit. Gusts of wind blew clouds of white dust into the air. Beyond the car park was a narrow road, a strip of cracked gray bitumen, crowded with people and animals. She walked out into the sun and across the car park, placing her hands flat on the hot metal roofs of the parked cars as she walked between them. On the side of the road, a team of men and women were working. The women carried baskets filled with hot tar on their heads and upturned them into potholes, while the men smoothed and filled the holes with shovels and rakes. The soles of the women's feet were black with the tar. Children sat on the side of the road, playing in piles of sand and stones, lobbing fistfuls of warm tar onto passing cars.

It made her feel foreign. Completely foreign, too, in a profound way that she did not quite understand. She had always imagined that she could be Indian if she wanted to. She looked Indian. Her parents had grown up in Bombay and immigrated to the States before she was born. Sitting in a living room in New Jersey, she learned about India from the tropical disease textbooks of her father. The India she had imagined from afar was a place of cholera, dysentery, typhoid fever, and old-fashioned bubonic plague. People dying of tuberculosis of the lung, spine, and brain. When she was a girl, she sat with the books flung around her, looking into photographic plates of ulcers and pathology specimens, and color-coded maps of the cholera belt. Now she was in Bombay for the first time. She had not expected the vividness of it all, the colors, the calamitous smells of decay and animals. She wondered if there was any part of her at all that could really be Indian.

She blinked in the bright light and walked along the road. Two young girls, no more than five years old, with tarry knees, ran toward her clutching straw baskets filled with packets of glucose biscuits, blackened bananas, and warm bottles of orange fizzy drink. Elizabeth bought biscuits and orange drink and watched the children move among other people on the road. A group of men got off a bus and gathered around the two girls. They reached into the baskets and took what they wanted and then dropped coins into the baskets. The girls stood with dusty legs and thin knees, looking at Elizabeth. After a few minutes, they ran back and forth collecting the empty bottles and when they got to her, they took her bottle and put out their hands for money. She got down on her haunches and looked at their hands, so adult and finely formed, and yet so small, and dropped some change into the palms. When they turned and ran away, she knew that they would not remember her.

Plain. That was how her own mother had described her. Too tall and too thin, with a chest that was too flat and a nose that was too large to be considered noble. In her bright and unforgiving passport photograph, taken five years earlier, she looked sad and beaten. Slightly damp. Resigned to her fate. She tried to hide when she was growing up, grew her hair into long, waving tresses and wore baggy clothes and played boys' games. She broke two fingers on her right hand playing baseball when she was twelve years old. When her father left, she thought he had left because of her. Indian girls were supposed to be exotic and beautiful. She thought that she deserved to have her father leave. When he walked out, her mother was so shocked, so unbelieving, that they did not talk about his absence for weeks. Just let it hang there above them like a great gaping hole in the roof. Three months later, her mother got a tatty letter from Toronto that at least gave her something to get angry about. He had left with a computer programmer, barely older than Elizabeth herself, and was living in a studio apartment with four cats and rented furniture. "Now at last I am free," her mother said, sobbing into her hands at the kitchen table while Elizabeth did homework and chewed the end of a 2B pencil.

She lived alone outside the beltway in Atlanta in a new California-style house on two acres of woodland. Deer grazed on her lawn and shed hard red ticks loaded with Lyme disease onto the leaves of garden shrubs. She had remodeled the house and put in extra windows and skylights, filling the wooden rooms with light. Her living room was her workroom and in the center she had placed an enormous desk, her father's desk, the only remnant of the man who she had learned to forget. On the desk, she arranged her journals, textbooks, articles to be written, correspondence, and other day-to-day papers in neat piles next to a fax machine and a laptop computer. Through the window was a bird feeder and on the desk she put fresh flowers every day, in a clear glass jar. These flowers, bought from the De Kalb farmers' market, were her only luxury. By the time she got them home, the flowers would already be sagging in the heat, limp fistfuls of color that she thrust immediately into water.

Raj Singh appeared alongside her in the sun with a cup of tea on a saucer. He had carried it across the car park without spilling a drop. Four flat tan-colored biscuits were fanned out around the saucer, like the petals of a giant tropical flower.

"You must get your strength up," he said. "Perhaps you should come out of the sun."

She took the tea and held it in front of her. "I'm feeling better," she said.

"It is excellent that you have come."

"I'm glad I came."

"Infectious disease is very popular here," he said. "Very close to people's hearts. People are very keen to come and hear you speak. You are an authority."

"I hope it is useful."

"It is more than useful. It is inspiring. People like it when they see an Indian who has made it big in America."

"I was born there."

"But really, you are Indian at heart. That is how I see it."

Raj Singh straightened his spectacles and took the cup and saucer from her. He took her elbow with his other hand and steered her away from the road and back toward the trees and the conference hall. He wore a white shirt and had a comb in his top pocket. He had met her at the airport the day before in his white Ambassador. The inside of his car was spotless and smelled of pineapples. He sprayed it every night, he told her, with a pump-action can of insect repellent to kill mosquitoes and other creatures with wings.

She finished the first day of training an hour late, but managed to make up for the time she had lost. Raj Singh was delighted. He considered the first day to have been a success and took her out to the Gate of India late in the afternoon. But she did not feel as if she had recovered. She felt weak and breathless in the heat, too tall in the milling crowds and embarrassed when stared at. There were too many people. She was so dizzy that she reached out and leaned on his shoulder. He ushered her into a tea shop and away from the crowds and bought her a Coke and four oily samosas on a thin plastic plate. "When you are not used to it, it is too much," he said with a flourish of his fat hands, and she nodded and tried to smile.

On the flight from New York, she had learned the most important street names of Bombay by heart and marked her guidebook with long streaks of yellow highlighter pen. It took a lot of effort to keep André out of her mind, and she wanted desperately to forget him. When she thought of him, she could not see him as a whole. She remembered only a few details: his fingernails, the smell of coffee on his breath, the angle of his chin.

She had met André the previous summer. He was from Argentina and had come to Atlanta for a year to continue his work on Chagas disease, an infection transmitted in the feces of the *Reduviidae* family of cone-nosed beetles. He was put in a free laboratory down the end of her corridor to work on developing his serologic tests and she saw him there in the early mornings before anyone else arrived. He was distracted by his work, looked up at her but did not see her. On one wall he had a large calendar, and every morning he crossed off the day with a large red stroke. He missed his family. They sent him a fat letter, smothered with blue-and-green Argentinean stamps, every week. He read them slowly and carefully with a cup of coffee and wrote letters back with a fountain pen.

His eyebrows met in the middle and he had a fine white scar running along his top lip. He liked red meat and coffee. She surprised herself when she asked him to a meal at a Caribbean restaurant and barely noticed that she had drunk four bottles of cold lager with the food. She was taller than him by an inch, and it was she who had fallen into him in the alley between the restaurant and the car, pushing her fingers up under his shirt as they stood there in orange streetlight. She surprised herself and didn't care as they stood in the street and she recognized that there were parts of herself that she did not want to understand. She had hidden impulses. On Sunday afternoons, she smoked a pack of cigarettes, sometimes more, sitting in her own garden facing the forest, the world still and quiet apart from the flick of the lighter and the warm pillows of smoke reaching back into her lungs, as deep as she could drag them, and the hard, dry rattle of the cicadas in the long grass.

André had warm olive skin and a wedding ring. When she thought of him, she thought of the pampas, a gold-and-brown ocean of grass teeming with brucellosis, yellow fever, and scrub typhus. She looked at the smooth skin of his chest at night, swept down the length of it with her open palm, and thought of the *Aedes aegypti* mosquito, its gizzard loaded with flavovirus, its tiny sharp proboscis sliding through that soft olive skin and into his bloodstream. When she had him to herself in her bedroom, with the sound of trees in the wind outside, he felt fragile. At risk. A precious and unique thing.

She took André home without his children or his wife, without her calm and orderly scientist's mind, and without consequences. When he laughed he giggled, like a girl, a surprising high-pitched laugh that shook him from the waist. He had thick square hands that held small everyday objects with such delicacy and care that she found herself staring at them when he was there, watching him lift a fork or a book as if it were something to be treasured.

His family was all in Buenos Aires, in a three-story apartment in Palermo Viejo. The apartment building had the cast-iron railings, balconies, and window pots of a building you might find in Paris, and when he was home he ate breakfasts of empanadas and real butter croissants in smoky cafes heavy with the aroma of strong coffee. He showed her photographs of his life at home. She saw his children, too, pale faced, with snub noses and blond hair, in perfect navy blue school uniforms and caps. She saw a picture of his laboratory, where he stood with crossed arms in front of a microscope, a pair of bifocals hanging from his neck by a gold chain.

Newspapers were the reason she had given him for not letting him stay with her at night. She had her rituals. She got up every morning and read the *New York Times* and the *Atlanta Journal Constitution*, cover to cover, with a pot of coffee and a bowl of raisin bran. In the morning she read mail, made lists, and read the newspapers, and she did it alone, staring out at birds landing on the wooden tray of the bird feeder. She needed that time, she told him, needed it like other people needed exercise.

On a Sunday evening in the summer, she sat with him on her porch and drank beer. The forest was loud and it was warm in the dark.

"I can't tell anyone about you," she said.

"You are ashamed of what we are doing," he said.

"I'm not ashamed."

"But you cannot tell other people."

"You're married. And you're going home."

"But that is why you like me. Because I am temporary. You are terrified of anything that could be permanent with a man. Terrified. You think it is weak to want to be with anyone."

"I don't think that."

"You do think that. I know you better than you think. Your work and your routines, they are tricks. You are the one who doesn't want to get involved. You are terrified of what will happen to you."

André wanted to be the center of attention when he was there. He thought that he was doing her a favor, she knew, expected gratitude and a nice breakfast. When she imagined him in the mornings, with his heavy white arms and gray stubble, she had a sense that she had made a mistake, and could not let him stay with her at night. She knew that he did not love her. He had a family. In bed, she felt his wedding ring against her skin and looked up at the ceiling and resolved that she would make him leave as soon as it was over. He would bump into furniture in the dark as he let himself out. Then she would wash herself clean and push open the window and sleep alone with the sounds of the forest filling her room.

There was cholera in the slums of Bombay when she arrived. On the second day of the training, she told Raj Singh that she wanted to visit the slums and see the epidemic for herself. Her parents were Indian, she told him, and she wanted to understand how people lived. She needed observations, real data, to help her understand. The density and chaos, the crippled people, the sheer desperation of the streets were things her parents had never talked about. Her parents remembered houses with trees and servants. They had gone to English schools where they read Walter Scott and Conrad, heard bagpipes played at morning assembly, and stared up at the names of prefects recorded in gold lettering on oak boards in the school chapel.

She had never seen a case of cholera. In the laboratory at home, she had admired the flat yellow colonies of the bacteria growing on culture plates. They came out of the heavy steel incubators smelling warm and yeasty, like bread. She had a clear understanding of how the cholera *Vibrio* elaborated a potent enterotoxin that made the cells lining the small intestine pump salt and water into the gut. She knew that people with the infection watched a river of salt run out of their bodies like dirty bathwater, until they died of shock. But she had never seen a person with the disease. In her hotel room, she unpacked her books and papers first and arranged them in neat piles on the bed. She ran her fingers over her hard copies of *Hunter's Tropical Medicine and Emerging Infectious*

Disease, the *Atlas of Human Parisitology*, and *The Manual of Clinical Microbiology*. When she looked out of her window and out across the chaotic skyline of Bombay, shrouded in tan-brown smoke, half hidden in the gloom, it was as murky as her own visions of the country where her parents had been born.

Elizabeth met Raj Singh under the mango trees at the end of the second day. His NGO was working in the Jogeshwari slums, and he took her there in his Ambassador. "I am taking you to see my colleague. He is a doctor there. He is working very hard indeed," he said and mopped his face with a piece of lined paper, pulled from the notebook he was carrying. They drove through streets heavy with the hard metallic smell of car exhaust. Thin men in white shirts stared in at her and children hammered on the windows with brown knuckles. She wanted to see the real India and sat still on the slippery red vinyl seat with both hands pressed between her knees.

They walked the last half mile through narrow alleys lined by ramshackle market *chawls*. The alleys were dark and moist and smelled of sewage and wood smoke. In a market square, they came to a large tent that had been erected on some open ground. The tent was made from bamboo poles, lashed together with rope, and had a loose hessian roof that bulged outward in gusts of wind. The sides of the tent were open and people in the market were staring at the cots inside. At one end, a long line of people were waiting to be seen by a nurse who was standing at a small wooden school desk. The air around the tent smelled of disinfectant.

"This is one of our treatment centers," Raj Singh said. "It is the only way we can handle the numbers that are coming. You see. There are not enough clinics and no hospitals for the people here. The only way is to set up these impromptu centers. They have to be large enough to handle the volume. In slums like this, you have a lot of transmission and large numbers of people getting sick."

The nurse stood at the desk with her arms crossed and looked at Elizabeth with desperate eyes. She wore a white uniform and a white cap. The front of the uniform was stained brown and the sleeves were blue with streaks of pen ink. A tall man with a thin neck and prominent Adam's apple came out from under the tent wearing a long white coat buttoned up the front despite the heat. Ajit Koomar shook Elizabeth's hand. He pushed a thick lock of very black hair away from his face and then put both hands deep into the pockets of his white coat.

"Please wait for a few minutes and I will be finished here. We are understaffed. There are many cases of cholera. I am terribly sorry you had to see this."

He took a red-felt marker pen from the desk and walked, with long, loping strides, down the line of people waiting to be seen. Raj Singh asked her if she would like to sit down under the tent, but she said no and they followed Ajit Koomar. The clothes of the people waiting by the tent were wet with diarrhea because they did not want to leave the line. The sickest had straw-colored liquid running from them continuously, down their legs, onto their feet. They held wads of cloth up against their buttocks, and cast wide and surprised eyes at Elizabeth as she walked past. The women looked away with embarrassment. Many were on stretchers and Ajit Koomar stooped down and examined the eyes and skin of these cases carefully. In a few minutes, he saw forty people. On the backs of their hands, he marked their treatment classification with the red pen.

"We use the World Health Organization system here, you see," he said over his shoulder. "Identify the degree of dehydration, classify, and treat. Mild and moderate dehydration gets oral fluids only — oral rehydration solution. Severe dehydration gets IV Ringer's lactate right away. The severe and the moderate get into the tent. The mild get instructions on what to do at home and then go back home. Everyone gets educated on how to prevent the transmission of cholera, you see. This is what we can do."

The market swirled around them. People ran past staring at Ajit Koomar as he examined the cholera cases in the street. Elizabeth sweated in the late afternoon heat. The sun was low over the corrugated iron roofs, reflecting off the metal and glinting into her eyes. Her hands hung limp by her sides and her feet were swollen and heavy in her shoes. She felt out of place, useless, and was still thinking about the look of desperation she had seen on the face of the nurse at the desk. Crows sat in a line on the top of the treatment tent, deep black even in full daylight, watching the ground with steady eyes.

Near the back of the line, a young woman in a green sari lay with closed eyes and sharp cheekbones. Her eyes were sunken and she breathed with shallow breaths through white, cracked lips. Her husband, wearing a blue shirt and a knitted brown-and-white-striped woolen vest, sat next to her. He held a piece of moist cloth in one hand and a banana in the other.

"This one is severely dehydrated," Ajit Koomar said. "She will need an IV line straight away. Help me please."

He bent down and clasped the woman around the ankles and Elizabeth took hold of her shoulders before Raj Singh could stop her. The shoulder bones of the woman were sharp and angular and Elizabeth felt the thin bony lattice of her ribs. She was as light as a bird. There were two fine gold earrings in her ears and her skin was the color of beaten egg yolks in a white bowl.

"She was all right this morning," her husband said. "She was cooking this morning. I saw her with my own eyes and now I do not know what has happened."

The woman was unconscious. The back of her sari was wet with diarrhea and Elizabeth's hands were now covered in it. She smelled sour apples and damp wool. The back of the woman's sari flapped down onto Elizabeth's skirt and the saturated cloth soaked through onto her legs as she walked. They carried her between them, low to the ground, and stumbled into the tent. Some of the people ahead in the line shouted at them as they passed, but Ajit Koomar ignored them.

Most of the cots inside the tent were occupied. Each patient was allowed one family member to look after them. A single open drain with a steel grill ran along the edge of the tent, and all the waste was thrown into it. Dogs milled at the edge of the drain with their noses in the air. The ground by the drain was thick with a mat of flies. A large steel garbage hopper was being used for the solid waste and there was a line of crows on the side of this container. The smell was palpable. "We have an issue with waste disposal, you see," Ajit Koomar said as they moved into the tent. "Please excuse the mess."

Inside the tent, it was calm and cooler. A thin brown light filtered through the hessian above them. There was a military sense of order and regimentation. Family members sat on stools by each cot with cups and spoons and plastic bottles of liquid. They gave sips of fluid and emptied the slosh buckets of diarrhea. People were grateful to have made it into the tent, and there was a sense of duty there, an eagerness to follow instructions. An old man with leathery skin and a long white beard looked up at Elizabeth as they walked under the tent and nodded to her, and she nodded back, trying to look as if she knew what she was doing.

They found an empty cot in the center of the tent. The cot was covered by a sheet of blue plastic and had a hole cut in the middle. They placed her over the hole so that the diarrhea could run directly out into a bucket positioned underneath. They squared her on the cot and Ajit Koomar asked one of the tent staff for an intravenous needle and giving set. It took him ten minutes to find a vein in her arm with the IV needle and to set up the line. He ran the first liter into her quickly and wrote instructions for the next three liters on a single piece of paper on a clipboard at the head of the cot. The IV bag was hung from a hook that had been screwed into one of the bamboo tent supports above their heads.

Her husband sat on the edge of the cot, clutching the banana and wiping his head with the strip of damp torn cloth. "Her name is Sangeeta," he said to Ajit Koomar. "She is my wife. She is a young woman and very healthy. Of course she will be fine. Of course she will."

But Ajit Koomar was no longer listening and walked away. Elizabeth bent down to the young man and clasped him by the shoulder. "She will be all right," she said. "You stay here with her. She will be all right." She could see that the man was terrified. Raj Singh took her by the elbow and led her back through the maze of cholera cots to the edge of the tent. As they walked away, the young man stood up and called after them, "I am accountant. Do you understand? I am accountant. I have means. I am not a poor man." He had a thin mustache and prominent ears and long thick eyelashes. The other people in the tent turned to look at him and he sat down quickly, putting his hands on his knees and watching his wife on the cot in front of him. "Now that you have seen it," Raj Singh whispered to her, "you can understand what it is like. You do not need to see it again. It is all most regrettable."

She arranged for the taxi to collect her every day after the training. She waited under the mango trees. Big green mangos fell to the ground around her while she waited, and in the warm air under the trees small flying insects attracted to the ripe fruit settled on her eyelids and arms. The taxi took her back to the cholera tent in the Jogeshwari slums.

On the day after her first visit, she arrived at the treatment tent a little after five o'clock. She wiped the sweat from her face with her fingers. Ajit Koomar was surprised to see her. When he smiled, his front teeth were crooked and stained red. The two nurses in the tent looked at her suspiciously and brought her a chair and a glass of hot sweet tea, boiled with milk on a gas ring burner on the floor. They stopped working and gathered around her, and she had to insist that she was all right, and that they should leave her alone. She felt as if she was being watched, and when she walked near the drain she tried not to gag. The dense heat, the vomiting and diarrhea, and the smells of cooking food drifting in from the market made her light-headed and dizzy. She told Ajit Koomar she wanted to see the woman they had saved, and he told her that she was not saved yet and led her through the tent.

Sangeeta, still wearing the green sari, lay flat on the cot with her eyes open. Elizabeth could see that she was very ill. Her skin had a yellow tint and she smelled of ammonia and something sweet and warm. The skin on her face was dry and pale and her eyes were sunken. Her hair, long and black with streaks of silver at the temples, was spread out beside her on the pillow. The IV tube had been taped to her forearm and ran upward to the bag of fluid near the ceiling. She looked up at Elizabeth and moved only her eyes, blinking slowly in the light. She did not acknowledge her but looked straight up into her face. On the narrow cot, she looked small and wasted and her toes were long, with brilliant pink toenails. Elizabeth took one of Sangeeta's hands and held it between her palms. The hand was cold and dry and she rubbed it carefully to try and warm it up.

A young boy, seven or eight years old, was sitting on a low stool at the head of the bed holding a green plastic cup in one hand and a white plastic spoon in the other. The boy had two fine silver bracelets on one wrist and was wearing a stained floral smock over a pair of white trousers. His eyes were almond shaped and wide and his hair was cropped to a short black stubble. He offered his mother sips of fluid with the spoon, held it up to her lips and gently tipped it into her mouth. His hands and wrists were tiny and delicate. When he took his hands away, he held them out in front of him, and looked down, away from Elizabeth, toward the floor.

"He is this lady's son," Ajit Koomar said. "Her husband is working and the young boy will be sitting here all day and all night if it is necessary. It is the son's duty, you see."

"Where is the rest of the family?" Elizabeth Dinakar asked.

"None of them have come, you see. She is very unwell. Her son will stay."

"But he is only a baby."

"He is the son."

The boy picked up the bucket under his mother and staggered over to the side of the tent to empty it into the sump. When he turned and came back with the rinsed bucket, his clothes were splashed with brown liquid. His eyes were bright blue. He replaced the bucket under the cot, sat down on the stool, and wiped his mother's face with a damp towel hanging on a pole.

Elizabeth wanted to say something but there was nothing she could say. She stood up and walked out into the dust and the people on the street. In the taxi, she sat back in the seat and let the tears run down her cheeks and into her lap, wondering when she had last cried, and where the tears had come from.

Her mother had given up on India. She blamed India for her husband and for her own sense of failure when he left her. The two of them moved into a small apartment with thin walls. She made Elizabeth American food and watched television in the evenings, crying desperately over the square-jawed men and doe-eyed women she saw embracing on hospital dramas and movies of the week. She saw life as a struggle, never learned to drive, and went everywhere by bus. Elizabeth thought she was beautiful. She had black eyes and a high forehead framed by a cascade of inky hair.

On weekends, her mother went to the houses of other expatriate Indians, told them that her husband was dead, and ate parathas and dhal. She came home smelling of cardamom and mustard oil. On these days, she dressed up in the silk saris that she kept pressed and stacked in the linen cupboard, sprinkled liberally with camphor and mothballs. When she went out in her saris, she wore pink sneakers on the bus, and carried thin leather sandals in her handbag that she would put on in the street to walk the last block to her friends' houses. She wanted to make Elizabeth forget her Indian heritage and her father, bought her a full set of encyclopedias, the collected works of Charles Dickens, the poems of Robert Frost. Educate or perish, she said. They read the dictionary together every evening, a giant heavy Webster's, and she made Elizabeth memorize three words a night. *Commingle, comminute, commisce. Commiserate, commisas, commissary.* "I will not have you spread-eagled between two continents," she told her. "You are here now. Accept it. Forget that other place."

Elizabeth read her father's textbooks to learn about India, studied green-and-orange maps, and rolled rich and unlikely place names off her tongue. India became impossible and exotic to her; the only constant thing in her life; something about which there was no doubt. Her father had disappeared. Her mother cut off all contact with him. When she was young, she sat in her room and wrote her father letters on pink notepaper, mailing them on the way to school, but she never received a reply. From his old textbooks, she understood that everything that seemed inexplicable could have an explanation. There was a precision and symmetry to the microscopic world that made her immerse herself in it. She was convinced that the bacteria that produced epidemics of diarrhea quickly and efficiently, the *Shigella* species, *Salmonella typhi*, *E.coli*, and *Vibrio cholerae* o1 El Tor, were perfect. Infinitely adaptable.

Her mother had been to university in India and had read Latin and French. She was an educated woman but had never worked. After her husband left, she got a job as a secretary at a firm that made bicycle parts, and worked six days a week. "Putting bread on the table," she said, "is more important than having a fulfilling life."

One September afternoon when she was fourteen years old, Elizabeth was sent home from school early with a cold. She walked home by herself carrying a green canvas backpack, kicking through clusters of wet brown leaves. The front door of the apartment was unlocked. Her mother was naked on the couch, straddling an Indian man with his trousers around his ankles. The man was wearing a white shirt and a tie, and a pair of polished black leather shoes. Her mother was sitting up high on the man, her breasts heavy and pendulous. Her eyes were shut. One of the man's hands was on her neck. The back of his hand was hairy and he was wearing a bright gold wristwatch. Elizabeth stood by the door and looked at her mother's wide hips and heavy thighs. She had never seen her mother naked. A thin line of black hair ran between her belly button and her groin. Her hair was hanging over her eyes and she was concentrating hard. Elizabeth stood in baggy jeans and a pink down jacket with the backpack hanging damp and heavy from her shoulders.

She knew what her mother was doing but could not understand why. She was more interested in her mother's naked body than the man lying underneath her. When the man noticed Elizabeth a few moments later, he said, "Bloody hell," and sat up straight on the couch with her mother in his lap. Her mother looked over at her and did not say anything. Elizabeth could see that she was angry, angry with herself, what she was doing, the man next to her. This is what could happen to you if you are not careful, her mother's face said, and Elizabeth walked out through the door, into a cool breeze that blew leaves along wet gray streets. She told her teacher that she felt better, sat through her last class with a tissue in her hand, wrote her name on the desk with a red marker pen, kept going over the letters of her name until she was left with a heavy red smudge.

.   .   .

Every day of the first week of the training, she woke up in the hotel feeling sick and tired. On the third day, she found a chemist shop on the ground floor of an office building, a bright room with fluorescent lights and walls stacked with multicolored boxes, smelling of sharp chemicals and perfume. She bought a box of pregnancy test kits with American dollars. She could not find the kits on the shelves and had to ask for them. The old chemist at the counter, a tall man with a large bald head and hairy ears, pulled his white coat tightly around his chest and looked at her suspiciously. She blushed as she handed over the money, pushed the box down into her shoulder bag without looking at him. No wedding ring, she thought. Loose woman.

Every afternoon she waited under the mango trees and went back to visit the sick woman and her son in the tent. She took the boy small gifts that she could find around the hotel — a box of colored pencils, gaudy stuffed elephants and tigers, a teak box carved with scenes of farmers and fishermen, small bottles of perfume, Cadbury chocolate bars wrapped in silver foil. Kneeling down by the cot she held out the gifts, but the boy would never look at her, always at the floor, and Elizabeth put them down on his mother's body, balanced there carefully in her lap, tucked into the folds of her sari. Sangeeta looked up from the cot with still eyes and said nothing. She never moved, just looked with her eyes, and Elizabeth felt judged under the flapping brown hessian roof, kneeling there on the beaten-earth floor. What did she expect? What did she want from this small woman and her quiet son in that tent? It was not clear what she could do to help.

She washed her hands furiously at a metal spigot with a thin sliver of white soap. Her hands looked smooth and soft in the pale brown light under the tent. She rubbed them over each other for a long time before rinsing them off in the trickle of clear water from the metal pipe. No amount of washing made them feel clean. Ajit Koomar walked with her slowly and showed her the food vendors on the street, and the public pump and how people stored and transported their water, and how they transmitted cholera. He showed her the tiny dark houses where people lived and she watched as sick people were carried outside. He told her about the public education they were doing using the mullahs at the mosques. She barely heard what he said. There were so many people, so many children, that she switched off. She saw a toughness and an openness in the faces of the people in the market that overwhelmed her.

On the fourth day, Sangeeta and her son had gone and no one told her. She walked to the cot and found it empty. The nurses kept their distance and the patients lying under the tent stared at her. She walked back to the side of the tent and saw the boy, Sangeeta's son, by the door. He was standing absolutely still with one thin arm resting up on the wooden tent support. As Elizabeth approached, he picked up a plastic bag on the ground behind him. He held up the bag. Elizabeth took it and crouched in front of the boy, who was staring at her for the first time. He stood there for a moment, his eyes as blue as sky, his eyebrows light and downy, and looked up into Elizabeth's face without smiling. And then he ran off, out into the market on his thin legs, out into the people and the dusty afternoon.

Ajit Koomar was outside in the sun.

"She died last night," he said. "It was very sudden in the night. Her kidneys failed. The son has gone back to his family."

"I'm sorry," Elizabeth said.

"We are all sorry."

Ajit Koomar took her to the carpenters' shops where they were making cholera cots for the treatment tent. The men standing at the back of the shops were old men with bony hands and the work was being done by young men and boys, lined up at chipped benches, ankle deep in wood shavings and offcuts, working with planes and saws. Dry wood shavings, curled into tight ringlets, stuck to their hair and the backs of their hands and legs. The fresh dry smell of cut wood made her feel better. Sawdust fell onto her bare arms and her shoes. She smelled it on her skin when she got into the taxi.

She opened the plastic bag on the backseat. All of her gifts were there,

each one carefully wrapped in two sheets of newspaper and tied around with lengths of thick twine. Nothing had been opened. She clutched the bag filled with little packages to her side and watched the hands of the driver on the wheel and saw motes of dust floating slowly upward toward the ceiling in the last of the afternoon sun.

When she arrived back at her hotel, the sky over the Arabian Sea was filled with yellow light and the streets were in darkness. In her room she double-locked the door. She pulled the curtains and took off her shoes and gritty socks. In the mirror she was red-eyed and pale, with heavy black rings under her eyes. She threw off her clothes and showered for half an hour in hot water and then wiped the steam from the mirror and stood naked in front of it. Her skin was a light tan. She looked dark against the white tiles on the bathroom wall and the white porcelain of the sink. Her thighs were long and heavy and tufted with fine black hairs. Her belly was flat and her breasts were small, with small brown nipples.

She left her hair wet and took a plastic syringe and a specimen cup from her bag and the pregnancy test from its cardboard packet and arranged them by the sink in the bathroom. She had always been methodical. Her mother told her that she was too organized to be good at anything. Too systematic. Brilliance came from thinking laterally, she told her, in the fast-food restaurants where they went every night after her father left. Elizabeth arranged things and followed recipes exactly. In her tidy room, she could forget that there were Indian men she didn't know sleeping in her father's bed. She understood that if you look at small things hard enough, then they become big things.

She squatted over the toilet and filled the specimen cup with urine and then took the syringe and drew up the warm yellow liquid and put two drops on the lilac-colored plastic test kit. It was shaped like a pen and there was a small window in the side. There were chemical reagents impregnated in the filter paper in the test that would combine with compounds in her urine. The tiles of the bathroom floor were cold under her feet. She was as tired as she had ever been. A black-and-white photograph of Gandhi hung on the wall above the bed. She brushed her teeth and lay down with the towel wrapped around her.

After a few minutes, she held the test carefully up to the light. Two thin purple lines had appeared in the test window. She had an impulse to run. She felt as if her own life, with its complicated procedures and protocols, had not prepared her. She drifted into sleep and saw, for a fleeting instant, that her instinct to escape came from her father, a man she had never known, whom she both loved and hated simultaneously.

She had learned about the hill station at Mahabaleshwar from a glossy tourist brochure in her room. The next morning she took one small overnight bag, put the rest of her luggage into storage at the hotel, and got on the first bus she could find from Bombay. She knew that Raj Singh would already be looking for her at the hotel. She could imagine him puffing through his small lips, adjusting his spectacles, and running up to the reception counter with his leather briefcase under his arm. It was the last day of the training, and two hundred people were waiting for her in the conference room.

The bus was full of women wearing saris. The road climbed into the misty-blue ravines of the Western Ghat Mountains. On the steep road, the bus slowed to a crawl and the driver grated the gears loudly as he changed down, his thin arm smacking the long gear stick with his palm for a minute before it fell into gear with the engine whining. Small cars loaded with people, heavy and low to the ground, sounded their horns and raced past the bus. As they climbed, the breeze freshened and banks of black clouds rolled over the tops of the mountains toward them. By midmorning, the sun had disappeared and they were plunged into a gray twilight. Gusts of wind from the deep valleys buffeted the bus. Elizabeth took a tissue from her bag and wiped her face and hands, then put her head to the open window and let the wind cool her skin.

A thin young man was sitting next to her. He was clutching a string bag filled with fruit and reading a Hindi newspaper that he held up close to his face. He had large childlike eyes, and wore American jeans and a white shirt. The wind from the open window blew his shirt around him. Under the shirt cuffs he had thin fingers and narrow wrists.

"You would like an orange? To eat," he said, reaching down into his bag.

"Thanks."

"Excuse me, but are you feeling well? I notice that the blood is rushing from your face. Excuse me. I can stop the bus. Give me the word. I will stop it instantly."

"That won't be necessary," Elizabeth said. "It's just the movement on the road. And I have eaten something perhaps. But I'm all right."

"Just give me the word. I can be stopping the bus at any time. This is quite fine with me. I would show no hesitation." Elizabeth nodded again and held the orange in her lap. She did not want to talk, and he went back to his newspaper, holding it in front of his face, licking his thumb and index finger every time he turned a page. The two top buttons of his shirt were undone and a thin gold chain hung around his neck. His skin was the color of olive oil, wood varnish, the crunchy peanut butter that she spooned from bulk tubs in the market at home.

She picked up the orange and plunged her thumb through the skin and deep into the pulp. She peeled it roughly, throwing pieces of peel out of the window. As she pulled pieces from the orange, juice ran over her fingers and onto her lap. She coughed as she swallowed the sour fruit and spat the seeds into the palm of her hand.

A baby began screaming in one of the seats behind her, coughing and pulling wet rasping breaths down into its lungs, while the mother talked to the infant and made clucking noises with her tongue.

The young man put his newspaper down and got out of his seat. He stood up carefully and walked unsteadily toward the back of the bus. She heard him talking quickly and then he came back and sat down and opened the newspaper again.

"I have told them that you are unwell," he said. "They must be keeping the baby back there quiet. It is a matter of common courtesy."

"You didn't need to do that," she said.

"It was important that I do it," he said. "People in this country do not understand. I have made it clear back there using plain language. The screechings from the lungs of a baby will not make it easier for you. I think the matter is in hand."

The cries from the baby were muffled as they rose farther into the mountains. She felt sick as the bus turned slowly up the road but did not want to stop and get off. The wet sour orange, the movement, the heavy smells of people in the bus only made it worse. If she stopped the bus, she knew that everyone would be watching her, a western woman, as she threw up on the road. It would be an admission that something was wrong. She ran her tongue over her lips, which were dry and cracked, and rummaged in the leather shoulder bag on her lap until she found a tube of lip gloss. She ran the sticky gloss, which smelled vaguely of strawberries, over her lips and watched flies land on the inside of the window.

Thunder rolled in the distance and the smell of rain and wet earth blew in through the window. The sudden darkness stopped people talking and they sat quietly in their seats looking out into the sky. When the rain came, it fell in fat drops like pigeon eggs onto the tin roof of the bus and exploded onto the warm road outside in dark circular stains, and then came down in vertical lines that were so dense and heavy that the valley and the mountains and the road ahead disappeared. The headlights of the bus were insignificant pinpoints of light into the rain. The water spat into the dry soil along the road. Elizabeth did not realize for a long time that they were passing through a small village, and that the blurred colors on the side of the road were people huddling under the lopsided roofs of narrow shops and stalls. The young man sitting next to her put down his newspaper and held it in his lap. It was not until the rain eased after five minutes that she saw that the bus had stopped and that people, barefoot and drenched, their clothes clinging to their backs, were walking quickly past them.

The bus driver shouted out of the window and then turned off the engine and pulled open the door of the bus. He got out of his seat, ran down the steps, and disappeared into the crowd outside. It was still drizzling and cars were stopped in front of them. Water ran down from the hill above in fast brown streams and filled the drainage ditch at the side of the road. Elizabeth got off the bus with the other passengers and felt the cool rain on her skin and smelled wet earth and hot oil. She sank into orange mud and held her arms out to her sides to get her balance. The women were all talking and laughing and holding their saris up as they walked through the mud and onto the bitumen road. The front of the bus was steaming and she put one hand up against the hot wet metal to steady herself.

"There is accident on the road, I think," the young man said as he came alongside her. She looked at him and wished she had brought a jacket or a sweater. They were in the center of a village. Stalls and shops made of wood and concrete block were set back from the road and people squatted in the shadows, looking out at the road. Groups of men walked past them, their sandals slick and muddy, their feet slapping flecks of mud up into the air behind them as they walked.

"Something has happened," she said.

"I am Suketu. It is pleasure to make your acquaintance, formally."

"Elizabeth. Hello."

She shook his hand in front of the bus and was grateful to have someone to talk to. Tiny droplets of rain had gathered in his hair in long silver rows. He had the air of an attentive nephew or tour guide. In the gray light, his eyes were as dense and impenetrable as coal or the hard bitumen on which they stood.

"You would perhaps like to sit down under cover."

"No, I want to see what is happening on the road."

"This may not be advisable."

"I want to see."

About twenty cars and a minibus were stopped in the road with people standing and squatting around them. Merchants from the stalls moved into the crowd with peanuts, cooked plantains and chicken, hard-boiled eggs, cigarettes, and bulging plastic bags full of cold water. People were shouting on the road ahead of them. A crowd had gathered in a wide circle around a truck and the man who had been killed. The truck had been coming down the hill too fast in the rain. The man had been crossing the road with a bag of rice. His body lay on the road in front of the truck, covered by a colored cloth. One brown hand was visible from under the cloth, reaching out down the hill. The bag of rice had burst as the man fell, spraying rice out around the body. The rice was brilliant white against the wet road.

The truck had slid at an angle across the road and was loaded with brown sacks tied down with lengths of orange rope. The sacks were piled high in the back of the truck and four or five men, naked above the waist and wearing white turbans, stood up on them, looking down at the crowd. Their chests were thin and black, the muscles of their upper arms well developed and shining in the rain. A bald man in a white dhoti was talking loudly and quickly to the driver, by the side of the truck. The driver was unshaven and had red eyes. He wore a sweat-stained lilac shirt and shiny dress trousers, frayed at the cuffs. People in the crowd were listening, trying to hear what was being said. The driver looked nervous and sick and he watched the man in white and the crowd with his arms limp by his side.

"The man talking to the driver is the head of the village council," Suketu said to Elizabeth. "He is saying that nothing must be moved until the police have been summoned. The driver says it was accident. The village man says that they must wait for the police to decide."

"Where are the police?"

"Not here, you see. Someone has been sent to fetch them at another town. Nothing can happen until they have been fetched. They will not allow anything to be moved. No traffic will pass. The driver says he will lose his job."

"And we're not going anywhere."

"Not until the police have come."

Elizabeth saw the children then, standing off by the side of the road in a tight group with their mother, looking out at the body on the wet road. The woman clutched her children on each side and looked down at the ground. She had black hair, pulled back tightly from her face, and a small gold nose ring that caught the light when she looked up. The man from the village council would not let the family go to the dead man because he did not want to disturb the body. He was already calling it a crime scene, Suketu said, had already made up his mind. It could be very dangerous for the driver, he said, since when there was a serious accident like this, people sometimes attacked the driver. Summary justice, he said, was not uncommon. Then the rain began again. It came as a heavy sheet, thumping down onto the dead man and sending thousands of grains of white basmati rice washing down the hill.

For a long time, Elizabeth thought that she was not capable of loving anyone. In college, she had had a four-year relationship with Ethan, who was studying civil engineering and who liked having sex on the Mary in a Bathtub in his parents' backyard. She liked him because he loved her and was good looking in an American way, and because he had a sound grasp of differential calculus. When she looked at him, she saw herself. When she got her first job, she moved without telling him where she was going. There had been perhaps five or six other men. She tried to concentrate on sex. For a while, she enjoyed some of it, the games involved, the jokes about the Kama Sutra, her technical skill in dimly lit bathrooms with her diaphragms and cold tubes of spermicidal jelly, the days or weeks of being chased and wanted by someone else. But she saw it all as a kind of experiment and she knew she didn't really feel anything. Later she realized that she thought of men systematically, as a thing to be cataloged, as a set of characteristics to be weighed and balanced. She gave up for a while, told her mother she didn't need men at all. In the light of what her own father had done, she expected her mother's support. "It is tragic," her mother said. "The only romance you have is with disease. You are wedded to things that cause people to die, for God's sake."

She understood that she was not able to think about the things that were most important to her. There were hidden places inside her. Impulses. She didn't know why she wanted André, but she knew that she loved him, of all people, someone she could never really have.

That summer she had made him dinner at home, filet mignon that she cut herself on a chopping board in her kitchen. She used a heavy-handled butcher's knife. When she had cut the meat, the board was slippery with blood. She wiped her hands on a cloth and got her diaphragm from the bathroom, walking back through the house with the flesh-colored dome on the palm of her hand. The diaphragm looked absurd on the bloody chopping board, garish under the kitchen lights, like a prosthetic appliance. She chopped it carefully into one-inch strips. It had the texture of a green leafy vegetable.

She cut the strips into squares, breathing hard through her nose, concentrating on the chopping board, feeling a sort of triumph. Then she held the knife horizontally in both hands and diced the thin rubber squares into tiny pieces, as she would dice an onion or a piece of ginger. After five minutes, she had reduced the contraceptive device to nothing, a bloody pile, nothing but a distant idea, and as she scooped it into the garbage, she felt as though she had run a successful biochemical test or laboratory experiment. Satisfied. She gave up contraception at the age of forty, the way other people took up exercise or a new hobby.

André never knew. When she slept with him after that, she felt closer to him, like the ocean, all currents and eddies, filled with invisible showers of phytoplankton. She understood what it meant to be an immigrant; to put yourself at risk, give up certainty, have a certain faith. The night of the filet mignon, when André had gone, she went out to her desk in the dark and turned on the reading lamp. She heaved her Webster's dictionary under the light and reread a word she had memorized when she was a girl: *cope — a hooded ecclesiastical vestment; a muzzle for a ferret; to find necessary expedients to overcome problems and difficulties; to fit or conform to the shape of another member.*

The rain fell heavily on the hill and rang on the side of the truck and on the cars in the road. Elizabeth ran with Suketu into a tiny tea stall with a rusty corrugated iron roof and three yellow Formica tables on steel pipe legs. The stall had a poured-concrete floor and a narrow veranda that was open to the street. They splashed through the mud and sat at a table. An old man with yellow eyes and tufts of gray hair in his ears came out from behind a piece of cloth hanging over a doorway at the back and they asked him for tea. He brought it boiling and steaming to the table in clear glasses. There was no gutter on the roof and water fell in a thick curtain from the edge of the veranda in front of them. The dead man was visible on the road outside, lying under the piece of saturated cloth. She held the tea to her face and felt the steam on her lips and sipped the sweet tea.

"This is most regrettable," Suketu said.

"It is terrible."

"There are people dying every minute in my country and no one pays the slightest attention. And yet when one man, just one, is hit in the street by a truck, everything must stop. This is an amazing thing."

"It is not a bad thing. I'm glad it happens."

"You are going to the hill station at Mahabaleshwar for vacation perhaps. To see the sights."

"I suppose so."

"Very wise decision, if I may say. The hill station is magnificent. Very decent. You know it was the summer residence of the British when they were in charge. Those Britishers knew how to live. Certainly."

"It was where they ran away to," she said.

"In a manner of speaking. It is cooler there. There are several lakes. You can look out over the entire world in Mahabaleshwar. It is a romantic place."

"I suppose I'm running away, too."

"I beg your pardon?"

"Escaping. I'm escaping to the hill station. Just like the British."

"You are married?"

"No."

"I am single and quite available. I am going up to visit my father, who is running a good hotel there. He worked his way up. I take him fruit."

"I see," Elizabeth said and looked out into the street. The rain had eased and people were gathering around the truck and the dead man again. It was dark and still in the tea shop and a radio was playing Indian music.

Suketu sat hunched over the table with his thin legs crossed. He had not touched his tea. He reached into his pocket and took out a gold pen and then said something to the old man who went out through the curtain and came back with a sheet of blue-lined paper pulled from the pages of an exercise book. Suketu took the paper and smoothed it flat on the table. His fingers were long and slender and he held the pen carefully in his fingertips as he wrote.

"Let me put down my assets clearly," he said. "Number one. I am having a good education, primary and secondary. At school, I received the Joginder Reddy Sugar Factory Gold Medal for standing first in my class. Number two. I am healthy and take daily exercise. I am a useful cricketer. Number three. I am keen in computers. I keep myself updated on hardware and software up gradations. Number four. I do painting — oil — and watercolors, as well as cartooning and sketching. I am also good at photography. Number five. I am not a bad-looking man. People have told me that I look like Mr. Imran Khan the great Pakistani cricketer. Please take this summary."

He finished writing and folded the paper in half. He wrote his name and address on one side and gave the sheet to Elizabeth. She held it out in front of her.

"I do not meet women from America," Suketu said. "You are not married. Perhaps you are looking for husband. This is for you to peruse at your leisure."

"Thank you," she said and finished her tea. His boldness made her feel like a girl. It embarrassed her. How would he have seen her if he had known the truth? Not as a virtuous woman. Not the way she appeared to be in her sensible skirt and shoes.

The rain eased and then stopped. Fast-moving white clouds blew over and snatches of blue sky appeared through the clouds. On the road, the man in white stood by the dead man talking to his family. People in the cars sounded their horns and shouted out of the windows. Others were walking along the road to crowd around the accident scene. White-and-black chickens wandered in front of the tea stall pecking in the mud. Elizabeth got up from the table and told Suketu that she was going to stretch her legs.

A small motorbike came down the road. Two policemen wearing khaki-colored uniforms were sitting on the bike and they pulled alongside the truck and got off the bike carefully. The legs of their trousers were covered in mud. They looked at the man lying on the road and walked over to the family. The head of the village council began talking to them quietly so that the crowd could not hear what he was saying.

Elizabeth walked along the wet road, out past the edge of the village and up the hill. It was bright and cool. The sheer mountains lay out in front of her, shrouded by mist that lay down in the valleys. Where the sun caught the mountains, they flared in the light, the red stone reflecting shades of purple and violet. Cool fresh air blew against her face.

She had seen André every night in the last month before he left. She knew he would never be back. She had decided to go to India for the training because he was leaving and because she did not want to sit in her house alone at night. His last day was a Sunday and he took her out to breakfast very early in the morning. They went to an outdoor cafe and were the first people there. It was a spring day and fine, but there had been a frost overnight. They wiped water from the table with their sleeves. There was a real chill in the air, a dewy crispness that made her shiver and drink coffee in big black mouthfuls.

They ate fried breakfasts that came on large, smooth, white china plates. She unfolded the white linen napkin, thick with starch, onto her lap and felt its texture on her fingers. In the cold morning air, she knew that this was how she would remember him, as a series of sensations in crisp light: the heavy eating instruments in her hands, the whites and silvers of the table, the fresh smell of black pepper on the yolk of an egg.

Far below, the flat plains stretched out toward the sea. The thin brown ribbon of the Krishna River ran through steep ravines in the mountains. She walked up to a bend in the road and looked out into the valley. The sun sparkled on the pools of brown water. In the clear light, tiny blue butterflies danced in the bushes at her feet. She crouched down and watched the butterflies bob in the sun, splashes of incandescent blue, flashing like slips of colored paper. She felt as light as air for a moment, watched the butterflies, saw the thick mud and the leaves of the bushes very clearly.

Someone called her name. She turned. Suketu was coming quickly up the road, waving his arms above his head. The sun was warm on the back of her neck. Thick mud stuck to her shoes. People had gathered around the truck driver and were shouting at him. The policemen held their arms in the air and were also shouting. She saw the driver climb back into the truck and slam the door shut. The crowd was angry now. Years later she would tell her daughter about that morning in the mountains. She would try and explain the moment when she had turned to walk back down the road toward the young Indian man advancing up the hill toward her. Such a clear morning. Everything washed clean by the rain. That was how I met him, she would say, that was how I met the man who would be your father.

2

ALL THE RIVERS
IN THE WORLD

Hardware

Vitek Kerolak, five foot six and fifty pounds overweight, shovel jawed and saucer eyed, tousled in appearance with an unruly mop of black hair that would not stay down, the son of three generations of fishermen, had not been in a boat since he was twelve years old. He was afraid of the sea. Large gutted and heavy limbed, with ham hands and paradoxically small delicate feet, he had a sharp memory for the two subjects that interested him: the constellations of the night sky, and hardware. Hardware was his special knowledge and his profession. He had an encyclopedic memory for the flotsam and jetsam of hardware: screw, bolt, flange, and bracket; pipe, faucet, and washer; the full gamut of glue, filler, plaster, spackle, and sealant; and the intricacies of wood, hard and soft, where to use pine, what to do with walnut, maple, or teak. He could give you an estimate for a job in his head without resorting to pencil and paper, in no time, but could not understand his father, or why he had run away. In the end, he had to do something about his old man, and that was what put him on the road to Florida with a stack of Peter Paul and Mary cassettes, a duffel bag of clothes, and a scrap of paper scrawled with an address in Key West.

Vitek drove south to find his father in October of his thirtieth year. He left the crisp mornings and burning leaves of Maine behind him, advancing into balmy sea breezes that made him uneasy. He knew that his fear of the sea was not justified but could not control it. Clutching the steering wheel of his small Japanese car with his big hands, hunched and squeezed into a compact cabin built for smaller people, he felt a kind of free-floating anxiety that made him eat. He wolfed doughnuts and pastries from thin cardboard boxes, powdering the seats with confectioners' sugar and greasy crumbs. He preferred driving at night and took comfort from the constellations above him as others might take comfort from good friends. When he was tired, he slept in the car, mouth open and gaping, legs up on the dash. Sand blew in through the windows as he got near the coast. He squinted through eyes more accustomed to twilight hues and began to see snatches of the ocean, which looked like sheet metal in the sun. Then the water was suddenly all there in front of him, out to the horizon, filling the dusty windshield, rippling and boiling in the wind.

His father did not know he was coming and this made Vitek nervous. His parents had been married for forty years. Now his father had been gone a year without a good explanation. Vitek had pushed this knowledge to the back of his mind, where it stood like a flock of sheep scattered on a distant hillside.

He arrived in the Keys late on a windswept day of pastel colors, the sky a checkerboard of high-altitude slipstreams, but put off going to the house. Back up the highway, he found a diner. He ate four fried eggs, washed them down with orange juice and coffee, noticed the color of the Formica countertop, the type of Phillips-head screws used to anchor the stools, the size of the hinges on the swing door to the kitchen. He smoked ten cigarettes and spread his map out on the counter in front of him, pressing maple syrup, egg yolk, ketchup, and greasy nubbins of hash browns into the highway system of southern Florida.

The waitress helped him find his father's street and gave him directions. She told him he was a northerner, no doubt, because of the color of his skin and his frown. The inside of the windows dripped with condensation. When he walked outside, the breeze had come up and carried the smells of fish and fresh paint from the marina. The day had disappeared and the night had welled in from the Gulf, moist and heavy, a great blanket of sea salt and turbulent air.

He pulled on a jacket and lay down on the backseat of the car in front of the diner. He heard cars starting. Voices drifted to him across the parking lot. Behind it all he could sense the wildness of the ocean, unfettered, looming out beyond the concrete of the barrier walls. There was something that he could taste in the back of his throat, something untarnished and genuine that he recognized from his childhood. It was a smell and a feeling that he only ever noticed at dusk or dawn, something that came sneaking up on him, and was always a surprise. He twitched with caffeine and fatigue, in equal measure, his mind spitting like a neon tube in the dark. In the morning, he would find his father. Not until then.

His father came from dirt-poor lobster and cod fishermen; lumbering red-faced men with square faces and meaty hands; tidy women with permed hair and stovepipe legs. His father had always wanted to fish, because of his family, the tradition of it, and this was the tragedy of his life. Vitek watched him work as a crewman on someone else's boat for thirty years, grew up in the squall of his thwarted ambition. He came home with bleeding hands and cracked fingernails, smelling of bilge and black tobacco; worked nights and sometimes drank all night; never had any money. He wanted his own boat and dreamed of blue-water fishing. Sitting by a coal fire in the rocky-gray afternoons of Maine, he talked of cobalt seas and fighting fish, and made Vitek see something bigger than himself in the ocean. He showed Vitek pictures of sailfish, short-fin mako, tarpon, and permit, could describe how they moved in the water. He took him to a bar in Portland where an eleven-foot Atlantic marlin hung on an oak backboard. That was where Vitek had his first taste of beer, sitting on a bar stool in Maine, looking up at the long blue body of an offshore fish. He was twelve years old and they sat under the stuffed marlin, the biggest and bravest fighting fish in the ocean, frozen forever in a moment of time. The marlin is a noble fish, his father told him, and catching a marlin will make you a king.

Now Vitek had walked away from the sea. He worked long hours and ate food heavy in saturated fat that he recognized was not good for him. Hardware was solid and safe. Landlocked. He liked the feel of new things: solid pieces of brass and steel; tools with engineered heads; fistfuls of new nails or masonry screws. A year ago, he had been cutting quarter-inch copper pipe at work when his mother called him and asked him to come home. He found his father sitting in a flower bed looking over the harbor, a bottle of schnapps in one hand and the keys to a new fifty-foot Bertram fishing cruiser in the other. He was rolling drunk, sprawled out in the damp soil, hair wild and aloft in the sea breeze, fishing clothes stained with engine oil and dirty saltwater. He had pulled off his steel-capped boots, and was sitting in his socks, taking pulls from the bottle.

Vitek took two mugs of black coffee outside and sat down behind him. Cabbage moths danced in the flowers. He looked at his father's neck, a red-brown slab tufted with hard white bristles, and focused on the softer colors of the harbor in the distance: a cotton-candy sky, seagulls floating on updrafts like icing sugar sprinkled on sponge cake. He felt inadequate. His father was as elemental as a rock seawall. Talking to him was a daunting undertaking at the best of times. Sitting there in the garden, his father told him that he was going to fish big game and run charters out of Key West. His mother could come with him if she wanted, he said, although they both knew that she would not. His father had resigned from the job he had held in one form or another since he was nineteen years old.

It turned out that he had been quietly putting away small sums of money for thirty years, and had managed to save enough to secure a loan for the boat. It was a heavy loan, over two hundred grand, and the payments would be difficult. In the fall, his father took off on the beautiful new Bertram with a bag of clothes and a wallet of credit cards and motored down the East Coast on his own. He knew what he was doing on the sea, understood navigation and could read charts. He sent Vitek a postcard with a telephone number and a postmark from the Keys. Vitek gave the number to his mother. Both of them kept quiet about what had happened and why, clung to some blind hope that time and patience would make it right.

His father stayed away, never called his mother, hung in the distance like a storm front. Vitek telephoned him at night, found himself listening more carefully to the silence between his father's words than to the words themselves. Six months later, a woman's voice began answering his phone, and Vitek hung up rather than say anything to her. In the Keys, his father had outfitted the boat on credit and put small ads in local newspapers. He borrowed money to set himself up as a charter business and slept in the boat for the first few weeks. It was expensive and reckless, but he believed that he would make the money back with a few good charters. He loved the warm water and blew two or three tanks of expensive fuel going out on his own to test his equipment. Fishing was all that he knew. He took his first sailfish on new gear, fifty pounds of flashing fish, and told Vitek that at that moment he knew he could never leave. He had been gone a year when he called with the news that he had not yet had a charter and was going to lose the boat. That was two days ago. On the telephone, his voice sounded like the ocean in a shell, all air and static. Vitek stood in plumbing supply with the telephone pressed to his ear, leaned on a pile of five-inch-square bathroom tile, tapped the top of his head with a carpenter's pencil. Then he went to the manager's office and asked for a week off.

Cold Mutton

Vitek awoke with the sun already high in a pale blue sky, his mouth dry and gaping, his neck twisted. He got out and stamped his feet on the parking lot. A yellow parking ticket fluttered on the windshield, and the diner was full of people. He flattened his hair in the rearview mirror, then went inside and washed his hands and face in the bathroom. He fell into a booth and ordered black coffee and a stack of flapjacks with

eggs and bacon. It was midday when he drove back into town to get his
bearings.

His car was flooded with air and light. He could not bring himself to
go and see his father. It was warm and he drove out to the southernmost
point on the island. A painted concrete marker overlooked the water.
Vitek sat and looked out to sea, smelled sea salt and fresh-poured asphalt,
found himself estimating the number of cans of ten-gallon outdoor paint
needed to cover the marker. Tourists in pastel shorts and broad-rimmed
hats snapped photographs and posed in front of the sky and water that
lay in front of them as flat and uninterrupted as a painted backdrop.
Vitek felt huge and gaseous, could see his skin burning red in the sun.
A thin Japanese man wearing white kneesocks and a tour badge asked
him to take a picture of himself and his wife in front of the water. He
swayed as he squinted into the viewfinder. The couple stood to attention in front of him, rigid and erect, vinyl traveling bags slung from
their shoulders, the woman wearing a pair of oversize sunglasses like
giant tinted mussels, her mouth a slash of arterial red lipstick. He squared
them in the picture, brought them into focus against the emptiness
of the water behind, and understood the power of being at the edge of
land. The full weight of the North American landmass lay behind
him, fading, dwindling to nothing, and the open water ahead was clean
and unencumbered. There was a sense of something unknown opening up ahead that drew you on, something optimistic and filled with
possibility.

He was quite calm when the water was at a safe distance. He thought
of the sea as a predator in the grass, hidden, coiled like a spring and ready
to pounce. At home he stayed inland except when visiting his parents.
When he was younger, he had feigned ear infections or the flu to avoid
beach days with his friends. He no longer owned swimming trunks. It
was clear to him that it was not the sea itself, but rather the concept of
it that made him uneasy. Looking into nautical paintings (ships, whale
hunts, fishermen and seascapes, rumpled stormy water) threw him badly,
made him perspire and feel as if he was walking a high wire without a
safety net.

He was sweating and red nosed when he drove back into the old town along Duval Street, and found the aquarium near Mallory Square. In a press of parents and children, he walked between the tanks filled with grouper, parrotfish, and barracuda, ate overflowing fistfuls of Cracker Jack, eyed a mako shark from a distance. The terrors of the ocean were manageable when they were contained in tanks. He was grateful to be out of the sun. The solid stone walls and damp concrete made him feel better. He emerged blinking in the late afternoon and walked into Mallory Square where groups of people were drinking coffee and looking out over the Gulf of Mexico. They were waiting for the sun to drop below the horizon, to flare and die, a momentary testament to the revolution of the earth, and Vitek found himself wondering what they saw in it, what they were looking for.

He had feared the sea since he was twelve years old. In early fall of that year, they got the news about his brothers, lost in a storm. It was a blustery day with a rolling gray sky. Vitek found his mother in the front room of the house in Maine, coal fire blazing, rain sleeting against the windows. Above the mantel was the clock in the shape of an Atlantic crab, with brass pincers and rhinestone eyes on tiny metallic stalks, and down on the tan carpet in front of him was his mother, knees to her chest, hugging her shins and crying.

Then he was out through the door, tripping as he went through, and running up the stairs to his bedroom. On the wall, he had a picture of a wool clipper under full sail, three-masted, at full tilt in a strong wind with cascades of white spume springing from her hull. Looking into the picture, he had a sense of the speed, of being carried along and self-contained, as if the tiny red and black and green figures of sailors on the afterdeck were moving toward some glorious destiny, and as if the figure in blue on the bridge with an arm outstretched, the captain, Vitek imagined, was in control of the whole tumbling, racing, whipping affair. He stared into it hard and could imagine himself out on the rolling water. His rain-driven bedroom window looked out at the harbor down the hill, and he saw pale gray water glossed with whitecaps. This was where he stood looking for a sign of his father, on a patch of carpet that had grown flat and thin with his own weight.

That afternoon he knew his father was days away on a cod boat, separated from shore by a hundred nautical miles, and from death by drowning by a tempered steel hull a foot thick. Vitek did not know whether he had survived the storm or not. His father was not there when it counted. He was always out, making a living, taking skin off his extremities, spraining joints and pulping fingers, cracking the tiny castle ramparts of the bones in his hands. There was always a chance he would not come home. Vitek grew up waiting for him, learned to avoid his mother when the weather was bad or the boat late into harbor. Now his mother was lying on the floor in the living room below him. The waves tossing in the bay were the color of cold mutton. He stared at the picture of the wool clipper and imagined himself somewhere else entirely.

Vitek's two brothers, ages nineteen and twenty-two, had been out on a trawler off Newfoundland when a huge storm blew in from the north Atlantic. It came in at night, hurricane force, with waves as steep and hard as reinforced concrete walls. Every ship within five hundred miles was blown off the water. The lucky ones found safe harbor quickly enough, but the trawler was near the end of a trip and already heavily loaded with cod, probably overloaded, and riding low in the water. She was broadsided and took in water quickly and then went down in less than half an hour. They got off a single volley of SOS signals on the radio, but when the Coast Guard helicopter arrived, there was nothing to be seen, not the boat, not a life raft or any debris, just empty black water and the crew lost and gone. The two boys were on the boat by chance. They were both there for six months of casual work. The younger of Vitek's brothers, Teddy, had just finished high school, and wanted to make some money before college. Leon, his older brother, had just finished a B.A. at the University of Maine where he had majored in English and history. Leon was broad and strong like his relatives, and the great hope of his mother, who thought he had the stuff to get out of fishing altogether, make her proud, set himself up doing something with his brain. Vitek's father had got them the job on the trawler. He thought he was doing them a favor, knew the skipper personally and convinced him to give them a chance for full wages, four weeks on, two weeks off. It was just for six months, to make some money. Any father would have done the same.

Then they were gone. His father would not be in from the sea for another three days. The house filled up with his relatives, baking bread and cakes, steaming pierogies, drinking endless cups of tea on cracked china saucers. There was safety in numbers. They came out of the woodwork when there was a tragedy, huddled together in silent groups. Vitek lay in bed and shivered when he thought of that trawler slipping into the freezing-cold water at night, nothing to see, the vast emptiness lying below, and cried silent tears that tasted like the salty water that had taken his brothers away.

Vitek was born seven years after Teddy, an admitted accident, a happy surprise, always the baby of the family, and was spoiled and looked after by his older brothers. They took him to football games when he was barely old enough to understand, took him swimming and bowling, kept a supply of lemon candies and licorice and all-day suckers that they would delight in giving him at night. They took him along when they went to drive-ins, when they met girls, made him a part of them in a way that he did not miss until it was gone completely. Vitek did not feel separate from his brothers, he felt a part of them. He shared a room with Teddy until Leon moved out, went to sleep listening to Teddy talk about the colleges he would get into, his dreams of living in the desert, learning to ride, raising cattle or ostriches. The night before Teddy and Leon went out on the trawler for the last time, they were all together. Leon had graduated and was home from college. They went down to the pier in the early evening and got ice cream. Seagulls shrieked at their feet. They ate the ice cream leaning against the railing, watching boats move in and out of the harbor. Next to them on the pier was a line of evening fishermen, old men with blank expressions and heavy, wrinkled hands, who smiled at them and said nothing. The men on the pier were the survivors, Leon said, the ones who had fished all their lives, seen the worst the sea could throw at them, stayed alive, and in their retirement still came down and fished from the pier at night. It is a powerful force, he said, something you can't easily get out of your blood. Sometimes you can't fight the need to fish, he said. It's just there. The ice cream was cold and sticky on Vitek's lips. He was twelve years old, and that was the last thing he remembered Leon saying.

He found the house, the map spread open on the steering wheel. It was in the Spanish style with a flat roof and dirty-brown stucco walls. The front yard was dry and sandy and covered in dull green islands of couch grass. Vitek sat in the car for five minutes smoking a cigarette, watching wind tousle the fat leaves of the palm trees on the street. He knocked on the door late in the afternoon and the woman he had heard on the telephone answered it. She was no more than thirty years old, big hipped, with firm round calves. Her name was Chika. She had an Arabic nose and big eyes and she didn't take her eyes off him from the moment he walked in. His father was red faced, looked at the floor and ran his hands through his hair. They stood in the small kitchen on black and white linoleum tiles. A fishing calendar hung on one wall. Chika stood next to his father with her arms around his waist. She could have been his daughter. His father held her hand and Vitek knew immediately that they were sharing the bedroom.

They took kitchen chairs outside into the warm evening and his father got bottles of cold beer from the fridge. Vitek sat down and drank the beer in thirsty gulps. Beads of condensation dripped from the bottle into his lap and he drank two bottles quickly, while his father held the beer between his knees and stared at the ground. Chika went back inside and when she had gone, Vitek said, "She's my age."

His father worked at the moist beer label with his thumbnail. "She needs someone to look after her," he said.

"For God's sake. You're married. Your wife happens to be my mother."

"It's more complicated, boy. I'm doing what I always wanted to do."

"You're running away. That's what you're doing. I can't believe it."

"Your mother could have come with me. It was my dream. Thirty years I wanted to come here. She wouldn't come. Spat in my face. You don't know the half of it."

"You haven't even called her."

"I'm getting things started here. Been busy. I've outfitted the boat."

"I'm very happy for you."

Vitek was no expert on relationships, but he had a firm sense of right and wrong, a kind of rigorous loyalty that came from his family. It had kept his relatives fishing for almost one hundred years. He was proud of his family, their toughness and silent work habits, a sense that the sheer hostility of the ocean made it a reasonable option. Men and women were partners in a larger enterprise, and it was not really a question of love.

He had never been able to talk to his father. He seized up. They sat outside for half an hour without saying anything important. His father asked him about the details of his road trip: towns encountered, roadside stops, traffic conditions, portions of the route where he had made the best time. Vitek felt as if there was a vast area of uncharted territory lying between them. Now that he was sitting there with his father, face-to-face, he felt as if all the anger and momentum had left him. He drank the beer and slapped large black mosquitoes when they landed on his legs and arms. The western sky flared into a nebula of peach and vermilion light and then faded, and they were left facing each other in the dark, sitting on the hard kitchen chairs. He could already feel the mosquito welts rising on his skin.

Rough-shelled Oysters

Chika Portini grew up in Brooklyn, New York, the only child of second-generation Italian parents who had wanted a boy, not a girl. Her father, a squat stoic with elaborate black mustaches and a wild temper, ran a convenience store. Her mother, impossibly short, sharp as a tack, with a zany sense of humor, was a primary school teacher. Chika grew up helping out in the store — manning the cash register, stocking the shelves at night, learning how to maintain an inventory and manage cash flow. As she got older, she increasingly acted as a peace broker between her parents. They argued, fought running battles, and her mother began disappearing for the summer to stay with her sisters in Queens, Buffalo, and

Rome, Italy. Her father drank and taught her how to do practical things: maintain an engine, repair a toaster, understand plumbing and house wiring. Her mother sent her long letters from distant places, and taught her to be skeptical. From her mother, she learned to trust nothing, and to become self-sufficient as quickly as she could.

In her last year of high school, she was in the store one night with her father when a man wearing a ski mask burst in and demanded money. He held a small black pistol in his hand, and her father, indignant, made a lunge across the counter for the weapon. There was a struggle. The gun went off and put a bullet into her father's upper arm. The man with the ski mask appeared to be more surprised than her father, and fled with nothing. Chika wrapped her father's arm in a piece of cheesecloth to stop the bleeding, then called 911. She surprised herself with her calmness and clarity, even as she realized that her father could have been much more severely injured or even shot dead. As she stood holding the telephone, she caught sight of herself in the mirror in the back room: short, dark-haired, thin-wristed, with a heavy white neck. She had a sudden vision of herself in ten years, broad, fat, and unwieldy like all the Italian women she knew, by which time, she imagined, it would be too late to find a man or experience whatever life had to offer.

She enrolled in nursing school because she wanted to see something of the world. That was the heart of it. She wanted to travel, and when she had finished the training, abandoned the bedpans and the smell of people dying in hospitals, and joined Doctors Without Borders — Médecins Sans Frontières — an organization she had read about in a newspaper article, standing at the front counter of her father's convenience store. She went to Amsterdam, where they had an office, and joined on the spot. Twenty-three years old, refusing steadfastly to shave leg or armpit, with a fondness for heavy desserts and battered seafood, she had no idea what she was doing. She smoked dope in Amsterdam for the first time. They gave her a rudimentary training. The rest she would have to learn on the job. Then she was on a flight to Afghanistan, holed up in the north near Mazār-i-Sharīf, helping to run a camp of five hundred refugees from Tajikistan who had cholera and typhoid. Trial by fire is what it was. Children with measles, corneas eaten away because they didn't have enough vitamin A. Pneumonia. Malnutrition. Women dropping babies where they stood. She had to learn a lot fast, but had a knack for it — the hours and the danger didn't bother her — she never really thought the Afghans would sack a refugee camp. She did not mind having to do things on her own. She liked the mountains. It was beautiful, and this is what she discovered about many of the desperate places she went: they were breathtaking. She went to four countries in six years. After that, she went home, knowing only that she could not live a normal life.

She saw the father in the son. The son came over the threshold that evening like a lumbering mastodon, pale skinned and sweaty, panting, and she saw the same dogged, slugging determination in him that the father had. A kind of soundless fury. They were like hoary rough-shelled oysters on the outside, both of them. It was the rough ones she liked. The hard ones. If you could get them to open their shells for long enough, there was a chance you could find a pearl. Like any prized jewel, it took work to get at it, but that was what she needed in a man. She wanted someone she could throw herself against, as unyielding as a stone wall, someone who had to be scaled.

Bread Thrown for Chickens

They came inside and sat down at the cracked deal table in the kitchen. A pile of dry buoys and some coils of frayed nylon rope lay in the corner. Chika was frying cod and making hash browns on a flat iron skillet. She brought the food over to them and touched his father in a way that was intimate and unthinking, put a hand on his neck when she leaned over the table, rested her hands in his hair. Her eyes were green with brown-flecked irises. She was olive skinned and businesslike, talked quickly and knew what she wanted to say, wore a pair of heavy construction boots. Vitek blushed and forked the cod and potatoes into his mouth in huge chunks. His father took out his papers: mortgage papers for the boat, a business plan, a file on advertising expenses. Chika had organized him, brought a word processor with her and was doing her best to help

him out. She smiled with her eyes and told Vitek that they would manage if they could make the next couple of boat payments. He understood
that there was nothing flimsy about her. Sitting at the kitchen table in a
cloud of grease and black smoke from the skillet, surrounded by the business papers, he felt more comfortable than he had imagined he would.
He knew that something fundamental had changed in his father, but
could not pin it down.

When they had finished eating, Chika cleared the plates and brought
them mugs of black coffee and put a bag of Oreo cookies in the middle
of the table. His father dunked a cookie in the coffee and ate it whole.

"Credit is not a sin," his father said. "You've got to borrow to make
capital investments. You've got to have a vision."

"What the hell is that?" Vitek said. "Vision? You mean a dream. A
risky pie-in-the-sky idea. Is that what you mean?" He put four heaped
spoonfuls of white sugar into his coffee and then said, "You've never used
the word *vision* in your life."

His father sat square to the table with his hands flat in front of him.
"I've got a business plan here," he said. "I've had to learn about it. You've
got to speak the language of the people who have the money. I've got
experience on the water, that's not the issue."

"Advertising is the key," Chika said. She sat next to his father with
the coffee mug held up to her face. She was watching Vitek.

"Advertising. Word of mouth, too," his father said. "Get a name and
everything follows." He leaned over and grabbed Vitek around the arm.
"I can do the job. You know that. I can fish big game as well as any."

"You're sixty-three years old," Vitek said.

"Sixty-three years young," his father said, then smiled and called him
a skeptic. "He's his mother's boy," he said to Chika. He stood up and
walked slowly to the sink. He was broad chested, with big forearms
and square hands, and he moved slowly and deliberately on stiff hips
and knees. Years on the sea had turned his skin to leather and his hair and
mustache were a brilliant white. He was stronger and bigger than Vitek,
who had the soft thighs and plump hands of his mother. Vitek had never
seen his father as an affectionate man but at the table he had clasped

Chika's fingers in his own and rested a hand on her shoulder when he talked. He had never done anything like this at home. Vitek sipped his coffee and watched his father run water into the sink and wash the dishes by himself, then dry them and stack them back in the cupboards. He had never done that at home either.

Vitek felt exhausted and gritty eyed and let himself rest heavily on his elbows. The hardware business was owned by the father of a high school friend, Johnny Yanulis, and the job had been given to him, no questions asked. It had been an easy option, something handed to him on a plate. He had stuck at it because he did not want to let Johnny Yanulis down. He convinced himself that he was providing an essential service like construction or plumbing or fishing, for that matter, a backbone industry. Later he realized that he had never had the courage to go out on his own, was terrified of ending up like his father. He had meant to go back to college, knew he was not stupid, but never found the inspiration. There was something reassuring about the textures of his work and he liked the airy, contained space of the warehouse, and the shimmering banks of fluorescent lighting that made everything clearly visible. When he decided not to fish, he thought he was making a rational decision, but he now knew that it had nothing to do with being rational and everything to do with fear. Vitek had stuck to hardware because it was safe. Dry, as his father would say. No water involved.

His father sat down again and said, "Chika here saves lives."

"Used to," she said. "Not anymore."

"You're religious?" Vitek asked, thinking he was going to have to deal with a Bible thumper, someone who had taken on his father as an act of charity. He already resented her, felt as if she had looked after his father in a way that he had not been able to.

"I'm a nurse," Chika said. "I worked with refugees. Not now."

"She's done something worthwhile," his father said. "Trying to help people. Takes guts to do it, if you ask me. Most people wouldn't have the mustard to go where she went, truth be told. You tell him. Tell Vitek."

She took a swallow of coffee. "Nothing much to tell. Afghanistan was the start of it. I went on for six years — two in Afghanistan, another two in Thailand, on the Cambodia border, another one in Burundi. Then I was in Rwanda in 1994. I felt as if I was doing something useful for a while. It's not exotic or exciting. I guess I helped some people, but I'm not sure it did much good in the long run. The whole thing was like patching a roof with bubble gum." She talked quickly and directly, looked Vitek squarely in the eyes when she spoke. There was no nonsense there, he saw that, she could handle herself. She wore no makeup, probably never did. Whatever she saw in his father was real, that was clear, and he shifted uneasily on the chair and let his father refill his coffee mug with the heavy dark sludge at the bottom of the pot.

"That's pretty solid," his father said. "Makes me feel like I've not been doing my part."

"You've fished," Vitek said. "That's plenty."

"I haven't saved any lives, boy. Haven't made any real difference to anything. Neither have you."

"That's not fair," Vitek said.

"You're capable of more."

Vitek excused himself and went to the bathroom, let a long parabola of urine arc into the bowl. He noted the line of polished cowrie shells on the windowsill, a poster of Miles Davis blowing a horn, two toothbrushes, a stack of twin-blade razors, fancy herbal soap that smelled like vanilla, and three brown-tinted medicine bottles with child-proof lids and typed pharmacists' labels, his father's, containing white and blue parcels of Captopril, frusemide, and slow K potassium. The shower curtain was clear plastic and covered with tropical fish in primary colors. Domestic. That's how it looked. If it hadn't been for the heart medications, he would have taken his father for a much younger man.

Vitek knew his father was right about his lack of ambition. He hadn't really done anything with his life, he sometimes thought, had watched it race by as if he was a spectator. But he didn't know what he could do. In the mirror, he looked huge and pale, dark rings under his eyes, gut tight against the rucked shirt, his hair standing up straight, as if he had just walked in out of a strong gale. He had the sausage nose and jug ears of his father's family, men and women alike, huge people instantly recognizable by their ears and mottled red coloring, and their high and wide buttocks. They were elephant seals, that was how Vitek imagined them when he was growing up, huge, patulous-mouthed, rippling with subcutaneous blubber, awkward on land — but at home on the sea and useful in a fight.

Some women took to him wholeheartedly, with a passion and vigor that he found shocking. He had chalked up four girlfriends in four years, each one confident and assured, knowing precisely what they wanted in bed. Strong and opinionated these women had been, if they shared a common characteristic. Better than him, he thought, and properly educated. They had always chosen him; he was always the silent partner. Two had been older, one the same age, one much younger, and this youngest a kind of sexual athlete whose antics had frightened him at first, then taught him a thing or two, then made him feel like some kind of pervert.

He had never believed himself attractive or even moderately acceptable, because of his size and his silences, his inability to talk freely. But there were girls who liked the incongruity between his physical bulk and what they saw as thoughtfulness. Vitek recognized that they read more into his awkward shyness, his cringing reluctance to let down his guard, than was actually there. But it had allowed him to come out of himself a little. To understand the difference between love and sex. To realize that a part of him was all right. And he learned, quietly, that you did not have to love someone to be loved back. He could not understand what prompted women to like him, just as he did not understand why he agreed to let them.

Vitek went out into the living room, low ceilinged and sparsely furnished with a purple sofa, a square coffee table topped with orange tile, a portable television on a stack of packing crates, and a tall bookcase made of pine boards, heavy with books. He read the spines of two of the books at a glance, *The Oxford Textbook of Tropical Medicine* and *Eye Care in Developing Countries*. A small framed photograph hung on one wall and he had to get up close to make out that it was a picture of African children, hundreds of them in a dense crowd, all pushing toward the camera, blue-black bodies, dazzling teeth, staring eyes. Hopeful eyes,

Vitek thought, and desperate. There were so many of them that they looked like an ocean, a sea of people stretching to the distance. He could imagine them pressed together, undulating like swell in the deep blue, moving like waves toward a distant shore.

Chika came up behind him and said, "Rwanda. Those are refugee children. I took it when I was leaving. That was the last place I worked, before I came back here and got out of it. I liked the children best, but they'll break your heart if you let them."

They were alone in the room. "I've got to ask why you're here," Vitek said over his shoulder. "Of all places."

"Truth is, I was burned out," she said. "I did it too long, and it was a lot of pressure. I didn't even realize how bad I'd got, but something was wrong. I couldn't relax, had nightmares, worked all the time. I saw some terrible things, but after a while I wasn't feeling any of it."

"What about my father?"

"What about your father? He's not a father to me. He's just a person I met, and I don't care about age or anything else. I'm fond of him."

"He's my father."

"That's right," Chika said and sat down on the edge of the coffee table.

His father came into the room then, clutching three more opened bottles of beer and a large nautical chart. He handed them the beers and then unfolded the stiff map on the coffee table, smoothing the creases carefully with his palms, as if he was petting the flank of a sick animal. "Here we are," he said. "This is what you need to see. Get oriented. Understand where we are."

Vitek squatted by the coffee table and watched his father's fingers, as brown and thick as cocktail franks, move over the map. The Keys tapered off into the Gulf of Mexico like a bullwhip, dangling out into the water, a tiny uvula in the great apple bite of the Gulf, drifting in the current toward the coast of Cuba. He followed across the island chain below: Haiti, Dominican Republic, Puerto Rico, Virgin Islands, and then the Bahamas, as random and irregular as bread thrown for chickens; Andros, the Biminis, Abaco, Eleuthera, Great Exuma, Acklins. It struck him how close it all was, how only a few nautical miles separated complete cultures, communists, despots, languages, and beliefs, the whole history of colonialism laid out in the geography of a handful of small islands.

His father ran his finger along a stretch of blue and said, "This is the place."

"What do you mean?"

"The Gulf Stream runs right through the Florida Straits. When you're out there, you can feel it under you. Moves more water through the Straits in a single day than all the rivers in the world combined. Just keeps moving all that water, day in and day out. When it passes over the continental shelf here, it brings food up from the bottom. More fish here than you've ever seen."

Vitek nodded, drank a mouthful of beer, and looked into the patch of empty blue, nothing but a map reference, a point on the grid, an imagined sheer drop. It was the edge of everything. The place where North America disappeared in a thousand-foot free fall.

His father kept tapping the map. "The rich water comes to the surface from two thousand feet down. It's a buffet. The big fish come to feed — marlin, blackfin, yellowfin, skipjack, tarpon, permit, you name it. Dolphin — bottle-nosed, Riso, spotted dolphin, too, out there, I've seen them."

"You can do catch and release," Chika said. "Conserve the resource."

"I know where to go," his father said. "I've talked to some old-timers, worked it out. Got some local knowledge. I know where to go. It's just a matter of getting some punters to pay me for it."

"I believe you," Vitek said and stood up. "But I don't have any money."

His father refolded the map. "I'm not asking for money," he said.

"He doesn't want charity," Chika said, sitting down on the purple sofa.

"You know all about charity, don't you?" Vitek said. "That's why you're here, I suppose. Looking after my father like he was some kind of refugee."

"I'm here because I want to be," Chika said. "No charity involved."

His father stood holding the map out in front of him like an offering.

Vitek swallowed his beer and looked at Chika. "He's an old man. He's been confused, that's all. My mother is very upset about it. They've been married almost forty years," he said.

"That's none of my business."

"I'm going to take him home," Vitek said.

"Think about what he wants to do. He won't go."

"You're half his age, for Christ's sake. You can tell him to go."

"I'm not telling him anything. He's been miserable half his life. I don't think you understand your father at all."

"I understand that he needs to come home."

His father threw his beer bottle down hard onto the floor, but instead of breaking it bounced with a dull thud, and a stream of white frothy liquid ran onto the carpet. He stared at them both for a moment and then walked out. Vitek heard the front door open with a creak and then slam shut. Chika told him that he was gone now, who knew where, and they wouldn't find him until he was good and ready to come back.

Vitek walked outside, across the sandy yard, and stood under the line of windblown palm trees. He felt fat and sluggish in the heat, was self-conscious about his white legs and heavy gut. He looked up at the leaves, dense dark hexagons floating in the air above him. Chika came out with two kitchen chairs and mosquito candles and told him they might as well wait as anything. He didn't want to talk to her. She put the chairs under the palms and lit the candles. They burned steadily with long orange flames and released a pungent smell of citrus. She knew Vitek was trying to be a good son, she said, trying to do the right thing. She hoped they hadn't gotten off on the wrong foot.

Vitek didn't want to talk, but he couldn't leave either. He sat down on a chair and looked up at the spangled sky, a shimmering arc that felt close and daunting near the ocean. The stars anchored him. When he was alone at night, he went outside and looked up into the sky like a child, felt he could manage his life in the face of the terrible insignificance of his own solar system. Chika started talking to him in the dark and he sat back and kept the stars in full view. The long flames of the candles felt faintly warm on his bare legs and he drank the beer she had brought him and let the alcohol calm him down.

.   .   .

Red Mud

She was in the mountains in Africa with about four hundred refugees —
displaced people who were being hunted by bands of militia with knives
and guns. This is what she told him there in the dark. She had not been
afraid, she said, they had the big blue UN flags with white laurel leaves
on them fluttering over the buildings of what once had been a middle
school, which gave them a type of diplomatic immunity. They had treatment and feeding centers in the school buildings and people had put up
tents on the dirt playground. There was enough clean water from a bore
well. They had a good supply of rice and oil, and beans and some fruits
and vegetables. The air was very clear in the mountains, and it was cool
and misty in the early mornings and at dusk. You could see a long way
down into the valleys and across the tops of the hills. Everything was brilliant green. Most afternoons it rained for half an hour, a dense downpour
that disappeared quickly and left the ground steaming and after the
rain the trees seemed greener and more vivid. They collected the rain
in stainless-steel tanks that had been shipped in from Paris and stored it
in big inflatable bladders. The water was distributed through standpipes
and used for washing — three to five liters per person per day, the international standard.

The point is, Chika said, they were organized and it was not as bad
as some places. It was quite calm. Everyone got measles vaccine when
they came in and they taught the people to come for treatment as soon
as they noticed fever or fast breathing, or the bloody diarrhea that was
everywhere then. She'd had the bloody diarrhea four times herself, but
it was all right because they had a supply of the new-generation cephalosporins that still worked well, although they were too expensive for the
country to use under peacetime conditions. This was the irony, she said.
You got better care during a civil war than you were likely to get when
the country was at peace.

There were two others running the camp with her — Comfort, who
was a local nurse, from the capital city, and a male nurse who was older,
around sixty, called Vince Head, whose name was a standing joke. Vince

Head was English and had left a complete life behind him, two marriages, three kids in Sheffield, England, and now looked to go to places where he could not be reached. But they got on well and could do the job, no problem, everything seemed calm and clear in the mountains.

They had all agreed to do some clinics for the Catholic priest who came down the white gravel road one day on an old steel push-bike, sweating like a pig, wearing a black shirt and high white dog collar. He kept the regalia on for security purposes, he told them, did not think the people doing the damage would touch a man of faith. The priest explained that he had many frightened people coming to his church with minor complaints who could use some basic first aid and some medicine. If they would come to help, he would let them set up in the church. The people were too frightened to come to the camp, he told them, but it was only a one-and-a-half-hour bike ride, perhaps half an hour by Jeep. They had all agreed that it was a good idea. They did not imagine that the people who came in to give medical care would be at risk, Chika told him, everything seemed clearer and more sensible than it really was. It was hard to read. They didn't imagine that there would be trouble, which was why they let Comfort go out to do the clinic at the Catholic Church. She went out on a Sunday morning in one of the Land Rovers, loaded with basic supplies and vaccines in cold carriers. She took two men from the camp with her to help out and to translate — they had been health assistants before the crisis and wanted to help.

They had an arrangement, Chika told him. They were not stupid or naive enough to have left it open. Comfort would be back by two, three at the latest. If there was more to do, she could go back the next day, or the day after. There would be no staying out in the countryside alone. That was the agreement, and when she was not back by three, Chika knew she would have to go out and get her, although she thought at the time that it was nothing, that Comfort had lost track of time or been unable to turn people away. At the very worst, it would be a problem with the car. She took their second car, a reliable Jeep covered in blue-and-white UN markings, and left Vince Head to hold the fort.

It was a tortuous road built into the side of a steep hill and slow going. She passed through one village that seemed to be deserted. At the second village, there were a few people milling about and she drove through very slowly, and the people stood back and stared nervously at the car. She could see that something was wrong, something in the air, you can get a feeling, and she stopped and wound down the window. No one came up at first, but after a minute or so, an older man wearing a tattered brown shirt and trousers held up by a piece of rope walked up and stood by the window with his arms by his sides, as if he were at attention, and told her in broken French that there was trouble at the church, and they knew there were nurses up there. A group of soldiers, *militaires*, was up there, he said, with guns, and everyone had run away. She should go back, he told her, get out of there.

What would you do? She asked Vitek this question and did not want or expect an answer. It was another mile up the road to the church and she drove halfway and then pulled the car off to the side in a clump of eucalyptus and walked the rest of the way. She kept off the road, walking through small fields planted with maize and cassava and potatoes, and when she got to the church, her shoes were caked with the red mud from the fields and her trousers and hands were covered in it. That's what she remembered, the mud, the feel and smell of it.

The church compound was completely deserted, no sign of life in the houses, no animals, no noise whatsoever. The Land Rover was parked by the side of the church with the keys in the ignition and she reached in through the open window and took the keys instinctively. At the front of the church, a dusty black Mercedes was parked at an angle with its two front doors open. She felt quite vulnerable on her own, but walked up to the car and looked inside. It had white leather seats and a walnut interior. The floor was littered with shell casings and cigarette ends, and on the backseat was a gun. She did not think she had ever held a gun in her life, she said, not even picked one up to see what it was like, but she didn't hesitate, just took it from the car and walked away. It was an automatic weapon, she thought, a big thing, surprisingly heavy, with ribbed plastic grips and a wide canvas strap.

She knew they were all in the church. She could hear noises now that she was close. She went along the side of the building. It sounded like people were talking inside — there were a few high windows, covered with wire mesh, but open, and she heard voices. At the back of the church, she found a door, for the priest, she assumed, and it was ajar. That's where she stopped, she told Vitek, because she did not know what to do, whether to go in with the gun, whether to go in at all. Perhaps everything was all right. She didn't want to blunder in with the gun in her hands, make it worse than it already was. Then it started raining. One of those solid downpours that came up in the afternoon, fat drops that felt heavy on your hands and face. It was suddenly dark as the thunderclouds came over, and somehow the rain and the cooler air made up her mind and she pushed open the door.

Three-vessel Disease

They sat under the palm trees until midnight and then Vitek got his duffel bag from the car and let Chika show him the small spare room. She pushed aside stacks of packing crates and two outboard motors on blocks, then put a sheet and a blanket on a narrow single bed in the corner of the room. There was no sign of his father. Vitek fell asleep instantly and had riotous colorful dreams that he would not remember.

He awoke early the next morning, cotton mouthed and gasping, to find his father standing at the end of the bed. It was still dark. His father stood like an apparition, framed by the hall light behind him, and had a wild look. "Let's go out in the boat," he said to Vitek. "No time like the present. Give you a chance to see her in action."

"Are you all right?" Vitek asked.

"I'm fine. I appreciate your concern for me, both of you." He was wearing his orange fishing overalls. He had fueled the boat, loaded some supplies from the E-Z Mart, and then slept down on the water. He had already woken Chika. She appeared behind him, bleary eyed and yawning, wearing a large jacket.

"It's early," Chika said.

"Not that early," his father said and walked back to the kitchen. "Get some warm clothes, let's go. It's calm. I'm getting coffee."

Vitek should have said something to his father, stopped him, told him that he didn't need to prove anything. But he didn't say a word. They went down to the boat. It was a huge white behemoth in the dark, bigger than Vitek remembered. His father showed him the cabins and the navigational equipment, got down on his haunches to point out the quality of the joinery in the galley woodwork. Vitek could smell alcohol on his father's breath.

His father took the helm and throttled up into the harbor with the water sparkling in the orange harbor lights. The engine rumbled under them, throaty and surprisingly quiet in the silence of early morning. The thin pale line of dawn shone on the horizon. Chika went below to sleep. The dark water sparked with green phosphorescence as they slipped away from shore.

Vitek stood on deck, silent and immobile, full of emotion, bundled up like steel wool. He was mute and furrow browed when something should have been said, stood with his jaw clenched and his hands hanging like steaks by his side. It was the first time he had been on the sea since he was twelve years old. Time slowed down. He began smoking cigarettes, one after the other, pulling them from the pack as if they were candy for the taking. He watched the sun come up over the horizon, a soft streak of red and purple that expanded to dazzling white light. Everything was clear and distinct in the morning light: the wash on the bow; the burnished wood of the steering wheel; the black hairs on the backs of his white hands.

Clarity was what he needed. He felt mired. More like the parent than the son, with a crushing sense of responsibility that bogged him down. Out on the open water, he recognized that his father had made his remote dreams real, absolutely so. His father's dreams were clear and palpable: the powerful boat; the shivering curtains of cold water on the prow. And yet he found himself resentful of what his father was doing, the recklessness of it, the money he owed. All of it on credit. Nothing real. Nothing certain.

An hour later his father throttled down, turned off the engines, and let them drift on the current. It was suddenly quiet. Hard diesel fumes from the engines hung in the air. Vitek looked out over the water as if there was something to see.

"This is the place," his father said. "The Gulf Stream."

"You mean you want to go fishing?" Vitek said. "We don't have to."

"This is a fishing boat. Nothing more natural than fishing in it. That's why I'm here."

"I like your boat," Vitek said.

"I'll tell you what this boat is," his father said. "This is a piece of freedom. If I wanted to go to Cuba, could do. If I wanted to go to any island in the world, I could go."

"You proved your point."

"You don't feel old out here," his father said.

"I see that."

"I'll get a drink."

"I don't need a drink," Vitek said. "It's too early."

"I need a drink and you need to celebrate," his father said.

"Celebrate what?"

"Celebrate that your old man is sitting right here, boy. Right here."

His father went below. The boat rocked gently in the swell. He came back on deck with a bottle of malt whiskey and two plastic cups. He poured a measure of whiskey into the cups and gave one to Vitek.

"Just over there is Cuba," he said. "Not far away. If I can get to Cuba, I can get just about anywhere." Vitek took a sip. His father drank quickly and drops of whiskey ran down his chin. He sat down in the fishing chair and held the bottle in his lap as if it were a living thing.

"You don't want to go to Cuba," Vitek said.

"Of course I don't. It's a principle. I could go. I have the power to go."

"Is it safe out here?" Vitek said.

"It's safe."

"Let's go back," Vitek said.

"You have to admit that it's beautiful on the ocean in the morning," his father said.

"It's beautiful when it's calm."

"Calm is a state of mind. I'm very calm."

"We should get moving," Vitek said.

"You can see that anything is possible with a boat like this." His father poured more whiskey into his own cup.

"I suppose so."

"Have another drink," his father said.

"I think we should go back." Vitek finished his cigarette and lit another.

"You've become a practical man," his father said. "That's what I always was. Practical." He stood up, undid his overalls, and pulled up his sweater and shirt. He pointed at the long thin scar running up the center of his chest to the base of his throat. The scar gleamed white on his brown skin.

"Open-heart surgery. That's what I got from being a practical man. Trying to put food on the table, working every day. Look at it."

"I know," Vitek said.

"You remember. Worked every day of my life for open-heart surgery. That's what being practical did for me. No good. That's what. No damned good." He stood there holding up his shirt as if he was holding a painting for display. Five years ago, he had come in from the water with crushing pain in his shoulder and jaw, and within a day they had him on an operating table. Three-vessel disease, the doctors said, arteries like clogged pipes. Without the operation, he would have dropped dead.

"This is revenge, that's what this boat is, boy. Revenge."

"It's not my fault."

"Not saying it's your fault. I'm trying to explain it to you. Trying to get it clear. If you don't look after yourself, no one will. I wasn't happy at home."

"You weren't miserable."

"I wasn't happy."

"No one is happy. Not completely happy. It's just the way it is. Everyone makes choices about what they can do. My mother stayed with you a long time."

"She's glad I'm gone."

"That's not true."

"You ask her."

"I won't ask her that."

"You should ask her that. I've done her a favor. She's free to do what she wants — I'm not holding her to anything. She's been off me since your brothers died. She blamed me for what happened to them."

"That's not true."

"You ask her."

"I won't. It was years ago."

"She thinks I killed them, your brothers. Holds me responsible. You try living with that for twenty years. She made me keep fishing because of your brothers."

His father pulled down his shirt and threw his cup over the side. Vitek listened to the water against the side of the boat. A thin breeze ruffled his hair. He shivered and put his hands into his jacket pockets. The blue water filled him with dread.

"They're not going to let me keep the boat," his father said.

"I know." Vitek took the whiskey bottle from his father and held it by his side.

"Can't pay. Can't raise the cash. It's too much for me."

"There's nothing we can do about it."

"I should have been stronger. Gone harder. I was weak."

"It would have been difficult for anyone."

"I was weak."

"It's all right."

That was a lie. It was not all right. He could not stand to let his father lose something that was so important to him. He knew that his mother had blamed his father for his brothers. It was in what she did not say, the silences, her refusal to speak about it at all. It was all wrapped up in her sense of unquestioning duty to him over the years, as if he was paying some kind of debt in the slugging monotonous work.

Three days after the accident, his father got back from the boat and came straight home. He was still in his fishing clothes, unshaven, flushed from sun and wind, hands the size of bread-and-butter plates. Vitek shut himself in his room and listened to the voices of his parents in the room below him. He looked into the wool clipper. An hour later, his father knocked on his door and came in and sat down on his bed. He looked vastly out of place in the small room with whitewashed walls and pale colors, and he smelled sour and fishy, like something you might find washed up after a storm. He stared at the floor, put both hands on his knees, and told Vitek that he would never let him fish. He would never let him do it, he said, not a snowball's chance in hell. It was a terrible life, a cause of great misery, now look at what had happened to the family. Vitek stood by the window and watched his father, nodded and told him it was all right. That night he took the picture of the wool clipper off his wall and slipped it under his bed. He could no longer bear to look at the sea, even an artist's rendering of it, static and fading behind a piece of dusty glass.

That was the way it stood and then later that same year his father took him lobster fishing one bitterly cold morning in September. Vitek was shocked by the blackness of the ocean, the ruthless cold, the sharpness of the rope and the lobster pots against his skin, the stink of fish and brandy on the men. His father put his head down and worked with his feet wide on the deck. The lobsters were hard and gray as they came out of the black water. Vitek tried to help, slipped on the wet deck and grazed his palms red. His father pulled him away and spoke to him against the wheelhouse in the dark. "You don't have to do anything. You're not here to help, boy. Don't want you to help. This is to show you what it's like out here. I know how bad it is, see. Now you know how bad it is. I'm doing it, but I know how bad it is. Every single day I think about how to get off this boat. Understand? Every single day."

His father tied a plastic bucket to the rail with a piece of nylon rope and then threw it over the side, filled it with seawater, and pulled it onboard. He unhooked his overalls and took them off, then peeled off his sweater, shirt, and pants. He stood on the ribbed deck in his underwear and upended the bucket over his head with a shout. He took a piece of soap from his tackle box and washed himself all over, then threw the bucket over the side again and rinsed with another shower of saltwater. His chest and back were light brown and covered in blond hairs. He wiped himself down with a towel. Vitek felt the heat from the engines when he stood in the stern and felt tired and jumpy from the cigarettes. Water lapped against the engine casing. They were floating in the Gulf Stream, moving at a barely perceptible two knots toward the northeast. Vitek took a deep breath and filled the bucket for himself. He took the bucket into the sun on the bow, took off his clothes, and upended the freezing water over his head. He gasped and shivered in the sun, watched the tips of his fingers turn blue, then repeated the process and put his dry clothes back on. The water cleared his head and made him feel fresh and awake.

Chika was cooking eggs, tomatoes, and pork sausages on a gas burner in the galley. She had made a loaf of bread into toast. The smells were wonderful in the cool air. His father brewed half a gallon of hot coffee and stirred in spoonfuls of white sugar. They carried the food and coffee up onto the deck and sat in the sun. Vitek surprised himself with his hunger, ate chunks of egg and sausage wrapped in pieces of the crisp toast. He soaked up the pork grease with toast and washed it down with pulls of coffee and the food and the spreading warmth on the deck made him feel calmer. A balmy breeze came up from the south and the sea was comfortable. The water was deep blue and shimmered with triangles of refracted light.

His father rigged his lines for marlin. He used one-hundred-and-thirty-pound test line and doubled the last six feet for extra strength. He tied the lines to the swivels with offshore swivel knots and used 80W reels on heavy game rods. At the end of the lines, he strung his artificial lures, big lures that resembled skipjack tuna when striking the surface of the water. The lures concealed huge knucklehead hooks. Vitek watched his father's hands as he tied the rigs. His fingers were fat and thick skinned and made everything he touched seem small. He manipulated the line with surprising care and dexterity, held it as if it was made of human hair. He rigged four lines and rods and set them at the back of the boat. Then he took out two gaffs and put them on the deck. He stopped to eat a plateful of eggs and sausage, then sat back in his chair and sipped coffee with the sun in his face.

"Bet you never thought you'd see me sitting here," his father said.

"Guess I didn't."

"Feel like I've lived my life in the dark when I sit here."

"It doesn't feel real."

"If you can kick it, it's real. Put your foot to something, boy."

Chika laughed and then Vitek laughed, too, laughed that he was sitting on the open sea on a bright morning with his father. They saw two or three other fishing boats then, off to the south, moving along the continental shelf. One of them had a problem with its muffler that made the engine sound loud and explosive. The boat was long and low in the water. Terns and man-o'-war birds flew overhead and hovered over the water to the south. A school of silver bait fish flashed and shimmered at the surface. The birds plunged into the water after the fish.

"Fish in the water," his father said. "That's where we need to be."

His father set his four lines and motored slowly along the continental shelf, out toward where they had seen the birds. The lures spanned out behind the boat. Chika cleared the breakfast things and came on deck wearing shorts and a T-shirt. Her legs were thin and white. They moved past the boat with the loud engine and saw three men in large straw hats bent over the engine with tools. The men waved and his father waved back. Fine cold spray came onto Vitek's face and the water and clear air made the night seem smaller.

Chika stood next to him and ran a hand through her hair. She looked older than her thirty years in the bright light. Her cheeks were hollow and scarred from acne. Deep gray rings lay under her eyes. Vitek could imagine her as an old woman. There was something reliable about her, a certain uncaring loyalty, a sense of conviction that he knew was from love. "You know, you can take him home, if you want to," she said to him. "If it's important to you. If that's what you want. You take him home."

A Land Rover Key

It was cold in back of the church, Chika told him, and dark. She had to stand there for a few minutes before she could see anything and she was frightened, frightened in a way that made her bowels feel loose. The gun was heavy in her hands and so she slung it around her neck with the canvas strap. She walked though a dark room that had a table and some chairs in it, through another door and a short hallway, and then she was in the back of the church itself. The rain was hammering down on the cast-iron roof like a cascade of ball bearings, and she was glad because it masked sounds, made it feel less real, easier to be invisible.

She squatted down out of sight at the back. Four men in green uniforms stood in the middle of the church, armed, pointing their guns around. They had a wild look, she could see that, and seemed ready to do something terrible. The priest was standing up talking to them, or trying to. He was using a local language she did not understand, and it was surprising to her, but the men with the guns seemed to be listening to him. About a hundred people were sitting, absolutely silent, on the floor. They were watching the priest as he talked to the soldiers.

Comfort was sitting at one of the tables they had set up for the clinic, watching the men with the guns. The two health assistants who had come with her were on the floor in front of the tables, wearing dirty white coats. The coats seemed inappropriate, Chika said, out of place in the dark church that was surrounded by fields filled with all that red mud.

What could I do, she said, what would *you* do? All those people in that church, and Comfort, her friend, and the two health assistants. She'd seen many dead people, of course, she told him, but never people she knew. It was different when the people at risk of being killed were people you knew. When she thought about it later, she was very angry, blind angry, and imagined herself taking that gun she had, lifting it up, and running into the church shooting. She did this over and over, in daydreams — shot those soldiers with that gun.

Squatting in the back of the church, she felt shocked and out of breath, as if she had been knocked over. She couldn't do anything at all. She sat there, lost track of time for a moment, and then just wanted to disappear. It was easier if she imagined that she was invisible. It seemed as if she must have been there for a very long time, but in fact it couldn't have been more than a few minutes. She went back through the church and outside, and then jogged away, back along the road. She left them there, all those people, the priest, the health assistants, and her friend Comfort, and went back to the car. She threw the gun down in a field, kicked some heavy mud over it and left it. She still had the key to Comfort's Land Rover in her pocket, forgot about it completely for hours. She was in a kind of purposeful daze and not thinking at all. She got back to her car and threw up until she was just dry-heaving and everything smelled like sick. Then she drove back to the camp, down that winding road, very slowly, very carefully. She didn't remember a thing about the drive itself. She was still amazed that she hadn't driven off the road completely.

She told Vince Head and everyone else that she hadn't been able to reach the church, that she had been stopped by villagers, that the road was barricaded. She lied through her teeth about it, pretended that nothing had happened, told everyone that she was sure the people at the church would be all right. She lay awake, couldn't sleep. Then everything seemed to work out, because early the next morning Comfort and the health assistants *did* return, unscathed, having spent the night with the priest. There were no keys for the Land Rover, of course, so they had walked. In the end, the priest had convinced the men with guns to leave them alone and had given them money. The priest had seen this as a kind of triumph of righteousness and faith. Comfort told them they had never been at real risk, but Chika had been there and knew that this was a lie.

She knew with certainty that she had failed in a profound way, she told Vitek, because she had not tried to save those people when she'd had the chance. She had done something inexcusable that she could not tolerate, would not accept in others, and would not accept in herself. Nothing really matters, she said, nothing at all, except what you do in those few moments when you have to put yourself on the line for others, to overcome your own fear. That's all that counts and when you can't do that, you need to stop pretending you will. It is all right to fail, she said to him, she understood that. It is more important to try, to do your best. This is all that makes failure acceptable.

She got out — stayed to finish her time in the mountain camp, then did not sign another contract, and got out. She came to the coast because it felt temporary, not quite solid, and at the time she needed to be temporary. Then she met his father and somehow he had calmed her down, and given her some sort of grounding. He seemed so sure and certain of what he had to do.

She still had the key to the Land Rover, and sitting there under the palms surrounded by the mosquito candles, she showed it to him. It was strung on a chain around her neck. She pulled it out from under her T-shirt and let it rest on her open palm. In the yellow flickering light from the candles, the key flashed and blinked. This reminds me to be a stronger person, she said, reminds me that you need to give up something of yourself to be useful, let go of your own fear. Fear was the impulse she wanted to overcome, she said. His father was better at facing his fear than most, in fact, and you had to respect him for that.

Stack of Bibles

The deck of the fishing boat was brilliant white under their feet. Vitek turned to Chika and said, "I do have money saved. I didn't tell him. I can give him the money. I want to help him out if I can." The sun was bright in his eyes, flashing and glinting off the rippling water.

"I don't think he'll take it," Chika said and smiled. His father was standing at the wheel, looking down at them, his hair blowing back off his face. It was where he belonged, out there on the open water.

"I'll make him take it," Vitek said.

"You can't make him," Chika said.

Vitek slipped off his sneakers then, felt the cool gritty fiberglass deck under his feet, and had a sense of carelessness that he did not recognize. He hoisted himself up on the stern rail. Chika watched him, asked him what he was doing. If she had told him to stop, he would have done so, but she said nothing. He looked into the sky, away from the water. His heart pounded. He stood on the edge of the boat as if he were at the edge of a cliff and said, "I'm going to help."

He felt lighter than he should have standing up high on the rail, impossibly tall and commanding, as if he was on the wool clipper of his childhood, racing toward some kind of destiny. The swell rolled under him in big slow pillows that lifted him up toward the sky and then dropped him back. He let himself go.

Vitek lifted his knees to his chest as he jumped. There was a moment of exhilaration, a childlike sensation, an ecstatic feeling, somewhere between the jump and striking the water, perhaps just before he broke the surface. The cold water rolled over him, swallowed him up, and he had a moment of gasping panic. Then he sank below the surface, watched the blue sky give way to a hazy veil filled with blue-green light, and saw the bottom of the boat, the dancing silhouette of Chika leaning over the side, his own legs hanging in front of him. He kept going, felt as if he could sink for a long time, used his arms to push himself down, and in a few seconds felt warm again and full of energy. He kept sinking. The hull of the boat became a little smaller. He felt free in a way that he could not have described. Everything is arbitrary, he thought, and when he felt the need to breathe he stopped and looked back up to the light, warm and clearheaded, and decided to go back to the surface. He let himself rise slowly. He came up through the cold water with his hands waving figures of eight in front of him. He rose through the incandescent light, looked down to the absolute emptiness below, felt no fear, and broke the surface with tiny rainbows of saltwater spinning in front of his eyes. He was a hundred yards from his father's boat. A breeze blew across the water and rippled the surface. Vitek waved his arms in the air, slowly at first, and then more quickly. He knew then that he would not be taking his father home.

It is remarkable, Chika had said to him in the dark, that your whole life can come down to just a few key moments. When you boil it down, it is all about fifteen minutes here and fifteen minutes there, the moments when you are really tested, when what you do will make a real difference. Everything else is just biding your time for when you're needed. In that church in Africa she had realized this, she said. You have to be able to grab those moments when they are presented to you. The day after Comfort and the others returned, they had all gone back to the church with the spare key to collect the Land Rover and drive it back to the camp. People had reappeared in the villages, and children were running along the road and playing in front of the houses. Chika went back into the church and found a young boy playing with a stack of Bibles on the floor. He had big eyes and thin arms. When he looked up at her in the dim light of the church, Chika said, she cried for the first time, cried like a baby, because there was something terribly innocent about that child, and she knew that this innocence would not last.

She had told him her secrets. Vitek had his own. He recognized that something had clicked and turned inside his own twelve-year-old head the night his brothers disappeared, something as difficult to pin down as the stormy water he saw through his own bedroom window. The night they got the news, when his father was still out on the fishing boat and his mother was inconsolable, he had gone out into the wet night on his own. He walked down the hill through streets slick with icy rain. At the dock, he looked out at the boats moored in the harbor, dim shapes beyond his vision. The black water, the cold metal of the boats, the hidden things below, all of it was terrifying for the first time. He stood in the rain. It soaked the canvas jacket he was wearing, ran in cold rivulets down his neck and onto his chest. When he looked back, he felt as if he had been frozen there, held at that moment, looking for something certain on that dark harbor that he had never been able to see. That moment had become a part of who he was.

They pulled him back onto the boat, dripping and shivering. Black terns flickered in the sky. It was hot on the deck and his father looked at him carefully, shaded his eyes with his hands, and asked him if he was all right. Chika laughed and gave him a towel. Vitek put his hand on his father's shoulder, awkwardly, lightly, a big red ham of a hand that shook with cold, and had the sensation that his life had been rushing past in a torrent. Why had he jumped? He barely understood himself. He felt as if he had jumped through a plate-glass window, cleared some kind of transparent barrier.

He wanted to tell them both that he understood why they were there, that he understood *them*, but no words came. He looked down at Chika and laughed at his own tears, coming now into the corners of his eyes. He would remember the cold water dripping onto the tops of his feet, the rough fiberglass against his toes, the sharp saltwater in his mouth. What was there to say? He shivered and shut his eyes. With his eyes shut, he saw himself standing in that church in Africa with the thin-armed child. He knew what he had to do. With his heavy red hands, he lifted that child up, lifted him into his arms and held him tight, told him to watch the stars, to keep his eyes on distant galaxies, because every point of light is a wish made a million years ago, and it was available to him, it was available.

3

A FEW SHORT NOTES ON TROPICAL BUTTERFLIES

1. Danaus Plexippus: *The Monarch Butterfly*

Last night Maya locked herself in the bathroom again with her copy of *The New England Journal of Medicine.* She likes to memorize the most interesting articles and quote them to her patients. She is a lover of small details, tiny pieces of information, maps, diagrams, and the tortuous skull anatomy of the twelve pairs of human cranial nerves. Maya is spending longer and longer periods of time locked in the bathroom, and I know that she has been crying because the wastepaper basket fills up with tissues. Her decision to become a neurosurgeon was partly an attempt to control the surrounding world, which she sees as unmanageable. It is the ultimate test of her ability to remain calm in the face of difficult, and often dangerous, clinical situations. She has buried herself so far in her knowledge of details that she cannot properly feel what is happening in her own life. I know that she needs me to reach out to her, but I can't do it. She does not understand how much she has hurt me, and I clam up whenever we are together.

At dinner, I watched her eat chow mein and looked for an opportunity to say something about what has happened to us. It is fall, my favorite season, and I remarked that the monarch butterflies of central Texas would soon begin their annual migration. These remarkable butterflies follow the Sierra Madre Oriental south across the tropic of Cancer and then turn west over the neovolcanic mountains of Mexico.

"Can't you forget about butterflies for a change?" she said to me.

"I'm just interested. They *are* fascinating."

"We'd be better off if you were more interested in children."

"I'm not ready for children." I concentrated on my food.

"You may not be. But I am. I'm already thirty-eight and not getting any younger. And neither are you."

Maya is twenty years my junior and we were desperately in love when we married. She was a resident, working for me as part of her surgical rotation. It was such a cliché—distinguished older surgeon with ambitious younger woman—that we kept our affair secret for three years. The illicit nature of it appealed to her. For months, we met in the pathology laboratory at night when we were both on call—we got to know each other surrounded by jars labeled "Normal Human Lung," and "Chronically Inflamed Gallbladder." The laboratory was the only place where we could be alone and we were never interrupted there. It had a strangely peaceful feeling—like that of a deep pine forest where all you can hear is your own breathing.

Before Maya, I'd had a series of relationships with women my own age. These were comfortable and easy affairs, filled with companionable silences, safe dinners, and weekends away. But I was never in love, and I never married. I chose convenience over everything else, and I did not want to be too close to anyone. Seeing Maya in a surgical mask and blue paper hat, I was bowled over for the first time in my life. She was different in a way that I cannot exactly explain. Maya looked like someone with secrets. She was utterly self-contained. It was this sense of isolation that reached out to me.

Last night, after an uncomfortable silence filled only by the slurping of wonton soup, I said to her, "Perhaps we should try getting pregnant in the summer."

"You said that last year," Maya said.

"I mean it. You know I do."

"You don't convince me."

"How can you say that?"

"Because I think you're lying. That's how."

She is quite right. I have not thought about children. I am putting it off. After dinner, I had trouble walking to the kitchen to make the coffee — I had to hold on to the wall to get my balance. Maya told me again that I drink too much and I shouted that I could damn well do as I please. She followed me into the kitchen then and wanted me to hold her. "Just hold on to me," she said, "and put down that bottle, for a change."

Watching Maya operate on the brains of strangers brings back memories of my childhood. Last week, I stood in an operating theater and watched her remove a tumor from the head of a sixty-nine-year-old retired tax accountant from Queens. The care with which she used the bone saw, cauterized each bleeding capillary with a sharp hiss of burning tissue, and gently cut through the layers of dura surrounding the brain reminded me of my father when he handled his butterflies. Maya treats every brain she works on with such respect that I am always amazed that she manages to operate on them at all. Her touch is as light as that of a butterfly on a leaf. Her hands seem to flutter and waft in the air, barely in contact with the solid stainless-steel handles of her instruments. It is always a surprise when the brain opens up beneath her hands.

Maya is fascinated by the story of my grandfather, partly because she is from an Indian family and has a deep understanding of how important relatives can be to what we all become. And partly because she has a professional interest in the disease that eventually killed him. "He is the only man I have ever known who was killed by a butterfly," Maya says. She likes to hear the full story, and I have told her most of it, often at night, lying in bed. Telling the story has become like a ritual for us. Sometimes I wonder whether she married me for it — for a piece of my

legacy. Maya, like me, has an admiration for the spirit of my grandfather, who was driven by a desire to understand the world around him.
He was a man obsessed with butterflies, and sometimes an obsession is the
only way to live. "You come from butterfly people," Maya says, "and you
are a butterfly person."

In September 1892, my grandfather chopped off his left thumb with a
butcher's cleaver out of frustration that he could no longer use his
hands. The force and accuracy of the blow were sufficient to remove
the thumb cleanly at the level of the first metacarpal joint. This violent
and painful act was the result of what my grandfather described as a
"compulsion that could not be denied."

I imagine my grandfather examining his own thumb with scientific
dispassion. He wrapped the bleeding stump in a handkerchief and drank
half a bottle of whiskey to numb the pain. The thumb and bloody cleaver
were left on the kitchen table, where they were discovered by a housekeeper. There is nothing more alarming than a severed digit — so vividly
human with its fine hairs and fingernail intact — and the housekeeper
dropped the tea tray she was carrying when she saw it. A doctor was called
and the thumb collected, and my grandfather was escorted to New York
Hospital where, under chloroform, a surgeon made crude attempts to
reattach it. There was no such thing as microsurgery at the time — the
instruments and techniques were unavailable — and the procedure was
unsuccessful.

If the accident happened today, of course, the result would be very
different. I would have had the thumb back on in eleven or twelve hours
and my grandfather would be using it again in six weeks. I have a natural affinity for the detailed work that is needed for microscopic surgery
of this type. I have always enjoyed details. I am sure this comes from my
grandfather, who was a cataloger by nature. He was famous for his collection of butterflies. He had hundreds of them from all over the world
pinned to felt boards in glass-fronted display boxes. As a child, I spent
hours looking at rows of these brilliantly colored insects. They were vivid
and exciting to me. Each splash of turquoise, mother-of-pearl, and burnt

orange represented a distant tropical forest that seemed impossibly lush and colorful. My world, New York City, was gray and brown. I grew up looking at oily concrete, cast-iron railings, and slabs of fatty corned-beef on flaking white bread.

My grandfather's thumb became a part of our family folklore because — true to his nature as a collector — he demanded that it be preserved in formaldehyde. He came home with the severed digit bobbing in a small glass jar and put it on top of his desk. It sat there for many years. My father kept it after my grandfather died, and I grew up looking at the thumb. It was the only connection with my grandfather that I ever had.

As children, we were not told how he lost it, and so I created elaborate scenarios in my mind to explain its removal. He was an unknown but exotic man to us, notorious for his trips to remote and wild countries. As a young man, he wore emerald waistcoats and carried a walnut hunting stick capped with a silver monarch butterfly, *Danaus plexippus*. His house was filled with artifacts that included the dried scalp of a yeti — a leathery dome covered in tufts of black hair — and half a dozen shrunken heads. These small dry heads, shriveled like raisins, but with their essential features intact, made me feel as if I understood something profound. They represented a dark and violent part of my grandfather's past that was never discussed. They were all dark native heads with shocks of long black hair, with the exception of one that had a brilliant red beard and was clearly European — a small brass plaque screwed onto the back of the scalp said "Captain Cutter, 19th Bengal Lancers Cavalry Regiment." I hung the unfortunate Captain Cutter in my bedroom and showed him off to my friends. He was an impressive sight to twelve-year-old boys and earned me a reputation for being dangerous. I lay awake at night staring at Captain Cutter's dismembered cranium and imagining the terrible scenes that must have preceded its removal. I am not a morbid person by nature, but I cannot control my imagination. I'm a daydreamer — a worrying quality in a surgeon.

Sometimes I wonder whether his thumb was the reason that I chose plastic surgery. Perhaps I have always wished I could have reattached my grandfather's lost digit. I have the thumb in front of me on my desk as I write. It is surrounded by swirling motes of particulate matter and seems to be moving slightly in invisible currents and eddies. I consider it to be a kind of talisman — whenever I travel for any length of time, I take it with me in my luggage. A customs official at the Bombay airport once found the thumb during a routine search and fainted.

Two years ago, I realized that I could not let Maya disappear from my life. We were bobbing in an apartment-complex swimming pool in Manhattan that smelled strongly of chlorine, the only people in the water. Dark blue tiles surrounded the edge, and long lines of orange floats marked swimming lanes. It was late and we had come from the hospital.

"You're risk averse," Maya said, blowing water through her nose. She had just finished several laps of breaststroke and was hanging in the water in front of me. Droplets gathered on her eyelashes.

"No more than most people," I said.

"You get upset if you don't eat breakfast at the same time every morning," she said, ripping the yellow bathing cap from her head and shaking out her hair, "and you've lived in the same apartment for twenty years, even though you hate it."

"I don't hate it."

"You'd rather not live there."

"So?"

"You're terrified of change."

I could see the blurred shapes of Maya's legs treading water beneath her and little flashes of reflected water on her cheeks. The lights in the pool were turned out suddenly, leaving us floating in the dark, with just street light filtering in through the windows.

"I'm organized and logical, that's all."

"No, *I'm* organized and logical. And I can take risks. You go to the same restaurants, have for years. You're terrified of traveling. You get worried if I'm more than a few minutes late — you imagine the worst."

"I do imagine the worst."

"I grew up in a large family," Maya said. She floated toward me and I felt her naked breasts against my chest. She flung her bathing suit onto the edge of the pool. It landed with a wet slap. "In a large family, you have to take risks to be noticed. I was always trying to better my brothers. Screaming for attention. I had to assert myself."

"There's no doubt that you can be very assertive." She moved herself against me, and I felt her fingers, those delicate surgeon's fingers, fluttering on my shorts. She loosened them and pulled them down to my ankles with her feet. She wrapped her legs around me, and I felt scratchy pubic hair against my stomach.

"That's why I smoked. And why I had sex with a boxer." Maya's hair floated behind her like oil on water.

"You had sex with a boxer?"

"He claimed to have broken his nose twenty-three times. He was nineteen, I was sixteen. I took him home with me. My father was a pacifist, you know, believed in nonviolent protest and all that. When he saw that I was going out with a boxer, he was speechless. He didn't speak to me for months. I only did it once — to embarrass my parents. This boxer — he was only nineteen, remember — was already losing his mind. He couldn't remember my name from one minute to the next. Kept calling me Mandy, Molly, and so on. I was laughing the whole time I was with him. We did it in the training gym. Right on the edge of the ring. Under the ropes."

"So this makes you assertive, I suppose." My first sexual experience was terrifying and involved a geneticist, half a bottle of vodka, a darkened room, and a borrowed apartment. I left before she woke up in the morning and never saw her again, out of embarrassment.

"You're still afraid of losing something, aren't you?" She floated on her back with her legs clamped firmly around me.

"I'm afraid someone's going to come in through that door and find us," I said. She had begun rubbing herself against me.

"You act as if everything is about to be taken away. So you try not to invest in things. You've tried to avoid investing in people. How many real friends do you have?"

"I've got friends." She was moving rhythmically against me now, and the water had begun lapping gently against the sides of the pool.

"I don't see them. You avoid getting too close to anyone."

I spent my childhood ordering my collection of butterflies. Family, genus, species. I was devoted to the act of putting the world into ranked order. I could recite my grandfather's collection from memory. I remember hearing children my own age playing outside on the street as I lay on the floor of my bedroom, feeling lonely and different. But I felt safer away from them.

"I'm close to you," I said as she slid down my body.

"And I'm a risk," she whispered.

"I suppose you are." It was there, in that warm pool, with Maya's gasps echoing in the tiled space, that I suggested we get married. It was my first real risk in years. When the lights came on again, we were blinded instantly, and fell away from each other as if under a police searchlight.

My grandfather came into a substantial fortune in rubber and tea from his father's family, who owned plantations in India. He was a gentleman scientist. Sepia-toned photographs from the period show him to be a small compact man with enormous muttonchop whiskers and staring eyes. I have made a close study of his diaries, big heavy volumes bound in calfskin. They make fascinating reading. He kept daily records of his life from the age of twelve. He had a tiny, cramped hand, and I have to get down near the dusty yellow paper to make sense of his words.

He became an amateur naturalist of some standing. His money allowed him the freedom to travel and he spent a great deal of time in remote locations in South America, Africa, and the Pacific. He was enthralled by the highly colored species of the tropics and his diaries are full of his trips to butterfly breeding grounds all over the world. He collected beautiful examples of *Ornithoptera victoriae victoriae*, the Queen Victoria birdwing, from the Solomon Islands, and of *Papilio antimachus*, the largest butterfly in Africa with its distinctive black-and-orange coloring. The specimens were transported on beds of cotton wool in airtight cast-iron cylinders. He spent weeks cataloging his finds according to the taxonomic classification system and then mounting them in display cases.

The bodies were pinned through the thorax with such care that even today most of his specimens have six legs, proboscis, and antennae intact. Until he went mad, my grandfather was a patient man with a steady hand.

Somehow butterflies became the center of all of our lives. My father grew up with them, was given butterfly nets for birthdays, and knew the Latin names of the Papilonidae family of tropical butterflies before he started school. My grandfather took him to watch the fall migration of the monarchs when he was little more than a baby, bundled up in wool, with dimpled elbows and knees. It infected my father, and it infected me. There is something about the transience and the beauty of these insects that gets into your blood. "Butterflies are a metaphor," my father said to us, "for life. Beautiful, fleeting, fragile, incomprehensible." Even as a young man, I understood this. I collected them like my friends collected baseball cards and stamps — each one had a personality to me. There was something free and audacious about these flimsy, absurdly colorful insects that was appealing. What possible purpose could a butterfly have other than to brighten up the world?

I have tried to explain this to Maya. But she is the daughter of a physicist from Pondicherry who emigrated after partition and she inherited his brain. Everything needs a physical explanation for Maya — the world is nothing but a mass of electrons, neutrons, and quarks, each with clearly defined rules of action and interaction. My abstract love of insects is lost on her. She grew up in Washington, D.C., cut her teeth to the sounds of Elvis Presley and learned to drive during the last days of the Johnson Administration. She understood the first law of thermodynamics before her first kiss. Maya is a mass of cross-cultural contradictions — Levi's and saris; Twinkies and dhal; David Bowie and Mahatma Gandhi; the Kama Sutra and *Casablanca*. She lives on cappuccinos, wears leather pants, and voraciously reads biographies. She has none of the elaborate superstitions of her parents, but since we returned from our honeymoon, she has started getting emotional during her period.

"Here I am bleeding to death," she said last night, "and you don't seem to appreciate what is happening to me."

"Nothing's happening to you," I said.

"Life is running out of me. Don't you understand? All my eggs are drying up. You're so cold. I'm shriveling like a flower in the sun."

"You're being emotional," I said. She was crying into my shoulder.

"Yes, I am. I want to have a child. It's as simple as that."

Maya has long thick eyelashes that I sometimes think can be heard rustling against her cheeks when she blinks. She wants to believe that the brain is nothing more than a machine that can be serviced, faulty parts ripped out and replaced — thoughts and emotions little more than functional circuits that need good spark plugs and a starter motor. With the round thighs she inherited from her mother, she looks like a wrestler in her tight surgical scrubs. Her father died of a temporal-lobe brain tumor that caused him to speak in tongues and have visions of Lord Krishna in bowls of Indian food. She sees her father every time she saws open a skull.

"You're worried about Mr. Oomman," I said to her.

"It's got nothing to do with Mr. Oomman," she said with a jerk of her head. "Don't patronize me. It's about having a child, not about Mr. Oomman. I don't give a damn about Mr. Oomman. Mr. Oomman's brain is nothing compared to the current state of my ovaries. They're withering, I tell you. Withering! Withering like two pathetic grapes on a vine. And all you can do is bring up Mr. Oomman. Mr. Oomman can go to hell." Mr. Oomman is a family friend of her parents and she is operating on him in the morning to remove a subdural hematoma, a relatively benign condition with a very high cure rate.

"Why is this so important to you?" I asked.

"How can you ask that?" Maya was sobbing.

"I just want to try to understand."

"If you don't understand now," Maya whispered, "then when the hell will you understand?"

She ripped the bottle of claret from my hand and threw it onto the ground with some force. It exploded into a blossom of pink liquid and glass on the kitchen floor. I turned and walked out of the room as quickly as I was able in my condition. As I came up the corridor toward my study, Maya ran after me. She was still carrying two chopsticks from the Chinese food and she wielded them like daggers above her head; a small dollop of sweet and sour pork had fallen onto her upturned cheek. "Don't you walk out on me," she shouted at my back, "let's get this decided. You can't keep hiding in your chicken-shit room with those stinking butterflies. They're more important to you than I am. Your bloody butterflies and fucking Mr. Cutter."

"That's *Captain* Cutter," I called over my shoulder.

"Whatever. He's a bloody shrunken head! You spend more time talking to the head of Cutter than you do to me! You and Cutter can go to hell." I reached the door and tripped on the rug as I entered the room, falling onto my knees. I caught my weight on my outstretched palms and waited for the dizziness to pass before getting up and locking the door.

My father took us every year to count monarch butterflies as they streamed down the coast on their annual migration. He packed us all up in the Oldsmobile and we went to Cape May Point on the New Jersey coast. In those days, it was a wild place. Sharp-scented forests led onto sand dunes, and empty beaches; in September bright sunshine appeared and disappeared from behind racing bundles of cumulonimbus clouds. Distant smudges of rain raced in from the sea and blew over quickly in sudden blasts that barely wet our hair. The breezes that blew off the Atlantic were sharp and constant and filled our eyes with shell grit.

My father set up our lime green canvas tent with two bedroom annexes in sheltered clumps of pines. We built cooking fires and unloaded huge hampers of food that included potted shrimp, sardines, and armfuls of preserved meats — hams, lengths of salami, and pregnant blood puddings. My sister Hannah and I felt like explorers in a wild country. Each of us was issued a pair of binoculars, a magnifying glass, and a color plate of the mighty North American monarch butterfly, five times life size. Above us, bay-breasted warblers, sharpies, Cooper's hawks, and tan peregrines hovered and plunged, soaring on violent coastal updrafts.

My father counted the migrating monarchs for several years. The figures were meticulously recorded with red ink in oilskin-bound notebooks; every year he sent his data to the head of the entomology department at

Princeton. He treated the exercise like a big-game hunt, wore Hemingway jackets with rows of front pockets, did not shave for several days, and rolled his own cigarettes in the open air. He became quite a different person for a short time. For most of his life he was a high school science teacher who saw everything as a set of first principles. He was a regular and ritualized man, not given to doing anything that had not been fully deliberated. But on Cape May Point, I was allowed to take occasional puffs on his taut little cigarettes. I still remember the feeling of loose shards of tobacco against my lips and acrid smoke on my teeth.

My father could have been on the savannah hunting wildebeest — indeed, I have often thought of the butterfly migration as the insect equivalent of the famous migration of wildebeest down the Rift Valley in Africa. The African version is noisy, dusty, and terrestrial, while the North American version is utterly silent, clean, and airborne. You could live right under a monarch butterfly migration and never know that it was happening.

One of the most amazing features of the North American monarch is its ability to migrate fantastic distances to avoid the winter. How it does this remains a mystery. It was the sort of mystery that the naturalists of my grandfather's generation would have relished solving. They fly in vast flocks to the mountains of northern Mexico, where they perch in Oyamel fir trees three thousand feet above sea level, on the steep southwestern slopes. I have always thought that it must be lonely down there, in the Mexican fog, hanging from the limbs of those chilly trees.

In September 1937, my father brought along a college friend of his, Mr. Albert Gissendander, who worked with a firm of book publishers in Manhattan. He was a plump man, prematurely gray, who wore baggy linen suits that were stained yellow under the armpits. He broke his small wire spectacles on the first day and tied them together with a large wad of gauze padding. He had crooked front teeth and sharp bristles on his chin, and consumed huge volumes of luncheon meats, often straight from the tin. My father liked him because he was one of those people who could call up a Shakespearean quotation for every occasion. He had a nasal voice and a precise, flat diction that made the words lifeless and mechanical. In the evenings, my father discussed butterflies with Albert Gissendander and shared with him his hip flask of whiskey.

On our second day out, we began seeing the first of the monarchs coming down the coast, bobbing and wafting like leaves in the sky above us. These flimsy insects make for a strange sight as they bounce through the air, especially when one reflects that they will continue this way for more than a thousand miles southward. It is a biological act that strains credulity. My father stationed himself in the dunes at the eastern end of the shore, and Albert Gissendander and Hannah at the other end, looking west into Delaware Bay. Even as an eight-year-old, Hannah was a better counter than most adults. She could maintain her concentration for long periods of time while standing absolutely still, and she had perfect vision. She had a small ring-bound notebook and pencil in one hand and a pair of binoculars looped around her neck on a thin leather strap.

I remember the day vividly. I was considered too young to participate, so I walked barefoot along the beach. A pale sun glimmered from behind a solid sheet of high white clouds. A tremendous gale was blowing along the front, and blasts of sand kicked up against my cheeks. The surf was flat and gray, with lines of foam gathering on the wet sand. I picked over strands of sea grapes, jellyfish, and chunks of frayed green rope and net shards thrown overboard from distant ships. The sand was cool and smooth against my toes. Because of the wind, many of the butterflies were landing on the beach to rest. I saw the tiny orange-and-black bodies clinging to rocks and clumps of sea grass, their wings opening and closing slowly. Some of them were landing on the water, too, sitting on the rippling surface behind the waves. Some of them were dying out there and washing onto the sand. I came back up the beach and walked carefully along a long jetty made of cut-granite boulders extending a hundred feet out from shore. I picked my way to the end of the jetty, hearing waves break against the black rocks and crouching to inspect clear pools of water filled with tiny silver fish and the hard white domes of barnacles. Monarch butterflies were landing on the jetty, too, clinging to the rocks in flimsy orange groups, braced against the wind.

I was sitting out on the end of the jetty, balanced carefully on the rock, with feathers of sea spray blowing into my face, when I saw Hannah running out of the dunes. At first, I thought it was a game. She had a short bobbed haircut with a high fringe; she seemed to be running toward me. I waved. She did not see me. Gusts of wind numbed my face and blew my hair into chaotic swirls. Hannah was wearing blue patent-leather shoes with silver buckles. Her skirt blew out behind her as she ran, and her thighs were red from the wind. I realized then that as she sprinted forward she was looking behind her, at Albert Gissendander, who was lumbering after her out of the dunes and onto the beach. He ran with arms outstretched and was shouting something that I could not hear over the wind. He had his binoculars in his left hand. The leather strap was broken and dragging on the ground. Hannah ran down to the jetty and began climbing out toward me. She jumped quickly on the slick rocks. She was looking back over her shoulder when she slipped. Her arms grabbed at the air. She fell onto a piece of sharp granite on which I would later find strands of her brown hair. She hit her head and then splashed into the water, and her fall seemed so instantaneous, such a momentary thing, that I expected to see her come up laughing immediately. I was perhaps fifty yards away. I had a last glimpse of her face as she went down — she was concentrating hard and her mouth was firmly shut. Without a sound she fell, down onto those hard rocks, down into the clear, cold water of that September afternoon.

2. Ornithoptera Alexandrae: *Queen Alexandria's Birdwing*

One night in May 1874, during a violent downpour, a man appeared at my grandfather's house in New York City. Unable to afford a hansom cab, he had walked all the way from the wharf district, and when he pounded on the door, his thin dark fingers shook. He introduced himself to the servant as Thomas Gray and stood in the entry hall surrounded by heavy vases filled with camellias. Water streamed from his slick oilskin and pooled at his feet. My grandfather, who was entertaining dinner guests, was called away from the table and came to the door dabbing his mouth

with a napkin. Behind the heavy ginger beard and hollow eyes, he recognized his friend, who had left the country three years earlier on a
Nantucket whaler, and whom he had given up for missing, drowned
somewhere on the southern ocean, sucked into the belly of the deep like
so many.

My grandfather threw off the oilskin and embraced him. Thomas
Gray was so skeletal that he had a birdlike quality. He walked quickly into
my grandfather's study. His breeches were smeared with street mud and
his boots were thin. He wore a rough nankeen jacket and a blue cotton
vest. Long strands of hair, bleached white by the sun, hung around a
jaw that had become thin and angular.

They had been the best of friends and had grown up together. They
shared a genuine interest in entomology, which connected them even
after Thomas Gray's family had lost their railway fortune in South American gold speculations. Butterflies had united them — a shared love of
the insect world and a need to order, catalog, and list. They spent summers preserving specimens of *Saturniidae* that they found in groves of pin
cherry, larch, maple, and walnut trees.

Thomas Gray was now a poor man struggling to build a reputation.
He had left to make his fortune in the tropics, believing he would find
insects that he could sell to museums and private collectors for a profit,
while at the same time contributing to the natural sciences. As boys, both
of them had read A *Voyage up the River Amazon* by William Edwards
and the journals of Charles Darwin aboard the HMS *Beagle*. They knew
of the astounding collections that Alfred Wallace had assembled in the
island groups of the Pacific, and were familiar with the theories of both
Wallace and Darwin, presented separately to the Linnaean Society in July
1858. My grandfather, who had a strict Protestant upbringing, was skeptical of the theories of natural selection and still believed that they could
be disproved.

Thomas Gray spent two years in the Malay Archipelago and the
Dutch East Indies, where he found jungles whose density and lushness
paralleled the extraordinary variety of the insect life that he found there.
He told my grandfather that he had collected over five hundred new

species of butterfly, the same of beetles and flies, and several hundred of wasps, moths, and bees. He spent the last of his money on a return passage on a spice cutter out of Surabaja. They put in at Mauritius for supplies. The captain, sensing perhaps that Thomas Gray's collections were more valuable than Thomas Gray himself, had departed late one night with his collection, while Gray was ashore. Two years of careful work, and all his dreams and aspirations for the future went with the ship, out across the phosphorescent Indian Ocean. Penniless, he had worked his way back on trading vessels.

Now, standing in my grandfather's study, Thomas Gray was trembling violently. In the soft lamplight, my grandfather noted that his skin had a yellow tint. Later, unable to sleep, he would record everything that happened that night in his diaries.

My grandfather poured them each a healthy measure of brandy while Gray stood with his back to the fire.

"You will be pleased to hear that I have retained one specimen," Thomas Gray said to my grandfather. "I have kept it on my person, never wanting it out of my sight. You have never seen anything like it. I have had it with me for more than a year."

From his jacket he pulled a thick oilskin bundle, tied with a piece of hemp rope. He put the bundle on my grandfather's desk and unraveled it. Inside, wrapped carefully in sheets of sandy parchment paper, was the wing of a butterfly. It was just a single wing. It shone with a green-and-blue luminescence that seemed to pull light from the room. The wing was enormous — seven inches across from the lateral tip to the attachment point with the body. It shimmered on the dark oak of the desktop, was mottled with black striations and partitioned into corrals of color that shimmered and flashed as the men moved it under the lamp. "Can you imagine the size of the butterfly it came from?" Thomas Gray inquired of my grandfather, who could not. It was the largest specimen that he had ever seen. It had a mythical quality that was difficult to believe.

Thomas Gray had been given the wing by a sailor who claimed to have found it on one of the tropical islands to the northeast of Australia, across the Torres Strait. The butterfly was so large that they brought it down with a shooter, the sailor said. They had fired three times before it fell to the ground. "This is the largest butterfly in the world," my grandfather wrote, "the dimensions of which cannot be believed."

"I want you to help me find this creature," Thomas Gray said to my grandfather. "What a find it would be. We would make our reputations. And we would make our fortunes, at the same time."

Surrounded by solid furniture and dark teak paneling, they stood examining the wing for some time. I imagine the fire raging in the grate and blasts of rain pounding against the windows. My grandfather was entranced. Thomas Gray's eyes danced with fever and exhaustion. Later, after the guests had been seen to the door, and my grandfather had given Thomas Gray a dose of quinine, a hot bath, and a bed, he sat in his study and pored over his maps of the Pacific Islands. Everything else was swept from his mind, as if it had been carried away in the torrent outside his windows. "If this creature exists on the earth," he wrote, "then I am resolved to discover it." In his heart, he believed that the butterfly would disprove the theories of natural selection elaborated by Darwin and Wallace. "When there is only one of its kind," he wrote, "with no clear survival advantage to being of such magnitude and color, then it must surely have been placed here by a divine hand." This was the beginning of his obsession with finding the butterfly that would later be called *Ornithoptera alexandrae,* Queen Alexandria's birdwing — the largest butterfly in the world.

Maya and I were having our wedding dinner with her parents when her father had his first seizure. Earlier that day, we had gone to the registry office in Washington, D.C. We stood on blue fireproof carpet for the brief ceremony. A handful of Maya's friends came and flashed photographs of us standing before the justice of the peace, a man older than I who had a set of poorly attached, clacking false teeth. Her friends threw rice at us as we walked out.

At dinner, with fork raised to mouth, her father went suddenly glassy eyed. Drips of curry fell onto the tablecloth in front of him. His breathing became quick and shallow. Then he tumbled back in his chair and started jerking as he slipped sideways. His neck arched backward and his arms pounded stiffly on the floor. I could smell the urine, sharp and acrid, when I bent over him.

I had always admired Maya's father. He had a rigorous mind and a sense of humor. He worked on subatomic particles and was a skeptic by nature. He could do differential calculus in his head and was passionate about old movies. "I will tell you the most significant improvement in my life since leaving India, in two words," he said to me. "John Ford." He wore sandals all year, even in winter, and had delicate pink toenails and soft brown toes the color of maple syrup.

Maya drove him to the hospital herself, got the MRI scans and angiograms done quickly. There was a solid white ball filling the left temporal lobe of his brain, exploding into his head like some sort of celestial event in deep space. Her father had visions, saw lights in the sky, and heard voices from his childhood — his mother calling him inside, his father teaching him to read, distant coughs from his own grandfather, who was long dead. He cried like a baby. "For God's sake don't let me become a vegetable," he said. "Pull the bloody plug. That's all I ask. *Pull the bloody plug.*"

Maya assisted at his surgery. "It's my responsibility as his daughter. Who else can you trust? He knows I'll look after him."

"But he's your own father," I said. "How can you bear to see his brain? It's not something a daughter needs to see. How can you stand that?"

It was a seven-hour procedure in a cool operating theater resounding with the rhythmic clack of the respirator and the twang of taped sitar music. Maya shaved the head of her father smooth. His thick black hair fell onto the floor in clumps. Clear glass bottles at the end of the suction probes filled with blood and tiny pieces of connective tissue. I have never seen her colder or more isolated. In her protective goggles, double gloves, and green surgical gown tied behind her neck and waist, she looked prepared for battle.

I never saw Maya cry. She retreated into an inner place where she could dispense advice and give professional support. She made tea for her mother and brought dishes of rice and vegetables to the hospital room. She reassured her brothers and explained the pathology to them. Her white coat was wrapped tightly around her. "I have to take responsibility," she said to me. "I can't think about it. I just have to get on with it." She concentrated on the neuroanatomy, histological findings, and her father's intracranial pressure. Maya the clinician. I watched her slip away, slowly and for good reason, into a safe world somewhere behind her black eyes, somewhere behind those eyelashes.

As I get older, and especially at this time of year, I find myself thinking more and more about my sister Hannah. She understood butterflies. When my grandmother died, my father inherited the house, and we grew up in the creaking old place, full of dark wood, antimacassars, plinths, and vases. Hannah was three years older than I was and I worshiped her. I remember lying on piles of my grandfather's Turkish rugs with her and learning the names of the objects and artifacts around us — Ethiopian wooden head pillows, rows of carved penis sheaths from New Guinea, garish yellow-and-red face masks from the Ivory Coast, the stuffed head of a salamander, one goatskin side of a yurt.

Hannah had a photographic memory. She knew all of the butterfly names and species, and could remember the notes from my grandfather's logbooks — "I saw the pink hind wings of two *Atrophaneura horishamus* in a clump of tropical climbing vine," she would quote, "mating in the sun." Hannah inherited my mother's chestnut hair and my father's buckteeth, which rested neatly on her lower lip and left red indentations there when she concentrated for a long time. She had stumpy fingers and thumbs that curled back to her wrists. If she had lived, she would have had dental work, my mother said whenever she saw an old picture of Hannah.

Hannah took charge of me, led me around by the hand, and let me sleep with her at night. I never felt safer than in the crook of her arm, my face buried in her nightdress, smelling a strange mixture of pumice soap, milk, and burning hair. She dressed me up in her old dresses and tights, treated me like a doll, and took me for long walks with the dog in Central Park. I sought attention from Hannah, so I preferred being dressed as a girl, because it pleased my sister and because it allowed me to accompany her.

Even as an eight-year-old, Hannah had ambitions that I'm sure my parents did not believe or think about. But I believed. In 1937, Amelia Earhart was in the headlines — there was a new acceptance of women as tomboys and adventurers — and Hannah wanted to fly a plane, too. She cried for days when Earhart's plane disappeared in the Pacific that July. And it was she who wanted to be a doctor, not me. She had solid fingers and a light touch. She was able to concentrate on details for hours, and was charming to everyone she met. I never had any of these qualities, but growing up, I tried to become more like her. By nature, I'm much more of an introvert, slow-moving and unaware. I lose things, forget birthdays, put metal objects into microwave ovens, buy food that I never eat. Sometimes when I am alone, I feel like a kind of human chameleon trying to perpetuate the memory of a lost eight-year-old girl.

My grandfather would have looked for answers in the natural world, specifically in the biology of butterflies. There are interesting parallels to be found in the work of Henry W. Bates, a nineteenth-century English naturalist and explorer. I have perused his famous paper in the *Transactions of the Linnaean Society in London* (1862), entitled "Contribution to an Insect Fauna of the Amazon Valley." Bates captured over one hundred species of *Heliconian, Ithomid,* and *Pierid* butterflies in Amazonia. He found that butterflies that were toxic to predators, and therefore had good defenses against being eaten, were mimicked by butterflies that had no defenses. These weaker butterflies changed their coloring and markings to match those of the stronger butterflies. By copying the appearance of butterflies that had natural defenses, they avoided attacks by predators. Bates's field observations began the study of mimicry in biology.

Biology is a powerful force that cannot be denied. I am a surgeon for my sister and because of my sister. And for her I learned to fly a plane, spent endless weekends with my stomach in my throat, fighting with the rudder while bobbing over the summer beaches on Long Island. Hannah would have enjoyed all that sky and sea and the little pink figures staring up from the surf far below as she buzzed overhead.

My grandfather corresponded with Henry W. Bates in the 1870s. He also had a lifelong friendship with Fritz Muller, the German naturalist who collected and observed butterflies in the Amazon. In 1879, Muller published "Ithuna and Thyridia: A Remarkable Case of Mimicry in Butterflies," in the *Proceedings of the Entomological Society* (London, 1879). I have read the article several times. My grandfather owned a dog-eared copy of the volume, in which he made spindly marginal notes. The precision with which these striking butterflies can mimic each other's markings is astonishing. My grandfather was fascinated, and would later do his own experiments on butterfly mimicry. In the nineteenth century, it was still possible for educated amateurs to make contributions to field biology. Driving these men was a certain curiosity of spirit that I admire.

In 1875, my grandfather sailed for the islands of Southeast Asia in a four-masted iron sailing barque. Thomas Gray went with him. He was still weak and suffering periodic relapses of fever, but he was stronger than he had been, and was determined to take part in the expedition. From San Francisco, they charted a southwesterly course that took them to Hawaii and then Guam, the Philippines, and the island of Borneo. Later they would loop southeast to the Solomon Islands, and Fiji, before returning west to Papua New Guinea.

In the pockets of his jacket, my grandfather carried butterfly nets, bottles of chloroform, and a portable microscope with brass fixtures. He collected several butterflies of the genus *Atrophaneria* — there are striking examples of the red furry-bodied *Aptophaneria semperi albofasciata* in his collection. In the jungles of Borneo, he found *Troides brookiana* — Rajah Brookes birdwing — with its deep blue-and-green coloring. The second largest butterfly he found — *Ornithoptera goliath procus* — came from the Malaysian islands. One of his specimens has a nine-inch wingspan.

In New Guinea, my grandfather hired a Dutch missionary named Rhin Postma to guide them into the jungle. The Dutch Calvinist was an alcoholic, with veined cheeks and heavy thighs. He wore stiff collars over a mottled red neck. Although he was familiar with some of the coastal tribes — groups who wore the plumes of parrots in their hair and decorated themselves with silver pearl shells — he had little understanding of the interior of the country. My grandfather looked at dark, shimmering jungles and saw only butterfly habitats. They walked into the hills through morning mists and trees interspersed with kunai grass. Around them in the forests they saw giant crowned pigeons, pygmy parrots, cassowaries, and cockatoos. The dusk sky was rainbow colored with flocks of darting parrots and kingfishers.

It was densely humid and they were beset by flies and biting insects. Thomas Gray continued to lose weight and was immobilized by fever. Rhin Postma was in no condition to hike through dense undergrowth. They decided to set up a temporary camp on the shores of a lake that the locals called Kutubu and to let my grandfather press into the highlands on his own. "My friend is sick," my grandfather wrote, "and I am faster without him. The Dutchman is drinking too much and cannot walk well. I will be back in a few weeks. I cannot wait." He was unafraid of the unknown territory ahead of him. None of them knew what it contained or understood why he insisted on pushing ahead alone.

He continued with four native porters, haunted by visions of the largest butterfly in the world. Shortly after my grandfather left the lake, Rhin Postma abandoned the camp, leaving Thomas Gray on his own, sick and unable to move. He lay on a camp bed for several days in a state of delirium before he was killed by warriors from a mountain tribe, naked men with wild balls of feathered hair, who ran him through with stone-tipped spears. He was dismembered and the camp supplies taken. My grandfather was also pursued as he marched quickly on his short thick legs, but was saved by his fire flints and his rifle. He was observed starting a fire in a few seconds with some dry grass and twigs, and once he shot a tree kangaroo with his rifle. The highlanders saw him as a figure invested with supernatural powers. He was the first European they had encountered. They approached him cautiously and examined his white hands, covered in fine brown hairs, with suspicion. The magnified images visible through his glass made people jump back in terror. His knives and fob watch, his microscope and other scientific equipment, and his fine

brown hair and freckled skin were understood to be the trappings of something heaven-sent.

It was not a comfortable alliance. My grandfather was nervous, surrounded by spindle-legged men covered with thick scars, whom he could
not understand. But standing in the heavy heat one day, he noticed that
a warrior had the shimmering blue, green, and yellow wings of a butterfly strung from his neck. "They are wearing what I seek," he wrote, "and
I know I have to befriend them."

He was taken to villages set in baked-dirt clearings. Quick-limbed,
potbellied children hid behind trees and pointed at him. He was treated
as a guest, given food and shelter in grass lean-tos. They took him on hunting parties. He lived with this remote mountain tribe for several months.
This was at a time when cannibalism was still widely practiced in that
part of the world. Ritual marks were tattooed on his back. He learned to
speak fragments of a mountain dialect that involved guttural throat sounds
and clicking noises made by pressing the back of the tongue against the
hard palate. When he made it clear that he sought the large insects that
hung from the limbs of trees in the thick forest, he was taken to places
where he could find them. In this remote and untamed place, among
people living in a different age, he found magnificent examples of *Ornithoptera alexandrae*, the Queen Alexandria's birdwing. Over fifty butterflies were gathered and stored in caulked oak barrels.

I have read through the New Guinea volume — he recorded the daily
routines of the tribe and made comments on what he saw. There were
moments when he felt he could understand their lives and take meaning from them. It is clear from these pages that my grandfather also par-
ticipated in cannibalism. Skirmishes between tribal groups were common;
they were undertaken with long spears and wooden clubs. Victories were
celebrated by roasting the bodies of the enemy and consuming their flesh.
I recognize that my grandfather might have had no choice in the matter. The internal organs, including the brain, liver, lungs, and kidneys,
were a particular delicacy. The brains were often eaten raw, and my
grandfather consumed "the cerebrum of a poor unfortunate" on three

occasions during his time in the mountains. It was a matter of survival for him — he had to participate fully or risk death, I can see that. I do not judge him.

When he walked out of the jungle, he found the remains of the camp by the lake and understood what had happened to his companion. He believed he had let Thomas Gray down. His hair was matted and uncut. He returned to the coast with a heavy feeling of loss and failure that he would never quite lose. He carried three species of worm in his large intestine and on his arm a tame cockatoo. On the voyage home, he wrote a long letter to the parents of Thomas Gray, which he never sent. Instead, he went to see them in New York and gave them several specimens of the butterfly their son had gone to find. He knew that even this butterfly was poor compensation for a son. The cockatoo lost all its feathers, refused to eat, and was dead before the year's end.

3. Parnassius Hardwikii *and* Parnassius Maharaja: *The Himalayan Butterflies*

Seeing Maya's father after his surgery, I understood that we are more than just anatomy, more than just a set of structures. With his hair cut off, the long scar along one side of his head, and a spiderweb of tubes and wires emerging from neck, arm, and bladder, he was barely recognizable. He was paralyzed down the right side of his body and could not speak. Maya checked his intracranial pressure and muscle strength and examined his wound several times a day. There was something comforting about seeing his feet sticking out of the bedsheets — small and delicate with their maple syrup toes.

Although the man was paralyzed and swollen, his spirit had not left him. I felt it there with me, behind his eyes, which were dark and more understanding than mine. When I brought in a video of *Stagecoach*, I could sense his joy, and when his left thumb went up into the air, I could feel him there with us. He watched dozens of westerns in his last days. We are more than just the sum of our parts, I said to Maya. I tried to break down her objective view of the human brain. His spirit was walking on some forgotten prairie, kicking amongst the tumbleweed, while his brain was less than complete.

We knew immediately that the tumor would recur. He had only weeks to live. At home, he tried to walk and fell over. Maya read physics journals to him. Maya's mother made him his favorite foods and fed him with spoons they had been given for their wedding. With a trembling left hand, he wrote me notes that he didn't want his family to see. "Pull the bloody plug," he wrote, and when I looked into his eyes, the eyes of his daughter, I understood my grandfather more clearly.

Toward the end, Maya's father had more seizures. During one of them, he kicked himself off his wheelchair, in the garden. When they found him, his face was pressed down against the ground as if he were listening carefully to insects in the grass. He wanted to be outside. They laid him on a mattress under a clump of beech trees to stare at the sky though the white boughs. That was where he died, on a summer day, surrounded by bees, his forehead dusted lightly with yellow pollen.

In 1890, fifteen years after my grandfather's return from New Guinea, there were clear signs that he was going insane. He became obsessed with vaudeville, burlesque shows, and the circus. He had always been a quiet and meticulous man who believed firmly in Victorian morals and the importance of hard work and personal discipline. But in 1890, he began spending all of his nights in music halls — he saw over one hundred shows by the comedy team of Joe Weber and Lou Fields and went drinking with music hall comedians John T. Kelly and Peter Dailey. He spent days at the circus, becoming enthralled by the clowns. Because he was a wealthy man, he was allowed backstage. He became acquainted with Dan Rice, the famous Civil War clown. He filled many pages of his diaries with sketches and descriptions of clowns — almost as if he were trying to make sense of the theatrical world by applying scientific methods as rigorously as he could.

He began asking circus and vaudeville performers home for musical and burlesque evenings; he staged several shows in his house on the Upper East Side, inviting wealthy friends and acquaintances from all over New York. There were displays of slapstick, magic tricks, funny songs, sight and sound gags. This new interest in the theater was quite out of character for my grandfather, who had the personality and brain of a scientist, not an entertainer. When he began participating in these shows himself, dressed in baggy suits and suspenders, flopping shoes, makeup and wigs, everyone realized that something was wrong.

He became a clown in real life — making gags and giggling at dinner, finding eggs and flowers in the hair of visitors, and installing a trick chair in the living room that disintegrated into pieces when sat upon. In March of 1890, he induced a rhubarb tart to slide the length of his dining room table with a hidden magnet and a system of wires and pulleys. The dinner party consisted of "three Irish comics, a high-court judge, a physician of some standing who has pioneered the use of ether for minor surgical procedures, and the third cousin of Theodore Roosevelt." He reported that after dinner he bemused everyone (except the comics) with a trick bottle of tawny port which, although uncorked, would not pour. The cigars offered to the judge and the physician were of an explosive nature and resulted in "a very satisfying percussion that sent the smokers crashing back into their seats with a flash of gunpowder and a blast of black smoke."

My grandfather continued to document daily events in his diary. He was filled with a compulsion to "make flippancy of everything" and to "jest without restraint," recording that he often laughed uncontrollably for several minutes at commonplace sights such as a decanter of sherry or a conical pile of horse dung in the street. My grandmother must have been alarmed by the dramatic changes that she saw in her husband. My grandfather recorded that she packed several trunks and went to live with her family in Boston, leaving him to practice his tricks and gags alone in their granite-fronted house.

I sometimes drive past my grandfather's old house on my way to the hospital. It is a huge old Victorian with four floors and servants' quarters. My father sold it years ago. Now it has been subdivided into offices and the ground floor is a health-food restaurant. I'm sure my grandfather would have been amused by the waitresses in Ethiopian muslin shawls.

He would have seen their uniforms as an example of cultural mimicry. He had been to Ethiopia — then Abyssinia — in the early 1870s. He had walked around the solid rock ramparts of the Coptic churches in Gondar hunting specimens of *Papilio dardanus* and *Papilio lormieri*.

After her father's funeral, Maya and I both needed to get away, so we spent a month in India. My images of India had been formed by an early love of Kipling. I had imagined turbaned infidels (as black as night, with crescent moon swords), tigers on leashes, and polite English conversations under fans pulled by emaciated fan-wallahs. The withered limbs, animals, and death in the streets, and delicate children with staring eyes, were a revelation. There are many butterfly species on the subcontinent, but it is hard to believe it when passing through the cities. I was eager to find specimens of *Parnassius hardwikii* and *Parnassius maharaja*, both of which live on the southern face of the Himalayas above 2,500 meters, but I never found the time to make any field trips. Maya bought me a white dhoti and the most dramatic and shocking lingams that she could find. She found an electric one that could be plugged in and flashed rainbow colors. I felt as young as I have ever felt. There was something invigorating about the place. It was chaotic, teeming with fecundity, as busy as a human beehive. After a while, I forgot the squalor. One night as we lay on thin cotton sheets under a ceiling fan, Maya said to me, "You have the sexual energy of a twenty-year-old."

"Do you think so?"

"I do. I'm not complaining. But I wonder how you do it."

"I don't feel as if I'm doing anything. But I feel better being away from home. I feel a sort of freedom, I guess. Don't you?"

"Not like you. This is partly my home. I don't feel as if I've exactly escaped from anything. You know India. About one in five people you meet are probably related to me in some way, distantly."

"There's something liberating about being away from your family."

"I suppose there is." She rolled onto her side with her hands flat on the sheet, in front of her. Indian pop music floated up from the street below and I could hear the distant bellows of water buffalo. In the dim light, her black hair fell like ink onto the white sheets. Her feet and hands had been hennaed for our wedding and a complicated spiderweb of purple lines and flowers curved over her palms and the backs of her feet. There was a timelessness about this moment. I realized then that I could never really escape from my family at all. I carry them all with me.

We spent sweaty afternoons with members of Maya's extended family, eating silver and bronze sweetmeats and talking about the quality of Indian pollution and computer software. I was accepted completely as an older man with a younger woman — in a society in which many marriages are still arranged, it was quite reasonable for us to be together. "It is more of an honor for me to be with you than with a younger man," Maya told me. We ate string hoppers and glutinous ice cream in outdoor markets. We rushed around like children, bought a carved teak chest and a set of solid brass doorjambs. I felt close to Maya then. She forgot about her father for a while. She put away her lists and schedules and I felt as if she was relaxing for the first time since I had known her. She joked that we should never go home and that we should spend the rest of our lives running a leper hospital. Maya told me the stories of her maddest relatives, where to stand on crowded buses, and key Hindi obscenities. The only thing Maya didn't tell me when we were in India was that she was two months' pregnant with our daughter.

I would be a foolish man indeed not to admit that my surgical skills have begun to suffer because of my drinking. I now find myself drinking whiskey in my office, quietly and subversively, like a criminal, before my morning operating list. Two glasses of malt whiskey stop the alarming morning tremor and keep my hands steady. For an hour or two, I feel as I used to feel in the morning — in command of my subject, calm and analytical. I swallow gulps of mouthwash and suck peppermints to mask the smell of my breath. And as quickly as possible after I have changed into my scrubs, I put on a face mask. I have always taken great pride in my work, and yet now I feel reluctant and cautious, unable to enjoy what I do, unable to be companionable with the staff who work with me. I get away as quickly as I can — after a longer list, I can think of nothing except the bottle in the locked lower drawer of my desk.

I can see that my skills have deteriorated, but I am convinced that it is not yet obvious to those around me. I notice a subtle diminution in the precision of my skin cuts. My sutures are fractionally less clean, less neat, more slapdash to my eye, but I am not sure this is noticeable to anyone else. Occasionally I drop instruments, something I have never done. All of this, I believe, is within the bounds of normal behavior. I am certain that I have not had a patient who has suffered as a result of my drinking. My surgical outcomes have remained good. There have been no complaints.

I recognize, too, that things are getting worse. Last week, I was repairing several extensor tendons, severed in a motorcycle accident, in the right hand of a professional musician. I was working under an operating microscope. Two hours into the procedure, I fell asleep standing at the operating table. My head was leaning heavily into the microscope eyepiece. My hands, still holding the instruments, lay immobile in the open wound below me. I awoke suddenly and still have no idea how long I was unconscious. I assume that it was a very brief time. The resident assisting me was still by my side and did not say anything. The surgical nurse stood ready with the suction. I stood back from the table carefully and pretended to be thinking. I felt something akin to panic. When I had gathered myself sufficiently to speak, I told the resident to take over. I stepped aside and watched her complete the task. I stood there watching, ostensibly as a supervisor, although I paid very little attention to what she was doing. I had crossed some kind of barrier, I knew. I did not want to contemplate what would have happened if I had fallen. I did not want to think about those machine-sharp instruments in my unconscious hands.

It is time for me to take some concrete action, this is clear. I should go to the chief of surgery, Dr. Touli, and do the responsible thing. This is hard for me. I find it painful to discuss the details of my condition, particularly with a man ten years my junior who has never possessed my level of skill. It is difficult to describe a weakness to a man whom I do not consider an equal. In truth, I believe that I should be the head of the department of surgery, not Dr. Touli. The reasons I was passed over for this position remain obscure to me.

4. Limentus Archippus: *The Viceroy Butterfly*

I can only imagine what my father thought when he saw Albert Gissendander heaving toward him along the beach. The fat wad of gauze on his spectacles was flashing in the sun. His mouth opened and shut noiselessly and he was waving the binoculars above his head. I stood at the end of the jetty and watched my father start to run. He seemed to move in slow motion, a tiny figure battling the wind, as if he were trapped under glass. It took him minutes to reach the jetty, by which time he had ripped off his jacket and thrown it behind him. He shouted at me with terrifying force. "Just stay here and don't move. Do you hear me? Don't move." I didn't move when I heard him cry out and jump into the water. I didn't move when I saw him wading back to the beach with my sister in his arms. Sometimes I feel as if I have been standing at the end of that jetty for fifty years.

Loss is a strange thing. My mother blamed my father and my father blamed the butterflies. The house seemed empty and lifeless. My parents were unable to talk to each other. My mother got a job as a secretary in a law firm and left us two years later for a man who sold theatrical supplies. In later years, I would visit her and sit in a living room filled with wigs in plastic bags and stacks of Neptune forks. My mother became suspicious of science and logic. She started dressing flamboyantly, wearing makeup, and going to parties. She took up astrology.

My father never again looked at butterflies. We never again went to see the monarchs migrate. He taught. He began a lifetime of renovating and remodeling my grandfather's old house. New plumbing was installed. Wiring was updated. Walls were added. He rebuilt his grief outside himself in that old house, hammered and nailed it into place, as if his misery was something solid and visible. "We must prevail," he said to me.

"We must go on." I read my grandfather's diaries and watched my father become a thin and dewy-eyed man.

There is a grave, a shiny marble tablet at one end of a small earthy plot. Every week my father and I went to visit her, and in the summer I brought butterflies. I caught them in the garden and kept them alive in glass jars with perforated lids. Standing there among the graves, I'd let a butterfly out onto her headstone and watch it sit for a moment and then drift into the air and float off. When I think of butterflies I think of Hannah — there she is in front of me, a little sliver of color.

I saw Albert Gissendander once more in my life. I was an intern in the emergency room when he came in with chest pain. He did not recognize me. He lay with his eyes shut, holding an oxygen mask over his mouth and nose. His lips were blue. I asked him about his pain — it had come on while he was having a full English breakfast at a diner. The twelve wire leads of the electrocardiogram hung limply from his chest.

I placed my hands on his sweaty white skin and listened to fine crepitations in his lungs. He had a thin, irregular pulse. His heart sounded distant and muffled. It seemed to be beating underwater, like a deep-sea creature. "Will I be all right?" He asked me, opening his eyes for an instant. I inserted an intravenous line and gave him morphine. I imagined this body, propelled by this ailing heart, pounding along the beach at Cape May Point. His toenails were yellow and curled. We had shared something, this man and I, but I didn't feel anything. For a moment, I thought of telling Albert Gissendander who I was and watching his heart rate rise on the monitor. I could imagine it speeding up. I could imagine the peaks and valleys of his heart tracing squeezing together, tripping over each other. "You'll be all right," I said.

I got him stabilized and he was sent to the coronary-care unit for close monitoring. The next morning, when my shift had ended, I went up to see him. In the elevator, I pulled my white coat tightly around my chest and did up all the buttons. I stood outside his room for some time, watching him in the bed. He was huge and white, lying beached in the bed like some giant aquatic mammal. I went into the room and pretended to look at his chart. He looked at me benignly with dark moist eyes and did not speak. The cardiac monitor bleeped steadily. I stood for a moment at the end of the bed and then said, "I am Hannah's brother."

He regarded me silently and I was not sure that he had understood. But then he suddenly tried to speak. He pulled the plastic oxygen mask from his nose and mouth. His fat lips moved against each other, but no sound emerged. His eyes bulged. He was clearly in distress. He lifted one forearm off the bed and indicated that he wanted me to come closer. I bent down and put my ear to his lips. His heavy breath blew against the side of my face. "I'm a very sick man," he said in gasps. "You leave me alone." I stood hunched down with my ear to his face much longer than I needed to. As I left the room, I realized that I did not want to know any more. I did not want to cheapen the memory of my sister by talking about her with this dying stranger. I hoped that Albert Gissendander's memories of the past were vivid and alive, and that they would hasten him along his way. It is surprising how serious illness can sharpen the senses and bring the past into clearer focus — perhaps in the end he held himself accountable for what he had done.

My grandfather's hands began shaking and got progressively worse. He chopped off his thumb in frustration. The tremor became so severe that he was unable to control his arms and could no longer do fine work with butterflies. His memory began to disappear, and this was perhaps his greatest loss. It was his mind that had always sustained him. He began writing lists for everything that he had to remember each day. He shouted mercilessly at the nurse his family had hired to look after him. As the disease progressed, he had increasing difficulty in walking and getting his balance. Eventually he was confined to a wheelchair.

He had seen the disease in the highlands of New Guinea. The locals called it *kuru*. There was progressive destruction of the brain, marked initially by moderately inappropriate behavior, which then progressed to diminished motor control and memory loss. The victims became ataxic and uncoordinated and were eventually unable to move at all. In six to nine months, they could not speak or swallow and lost control of their eyes. Unable to eat, they often died of malnutrition. Only those who handled and ate infected human brains got the disease. In New Guinea, the stricken individuals sat aimlessly in the villages, wild-haired and babbling.

Of course in those days nothing was understood about the neurodegenerative diseases caused by "slow viruses," or protein agents called prions. It would be sixty-seven years before Vincent Zigas and Carelton Gajdusek described *kuru* in the Fore Highlanders of New Guinea — a form of dementia transmitted by contact with infected brains. And it was still some time before we understood other related diseases — Creutzfeldt-Jakob disease, scrapie in sheep, and the notorious bovine spongiform encephalopathy, or mad cow disease. I have studied this collection of disorders. The end result is always the same. The brain is eaten away like Swiss cheese and there is no cure or treatment.

Maya is inherently interested in anything that eats away the brain. It is proof to her that we are little more than machines — noradrenaline, serotonin, and dopamine running through a set of circuits and pathways. Each loss of function has an anatomical correlate and this appeals to Maya's sense of order. There have been a handful of cases of transmissible neuropathies reported in neurosurgeons. They get the disease from operating on infected brains without appropriate barrier protection — a hole in a glove and a scratch on a finger can provide an entry point into the bloodstream. Perhaps a splash of infected blood in the eye is all it takes. There is nothing more tragic than a neurosurgeon who loses his or her brain. All that skill, all that intimate knowledge, all that manual dexterity, eaten away.

We were having afternoon tea with Maya's aunt and uncle when she miscarried. It was our last week in India. From the living room of their second-floor flat in Goa, I looked out over a beach covered in dull yellow sand. Shouts from a game of volleyball filled the afternoon — tanned young men in board shorts and ankle bracelets were playing to the music of Bob Marley, watched by thin women in saris at the food stalls. It was a sticky day and the tea was strong and milky. Maya clutched her lower abdomen and turned paler than I have ever seen her. She ran into the bathroom. Her aunt Priya followed. They emerged five minutes later with Maya holding a towel between her legs. "Don't ask," Maya whispered to me. "Please don't ask."

Her uncle took us in a rusty Peugeot to a private clinic with white-washed walls set in a grove of waving palms. I had to half-carry Maya up the front steps. The towel between her legs was already red with fresh blood. Her uncle ran off to find the obstetrician, who was his squash partner. I sat with my arms around Maya watching an old man sweep the green concrete steps in front of us with a brush broom. I felt Maya slump into me. "I'm sorry," she said. "This is my fault. I should have told you."

The nurses were wearing winged caps and solid white shoes with laces. They found her a bed in a small room. I was quickly ushered out and told to wait in the dayroom, a linoleum-covered space in which twenty or thirty men and boys were watching cricket on a wide-screen television. They found me a chair in front of the television and I sat down reluctantly, not wanting to appear impolite. "This certainly is a compensation, is it not?" the man sitting next to me said through a wide grin. "Although we are in hospital, we have this magnificent television and a front-row seat for the first test match at Headingly. It is not to be sneezed at."

An hour later, the obstetrician appeared and led me over to the windows. He was wearing a three-piece gray suit despite the heat. When he spoke, it was with a strong Oxbridge accent — he sounded more English than my English friends. He had the air of a sportsman about him — competent games of squash and tennis, an occasional flutter on the horses, lifetime memberships to cricket clubs. His tie was monogrammed with two crossed polo mallets.

"I'm afraid she has lost the baby, old boy," he said to me.

"Nothing we can do?"

"Nothing at all. One of those things, I'm afraid. A spontaneous miscarriage. She'll be absolutely fine. I'm going to keep her for a day or two, just to keep an eye on her. I may have to do a D and C later."

"She hadn't told me. About the baby."

"Indeed. She may feel some guilt about that."

"I wish I'd known. Perhaps I could have done something."

"It's unlikely you could have done anything, frankly." There was a clatter of porcelain cups as a tea trolley was wheeled past. "There are only three things certain in the world," the obstetrician said. "Tea, cricket, and death."

I walked back to her room. Maya was asleep with an intravenous line running into one arm. Her hair fanned out on the pillow behind her. I walked over and put my hand against her forehead and watched her breathe through lightly parted lips. The linen sheets were starched and heavy. I could smell the new blood on her. I stood by the window looking out at chickens pecking in the dust along the side of the building. A thin green lizard sat immobile, tongue flickering, on the wall above my head. I could hear children playing in the distance. For a moment, I sensed the life everywhere around me, so constant that it was almost invisible. It is only when it is taken away that we notice, and it can happen in an instant.

My grandfather was never able to believe that Darwin was right. In his mind, the perfection of butterflies, their elaborate patterns and colors, exceeded the requirements of mere survival. "I cannot believe," he wrote, "that other butterflies notice the fine details that are seen on the wings of these creatures. To my mind, this is art for the sake of art. This is not just survival. It is something higher." After New Guinea, he gave many of his specimens to the Museum of Natural History in New York. He continued to spend summers collecting, but made no more trips overseas.

During the years before he became ill, he spent weeks out west in the plains states, the Rockies, and the deserts of Arizona and New Mexico. He took the whole family with him on some of these trips. These were happy days for my grandmother and their three sons, the youngest my father. My grandfather built a greenhouse at the end of his garden and made it a large butterfly-breeding laboratory. He raised *Actias luna*, *Antherae polyphenus*, and *Automeris io* and looked for examples of mimicry among these butterflies. The year my father was born, 1888, he claimed to have proved that the monarch butterfly is mimicked by the viceroy butterfly. Unfortunately, his illness prevented him from publishing his findings.

He would have been pleased to see his own observations confirmed in the work of Jane Van Zandt Browner in the mid-1950s. She reported that in North America, *Danaus plexippus*, the monarch butterfly, is mimicked by *Limenitis archippus*, the viceroy butterfly, to obtain the protective advantage of the monarch's pattern and coloring. I have filed her article, "Experimental Studies of Mimicry in Some North American Butterflies" (*Evolution* 1958, 35:32–47) with the others in my butterfly notes. Van Zandt Browner noted this phenomenon in the population of New Brunswick monarchs that undertake a fall migration to the mountains of Michoacán in southwestern Mexico.

When my father was four years old, my grandmother and the children moved back to live with her family in Boston, and stayed there for the last two years of my grandfather's life. My grandmother made no attempt to understand what had happened to her husband. Mental illness, in any form, still carried a damning social stigma, and it was never really discussed. Because my grandmother never understood the cause of his disease, she lived in terror that my father would somehow inherit it. She was wary of her own son, watched him carefully, and made him a serious child ahead of his time.

My grandfather never forgot Thomas Gray. Every year on his old friend's birthday, while he was still able, he released all the hand-raised specimens, hundreds of them, from his greenhouse. A dense shower of speckled wings flew into the air around him as they tumbled into the sky. On this day, he toasted his friend with whiskey and reviewed his butterfly specimens from the Pacific.

It was my grandfather's drive to possess the luminescent beauty of *Ornithoptera alexandrae* that had doomed him to a slow, progressive death. Somehow, when I look at the marvelous splashes of life and color that these butterflies still provide, I feel certain that he believed that it had all been worthwhile. I imagine him standing over his display boxes, magnifying glass in one hand and his diaries in the other, recollecting the days when he'd caught his remarkable specimens. I imagine him reliving the dark wetness of the forest, the sudden bursts of fluttering color, the dappled light through the upper canopy. He must have taken comfort in the long and ordered rows of butterflies in his collection.

Impotence is an emotionally charged word, but it is an accurate description of my current condition. I have not had an erection since we returned from India. Last week, Maya hung over me in bed, straddling my pelvis, prodding my private parts as if they were a delicate archaeological find.

"I couldn't help but notice that there is nothing happening *down there*," she said to me.

"*Down there* is temporarily out of order," I said. Maya ran the tips of her fingers down my chest and put her mouth to my ear.

"Is there anything I can do about it?" she whispered.

"I don't know," I said. "I don't really think so." I have never had a problem with erections. Quite the reverse.

"It's me, isn't it?" Maya said. She slipped off me and sat on the bed cross-legged. "I completely understand. It's perfectly understandable." She was crying.

I lay rigid on the bed. "It's not you, it's me. I'm tired. I've been working hard."

"That's never stopped you before. You know it hasn't. You blame me for India."

"I don't blame you."

"You hold me responsible."

"I don't."

Maya got up from the bed and pulled on her robe. She stood over me at the edge of the bed with her hands over her face.

"How do you think I feel? I have to get up and go to work every day, just like you. I have to take all the responsibility. That's a lot to bear."

"None of this is your fault, Maya." I sat up on the side of the bed.

"You're terrified of taking responsibility for anything. That's partly why this has happened. Why can't you admit that?"

"Because I don't know what I feel. I don't know what has happened."

"You're drinking too much. Every night you drink."

In my mind, I ran over the biological causes of impotence — vascular and neurological chiefly — none of which seemed likely in my case. And I love Maya. I seem to be in a state of paralysis. Everything is seizing up.

"I think it's psychological," I said. But Maya had already left the room.

My grandfather ended his own life in the summer of 1894. He was weak and had difficulty standing on his own. It is a testament to his will and persistence that he was able to get the rope strung from the heavy iron roof supports of his greenhouse. It was summer and I imagine the garden around him swirling with dandelions and rye grass. He tied a noose at one end of the rope. It must have taken him hours to get up onto the top of the workbenches — he pushed equipment to the ground, knocked over pots, and scattered butterfly pupae around him. They found him hanging three feet off the floor. According to my father, the butterflies in the greenhouse were attracted to his hanging body. When they found him, his woolen suit was covered with red-and-black viceroy butterflies, clinging to him from head to foot.

Last night, Maya found the spare key to my study. I heard the key rattling in the lock and then she flung open the door violently. She was wild eyed and had a hammer in one hand. Her cheeks were black with streaks of mascara. Maya has made a full physical recovery after India and easily held the hammer above her head. She walked quite calmly, with the hammer raised, over to my grandfather's butterfly display cases. Paradoxically, I found myself chuckling — she was wearing only her underwear and a pair of thick gardening gloves.

"These butterflies are a curse," she shouted. "Give me one good reason why I shouldn't destroy them all." She was swinging the hammer around her waist in broad arcs and was ready to strike.

"Maya, calm down," I said.

"One good reason. That's all I ask."

But I was unable to speak. All I could do was watch. And for reasons that I cannot explain, as I watched, I felt relieved.

Today I needed some air. I drove down the coast to look for monarch butterflies — the migration should begin soon. It was a beautiful September day, with stiff easterly winds and bursts of sunlight through racing clouds. Getting out of New York put me in such good spirits that I started singing in the car — a terrible rendition of "St. James Infirmary." My thoughts become very clear when I'm standing on the beach and facing the gray smudge of the Atlantic Ocean. I find myself walking for hours out here with my head tilted upward, to the sky. I barely notice the ground under my feet, stumble on tufts of sea grass and turn my ankles in potholes and cracks in the sandy soil. Waiting for the butterflies is like waiting for old friends — I am impatient and anxious that they will not come at all.

When I arrived at the beach, I went down to the ocean to feel the water. The first thing I do at the edge of the sea is to put my feet into the waves. It is a superstition — I have to prove to myself that it is real and that I am here. It was a calm day and the water was flat and green. Rows of black-eyed sandpipers were running frantically on pink legs in and out on the surf line. I felt self-conscious as I took off my shoes and socks and rolled my pants to the knee. Stepping carefully on soft, white feet that looked like a stranger's, I walked into the shallow water. Pebbles and shells shifted under my toes. Looking down, my legs seemed like those of an old man — pale, hairless, mottled with subterranean veins and mysterious blotches — and it was surprising how removed from myself these pale limbs seemed to me. Long plumes of seaweed wrapped around my shins as I waded in. For the most part, I feel as young as I ever have. But when I see my naked limbs, in bright sunlight, I am chastened, brought back to my age, my job, what I am supposed to be.

I decided to stay the night down here on the coast. I have found a small hotel where I can be anonymous. A group of Mormons is meeting here at the moment, using the convention facilities. I am surrounded by well-groomed people who practice polygamy. I managed to get a small suite with a writing desk and have pulled the desk over to the window where, in daylight, I can see out over the ocean. This afternoon, I found a fish restaurant and ate fresh scallops for the first time in years. I haven't needed a drink today and am encouraged. There is a bottle of Black Label on the desk, and a glass of ice, but I am putting off pouring the whiskey. I find that I want to be clearheaded when I think about the past so as not to diminish it — I am too sentimental. I let things influence me too much. Hannah would have been more practical, would have told me to worry less and get on with important things.

As the sun went down this evening, I went for a walk along the dunes again. The sky was a raging pink in front of me. There are no monarchs to be seen yet. When I walk through the sand dunes, I think of Vladimir Nabokov, the most famous amateur lepidopterist of the century. He was obsessed with butterflies. One morning in 1941, he walked down a mule path in the Grand Canyon and found a new species of *Neonympha* butterfly. Up at the top, his wife, Vera, wearing a black dress with a white lace collar, also came across two previously unidentified species. Butterflies have the capacity for infinite variation. They are changing continuously. Nabokov would have agreed with my grandfather. He didn't believe that such beauty and perfection were required by nature for survival.

The average life span of an adult monarch butterfly is four weeks. Four weeks to be a momentary burst of color and to reproduce. There is a painful transience to it all. They are nothing but a drop of color in the ocean. A fleeting moment that dazzles and blinds, and then is gone forever.

It is fitting that I find myself by the ocean. I have wanted to sail for years. Being out of touch with land, carried on currents and winds that we cannot control, must be liberating. How enticing it is to imagine being at the mercy of the elements. There are boats out at sea tonight, flashing mooring lights toward the shore. It is reassuring to see them out there. And in those distant glimmers, across the coal-dark water, I can see my own past, drifting just out of reach.

4

WHITE FLOUR

Every family has at least one lunatic. In Joseph De Graft Johnson's family, it was his father, Thomas. Pay close attention to what happened to your father, his mother said, because there but for the grace of God go you. On summer days, she told Joseph stories outside, under the peppercorn tree behind their house. She waited for him under the tree after school, sitting at a faded baize card table at which she cut up chickens, deboned fish, dismembered cauliflower, and diced the dusky bodies of eggplants. Her hair was white, had been so since she was twenty-five years old. She ate pistachio nuts from a Chinese lacquer bowl and dropped the little mollusk shells under the table like discarded bones. He sat at her feet on a raft of peppers with brittle pink husks that cracked and popped between his fingers.

Lunatics, she said, they are everywhere. Insanity is the great leveler of men. Look at King George the Third — he was a porphyriac and a madman. Queen Victoria had a kind of posttraumatic stress disorder following the loss of Albert. Growing up in Calcutta, his mother had seen mad people on the streets herself — there was nothing to do with them then, no asylums or drugs, no one who paid any attention — and they wandered around in rags, raving, shouting to themselves, stinking. She had seen men who sawed off their own legs below the knee so they could beg for small change. Quite insane. She had seen them do the same thing to their children, too, healthy children, who had had their hands cut off or their feet — because people were more sympathetic to children and there was more money to be made.

His mother had rings — on her thumbs, on her toes. She was five feet, four inches tall, wore saris at home, smoked mentholated cigarettes with a certain practiced abandon, and did not believe in sparing her children. Give it to them straight, she said, let them understand that life is a cruel mistress, nothing pretty about it. She told him her stories, laughed with a barking cough, like a dog, thought she was preparing him for the world beyond. Joseph sat cross-legged on the peppercorns and breathed in her smells — lily of the valley, cloves, spearmint chewing gum.

She told her stories like a diplomat, with the right emphasis and small, precise gestures. She knew something was awry with his father, she told him, on their wedding night. They were in the nuptial bedroom. He removed his shoes, slipped off a pair of wool-blend socks, and then she saw his feet for the first time — astonishingly large, toes massive and splayed, each digit tufted with an explosion of black hair. He had the feet of a monkey. It was like discovering a terrible secret about someone you thought you knew well. He was covered in hair, she said. In the dark that night, she felt it with her own fingers. Thick on his back and legs, like the pelt of an Arctic black bear. She was shocked, perhaps even terrified. And his arse, she said, his arse was like a doormat.

Arse. She liked to be vulgar in front of Joseph. She was not trying to shock him, but she felt abandoned, and in her mind this gave her the right to be blunt. She was direct in a way that intimidated people who did not know her. Joseph grew up with the sensation that he was looking after her, not the other way around. He had to be careful with her, not say too much, let her speak. He was the eldest of the three children, and the others, Kate and Marguerite, were old enough to keep out of the way with their after-school sports and music lessons. That left Joseph listening to her stories and trying to believe them. He felt trapped by her, held prisoner by the full weight of his mother's indignation.

It was not just the hair that set off alarm bells on their wedding night, his mother told him, it was what he did. They were staying in the Galle Face Hotel in Colombo, Sri Lanka. He took a thirty-minute shower in cold water, while she lay petrified under the very white sheet, a virgin, wondering what was to become of her. He came out, got dressed in his street clothes, and told her he was going for a walk. To get things in perspective, he said. It was one o'clock in the morning. She called room service and asked for the first thing she came to on the menu — eggs Benedict — and ate it sitting in bed, listening to waves breaking on the shore below, sobbing. What kind of perspective can a man be getting when he should be engaged in the act of consummating his marriage? All the bad signs started to add up to her — he was a Capricorn, smoked pipes, wore claret ties. A university man. He had seen too much of her before the wedding. Perhaps he was too modern. All of this went through her mind. He came back two hours later, smelling of sea air and sewage, did not seem to be surprised that she was still awake, was quite oblivious to the time and pleased to see her. She had traces of eggs Benedict around her lips.

He had been walking in the slums and had given away all his money. He felt guilty staying in the large and expensive hotel — although it was her father who was paying all their expenses. Property is theft, he said, or something along those lines, because he had read *Das Kapital* and believed himself a Marxist — it was 1965 and Marxism was still believed to be a reasonable option. She knew then that she *did* love him, despite the oddities, because isn't that what we always love — the oddities?

Despite everything — despite the hair and the eggs Benedict and the Marxist rhetoric — Joseph was conceived in the early hours of that morning. But his mother knew that something was not quite right. He was an unusual man, to be sure. He didn't care what people thought. He dressed casually and messily. She should have seen the signs then, should have seen that he was going to be trouble. I'm not a bitter person, she told Joseph, but for the love of God, look at his feet. The missing bloody link.

She peppered her conversation with *bloody, hell and damnation, balls.* Joseph was embarrassed by her in front of his friends, didn't want to pity her but did so. She had a faded elegance, imagined she still had the money of her childhood. After his father left, they moved to a washed-out bungalow by the river with asbestos siding, patchy grass and thread-bare carpets in orange and tundra. She sat in front of the mirror at her mahogany dressing table, a piece of furniture that had been given to her by her parents, and applied makeup and unguents from a phalanx of china bowls. She barked instructions to them over her shoulder from in front of that mirror, wanted them to understand that they were superior. But there was no hiding that they were poor. They ate organ meats often — liver and onions, deviled kidneys, bowls of tripe, brain sandwiches. Poor people's food that she said was nutritious. They shared clothes, took buses, did not have toys or gifts. They kept a wood fire because they could not afford heating oil. She shopped for their clothes by herself, thought she could hide the fact that she bought them second- and third-hand from Goodwill or the Salvation Army.

It was vanity that made her keep a housekeeper — she could not really afford it. Mrs. Sedivy came in three days a week to cook and clean, a wide-beamed Yugoslavian woman with thick shiny fingers who grew vegetables for them, made pots of soup and stews, chopped wood, washed the floors. She treated his mother like royalty and was deferential in an old-fashioned way. His mother sat in the kitchen and drank tea when she was there, in her saris and makeup, luxuriated in the sense that she was being cared for by a *servant.* Mrs. Sedivy took breaks sitting at the kitchen table with his mother, poured herself a cup of white tea and smoked a cigarette. It was at these times that he saw his mother as most relaxed — talking about Mrs. Sedivy's two sons, her brother in Belgrade who had spinal tuberculosis, people they knew with cancer, pregnant daughters, where to get cheap turnips or rhubarb. It made Joseph angry to see his mother talking with Mrs. Sedivy because she could never be that way with him. With him, she had to put on airs, take a stance, main-tain her dignity. He realized that she had no real friends.

She laughed at Joseph when he came home with his small triumphs —

perfect test scores, a goal in soccer. She didn't belittle him exactly, but she gave him no recognition, no acknowledgment of his achievements. He was a good student and tried hard for her. He knew she was proud of him underneath, but all that came out was her self-absorption. "I was brilliant at school," she told him. "Valedictorian of my class, the world at my feet, and now look at me." She would blow a jet of smoke into the air, adjust the rings on her thumbs, stare down at him as if it was obvious what had become of her. As if it could be seen in the air. "A good education will stand you in good stead," she said to him. "Balls to that. Hear me? Balls."

She had loved his father once, she told him this, too. Blindly and without question she loved him, before the lunacy set in. He came to India from America as a final-year medical student to work with lepers. He was tall and painfully thin, naive as a schoolboy, heir to a fortune in discount car parts. Handsome in a gawky way. She laughed like a girl when she remembered him, his intensity, the way he got hold of you with his pale blue eyes and would not let you go. She was nineteen years old and she met him through her father, who ran the leper hospital, and who brought him home like a son. He was very serious and had notions of changing the world that she found amusing.

She was like many upper-middle-class Indian girls then: well-read, conceited, rebellious, full of her own self-importance. She was at university studying paleontology — that was what she really wanted to do, live in a tent in the Rift Valley, on her knees in a mass of shale, unearthing the ribs and pelvic bones of early man. She had pictures of *Australopithecus* on her bedroom wall. She was a dreamer and had romantic visions of what a man who was heir to a fortune in discount car parts could do for her. She barked with laughter when she remembered, made Joseph smile, too. Love, yes it was love, she told him, because his father listened to her, completely and with absolute faith. He believed her. She could be herself.

She was ambitious, she would not deny that, and she was not afraid of his father's inheritance either. Her parents were agnostics, free thinkers, and allowed the marriage to be a small and simple affair in Calcutta.

His parents flew in for the ceremony, contracted bloody diarrhea on the third day, and looked to be near death for the duration. He planned to go home to North Carolina to work in infectious disease. She was happy to go with him. She wanted to get away and make a name for herself, show her friends that she was moving upward. It was a great adventure to her. She imagined herself on exotic digs, making great discoveries, independent. She had dreams of living on an estate with horses and tobacco plantations and large tracts of perfectly manicured croquet lawn. On the plane, she read Dylan Thomas. She could still remember pieces of *Under Milk Wood*. Under the peppercorn tree she recited the lines to him:

> *We are not wholly bad or good*
> *Who live our lives under Milk Wood*
> *And thou, I know, will be the first*
> *To see our best side, not our worst.*

On the way back to the States, they stopped in England. She had an uncle who lived in Wales and they went and stayed with him. He was a tobacconist and lived in a two hundred-year-old cottage with oak beams and low-slung ceilings. He gave them a running commentary on the inadequacies of the National Health Service, while his wife, Rhonda, a plump and fluffy Welshwoman with calves like melons, fed them kippers for breakfast. Wales was small and damp. Her uncle gave them a set of six new tea towels as a wedding present. They visited the house where Dylan Thomas had lived, stood in the broken shed where he had written masterpieces and drunk himself to death.

Her uncle was unflinchingly English. He did not believe in restaurant meals and practiced a kind of withering parsimony with food: root rather than green vegetables; meat once a week; puddings on holidays. He lived a small life, did not have any money, had never been to Europe. His mother wanted to shout at him. She felt as if her uncle was old before his time, squandering the freedoms that he had earned. He drove them to Heathrow himself in his Ford Escort. In the car, he recited

Wordsworth from memory, said that he was suspicious of America, and told them that he had more Indian friends in London than he had ever had in Calcutta. "It is better than actually living there," he said. His mother sat in the back of that Ford Escort and decided that she would live her life on a grand scale. Grasp opportunities. Be someone. It was the dead English poet that did it, she said. Hearing that dead English poet recited by an Indian tobacconist in the cabin of a Ford Escort, she told Joseph, filled her with loathing.

His mother never understood why his father left. His departure was as unfathomable to her as a cataclysmic natural event: a tropical cyclone, perhaps, or a tsunami. In the fall of 1975, they had planned a trip to India to visit her parents. By then, there were three children, Joseph the oldest, who was nine, Kate, who was seven, and Marguerite, who was four. Soon after arriving in Raleigh, North Carolina, they had moved into his father's parents' house on four acres of land, and she landscaped the garden herself and bought three horses. The house was on a river. She earned a Ph.D. in paleontology and was doing a fellowship that for the last two summers had taken her on a dig to the Koobi Fora site in Kenya. The very idea of Africa thrilled her. She bought leather boots that laced to the knee, enjoyed the sun and the dirt, the rough camps, all the things she would not tolerate at home. In 1975, she was still only twenty-nine years old, a blur of perfume, papers, ink-stained fingers, cigarette ash on the backs of her hands. She sat under her reading lamp at night. Joseph remembered the smooth white pages of her books, warm under the harsh white light, his mother tucking him into bed with a fountain pen in her fingers. She had odd bones on her desk: a piece of skull in the shape of Italy; a single metacarpal; a hoary lumbar vertebra the color of mustard. He wanted to be with his mother, but it was his father who was there more often, with his steady private practice and quiet enthusiasms over sporadic cases of botulism or imported cerebral malaria. His father was a listener, not a talker. He got down on his haunches with his children, tried to understand what they were talking about. He had a puzzling seriousness, a tendency to believe what they said, that made them love him. You could tell him anything as a child, anything at all, and he would give it careful consideration. He had a loud, deep voice that could be heard everywhere in the house, a constant low rumble like an underground train.

His parents had a tradition of throwing a party in the summer and they organized the party that August, the week before they were due to leave for India. His mother liked the bustle of planning and organizing, and made dozens of samosas and savory snacks, bowls of chicken and lamb curry and sag paneer and potato and chicken salads.

That night it was warm enough to go outside and people stood on the lawn by the French doors. His mother had strung paper lanterns in the trees. They set up outdoor tables for the drinks and his father put Joseph in charge of giving out glasses of champagne. His sisters were with a baby-sitter for the evening and this made him feel grown up. People huddled outside in groups on the lawn and looked out over the river, watching the sunset. There were perhaps a hundred people outside, mostly his parents' age, professionals wearing pale slacks and colorful shirts.

Joseph found his mother cutting cheese and cold meat in the kitchen with Brian Underwood, the head of the department of paleontology and her supervisor. He was in his fifties, bald, with a thin collar of black hair around the base of his skull. His mother was drinking champagne and wearing a cotton dress covered with a print of small pink flowers. She never wore her traditional clothes to parties because she said it made her seem old-fashioned. Joseph took a cube of cheese and ate it leaning against the sink. His mother seemed young and happy. She had just begun taking driving lessons. "At home, no one has a car," she was saying, "so there is no need to learn. But it would be much easier when you are younger than I am. Because when you are younger, you are prepared to take extravagant risks. I am terrified of the accelerator pedal. Simply terrified. I drive to the great metropolis of Raleigh at thirty miles an hour, for God's sake. The people around me on the roadway appear to want to kill me."

Brian Underwood laughed. "At least you are safe," he said.

"I hope I will be a better paleontologist than I am a driver," his mother said.

Brian Underwood said, "I am sure of that." His mother finished her glass of champagne, leaned toward him, and said confidentially, "I intend to make a great discovery. Something that will advance the field." She leaned over and put one hand on his shoulder. "Of course I need to get a job first, which is why I need to suck up to you." They both laughed, and she gave Joseph one of the plates of cheese and told him to take it out to the table. Brian Underwood got his mother a glass of wine and drank one himself. His mother drank the wine and decided it was time to start dancing. She rushed into the living room and asked Joseph to help her move the furniture. They pulled the couch and several chairs over by the window. She drank another two glasses of wine in quick succession, put Herb Alpert and the Tijuana Brass on the stereo, then grabbed Joseph and asked him to dance with her. A glass of wine sloshed in her hand. He came level with her chest and watched her feet, very brown, with painted pink toenails. She looked over his shoulder and called people to join them. "The people here seem very old," she whispered to him. "Am I really that old, Joseph, do you think?" He smelled wine on her breath and shook his head.

People began moving inside to dance and she let Joseph go then, and turned off the lights. He stood by the French doors and watched the Chinese lanterns swinging in the trees outside. His father was drinking champagne by himself in the dark, looking out at the river. Joseph walked outside and stood next to him.

"What do you think, Joseph?" his father said.

"They're dancing," he said.

"A perfect night for the boat," his father said.

He led Joseph down the lawn, toward the river. Fireflies flashed in the grass as they went down the hill. The lights and the music dwindled behind them. His father opened the doors of the boat shed, took the boat off the wall, and dragged it to the river.

The boat rocked and splashed as they climbed aboard. They pushed out onto the flat surface of the river and his father took the oars and rowed along the bank. A cacophony of frogs sounded in the reeds and tall grass.

"I never have been able to dance," his father said.

"Me neither," Joseph said.

His father laughed. "There is time for you to learn. If you want to. One day it might be useful. You can meet girls."

"I don't want to meet girls."

"Not now. One day you will. When I met your mother, I said that I liked dancing, actually. I was trying to impress her."

"You lied."

"Right. I lied and then had to spend the rest of my life avoiding dancing altogether. I have had to think up very convincing excuses. "

"You could just tell her."

"Not now. I'm trapped now. A prisoner of my own deceit."

They went downriver, sliding smoothly through the black water, unable to see anything on the shore. After ten minutes or so, his father turned the boat and rowed them back along the bank. Tiny droplets from the oars splashed into Joseph's face and he felt completely alert to the lapping of water on wood and the distant sounds of the party on the hill.

They were below the house again. A snatch of laughter and a man's voice came from the riverbank. They sat still in the boat and looked out through the reeds. A man and a woman were walking along the river, through the shadows cast by trees, in and out of the light. As they came closer, Joseph recognized his mother and Brian Underwood. He looked very tall alongside his mother. She walked carefully in her tight dress and clutched his arm with both of hers. He was smoking a pipe and the smell of tobacco drifted over the water. His mother was talking in whispers. They walked along the bank past them and his mother kept looking back over her shoulder. They stopped under a tree, in complete darkness. The frogs were loud in the reeds and water slapped against the hull of the boat. Joseph stared into the blackness without thinking. His father held the oars and sat still. Soft noises came from under the tree, gasps and moans that seemed to float over the river with the sounds of the insects and frogs and get lost there. When he heard the sounds of his mother, a mother he had never known, crying like an animal in the damp grass, Joseph whispered to his father. "Row," he whispered, "row us away from here."

Now his father lives in Bombay, near the Kalbadevi bazaars. He has the second floor of an old Victorian building. The building has a central courtyard reached by a narrow passageway from the street. On the walls of the courtyard, mosaic frescos depict Arab sailors, Koli fishermen, and Portuguese traders, in red, yellow, and gold tiles. The sounds and smells of the market press in from all sides and the sky is a distant white square visible high above.

Joseph is visiting him for the first time in fifteen years. He is twenty-six years old, with a hooked Arabic nose, baggy jeans, a small silver ear stud, and pieces of colored string around his wrists. He has a letter from his mother to his father in his suitcase, pressed between the pages of a Hindi phrase book. In the airport, his father approaches with one arm held in the air, clutches Joseph's elbow and pumps his hand. His father is shockingly thin for a man of his height, wears a blue pin-striped shirt, dark slacks, and sandals. He scrutinizes Joseph seriously, pays close attention, appears to be collecting data, fixes him with his pale eyes, cocks his head to one side, lets forth a blast of fabulously halitotic breath. This is great, he says, really great. Terrific.

Joseph does not want to know why his father left them, because he already knows. He has read the letters, stained aerograms filled with single-spaced typed pages. He knows what his father did with all of his money, even approves. What he does not understand is how. How his father could leave them so completely and disappear. How he could be gone for so long without talking to them again. He is full of his mother's stories. She read his father's letters, letters that appeared after years of absence, years of nothing at all, and cursed him under her breath. She called him a cur and a bugger, a bounder and a son of a bitch. She called him insane. Yet Joseph feels bound to this tall thin man in a way. There is a familiarity there that he recognizes. But he cannot understand *how* he left them.

His father gives Joseph a room on the second floor. The room has a high ceiling and a rotary ceiling fan with burnished brass blades. It is sparsely furnished with a single bed along one wall and a bare oak desk near the window. There is a small bedside table and a chest of drawers with steel handles. The walls are whitewashed and bare, the only color in the room from two heavy Persian carpets on the floor. In the afternoon, there is a strong breeze that cools the air and flings the cotton curtains out into the room. Through the window, he hears the market, the loudspeakers of the mosque, and water rushing down a rusty drainpipe when it rains. A local flour mill is working in the building opposite, and when he sits at the desk, he sees men and boys coming and going from the mill, naked above the waist and white with powdered flour. Clouds of flour dust hang in the air and blow into the room. He finds the desk frosted with flour at the end of the day, feels the fine powder on his fingertips as he goes to sleep at night.

His father disappeared for fifteen years. It was a vanishing, done quietly and with rigorous determination. He sold his infectious-disease practice. Then he sold his share of the family company, the discount car-parts fortune, worth a million dollars. The actions of an unstable man, his mother believed. He took out all his savings and sold everything that she had no claim on. He left her the house, told the children they could go to public schools, said it was probably a better education for them anyway. There is work to be done, he said, I have wasted my time. She screamed at him, belittled him, told him he had lost his marbles, went into blind rages. She would not follow him to the ends of the earth, she said, would not have her children sacrificed. She had her own career, was going to be successful despite him. He listened to her calmly, as if she was talking reasonably, walked through the house with armfuls of his suits and shirts, great piles of starched cloth, that he piled into the car and took to homeless shelters.

He moved to Bombay and devoted his life to working in the slums. He formed a nongovernmental organization, an NGO, set it up and ran it with his own money. He was not able to buy property himself, but later he persuaded a colleague to purchase four large flats along the southern shore of the city for him, three of them in buildings on the Nepean Sea Road and one on Malibar Hill, overlooking the Arabian Sea. The rent from these properties has kept things running.

He is ignored by other doctors, works alone, and stays because he sees a need. He trains local people to run their own health programs. They are Muslims, but this in itself is not why he is there — they are people, he says, that is what they are, just people. When he goes to the mosque, it is to talk, not to kneel and pray. He knows as much about the prevention and treatment of childhood pneumonia, diarrhea, and measles as anyone. He has a working knowledge of the management of tuberculosis and leprosy and has controlled outbreaks of *Shigella* dysentery, cholera, and plague. He has started programs to distribute vitamin A and is recognized by young children and old men all over the city. On Joseph's first evening, he opens his bedroom door and throws a copy of *Control of Communicable Diseases in Man* onto the bed. "Welcome home," he says and Joseph must look confused, disoriented perhaps, because then he adds: "No, I mean it. Really. Welcome home."

His father is enthusiastic. He wants to show Joseph what he has been doing. He takes him into the Jogeshwari slums, walking ahead with long, loping strides. The alleys are dark and so narrow that they have to walk in single file. The houses are made of painted mud bricks that are crumbling in the dim light, held together with corrugated iron, sheets of plastic, and cardboard boxes. In the market, a fury of people move between *chawls* that are hung with laundry, sheets of thin cloth with floral prints, rugs, tools, taps, and plumbing equipment, electrical fittings, the fat white carcasses of lambs and goats, cassette tapes, lottery tickets, pots and pans, Victorian porcelain, glossy posters of Indian movie stars. The merchants are men, bearded, olive faced, with scrubbed hands and quick eyes who stand with their hands folded in front of them. Open drains run the length of the streets. Young children carrying yellow plastic bottles of fresh milk on their shoulders stare at them. People are quiet and stand back when his father walks past. He is offered a chair at every house he passes. All the thanks I need or deserve, his father tells him, is the offer of a chair. He talks to Joseph over his shoulder, walking awkwardly through the narrow streets, hitting his head on shop awnings.

His father takes him to health clinics and introduces him to trained volunteers in white coats who shake Joseph's hand and flash rows of teeth when they learn that he is the son. He shows him drug cabinets neatly stocked with capsules and tablets and rehydration sachets; opens fridges and points to the stacks of vaccines; demonstrates the Salter scales and steam sterilizers. A little bit of knowledge, he says, can make a world of difference. Nothing is too small to escape his attention. He notices details — a chair leg broken, a patient register incorrectly filled out, how long people wait to be seen. Joseph feels intimidated by how people react to his father. They trust what he says. There is none of the doubt that Joseph himself feels.

Joseph feels like the nine-year-old who sat in a wooden boat with his father and listened to noises coming from the shore. They had shared a moment that bound them tightly and that they had never talked about. It was an understanding, a blanket of intelligence, as unyielding as tempered steel. The dissolution began with the party. They were due to go to India to visit her parents, but two days later she told them she could not go because she had an offer to present a paper at a conference in Stockholm. Brian Underwood thought she would be foolish to turn down the opportunity. This could help make her name and get her established, she told them, sitting at the kitchen table with a cup of coffee held to her lips and the morning sun falling, in a sharp white band, across the top of her head. Just a week in Sweden, a dull place, she had heard, but then she would join them in Calcutta, see her parents, tell them all about it.

How did Joseph know she was lying? How did he know that, somehow, it had always been a lie? It was nothing he could describe. The children went to India with their father. Their mother disappeared in the other direction. A week later, she called to say that she had been invited to make another presentation and would not be able to join them, because it was too important for her career. His father barely spoke on the phone, stood with the receiver pressed to his ear and listened with

the intensity of a man receiving instructions. Her parents were understanding, took them to films and markets, to a circus with tigers and dwarf
trapezists, and bought the children ice cream — chocolate and strawberry
balls that began melting in seconds, falling in moist globules onto the
backs of their hands and the toes of their shoes.

His father left the two girls with her parents for a few days and took
Joseph to Delhi on the train. They went to Birla House where Gandhi
was assassinated in 1948. The white building stood in grounds with leafy
avenues, swaths of lawn, and well-manicured flowering shrubs. The last
several steps taken by Gandhi were marked with red stone footprints on
a path beside the house. Joseph stepped in the footprints with his own
feet, followed them as they turned left up five steps to the lawn and then
stopped. A stone plinth marked the spot where Gandhi fell, shot in the
chest by a newspaper editor who believed that Gandhi's philosophy
would destroy Hindu India. His father explained all this to him at the
time, although he did not understand. He put his shoes over the red stone
footprints and when he came to the last one on the path, fell to the
ground and imagined being shot. The grass was cool and sharp on his
cheek. Dying, he resolved, was like that — like lying down on a piece of
very green grass, surrounded by flowering shrubs, and never getting up
again.

Inside Birla House, by a black-and-white picture of Gandhi after
death, his father's eyes pooled with tears. Joseph looked at the pictures
of the small man in white with skeletal hands. He had never seen his
father cry. He pulled on his father's sleeve. His father squatted next to
him, dabbed his eyes with his cuffs, smiled thinly, and stared up at the
photograph of Gandhi. "It's your mother," he said. "I'm afraid that she
is not going to come home."

His father lives in two whitewashed rooms with very little furniture. On
a low table, there is a stack of medical journals and a stack of newspapers and a chess set. "The Universal Declaration of Human Rights" is
mounted on the wall in a thin frame. He has no clocks in the house, does
not carry a watch, gets up with the Muslim call to prayer, washes in tepid

brown water that smells of sulfur. A silver tea service made of Sheffield silver plate and two Toby jugs are his only luxuries, he says, small concessions to British imperialism. For the first few days, he does not sit down when Joseph is in the room. He stands and listens with his hands held behind his back, his head pushed forward, and his eyes directed firmly at the floor.

He has a housekeeper, Mrs. Bhattacharryya, as tall as she is wide, who prepares lunch and dinner, spreads dishes out on the table with great care and is profoundly disappointed when she finds food uneaten. She watches Joseph while he eats, nodding and smiling every time he looks up. He is ravenous, for some reason, in the humid air, and eats the oily dishes without hesitation. Mrs. Bhattacharryya puts a new cake of soap in the bathroom every morning, as if it were a hotel. He finds her one afternoon at the kitchen table, scrubbing his sneakers with a toothbrush. He feels as if he is being observed.

His father eats with his head down, picking up the food with pieces of nan bread or chapati like a local, and talking with his mouth full. He eats so much that it is remarkable that he remains thin. He is full of optimism and plans for the future. There is no cynicism or bitterness in him. Joseph talks too much at the table, about things that he does not think are important — his life at home, his interest in being a geologist. He talks about Kate and Marguerite and how well they are doing, and about his mother's latest job as an editor of a training manual for telemarketers. He hears himself from a distance and has a sense that he is performing badly, overacting in a terrible family drama.

Three afternoons a week, his father takes a vigorous walk along Chowpatty beach wearing a pair of stained Hush Puppies. On Sunday morning, he has a massage from a malish wallah with thin sinewy hands and tea-stained teeth who comes up to the house specially. His father goes about his business. He lets Joseph do as he pleases. On the street outside, a man selling the *Times of India* claims to have memorized every postal code in Britain. Give him the address, he tells Joseph, and he will give the postal code in a matter of seconds, an extraordinary feat, he says, for a man of his class and means. Joseph walks in the bazaar. The colors and the filth dazzle him. The city is messy and exuberant, all at once, unfair and triumphant, shocking and deeply reassuring. There is a power there. It comes rushing up from the streets, from the bustle of commerce, from the sheer force of it, and he senses that this is running through his father.

They listen to the radio news in the evenings, without speaking, with the lights out. The smell of the sea comes through the windows and the sun sets in distant flourishes of indigo and violet. They hear mobs of men and boys running through the streets. People shout at night. The smoke from burning buildings blows inside.

"Hindus are attacking Muslims," his father says in the dark.

"It doesn't make sense to me," Joseph says.

"Nothing makes sense," his father says. "I'm sorry to say."

"There must be a reason."

"Now you know why I am here," his father says.

It is his mother who wanted him to come. She sees Joseph as an advance party. He is here to gather intelligence and to give weight to her speculations about the state of her husband's mind, his lack of moral fiber, his likely dissipation in the tropics. Joseph watched her writing the letter to his father that he now carries with him, folded in two and pushed into the top pocket of his shirt. He wants to give his father the letter but cannot bring himself to do so. His mother sat at her old desk and wrote with her head close to the paper. She used a fountain pen, and when she had finished her hands and cheeks were stained blood red with the ink.

Her desk is still piled with her old textbooks, bits and pieces of preserved human bones, a plaster cast of the pelvic girdle of an early hominid. The desk is familiar terrain to Joseph and a part of his connection to his mother. He knows the objects, the holes and divots, the place underneath where he carved the initials of his father and mother when he was ten years old, deep furrows that he can still trace with his fingers when sitting in the chair. He sat there to be close to her. As an act of solidarity. All her lost dreams and ambitions are littered across the surface of that desktop, and all her bitterness and resentment. She blamed his father for the loss of her career, although there was no one to blame but herself. She made her indignation real with her stories, repeated them often enough to bring them to life. Now he can feel the envelope against his chest, heavy with the pages she had written.

If I've got nothing else, I've got my pride, she told him. Pride was why she could never go back to India, admit that she had failed and was no longer living a privileged life. Pride was why she could not acknowledge that they were poor, would not accept help from his father's family, continued working at part-time and occasional jobs that did not pay. Her pride told her that it was just a matter of time before she got an academic job in paleontology, the job she deserved. She wielded her pride above her head like a cutlass.

She imagined that Joseph saw her as an innocent. She did not know about that night on the river all those years ago, about what he had seen, about how vividly each sound and movement had been impressed into his nine-year-old memory. She did not know that Joseph understood what his mother was then. A fling. A mistress.

She was never able to get a university appointment in paleontology although it was the only subject that had ever interested her. She did not understand. What had she done? Joseph sensed that something terrible had happened. She could upset people, he knew that, could push people away when she thought she was drawing them in. What had she said? There was no way for him to find the truth. Everything was clouded by her ambition. She did not have the capacity to see herself as being at fault. Her fellowship ended and she began applying for the jobs she would never get. Each rejection made her harder and more unforgiving. Joseph's father left her with no money. She could not ask for help. All she had was her independence. I would rather live the life of a pauper, she said, than do a job that is beneath me.

Joseph and his father are standing in a health clinic near a market when a group of men carrying sticks attack a Muslim bread seller. The bread seller has a long beard, a shaved top lip, and a white skullcap. There are twenty or thirty young men in the group and they shout obscenities at the man, who stands with his bicycle. The old man shouts at the group, both hands in the air. People in the market stop talking and move away. His father says, "This is ridiculous," and looks out through the window. Joseph asks his father what the old man is saying. "I know you. I sell you bread," his father translates. "I know you. I am nothing to you. I sell bread to you." His father is visibly distressed. He walks away from the window and paces the floor. The men push the bread seller to the ground and begin beating him on the back with their sticks. His father moves toward the window again and says, "I'm going out there. Let me deal with it."

"You can't do that," Joseph says and grabs him by the arm. His father is shaking. Through the window the bread seller is lying in a cloud of dust, still shouting at the men with sticks.

"You're right," his father says. "It wouldn't do any good. This is the problem. It would do no good. It makes me wonder what the hell I'm doing here."

Joseph feels his father's arm in his hand. It is thin and hard. He realizes that it is the first time he has held on to his father in a long time. They are standing in the middle of the health clinic. A group of pregnant women waiting to be seen are sitting on benches. Two of them have moved to the window and are watching the street outside.

"Incredible," his father says so loudly that the women look up at him. "Incredible that I am standing here with my son." He turns awkwardly toward Joseph and grasps him by both shoulders, as if preparing to push him to the ground. It is only at the last moment that Joseph realizes that his father is hugging him, pulling him into a gangly embrace. He is held there, pressed into the bony rib cage, enveloped by the smells of camphor and curry, and is so surprised that the kiss, when it comes, is as inexplicable as a moth, a soft winged creature, striking his cheek on a dark night.

They walk quickly down the nearest alley. His father puts his head down and walks with his hands in his pockets. A few minutes later, they stop in front of a butcher's shop with a white tiled counter open to the street. The fresh carcass of a goat hangs from a hook at the front and two men in aprons are using large steel knives to cut slabs of meat from the flank of the animal. Cuts of red meat covered in marbled fat sit on display. A dead chicken with bright orange feet hangs upside down from the ceiling.

Joseph speaks to his father over the street noise. "Are you all right?" His father is panting heavily and large sweat rings have appeared under his arms.

The owner of the shop emerges from the shadows. He wears a white robe with blue cotton embroidery over the chest and shoulders, and a white skullcap. He shakes their hands and insists they sit on two steel-pipe chairs that he brings from the shop and places in front of them. A boy wearing torn shorts is boiling coffee over a small gas ring inside. Next to him on the floor he has a plastic bag filled with white sugar that he spoons carefully into the pot with a beaten-copper spoon. The boy brings them two small cups filled with strong sweet coffee and after every sip he refills their cups.

"I am all right," his father says. He looks up at the butcher and says, "We have seen another mob." He is still breathing heavily. "We should not have left."

In the bright afternoon light, Joseph sees his father for the first time as an old man — the dark hollows under his eyes, the beginnings of jowls. His hair is thinning at the top of his head, and is flecked with gray. Joseph realizes that he has never really looked at his father at all — he is a series of memories and impressions.

The butcher stands in front of them and says in good English: "These are difficult problems to solve. We are humble men here." He waves his hands out toward the street. "We practice the rule of God. I try to be a good man, you see. But it is a matter of pride. When mobs attack people, we cannot sit by and let it continue. It is pride. I said to my son, I do not condone violence, but you must go to the street to make your voice heard. And he is doing that in the name of God. You see."

Joseph nods and sips the coffee. His father holds the cup between his knees and looks at the ground. "Both sides think the same thing," his father says. "This is the problem. Both feel they are equally justified."

The butcher smiles. "You do good work here. We are all exceptionally grateful. Everyone is grateful. I know you see no difference by Hindu or Muslim." He bends down and whispers to him, "You are right. Really you are. There is no difference — all people of flesh and blood. All just flesh and blood."

His father finishes his coffee and stands up suddenly, blocking the afternoon sun, and throwing Joseph into shadow. For an instant, he can see things clearly: his own hands, the creased face of the butcher standing over him, the luminescent blue of the butcher's clothes. His father looks down at him and says, "I did love your mother. That was why I left. You should know that." He starts walking down the street and then turns and says, "I know I've let you down." Joseph stands up as his father disappears into the crowd. He shakes the butcher's hand, finds himself clutching these large fingers like a drowning man being pulled from the sea.

Joseph lies on the bed in the late afternoon and watches waves of white flour float though the window and settle slowly to the ground. He holds his mother's letter in his hands. It is just paper and ink, thoughts organized as symbols, but he feels as if it could change everything. He wants to open the letter and read it for himself. Perhaps there is some truth there that he has never seen. A kernel of understanding or reconciliation. He still wants the past to be erased and his parents to be together. He wants this letter to do all of that.

There is a dusting of white flour on the floor of his room. He remembers the bones on the top of his mother's desk, scattered like tiny icebergs. The day his father told his mother that he was leaving, they were in her study. Did they know he was under the desk? Would anything have been changed if they had known? He looked out at his father's legs. His mother had kicked off her shoes. She was so angry that she could not speak. She turned away from his father and stood there with both hands on the desk. "You can come with me," his father had said. "I want you to come with me." Now Joseph realizes that his father was trying to hold on to her. She could have accepted. She could have changed everything at that moment. She could have turned the tide.

But she didn't speak. She turned and threw a bone at his father, a big piece of bone that he later knew to be the lower jaw of modern man. He still sees the spinning white triangle arcing through the air and striking his father on the forehead. A flash of blood appeared at the point of impact. Perhaps everything would have been different if he had come out from under the desk. But he didn't move. He sat and watched the tendril of blood run down his father's forehead, felt the carpet under his bare knees, heard his mother shout, "Never," and then repeat it, "Never, never, never."

It is just a letter. It is in his hands. Years later, he will remember the cloud of white flour, falling like snow in that small room. He will remember the sounds of the market through the open window. But it is the unopened letter that he will remember most clearly. It is heavy. The red ink is already smudged. The letter makes him feel as if anything is possible. The future and the past are in his hands. Everything is contained. Time feels as measured as the white flour drifting in the air and he understands, for a few slow minutes, the pleasure of not knowing.

5

WATSON AND THE SHARK

Early on that Sunday morning — it must have been five or six o'clock —
the first of the wounded began arriving at the gates of the hospital.
They came in on crude stretchers fashioned from eucalyptus poles, and
had been carried all the way from a refugee camp on the border with
the Democratic Republic of Congo. These were the first real injuries we
had seen. The men carrying the stretchers were gaunt and loose limbed.
They had haunted eyes.

Guy Buffington, the local Catholic missionary, came to wake us up.
I heard him knocking on the windows of the house for several minutes
before I opened my eyes. When I pulled open the door, I was still groggy
from sleep and a wave of cold wet air, tinged with the heavy scent of
cow dung, washed inside through the open door. It was dawn and thin
fingers of light were coming into the sky. Guy Buffington was a tall and
angular man with no visible eyebrows. He was wearing a bathrobe and
had a chunky wooden cross, made of polished dark wood, strung from
his neck by a leather thong.

"There are refugees arriving," he whispered to me, "quite a few of
them. I think some of them have been attacked. I *know* they've been

135

attacked. I'm sure of it. I thought you should know." Then he erupted in a sudden burst of coughing that lasted more than a minute. He was still coughing as he walked back down the hill.

Stefan and I had a triage system worked out with the nursing staff who were left — there were not many of them — and the incoming were dropped under three U.S.-issue mess tents that the MSF team had set up in the central courtyard. From there they were carried to the operating theater, a low building on the top of a small rise. This building was made of yellow cinder block and had a new corrugated iron roof and a poured-concrete floor. It was the best we could do. We got all of the stretchers and assorted family members settled under the tents and then handed round packets of Belgian biscuits and foil-wrapped chocolate from Germany. We were awash in donated snack food — high-energy sugar and carbohydrate that could be used in a pinch to stave off hypoglycemia and keep people happy for a while.

The first thing I noticed was how quiet everyone was — these people had walked for ten hours without food or water but none of them were complaining. More than that, none of them were speaking to each other, they were just looking, and not in a dumb way, but in a cool and somewhat appraising way. There was a nobility about them. They were big-boned people, lean and tall, with high, polished cheekbones and delicate lower legs and ankles. It was so quiet that Stefan and I assumed that the injuries were minor. So it was a surprise when Made in Detroit and Johns Hopkins Hockey, our triage nurses, started shouting and calling for help.

The hospital had taken a shipment of donated American clothing just before the crisis, and everyone had secured a hand-me-down T-shirt emblazoned with the name of some college or popular capitalist icon. We started using the T-shirts to identify people. It was easier and quicker. No one seemed to mind. We didn't have time to learn their real names.

The wounded were wrapped in sheets of mud-stained cloth that smelled of wood smoke and wet leaves. Under the first sheet I found a teenage boy, perhaps fifteen or sixteen years old, pale and clammy from shock. He had flecks of straw in his hair, fine cuts across the bridge of his nose, and dilated pupils. A wad of green palm leaves was pressed to the front of his body to stanch the blood. He looked up at me with such hope that I found myself smiling unreasonably, but when I pressed around his wound, an enormous blood clot — a baseball-size mass — fell into my hands, and the boy made a sound for the first time, a sucking gasp, and his eyes rolled back up into his head. It was a huge abdominal laceration, right through muscle, peritoneum, bowel, and a healthy segment of the lower lobe of the liver. I was assailed suddenly by the warm reek of gut contents and pulled back sharply. This needed immediate work. The wound was a vicious cutting injury made with a long sharp blade, at least twelve- to twenty-four-inches long, I estimated, and this was confirmed by the survivors around me. They had been attacked with *machetes*, broad-bladed farmers' implements that were used for clearing scrub and cutting cane sugar. I got Made in Detroit to put in an IV line, run in a quick liter of normal saline, then start a second liter, and give the first dose of ceftriaxone and metronidazole. I held off on the morphine because I guessed he was splinting the wound with his own muscles and didn't want him to relax for fear of starting a major bleed. Made in Detroit talked quietly to the man next to the boy, who was his uncle. The teenager's name was Gabriel, she translated, in his final year of school and a star player of *le football*, a center forward who had already tried out for the national team. All of his family had been killed.

Looking back into the tent, I could see that every eye was fixed on me and I felt that sense of power and control that I needed then — this was why I was a trauma surgeon — and I wanted life-or-death, all-or-nothing situations. Life or death. That was why I was there in the jungle, and I honestly had a tremendous feeling of being in the right place and of being filled with a certain glorious energy.

Stefan came up to me as I stood looking into the tent. He had already been through both of the other tents and I understood how slowly I had been moving. He had made all the critical decisions about the other stretcher cases in seconds and then moved on. It was what you had to do in high-volume situations. I was still working on American time. He had about ten individuals who needed major surgery under general anesthetic, and another twenty who needed smaller muscle and skin repairs that could be done under local. At least fifteen of the others were already deceased, he told me, all of them from big slashing wounds to the limbs and abdomen. There were some babies and pregnant women among the dead, he said calmly, and we stood there for a minute thinking about this, but did not take it any further. Objectivity. I prided myself on it. That was why Stefan and I were doing this job. We could control our emotions, put them away somewhere, and do what needed to be done.

I had taken to Stefan immediately. He was French, born and raised in the town of Poitiers, and had been a trauma surgeon for the ICRC — the International Committee of the Red Cross — for the last ten years. It was all he did now, rugged placement after rugged placement, in war-torn and decimated corners of the world. In between, he returned to his apartment in Paris, down near the Bastille, where he ate glorious meals, drank till all hours, tried to cut back on his smoking, and chased smart French women with a taste for cognac. He had seen some action. He had operated under fire in northern Afghanistan, helped patch up mujahedeen who had been blasted with AK-47 fire and rocket launchers, often working without electricity or water. Somalia, Angola, Beirut. He had seen the high-speed injuries induced by exploding bullets, shell casings, shrapnel of all kinds, land mines, and a variety of antitank armory. He did what he could. Resigned himself.

He'd picked up several useful skills that made him self-sufficient in a crisis — some vascular techniques for repairing the larger vessels, a little basic neurosurgery, simple plastics and orthopedics, and he had enucleated more eyes than most surgeons ever do. He had supple pale fingers and an enormous brush mustache that hung under his nose like some kind of mammal. There was an intensity to Stefan, a seriousness when he was working, that I respected. He did not take what he was doing lightly and he treated everyone around him as if they mattered. Including me. It was my first time in the jungle, and he was kind enough to treat me as an equal. I respected the man more for it.

Standing by the triage tent on that Sunday morning, Stefan and I looked up into a brilliant blue sky filled with the calls of tiny African brush warblers. Stefan lit up a Camel and walked with me between the stretchers. He was calm and deliberate, got down on his haunches with the cigarette burning in one hand to examine the injuries closely. Under his green surgical scrubs, he had white hairless skin and a surprisingly taut and muscular body, although he scorned exercise of all kinds.

"You can see that we are dealing with knives here," he said to me. "For everyone it is the same. Big knives. Big cuts. It takes a lot of energy."

"What do you mean?" I watched him take a deep draw on his cigarette and blow smoke out of the side of his mouth.

"To attack with a knife. It is a very personal thing to do. You have to be close. You have to mean it, really *mean it*. If you see what I am saying. There needs to be a brutality there. It is not so impersonal."

We finished triaging the stretchers in the last tent and saw the same pattern to all the injuries. Multiple cuts to hands, forearms, necks, and faces where knife blows had been taken or fended off. The worst of them were the abdominal puncture wounds. There was a great deal of open bowel and a high risk of infection. We ranked the surgical cases for Made in Detroit and Johns Hopkins Hockey and got them to set IVs and prep the cases for surgery. Then we asked Marlboro Man, a tall, very thin fellow who was the hospital caretaker and now did anything that needed doing, to find Chaswick Rashid, the third member of the ICRC team. Like a lot of anesthetists, Chaswick made himself scarce whenever he wasn't needed, took cover somewhere, and tried to avoid the messy business involved in managing the real problems. I am not being judgmental. Simply stating a fact. And I liked Chaswick Rashid, too, although he took liberties with the MSF girls that I thought were pushing the envelope of propriety a little.

Chaswick Rashid came rushing out of the billet house like a madman. Back in England, he had just finished his residency training and was studying for his college exams — he arrived in country with two boxes of textbooks and journal articles — and had spread himself out on the dining room table in the house. Before the first cases arrived, he read for hours, sitting quietly with his head between his hands. His reading was punctuated by bursts of energy, when he went down to unpack the anesthetic equipment, and to make a detailed drug inventory. He came down the hill over the moist grass wearing his white theater clogs, with a pile of rap and hip-hop cassette tapes in one hand.

"We have some business, I see, gentlemen," he shouted as he came down toward us. He straightened his grandmothers' spectacles, which had fine gold rims and tiny circular lenses, and looked into the first tent. "More refugees," he said.

"From up on the Congo border," Stefan said. "They were attacked with knives."

"Gottcha. Nasty stuff, init?" Chaswick Rashid took off his spectacles and began polishing them briskly with a handkerchief—he spent his life playing with his eyewear. It was a nervous habit.

"I should say about twenty abdominal cases, Chaswick, who will need generals." Stefan finished his cigarette and bent down and pushed the butt into the dark soil until it was buried there.

"We've marked them all," I said, "in the tents. They're getting them prepped."

"Gottcha. I'd better get on with it, then. Better make hay while the sun shines."

Chaswick Rashid was a tiny man, five feet tall I would say, with a high, domed forehead and thin black hair that stuck up at all angles. He had a small gold ring in his right earlobe, a big hooked beak of a nose, and the smallest hands I have ever seen — like the hands of a child — with bright-pink nails and shining white cuticles. His hands held my attention. I found myself watching them intently, as if they were butterflies, wafting around in the air in front of him. He ran off to do preop assessments on the surgical cases. He was very thorough and I never had anything but the strongest confidence in his skills. When he *was* working, there was no cutting of corners for Chaswick Rashid, and this is my style.

Chaswick Rashid was second-generation Indian, grew up in east London somewhere, and he had one of the broadest cockney accents I have ever heard. This made him a somewhat incongruous figure in my mind, because he looked like an accountant from Calcutta. I couldn't understand half of his sentences, although in the end it didn't matter. He was obsessed with the Full English Breakfast — fried egg, bacon, sausage and

tomato, with baked beans, toast, and tea — which he required every morning. He arrived in the country on a UN flight from Paris Orly with a ten-
pound carton of handmade beef sausages, plump pink cylinders bulging
under their own pressure. His father was a butcher. He stored the sausages
in one of the clinic refrigerators next to stacks of measles and tetanus
vaccine. The smell of eggs and bacon already hung in the air by the
tents — Groove Tube was the cook at the mission and he took personal
responsibility for the preparation of the Full English numbers for the
anesthetist– but I knew that Chaswick would miss his breakfast that
morning.

We quickly took in a hundred wounded, the only survivors, we were
told, of a camp of over four hundred people. They kept on coming
all morning, emerging like shadows out of the mist that hung over the
high, rolling hills. When they arrived at the gates, the stretcher bearers
paused to cross themselves and say prayers. Looking down the winding
red-earth driveway that morning, through the vanilla and mango trees, I
could see the new arrivals waiting at the rusty iron gates.

I smoked a Camel with Stefan in front of the operating block, looking back down the hill. It was wonderfully clear above the valleys, which
were filled with long white streaks of mist. We were on the crest of a
high *colline*, and towered over a landscape that was all hills and valleys,
light and shadow. The sun cast bright light on distant pastures, swaths
of deep green that rolled away like ocean swell. So much for the jungle.
A great deal of it had been cleared out there — many of the people were
pastoralists who farmed big-horned cattle. There were a few pockets of
real forest left, and you could still get a feeling for what the land must
have been like once — there was a thickness, a clinging density to the
jungle, when you saw it, that was unsettling.

Guy Buffington came up the hill to see us. When he reached the top,
he coughed into a white handkerchief for some time. He was in charge
of the mission where we were all housed. The mission had been there
for more than fifty years, and comprised a stone church, a one-hundred-
bed hospital, a large outpatient clinic, and an elementary school, all on
several acres of hilltop land. They baked their own bread and employed

local people from the surrounding villages. The operating theater was near the top of the hill, and from there we looked out over the mission buildings, which curved around the hill below us.

All the senior medical staff at the mission — there had been four doctors before the crisis — were gone now. Guy Buffington was from Oxford, England. He was a formal but well-meaning man, and almost certainly a homosexual. I say this simply to state a fact. Chaswick Rashid, who was a chronic insomniac, often walked alone when he couldn't sleep. Walking in the early hours of the morning, he had seen Groove Tube, the cook, sneaking out of Guy Buffington's bungalow on several occasions, wearing only a pair of loose shorts. Chaswick had seen Groove Tube going into the darkened house at night, too, after midnight, walking quietly in through the shadows of the spindly pine trees that grew along the front boundary in symmetrical lines. Groove Tube was a young man in his twenties, with round cheeks and full, sensual lips. He had a withered left leg from polio and walked with two stout wooden sticks. Groove Tube was always cheerful and laughing — of all the local staff, he was the one most inclined to talk with us, often sitting on the porch while we ate. He asked questions about America and England, wanted to know about French food, and bummed a few gratis Camels from Stefan.

"Good day to you." Guy Buffington came up along the gravel walkway wearing a black shirt with a dog collar. "You realize that today is a Sunday — an important day for us."

"Sunday," I said, "sure."

"Well, it's very important to us here. There will be a service, of course, and later we like to have a dinner for people from the villages."

"Very nice," Stefan said and continued to smoke.

"It would normally be a day of rest."

"Not for us, Mr. Buffington." Stefan waved politely over the triage tents that were steadily filling with stretchers.

"You can see that we have wounded today, Mr. Buffington," I said.

"It worries me, frankly. The numbers that are coming." He ran his fingers through his thin straw hair.

"It is disturbing," said Stefan through a mouthful of smoke. "Who knows how many will come. Maybe there will be many more. Maybe no more."

"All these poor people would not be coming here if *you* were not here."

"Nonsense," Stefan said. "They would be coming here because they think there is a hospital with some staff here."

"It makes it difficult for us. We don't have much food — the local people around us, they are resentful that these refugees are getting free food and medicine."

"We can't turn them away," I said.

"No. No, of course not."

"We will need to make arrangements for more food," Stefan said. "There are convoys delivering donated food, are there not?"

"You can use the radio, can't you?" I asked.

"I can. I can use the radio. The problem is the roads. They tell me that the main roads are all barricaded and held by armed rebels. Nothing is getting through. We'll have to make do with what we can get locally. Not much, I'm afraid."

"We will manage," Stefan said and finished his cigarette. He had smoked it down to the filter.

"You realize that it makes us a target," Guy Buffington said, fingering the wooden cross around his neck. "Now that we have refugees, even wounded refugees, then we become a target for the rebels."

"But this is a hospital," Stefan said, "they would not attack wounded people. We have a certain immunity."

"Perhaps you're right." Guy Buffington was shifting uneasily from one foot to the other. "I spoke with Pastor Meffin down in Muramvya yesterday, and he told me that they have taken a number of armed soldiers at the hospital there, for protection. I wonder if I should ask for the same. I mean, I think I *will* ask for soldiers. I don't see that there is a choice."

"You must do what you feel is best," Stefan said and looked at me and we moved off toward the operating theater. I heard the sounds of children playing on the soccer pitch. A choir was singing in the valley below us. Stefan went inside and Guy Buffington walked back down the winding path toward the stone church. In the distance, I could see lines of women, wearing dazzling indigo-and-yellow head scarves, walking between the trees, toward the church. The colors stood out as vibrant splashes in the deep green of the trees.

I saw some astounding churches in the hills. They were beautiful stone buildings built by missionaries who knew more about how to build a flying buttress and make a stained-glass window than they did about the dysentery and malaria that was killing half their flock. Guy Buffington's church had a small spire, a hand-carved granite altarpiece, and some very fine stone columns. The interior was dry and calm — it sealed out the chaos and made you want to be in there.

During our first week in the hills, when there was not much to do, Stefan, Chaswick, and I drove out along winding hill roads to look around. The interior seemed almost deserted then, the fields empty and overgrown with weeds, the villages quiet and filled with burnt-out buildings and wandering chickens. Whenever we saw people on the road, they ran away from us, tearing back through the undergrowth, not looking back. In one of the larger towns, we came across a big stone church in the Gothic style. It was an impressive building sitting out on its own surrounded by mud huts and dirt paths. We pulled the Jeep up at the front. The doors of the church, which were thick wooden slabs, were hanging from their hinges — they were pocked with bullet holes. The paving stones in the entry were worn smooth, furrowed from decades of moving feet, and littered with straw and leaves and firm black pellets of goat dung. Inside it was dry and cold, the vaulted roof in shadow. The nave was filled with long pews with tall backs and knee boards, a hymnbook behind every seat, and the place smelled like dust. We walked up the length of the nave. As our eyes adapted to the dim light, we could make out the cow. The tan-colored animal was standing stock-still in front of the altar and was staring at us with steady eyes. It had been drinking from the baptismal font and the fur under its mouth was wet and dripping onto the stone floor.

"Should a cow be in a church?" Chaswick Rashid said loudly.

"Who can say?" I said.

"They are, how do you say, one of God's creatures, are they not?" Stefan said, walking up and laying a hand on the animal's neck. The cow did not flinch when he reached out. It flicked its head to one side, sniffed briefly at his arms, and then walked past him, toward the front door. I could see now that there was a pile of loose straw heaped at the back of the church, behind the pews, and the cow walked back and started eating from the pile. Stefan looked up at the altar and crossed himself.

The baptismal font was a solid piece of white marble, elaborately carved with the branches of a tree filled with birds and fruit. The water inside was yellow and had stained the marble with rust-colored streaks. It was a beautiful object that seemed to gleam as it sat there in the dim light. It looked Italian, elaborate, rococo. It must have weighed a ton. Getting it into the jungle can't have been easy. Squatting down, I read an inscription carved into the side: "Rev. Thierry Lambrechts, Antwerp, 1925." Someone had carried it a long way, this massive chunk of marble, into a place that had never seen marble. I imagined the kicking feet and reaching hands of all the babies that had been lowered into the font, watched by parents and families who must have been in awe of the object itself, its perfection and weight. Like a big carved stone from heaven. There was a futility to the whole thing.

"It doesn't make sense," I said.

"What doesn't?" Chaswick Rashid was polishing his spectacles.

"This thing. Think of the energy spent getting it out here. Out into the middle of nowhere. The people out here don't have enough to eat, for God's sake. They're dropping like stones because they don't have medicine. And a priest in Antwerp decides that what they most need is a marble font, and a very large church. Does that make sense?"

"Faith is more important than food," Stefan said.

"And now they're killing each other anyway," I said, "despite the faith, the church and the marble font. Does that make sense?"

"The less you have, the more you need the church," Stefan said. He was sitting in the front pew, staring up at the ceiling.

"What shall we do with the cow?" Chaswick Rashid said. "I'm worried about the cow."

"Leave it. Leave the cow," Stefan said.

I reached over the lip of the font and dipped my fingers into the holy water. The smooth marble under my fingers felt solid and immovable. They would never get it out of there. The whole church could collapse, fall over in a pile of rubble, but that font would be there for a very long time. A big piece of marble from Antwerp.

I don't want to appear bitter — really, I've got nothing against the religious people who went into the jungle with their black Bibles and white skin, spouting their Hail Marys and eternal salvation. Everyone's got a job to do. And the locals believe in God, I can say that. They may not have any of the new-generation cephalosporins or a reliable supply of chloroquine or penicillin, but they can recite the holy Eucharist like there was no tomorrow. And there may not be a tomorrow, in that part of the world. You need to hang on to something.

I cast a last look at the wounded on the stretchers and walked inside. Things got going quickly. Chaswick Rashid already had the first two cases induced, intubated, and fully under on the respirators. He was using ketamine for the anesthesia, with infusions of diazepam and midazolam, and had cardiac monitors set up. Being the first in the room, he had taken the opportunity to put some heavy urban rap — his music of choice — on the cassette player, and the booming back beat echoed around the concrete room. Stefan made a face — he was a Gustav Mahler man — and we scrubbed and gowned. We had a supply of sterile kits with drapes and prep materials for a large number of cases. There were prepackaged sets for the abdominal work, and we had a steam sterilizer, so we planned to sterilize and reuse the instruments when we needed to. The kits included the usual range of scalpels and absorbable suture materials for abdominal work, as well as large-toothed scissors, toothed dissection forceps, curettes, hemostats, medium-lipped retractors, and a few self-retaining retractors. There were some sterile kits for head and bone cases, if we needed them. The regular suck and clack of the respirators calmed me down. As we began working, I looked out through the high windows along one wall, and saw lines of wood smoke from cooking fires rising into the sky.

Two Honda generators had been put in place to feed the theater, and Marlboro Man was in charge of getting these cranked up and working when we were operating. They provided enough juice to power the hundred-watt overhead lights, the suction and cautery equipment, and the respirators. If we needed it, we would turn on the air conditioner, as well, but it was brisk enough up in the hills not to need it. The generators roared outside, along the back wall. Every time someone opened the door, diesel fumes washed into the room and we had to keep all of the windows shut.

Virgin Atlantic and Madonna were the theater nurses and Stefan and I were impressed with their skills. They were neat and efficient, very useful with retractors and suction, and knew where to put their hands. They were both women in their forties and had beautiful round faces with shining coffee-colored skin and smooth fine-boned fingers. Each of them had five children at home. Like the others, they were quiet and self-contained, saying little, but laughing under their breath as they watched Chaswick Rashid jive his way between cases, in time to the pounding music. Chaswick did not care what people thought of him — he did his job well and said what he thought, and just got down to business. He made everyone feel better and I should have told him this when I had the chance.

Gabriel, the teenager, was my first case, and he set the pattern for the rest of the day. A lot of blood. I was cleaning the wound and having a closer look at the damage when a large arterial cut opened up and a jet of blood shot up to the ceiling. Then blood began to fill the abdominal cavity like water from a faucet. I got my hand in there and pressed down blindly, and we got a series of packs and the suction inside, but it was a struggle finding the vessel in the blood. I guessed that one of the larger branches of the mesenteric artery was cut. Stefan came over then, pulled on a new pair of gloves with a slap, and went straight in. He definitely had a sixth sense for bleeders. He got right in there with a couple of clamps, got hold of the offending vessel, and held it firm in a minute. "You can see the vessel down there," he said to me, "it is deeper than you may have imagined. The knives go further than you might think."

Stefan had a deft touch. He was quick but very effective, and he did the neatest suture work that I had seen. "I have done a lot of practice," he said to me, "with bleeding people."

This was the pattern with many of the cases we saw. Small arterial vessels punctured or cut that began pumping blood when we got inside. I was doing vessel tie-offs, and extensive debridement of damaged and pulped tissue on most of the cases. There was a lot of bowel work, as well, and we tried to do resections and primary repairs when we could. There were a few who were too traumatized and we did colostomies on these, hoping that they could be closed later.

It was fast and furious and I quickly got into a rhythm. There's a balance to this type of work, a sense that the instruments are under your control, where you don't need to think. Things just happen because they have to happen, and your hands are working automatically. I was getting into my rhythm on the second or third case, and feeling strong. By the time Stefan had badgered Chaswick Rashid into playing Mahler's second symphony, I was soaring and floating right along with the string section. I didn't understand that rhythm when I started my surgical training. All I saw was disorder and chaos.

We operated all day. Stefan was doing two cases for every one of mine, but we were getting through them. Late in the afternoon, Made in Detroit came in to tell us that Marlboro Man and Groove Tube had disappeared. She could not find them anywhere. None of us gave their absence any more thought at the time, and Madonna sent someone to find her two eldest sons to help out. We were filling the hospital with postoperative cases. The cast-iron hospital beds sat under whitewashed walls adorned with bloody color lithographs of Christ on the cross, mass-printed in Rome. Three MSF nurses were in charge in the hospital and seemed to have things under control. They were all from Brussels, young women who wanted a taste of the world, and they were getting it, too, up to their elbows in wound drains and catheters and piles of stained gauze bandages.

By midafternoon the number of refugees arriving at the mission began to increase dramatically. Most of these people were not injured, Guy Buffington told us, but were fleeing armed rebel soldiers with guns, and bands of civilians with knives. They were just innocent villagers, he said, running for their lives. Standing up on the hill in front of the operating theater that afternoon, Stefan and I watched them coming in along the road, long-limbed people with wrapped bundles on their heads, tickling small flocks of goats and sheep ahead of them as they walked. Guy Buffington had no choice but to let them in, and was beside himself with anxiety. "We have no food, no water, and no space," he whispered to us, "and I've radioed for assistance three times."

We took it in turns taking breaks. Outside, I went walking around the grounds, taking in big gulps of the fresh cool air and looking out into the valleys. I ate a few grilled goat brochettes with tiny new potatoes and fresh peas from the garden. The meat was smeared with a red hot sauce called *pilli-pilli*. Once the worst of the wounded were cleared from the triage tents, the situation appeared more manageable, but there were still a large number of people lying on the canvas floors of the tents, including many restless bare-bottomed children. The older children had been given chunks of sugarcane, and were stripping the husks and sucking the pulp loudly through their teeth. Colorful enamel bowls piled with millet balls, loose eggs, oranges, and tiny sweet bananas sat on the grass by the tents. Exhausted women lay with their forearms over their eyes. It felt pastoral. Like a quiet moment in the country on a fine spring day.

When I arrived in the country, four weeks earlier, I took a rattling taxi through dirt streets filled with people without shoes who looked over their shoulders nervously whenever they heard a car coming toward them. It was hot and dusty on the plains of the capital, and although there was no sign of the bodies that had littered the roads and drainage ditches only a few days earlier, I could feel the death there. I could smell it. There were hundreds of tar-feathered vultures sitting in plane trees and on the tops of the concrete walls of the housing compounds that lay along the main road from the airport. The hills in the distance were brilliant green. It was densely humid. Everything appeared to have been reclaimed by dust — it was in the air, swirling in eddies under cars and coating the slippery leaves of the trees like baby powder. If you got down close to the ground, you could see a perfect layer of dust on each individual blade of grass.

I met Stefan in the Novotel, the only working hotel left in the city. The hotel had a crumbling colonial charm — there were green lizards on the ceilings, thick black sheets of mold taking over the stucco walls, and a patisserie, still attended by an enormous shiny-cheeked man who wore a chef's hat. When you made a purchase, he delicately wrapped the cakes in thin squares of colored paper. Although most people in the country had no food, the hotel was still producing tiny glazed cakes filled with fruit, croissants, and eclairs every day — and they were all eaten, too, sold out by midmorning. The place was run by a nervous Frenchman who itched to get out of the country, but who acknowledged that he was making more money during the crisis than before it. He lived with his wife in the hotel and every morning his wife exercised their dog, a tiny ornamental shih tzu, on the hotel tennis court. She treated that dog like a baby. I saw her feeding the animal with pieces of croissant dipped in milky coffee.

The Novotel was filled with serious-browed, flak-jacketed international assistance people, shouting into satellite phones and negotiating for vehicles and fuel with cat-eyed young men wearing slip-on Italian leather shoes and baseball caps. Every evening, the crisis people gathered in whispering groups to drink foreign beer and discuss the devastation around them. They talked about what was happening up in the mountains, and took swims in the hotel pool that smelled strongly of chlorine. By dusk, the pool was shrouded in a heavy cloud of *Anopheles* mosquitoes and the water was filled with the bodies of thousands of dead and dying insects that had been attracted to the light — when I swam in the water, it was blood warm and I could feel the exoskeletons of these insects scratching against my cheeks and arms, splashing up my nose and into my mouth.

Stefan told me to ignore everything I heard down there — most of it was nothing but overexcited gossip, he said. But it was hard to turn off the stories of schoolchildren burned and babies cut up. Neighbors killing neighbors. In the end, I didn't know what to think, but I knew I had to get away from the expatriates who were tanning themselves around the pool during the day. I'd have a lot of trouble slipping on a pair of swimming trunks, rubbing in the coconut oil, and swilling down Cokes poolside when I knew what was happening up in those mountains.

There were five Russian military men staying at the hotel and obviously enjoying themselves. During the day, they lay around the pool. They were paper white in the sun. They chain-smoked duty-free cigarettes pulled from crumpled packs. Occasionally we saw them swimming vigorous laps, racing each other back and forth while shouting loudly in Russian. One of them — a captain — sat apart from the others under the covered patio, drinking black coffee and reading. Stefan and I got to talking to him one morning and he told us in good English that they were the crew of a transport helicopter and had been hired by the U.S. government to fly emergency supplies into the countryside. They had previously been doing the same thing in Somalia, he told us. The Russian military welcomed the hard currency. For the crew, it was like a long vacation, he said. It was easy work earning dollars. They stayed in foreign hotels, did occasional flights. He was reading Chekhov, he said, getting some literature while he had the chance. The crew had been hired by the local USAID office for ten thousand dollars a week including fuel and maintenance costs. Only after they had arrived did anyone realize that there were only a couple of places in the mountainous interior where it was possible to land a helicopter. They had little to do. He looked at us through reflecting sunglasses and sipped his coffee.

"Really, this is like an escape for us," he told us. "It is good for us to get out of Russia. To be frank, we are running away."

"What do you mean?" Stefan said with a smile.

"That is truth," the Russian replied, "we are running away. Like all the people who are coming in to help are running away from something. I'm sure of it. You don't come into these places out of goodness of heart. No. You come here because you've got your own problems. I've seen these people. They are all running away. I would not be coming here if I was happy at home."

Stefan and I were driven out to the mission in a Jeep. As we drove up the tortuous hill roads, past burned villages and stalled trucks, he smoked a fat stogie. "The Russian is quite right," he told me through a haze of blue smoke. "We come out here to find answers, not to provide solutions." And as we whizzed past roadside stalls selling tall bags of charcoal, trussed chickens, and pyramids of melons, I knew without a doubt that Stefan was right. I was looking for answers out in the jungle, even as I realized that there were no answers to be found.

The house where they were putting us up had been home to a family of American Catholic missionaries. It was sparsely furnished with locally made wooden furniture. The rooms were large and had tiled floors and white plastered walls. It was always cold inside and our footsteps echoed when we walked. A bookcase in the living room was tightly packed with thirty leather-bound Bibles that had been translated into Swahili. In the kitchen, each bowl and plate was painted with a small red cross. Jesus was nailed above every bed. Framed prints, in bright reds and blues, depicting Christ ascending to heaven, with outstretched bloody palms, surrounded by a crowd of disciples, hung in the living room, the kitchen, on the back of the bathroom door, and at intervals along the up- and downstairs hallways. I felt as if I was being watched. The continuous presence of the crucifixion made me feel as if the civil war had come inside with us. "There is a very high concentration of Christ in here," Chaswick Rashid said. "It's freaking me out."

The Catholic missionaries had also hung prints of classical paintings on the walls — dramatic paintings depicting heroic events. *The Battle of La Hogue* by Benjamin West hung in Stefan's room; *A Scene from the Beggar's Opera* by William Hogarth hung in Chaswick's. In my room, a color print of *Watson and the Shark*, painted in 1778 by John Singleton Copley, hung between two pieces of plywood that clacked back and forth against the wall in gusts of wind. The work depicts a real shark attack that took place in Havana Harbor, Cuba, in 1749. It was the first thing I saw when I opened my eyes in the morning.

Brooks Watson was a fourteen-year-old orphan serving as a crew member on a trading ship and was swimming naked in Havana Harbor when he was repeatedly attacked by a tiger shark. The first attack stripped the skin from Watson's right leg below the calf. The second took off his foot below the ankle. His shipmates put into the water in a rowing skiff and went to his aid. The painting depicts the action as they pull alongside him in the water. There is a sense of motion and of frenzied activity in the work, and the rescuing sailors show expressions of terror. Brooks Watson floats in the water with blood rising from his right foot — he is limp — and you can feel his shock and fear. Two sailors are reaching out to him, over the gunnels of the boat, and are attempting to drag him onboard. The boatswain is hanging on to the shirt of one of the sailors stretching out over the side and four sailors are pulling furiously on the oars. A sailor in breeches is standing upright in the bow with a boat hook raised in front of him, his face set in an expression of wild determination, and he is poised to plunge the sharp spike into the body of the shark below. It is a moment of rescue and salvation.

I found myself imagining all the things that could not be seen in the painting — the heavy water below the boat, the hold and cabins of the trading vessel floating in the background, the smells of food and tobacco on the wharf in Havana Harbor. It was strange to have a moment from the eighteenth century there on the wall. Lying in bed in the morning, with the smells of cooking fires and baking bread coming through the window, and the sound of rain hammering on the corrugated iron roof, I felt as if I was there in Havana Harbor myself.

At night, Stefan invited Chaswick Rashid and myself into his room to talk. Stefan's room was on the first floor and had a balcony overlooking the surrounding hills. When he was not working, Stefan sat in the sun on this balcony, bare chested, wearing colorful shorts and dark sunglasses, as if he were overlooking the French Riviera.

In his room, he lit three or four of the heavy beeswax candles made at the mission, and stood them on chairs. They burned with long slender flames that danced in the breeze blowing up from the valleys around us and cast tall eerie shadows on the walls. Stefan had brought several bottles of cognac with him, one of grenadine, and another of crème de menthe, and he had a set of small drinking glasses made of thick blue glass. He was proud of these glasses and carried them in a padded leather-ette case. He had one entire suitcase filled with cartons of Camel ciga-rettes, which he removed a pack at a time, with fastidious care, locking the suitcase carefully.

We sat in his darkened room and sipped the thick liqueurs. By nine o'clock at night, it would be absolutely silent outside and pitch-black. People were afraid of the dark, of what could happen at night, and dis-appeared early. From the balcony, everything appeared to be reversed — the night sky shone like some great luminous city, while the ground below was as dark and empty as outer space. I had the same sensation, looking out across that dark country, as I had when looking at the ocean — dangerous, terrible, impenetrable, all at once. Stefan set up his small shortwave radio, running a wire up onto the roof as an aerial. On some nights, he could get music from the French national stations or the BBC. Through a sheen of static, we listened to the songs of Edith Piaf and Bil-lie Holliday, Plastic Bertrand and the Bee Gees. On one occasion, we heard the entirety of Stravinsky's *Rites of Spring*.

"Tell me why you are here," Stefan said to me one night and I realized that I was no longer sure.

"I had the notion that I could make a difference," I said and smiled because sitting there on the dark African continent, I sounded impossi-bly naive, even to myself.

"Nothing we do can make a difference," Stefan said, draining his glass of cognac. "This is what I have come to realize. If you look for *common sense* — a very quaint English expression — then you are in trouble."

"There is nothing wrong with trying," I said.

"Of course," Stefan said. "Trying is everything. Absolutely, yes. But make no mistake. Trying will not change very much about the war. It is no different from attempting to stop the Niagara Falls with a postage stamp, or to hold back a deluge of rain with a scrap of paper. You see? Of course you must realize this if you are to work here." Stefan got up and walked out onto the balcony. He took a cigarette out of the pack in his top pocket and held it, unlit, in one hand. "I am not a cynic," he said.

Chaswick Rashid had been sitting on the balcony by himself in the dark with a glass of cognac clasped to his chest. "You sound like a cynic," he said and slapped a mosquito on his neck. "Sounds bloody cynical, if you ask me."

"I am a Catholic," Stefan said. "I am not capable of cynicism."

"Now you really are being cynical," I said.

Stefan came back into the room, still clasping the unlit cigarette in his hand. He pulled his chair over to mine and sat down, leaning forward until he was inches from my face. There were flecks of ash in his mustache.

"*Non, non,*" he said. "Listen. What you need is a philosophy. This is what you need. A way of making sense of the world. You cannot rely on what you see — because it will always be chaos, without rules. Wars are ridiculous. By definition, there is never any *common sense*. They will always happen — they will always be terrible. Many people will die in quite awful ways and we will never stop that. If you depend on what you see, *mon ami*, then you will be always disappointed. And of course you will go mad. I have a philosophy of disaster, you understand."

"And what is that?" I asked.

"That if you save just one life, then you have saved many. This is what I believe."

"What?" Chaswick Rashid called from the balcony.

"Each life counts," Stefan said. "Every life saved is a triumph. That is what keeps us human. You see. That is why I am here. Every day in the operating theater, I am affirming my humanity. You see that. This is how we will finally win. I cannot change the war, but I can affirm that every life has a value."

Sitting there with our glasses of cognac, listening to the night sounds coming in through the windows with the night breeze, with Stefan pouring drinks carefully from his bottles with fancy labels, I felt as if we were all mad. As if the world had gone quietly off the rails. "The painting in your room says it all," Stefan said to me. "Saving that person in the water allows us to save ourselves."

.   .   .

We were halfway through our last two cases when all hell broke loose. Made in Detroit ran into the operating theater in a cold sweat and told us that a truckload of rebel soldiers had pulled up at the front gates. By now, we had taken in at least two or three hundred refugees, and they were scattered across the mission, under the mess tents, in the school building, or just sitting in family huddles on the soccer pitch. They had been given blue UNHCR plastic shelters, and had begun erecting them on the grass. Stefan and I broke protocol and stepped outside, fully gloved and gowned, to look down toward the gates. A military transport truck was parked at the front and there were twenty or thirty soldiers, armed, milling at the gate. Behind them, fanning along the road, were another hundred or so men, short squat figures standing absolutely still, and clutching, quite clearly, a variety of knives. It was unnaturally quiet. The people inside the mission watched the gates intently. All I could hear were the sounds of children crying.

I saw Guy Buffington then, lanky, pigeon-toed, striding down the earth driveway. He stopped in front of the closed gates and snatches of his voice drifted up the hill. In his left hand he appeared to be clutching a Bible.

"Gentlemen," Chaswick Rashid put his head out of the door. "We have two customers still on the tables in here, if you get my meaning." Stefan and I went back inside. We were scrambling to finish up and get closure on the wounds when there were shouts and the sudden clatter of a few fast bullet rounds. Then people outside began shouting and screaming. Made in Detroit ran in again and said that the soldiers had ignored Guy Buffington and were firing into the air and coming into the mission. "They have ignored a Catholic priest," she kept shouting, with her hands in her hair, quite distraught. Stefan told her and Madonna and Virgin Atlantic to get the hell out of there, then, and spoke to them in some high-velocity French that I could not understand. They took off, out through the back door. Stefan told me to hurry up. I was suturing the abdominal wall in front of me as fast as I could when the door was flung open.

The soldier who burst into the room was wearing a mottled green combat uniform and smelled strongly of gasoline. His shirt was open to the navel. There was a big jangling collection of silver and gold chains around his neck, and he was incredibly young, no more than twenty years old. I could see immediately that he was out of his mind, spaced out on something. He had fat, swollen lips and his eyes were brilliantly bloodshot. In one hand, he held a Molotov cocktail — a burning rag hung from the neck of a bottle and thick black smoke was rising into the room.

I have seen a lot of punks like him in emergency rooms, trying to look confident, trying to look intimidating, but nervous as hell underneath. The key to dealing with punks like this is to not show any fear and treat them as equals. Make them think you understand them. I was confident. We'd had a good day of off-the-cuff surgery and I had power in my fingers. I did not think about the big black-barreled machine gun that was slung under his right arm, glinting like a wet seal. I wanted to prove something, too, wanted to show the others that I could hold my own when it counted. So I didn't skip a beat, just walked out from behind the table with my hands outstretched in front of me, and walked toward him as he stood swaying at the door. I smiled at him. He shot without looking at me. Let fly with a single round in my direction. I don't think he meant to. He just raised the barrel a few degrees and unleashed a cracking explosion that rattled in the small room.

I was thrown violently backward, smelled cordite and oil, and crashed into the instrument trolley behind me. The trolley collapsed and stainless-steel instruments scattered onto the concrete floor. The wall and ceiling passed in front of my eyes, and I was suddenly looking up. Stefan shouted something and I heard a bottle shattering against the wall. Then there was more smoke and the face of Chaswick Rashid down near mine saying, "Bloody hell, mate, bloody hell." With my left hand, I felt a wet mess on my shoulder, and chunks of what I knew was my own muscle. My arm was hanging open on a concrete floor in Africa and I knew it was bad when I felt blood running like a river through my fingers.

Stefan's mustache appeared above me. He was muttering in French as he and Chaswick took hold of my shoulders and legs and stumbled outside. There was a lot of smoke in the room and flames licked along one wall of the building. They put me down on the gravel path and then came back with the two postop patients we had just finished, laying them next to me. The gravel from the path felt sharp and cold on my shoulders. Stefan had put a clamp into my arm, and I could feel the cold metal, snapped around a branch of my brachial artery. The pain began sweeping into me, in heavy bolts that radiated up into my back. Then Stefan was above me again with a 10-cc vial of morphine in his fist, and I heard the vial crack as he broke off the top. I watched the needle slide into the glass as he drew it up, and felt the freezing alcohol swab on my left thigh. The morphine rolled over me and the warm rush into my brain was a welcome relief.

Stefan and Chaswick ran off down the hill, toward the hospital. People were screaming. Flames reached into the sky from the operating theater. There were birds high up above us, swirling on updrafts. When they ran back, they were breathless and red faced and had the MSF nurses with them. One of the nurses was crying and shouting at the others. As they came up, the nurses saw me on the ground and stared at my bloody shoulder. Stefan got down on his knees and ripped the shirt off my right arm and felt the fingers of my hand. "Can you feel this?" he kept saying as he pinched my fingers, and I nodded and looked up into the faces of the nurses from Brussels.

People were running everywhere. I watched them as I slipped in and out of the morphine. I pulled myself up onto my left elbow and looked down the hill. A few bodies were lying next to the soldiers and they had begun gathering people in front of the church at gunpoint. The sense of panic seemed to have disappeared — people were resigned or exhausted or both. I saw two of the soldiers find Groove Tube in Guy Buffington's bungalow — he must have been hiding in there. They pushed him out of the door and began kicking him as he lay on the ground. He was unable to get up without his sticks. They were kicking him, and Groove Tube was rolling around with both arms clasped over his head, when

Guy Buffington stumbled back up the hill. He ran up with the Bible still in one hand, shouting loudly, and got down on his knees. He took Groove Tube's head in his arms, and was bent over like that, talking to him, when the soldiers shot them both. Guy Buffington slumped down, as if he had decided to suddenly go to sleep. There was absolute silence from the crowd gathering down in front of the church, and I fell back, numb. Chaswick Rashid's tiny hands fluttered on my arm as he set up an intravenous line and I watched his fingers drifting in front of me. I was seeing waves of morphine in the sky now, felt deeply relaxed, and wondered if I had hallucinated the whole scene.

When I opened my eyes, a group of soldiers had surrounded us. Four or five of them stood with their big machine guns held in their hands like briefcases. I smelled fresh sweat on the soldiers. Their boots were clean and well polished. Their eyes were wide and dancing in the light from the flames next to us. None of the soldiers was looking at me, but they were eyeing the MSF nurses who stood with their arms clasped around their chests, blowing plumes of steam out into the cool evening air. Stefan stood in the middle of the group talking quickly in French, and I couldn't understand what he was saying. He kept on talking and the soldiers watched him carefully and occasionally looked back over their shoulders and down the hill, toward the church. Chaswick Rashid worked at his spectacles, running the lenses between his thumb and index finger, and turned to face the burning building. His theater clogs were covered in fresh splatters of my blood. I couldn't understand what was being said, but I knew that a negotiation was taking place. Stefan pulled out his pack of Camels and offered them around to the soldiers. They all took cigarettes and then he took out his lighter and walked around the group, lighting the cigarettes with a polite flick. I swam and drifted on the ground under them, listening to smoke being exhaled into the cool African air, and wondering how the hell I had got there.

Two months later, when I could use my arm again, I met Stefan in Paris. He looked quite different in his casual cardigans and buckle-down leather shoes. It was December and the City of Light shimmered in the cold air like a gemstone. At night, the Seine was like a mirror for all that light, seemed to reflect it in a thousand directions. I walked a lot in the city and preferred it at night. I stayed with Stefan in his Bastille apartment, which was clean and light, very modern. He gave me plenty of time on my own, and I was grateful because I was not good company. I couldn't make sense of the real life that I saw around me — families and children in the parks, warm bistros and shots of hot espresso. The buttery pastries reminded me of Africa. Real life seemed like a dream. Like something slightly improper. Stefan treated me to enormous meals in tiny restaurants where he knew the owner, the chef, the waiters, everybody. He poured wine into me, ordered foie gras and meat dishes and creamy desserts for us both from the menus. There was so much food and so much time to enjoy it that I was disoriented. We drank cognac and I walked.

Movement helped. In the City of Light, I felt like light. I felt the freedom of nomads, the need to move for the sake of it. I was a part of something outside myself in that city of spires and zinc bars. When I felt my shoulder creaking and aching, I felt stronger. On cold mornings, I blew steam and sat in tiny cafes with wet dogs and read three-day-old newspapers with hot cups of coffee. I ate big brown sausages in the street for lunch and made my heels ache with walking.

At one o'clock on a freezing morning, Stefan and I were walking across the Pont Neuf. We stopped to look at the river, which was sparkling in the frost, refracting through the thin cold air, and absolutely still. We stood shivering there for a moment and I said to him, "I don't think I've thanked you for what you did for me."

"You don't need to thank me," he said.

"I *am* grateful for what you did."

"So am I," he said, clapping his hands against the cold. "The fact that you are standing here now is thanks enough." Then Stefan turned and hugged me, a big bear hug on the bridge, and I felt his hot cognac breath on my cold cheek. At that moment, I thought that Stefan was perhaps my only friend in the world, and realized that this was enough. One real friend is enough. Then it began snowing and as we moved off along the bridge, under the heavy sky, I knew that I would not be going home for a long time.

I didn't see all those people being herded into the tiny stone church. They told us later. We were far down in the valley, out of earshot, when the screaming began. I have been told that Stefan and Chaswick took some flak for leaving, but they were trying to save our lives, and didn't know anything about what happened in that church either. How could they have known? What could the two of them have done? They behaved with great presence of mind under the circumstances.

Like Stefan, I can understand the healing power of rescue after catastrophe. The attack by the tiger shark in Havana Harbor made the reputations of both Brooks Watson and John Singelton Copley. Watson survived the attack, and although the ship's surgeon had to amputate his right leg below the knee, he made a full recovery and went on to become a successful merchant in London. He wore a wooden leg and was a distinctive figure who parlayed his tale of survival into a career in commerce. Popular enough to run for political office, he was Lord Mayor of London between 1796 and 1797 — his opponents mocked his wooden leg in satirical cartoons.

Watson himself commissioned the painting from Copley — the two men met in the summer of 1774 when the artist was passing through London en route for Italy. The painting was exhibited at the Royal Academy in London in April 1778, and praised as a work of genius. Copley was hailed as the equal of the Italian Renaissance masters. Both the painter and his subject had been transformed by this single violent moment.

Redemption after catastrophe must have influenced Copley when he was composing the painting — it is thematically close to the Old Testament account of Jonah and the whale, and *Watson and the Shark* has many compositional similarities with the Rubens painting of 1619 on the same subject. Watson was painted to bear a strong resemblance to the apoplectic boy in Raphael's *Transfiguration*, painted on panel in the Vatican in 1520. It was all about redemption. I'm not a religious man, but I know that survival from catastrophe can make you stronger. It can make you closer to people, too. I do wonder what happened to Gabriel and the rest of the wounded. Three or four days later, a UN team was sent to get the people we had left in the hospital. Many of them will have made it. Gabriel was young and healthy and stood a better chance than most.

In Paris, I went to sleep with my windows open and woke up with the room freezing and my shoulder stiff and aching, gusts of gray sleet blowing in through the windows and onto the floor. In an odd way, I felt as if I had been unhitched from my previous life. Something of my past had disappeared and I didn't need it anymore. Nothing that I had always believed to be important — my career, girlfriends, the books I read — seemed to have any real meaning. There is something insidious about being a distant observer, and that is what I had always been. An armchair moralist. A watcher of television news. A talker. I had believed I could make a difference with my surgical skills and my good intentions. Nothing is as clear as it appears to be from a distance. What difference can any of us make? This is the real question. What value is religion when a church is just another stone building with a roof and a floor?

In Paris, I had the sensation that I was weightless. Barely visible to the people around me. Perhaps you have to become nobody to understand who you are. I realized that I could not go home to the things that are comfortable to me. This was a strange kind of realization and it has come silently and imperceptibly, like a layer of frost gathering overnight on a piece of cold glass.

Now when I go to sleep, I think of the Copley painting. I suppose it is still hanging in that house in Africa. I imagine it there, accumulating dust, slapping the whitewashed wall in gusts of breeze, tapping out a rhythm into the empty room. A witness to the unseen events outside the window. When I shut my eyes, I can see it curling at the edges, growing brown and brittle, a whole universe perhaps to certain species of colorful tropical insect, small and busy, able to sustain themselves by eating the paper.

Stefan and Chaswick took care of me. We walked ten miles clear of the mission and were given shelter by people related to Virgin Atlantic. Stefan repaired my arm — vessels, muscles, the whole affair — in a straw-and-adobe hut. I was lucky that the bone was intact. Chaswick gave me an arm block, so I didn't feel a thing. They sent a team of Belgian UN soldiers in to find us. When the doctors at the American base in Germany saw the condition of my shoulder, they couldn't believe it. The neatest work they had ever seen, they told me, impeccable technique. They really couldn't believe it. I take my hat off to the Frenchman. I am using the arm already and have never felt better.

Stefan gave them everything we had. Everything we had in exchange for our lives. Bribery. That's what it was. He gave them the keys to the Jeep. He gave them five hundred dollars in American greenbacks, francs, and pounds and another two thousand dollars in travelers' checks. He gave them our clothes, our shoes, our razor blades, and the entire stock of Chaswick Rashid's beef sausages. Everything he could find. Then he gave them four twelve packs of cigarettes, shook their hands, and stood watching them troop back down the hill. I fell asleep as I watched them go.

When I opened my eyes, Stefan and Chaswick were standing over me with some surgical sets and boxes of supplies. Madonna's sons had appeared again and waited with fear in their eyes. "We're going to take you down to one of the villages," Stefan said to me, "we have to get off this hill." Chaswick Rashid polished his spectacles furiously, and cast long glances down toward the church. Flames rose from the roof of the operating theater. Some of the others picked up the two postop cases and set off in front of us. The two boys shifted me onto a stretcher and began carrying me. I swam in the dusk, felt no pain, looked up into the big arc of the sky. Gentle pops and explosions sounded in the distance like a public celebration on the Fourth of July. The night air and the smell of grass and earth made me think of the cool nights of my youth, lying on my back, watching fireworks.

We walked for a long time, down into the valley. They carried me along a steep path. I smelled burning wood and burning leaves and saw faces illuminated by cooking fires as we passed the houses. It was not until the morphine wore off that I realized that the soft explosions in the distance had been the explosions of guns. I called to Stefan, and when he appeared alongside the moving stretcher, told him I was sorry. I am not sure whether he heard me. The air was alive with the chirping of cicadas. It was getting dark and the sky was filled with a beautiful purple light. At one point, I saw the faces of Madonna and Virgin Atlantic above me, and then it was night, and there was nothing to see.

6

THE CARPENTER WHO
LOOKED LIKE A BOXER

His wife had been gone a year when he began hearing burrowing in the walls of his house and at first he tried to ignore the sounds. But as the weather got hotter, the noises got worse and he was waking up at night now, moist with sweat, and listening for hours. He called a firm of cheap exterminators who took cash only. He was finishing a building job and judged that he could afford to treat the house provided he didn't use one of the fancy American companies that advertised on television. Danny Dalton didn't like the idea of dark things living in his walls.

The exterminator was a stocky man with a red, peeling nose and buckteeth. He looked the house over and spent half an hour under the floor with a flashlight before telling Danny Dalton that he couldn't find anything.

"No rats, no possums, no insects or birds," he said, "and if there's a termite, or a wood borer, I can't see it." They stood at the end of his backyard, a rough brown-and-green slab of grass that sloped gently downward toward the cliffs. A salty breeze ruffled their hair. The exterminator looked young and had a withered right leg that gave him a swaying gait. He sounded like a salesman and Danny Dalton guessed that he had a second job in the restaurant or retail line.

Danny Dalton said, "I know what I hear. There's something in the walls." They both shrugged, and knew that the exterminator would treat anyway, without argument, for the cash. He agreed to spray for termites. Danny Dalton watched him clomp in heavy boots back up the lawn and along the side of the house. He heard equipment being unloaded onto the front lawn. When the exterminator reappeared a few minutes later, he was wearing rubber gloves, goggles, and a respirator. A bottle of chemicals was strapped to his back and connected to a nozzle in his left hand.

Katie and Tom arrived back from the beach then and Katie ran down toward him across the grass. The white sheets hanging on the clothesline were kicking slightly in the sea breeze and her brown legs flickered against the sheets as she ran past. She stood behind him clasping one of his legs with both arms. Danny Dalton went back to his painting. He stood with a box of watercolors in front of an easel that faced out over the bay. The jumbled coast looped around toward them and was dotted with the pink-tiled roofs of houses. While the exterminator treated the house, the children lay on their faces next to him. In the late afternoon sun, the bay sparkled and flashed and his paintbrush made a rasping sound against the paper.

Elsie Gannet put her head over the back fence and waved to him. She wore a one-piece bathing suit and stood at the edge of her vegetable garden, a huge landscaped area in which all the vegetables were arranged alphabetically. The Gannets had a quarter of an acre under cultivation and had installed a computerized irrigation system. Neat rows of green plants stretched out behind her, shimmering in the breeze.

"Everything all right?" she asked. Danny Dalton nodded and watched her hair float in long black strands across her face. She was twenty years younger than her husband, Henry Gannet, and had a firm Rubenesque figure. She was wearing gardening gloves. Danny Dalton had never seen so many vegetables growing in one place.

"Everything's fine," Danny Dalton said.

"What was that man doing with the spray?" Elsie Gannet had blood-red toenails.

"Treating for termites," he said. Sometimes he felt as if she was watching him. She knew Marion had gone but never said anything, and he felt himself tightening up whenever he saw her.

"Sounds serious." She shaded her eyes from the sun with a gloved hand.

"It's nothing."

He turned back to his painting and dabbed some streaks of cobalt blue into the sky.

When the exterminator had finished, there was a bitter chemical smell in the house that stung their eyes and made them dizzy, so he lit up the barbecue outside on the lawn. Tom carried dry kindling from underneath the veranda and he packed it with newspaper in the barbecue. The sun cast yellow streaks on the bay as Danny Dalton threw big fatty chops onto the grill and made a salad from lettuce and tomatoes in front of his children in a wooden bowl. There was a chill in the air as the sun went down, and he pulled on a hat and drank beer straight from the bottle. Tom and Katie sat on lawn chairs and watched him as he stood over the fire. He had big forearms spattered with red and blue and green paint.

"Dad, what did you hear in the house?" Tom asked.

"I don't know exactly"—he was turning the meat—"but it sounded like there was something in the walls or ceiling. Something living in there."

"What's living in there?" Katie asked.

"Well, I don't know. There are lots of things — insects and ants — that can get into houses. They eat them away. They can do a lot of damage. In a few months, we wouldn't have a house left."

"So that man came today to kill them," Tom said.

"That's right."

"I haven't heard anything," Tom said. The fire leaped as fat dripped into it from the chops.

"I hear it at night when you're asleep."

"Maybe you can hear Marion," Katie said. "Maybe she's talking to you."

"Maybe."

"I think she would want to talk to you. Maybe that's what she's doing," Katie said. The smell of cooking meat was heavy in the air.

He walked over and crouched down next to Katie. "I'm sure she would talk to me, if she could, Katie. But I don't think she is."

They slept outside on an old canvas tarpaulin under prickly blankets and stared up into Orion's belt and the Southern Cross. Danny Dalton played the harmonica that he had gotten from a drover when he was working in the country. He played "Wild Colonial Boy" and "Walking Man's Blues" as the last of the heat from the grill dissipated and the sea breeze struck up a gentle moan in the eaves under the house. He lay awake thinking about Marion, his wife, and imagining where she was now.

That was the first summer he had been alone with his children. Big Danny Dalton, the carpenter who looked like a boxer. He'd been the size and shape he was now since he was sixteen years old and he had suffered at school for it. His big brow and squashed nose turned off a lot of people. He was self-conscious about his face and large arms. He walked with rounded shoulders and a plodding head-down walk. His hands were square and covered in light blond hairs, and he had a long scar down his left cheek from a fall on a lump of reef coral in his surfing days. In the summer, his hair was streaked blond from working outside on construction sites. He looked like a murderer, he knew, but if you were perceptive, you could get past the face, and notice that he had laughing cornflower-blue eyes. To the children, he was a thing of wonder, an immovable object that smelled of sawdust, glue, and salt, who could hold them both under one arm. No one had been more surprised than Danny Dalton about his affinity for his children, the way he needed them, and the way he laughed as he ran his big hands over their limbs when he picked them up. He didn't feel awkward with his children, he felt right. He figured that this made up for a lot, and it made him stick to his routines.

In the morning, Danny Dalton slipped out from under the blankets while it was still dark and went inside to shower and make coffee. There was still a warm breeze off the ocean, and gum leaves swirled against the side of the house. He stood under the electric light shaving and looking at his own reflection in the mirror. He ran a hand over his lantern jaw and down the pale scar along his cheek. "You're an ugly bastard," he said out loud, knowing that he could live with it, and knowing that the people he liked had warmed to his face. It was not as bad as he had once thought. There were some good laugh lines around the eyes. It had character and was better with the children than a face like that should be. He knew that others had noticed this, too, and had given him credit for it.

While the water was boiling for coffee, he toasted four pieces of thick white bread, which he spread with butter and marmalade. He poured the coffee and drank it while eating the toast, standing, reading the art gallery schedule that was fixed to the fridge door. He pulled on his work shorts, socks, and steel-capped boots, and took his toolbox and the battered leather tool belt out to the back of the truck. He brushed his teeth, and was making two cheese sandwiches for lunch at the counter in the kitchen, when he heard the noises again. They came from above and behind him: dull humming noises, not like movement, but like the workings of a machine. He walked into the bedrooms and the living room, but could not pinpoint where they were coming from. The noises sounded like whispers in a church to him, like people praying quietly. He shrugged to himself and went out to the truck as dawn began creeping into the sky.

He felt guilty about his children. They were alone during the day now and he relied on Tom to take care of his little sister. It was too much for a ten-year-old on summer vacation. He knew that Tom was glad to have this new sense of responsibility, and in a way enjoyed telling his friends that he couldn't play with them because he had to look after Katie. But Danny Dalton felt that it wasn't right and wanted to spend more time with them when he finished his current building job.

Danny Dalton knew that Tom had been outside watching and listening through the kitchen window the night Marion left. He had seen the thin shadow of his son standing on the freshly cut lawn. It was a night so still, you could hear waves breaking on the rocks at the bottom of the cliff. Danny Dalton had sat slumped over the kitchen table, resting on both forearms, the salt shaker between his fingers. Marion paced in front of the sink with her arms crossed. Neither of them was angry — they had never argued — and he would have done anything for her. She was not there much, with her hospital schedule, which had her on call three nights a week, but he never complained. He did most of the housework. He washed their clothes and cooked the meals — "rough-and-ready affairs," as he called them, that usually involved grilled steak or sausages and a couple of boiled vegetables. But he was competent enough, and always seemed to have a meal ready on time. In the kitchen that night, she smoked a cigarette, and she never smoked. She still wore her white coat from the hospital, the one that smelled of antiseptic and latex, and had a stethoscope looped around her neck. He didn't understand her, but he couldn't get angry with her either.

When he got up in the morning, she had gone, and he told his children that she would be away for a few days, and that she would come back. That was almost a year ago now and Katie had stopped asking him when she was coming back. Her absence was like a great open wound that was visibly painful for him. For such a big man, he seemed so fragile and vulnerable when talking about his wife that they had all learned to avoid it. Somewhere along the line, the children had stopped referring to her as their mother, and had started calling her Marion, as if she was less personal to them.

He pulled his truck out of the driveway in the dawn light. It was already warm and he could smell heat on the gritty north wind. Elsie Gannet stood in her front yard watering hydrangeas with a hose. She dropped the hose, jogged over to the truck, and tapped on the door with her knuckles. He wound down the window.

"What's wrong? Do you have termites, Danny?" she said. Her eyes were puffy and she was wearing pink lipstick.

"It's not very likely."

"Because I was thinking that if you do, we should know about it." She smiled. She was his age but he felt as if she was older. She was a young woman who had married a retired bank manager and this said something about her. Marion had been friends with Elsie Gannet and they often spent weekends in the vegetable garden. They drank fancy cocktails that he had never heard of and Marion would come home tipsy and sunburned.

"Relax," he said, "there's nothing to worry about." He backed the truck out into the road. "I'll let you know if there's a problem." He waved through the window as he eased down the hill. Elsie Gannet stood watching him go, scratching her forearms. The sun suffused the sky with yellow and she stood on her lawn with rays of light burning around her head like a halo.

Danny Dalton pulled his truck up to the construction site and unloaded his tools. He put on his tool belt and got up into the scaffolding to begin work on the roof frame. The morning sky arced in a big blue dome above him.

He imagined his children walking to the steep zigzag cement steps with rusty pipe handrails that went down to the beach, still shaded from the sun. It would be cool, with a wet-earth smell on the steps. He knew they talked, but had never heard them have a conversation about Marion, and he wished he knew what they said to each other about her. Down on the front, it was slack tide. From where he worked, he could see firm wet sand stretching out to the water. The sun was already beginning to flash on the roofs of parked cars and a few blue-and-red-colored figures were walking far out on the surf line. It would smell like rotting fish and seaweed as they walked onto the beach. In the distance, seagulls were massing around the end of the jetty and they would hear the gulls screeching and see them swirling in white plumes around the heads of the fishermen. They would set the green-and-white-striped beach umbrella in the lee of the rock beach wall and run their toes through the cool sand. Later they would eat the sandwiches he had made them, wrapped in wax paper, and it made him feel better to think that they had the food he had given them. They spent all their days at the beach and were nut brown, with flat, splayed feet from walking without shoes. He guessed it was safer for them to be down there, around other people, than locked up inside.

He had tried to find his wife. He called all Marion's friends, none of whom knew anything, and stormed into the hospital in his work clothes to see the professor of psychiatry. He felt rough and awkward, with his snub-nosed boots and red knees, standing in the departmental office in front of the secretary. Professor Chalmers was used to dealing with crazies and seemed to treat him like a patient — he got Danny Dalton to sit down and carefully explain what had happened. But he knew what the psychiatrist was thinking and it didn't involve his mental state at all. It involved his suitability, his acceptability, his ability to live with a woman who was clearly his intellectual superior. He felt judged in that prefabricated office with the spleen-colored carpet and third-rate carpentry. Hong Kong, Chalmers told him, she's gone to Hong Kong for her doctoral work, that was all he knew. She would be there for three years. He didn't know why she walked out, it was none of his business, although she was one of the most talented residents he had ever had. She was going to be very, very good, and the Hong Kong move was important for her professional development.

Marion's parents had never liked him. To them, he was an aberration, an act of rebellion on her part. They were lukewarm with the children, saw them as part of the problem, and he could never forgive them for this selfishness. They hadn't heard anything from Marion either and were surprised that she had walked out, but he heard something in her mother's voice, a sense of relief, he thought, that suggested that they accepted her decision completely. They were both professionals, had lived in houses with tennis courts, and did not understand Danny Dalton. At one time, they had given him some credit for his celebrated father's status in the art world, but this was only slim recompense now that his father was washed up. His father was a fatally flawed man and people assumed that the son was the same. Sometimes Danny Dalton felt cursed by his father — for most of his life, he was ignored because he stood in the shadow of his father's reputation, and lately he was ignored because he was the son of a man who had disintegrated so rapidly.

He sat up in the roof with three-inch nails clasped between his teeth and a hammer in his left hand. By midmorning, the rubber grips of his tools were wet with sweat. There was a seriousness to him when he worked with wood, an intensity of concentration that shut out the rest of the world. He frowned and held the tip of his tongue between his teeth. When he ran his fingers over wood, there was a delicacy there, a sensitivity to it. His skin was the color of the planed boards around him. He was careful with measurements — he got his lengths and angles right — and carried the nub of a pencil behind one ear. He kept getting hired, and it was for the quality of his work, not his social skills. Under his T-shirt, the big muscles of his back fanned and contracted with each movement. Every time he squatted, he felt the muscles of his legs become taut and smooth and knew that he was physically stronger than he had ever been, and that this wouldn't last.

Late in the afternoon, Danny Dalton drove down to meet his children. He appeared at the umbrella in his work clothes and heavy boots bearing three orange ice-blocks. He had a tape measure clasped to his belt. He eased himself down into the shade and handed around the ice blocks. Katie draped herself over his shoulders, sucking her ice block in his ear. He sat with his big hands on her forearms. His hands were deep brown, with red knuckles, and there were little nicks and scabs on the backs of his fingers. As he sat, his shorts rode up, revealing a band of dazzlingly white skin.

They were sitting on the beach when Henry Gannet — a tanned, bandy-legged man, with a flurry of gray chest hair — walked up to them. Danny Dalton had never understood what Elsie Gannet saw in him.

He had a rumpled paper bag in one hand. "Thought you might like a few cucumbers," he said and dropped the bag onto the sand in front of them.

"Thanks, Henry." Danny Dalton squinted up at him against the sun.

"You've had the exterminator round, I hear," Henry Gannet said and raised his dark sunglasses onto his forehead. He was neat and fastidious, with a small clipped mustache and perfect pink fingernails. The plantation of alphabetical vegetables was his passion. He kept the vegetable beds as finely trimmed as his mustache.

"Yes. Had him yesterday. He did some spraying."

"Hear it might be termites."

"Might be. He didn't know. There isn't any sign of anything. He sprayed anyway, although I don't think he would have. I insisted."

"Right. Better to be safe than sorry. I'm always wary about these things. They can spread like wildfire. If you have them, the chances are that we have them, or will get them."

"Maybe, Henry. I don't know."

"Don't want the word to get out either. Property values."

"Don't worry, Henry. As I say, there may not be a problem anyway."

"Fine. How are you kids?" He bent down and leered at Katie, who had orange lips. "I'll get going then."

They laughed together as he walked down the beach.

"We know it's really Marion talking," Katie said, "not the ants."

"I need a swim," Danny Dalton said, undoing his boots and pulling them off. His feet were moist and pink. Then he pulled off his T-shirt, emptied his pockets, and took off his belt. There was a dusting of brown hair on his shoulders.

He picked up Katie by her waist and ran off toward the water. Her hair hung in heavy tendrils along the back of her neck and there were streaks of sea salt on her calves and thighs. She screamed and squirmed as he carried her. Tom ran after them and they plunged together into the surf. Danny Dalton was like a great whale, rolling about, dunking his head under and emerging with powerful snorts through his nostrils. He seemed to be washing days off himself, erasing memories. He knew that this was how his children most loved him. He shouted as he lifted them into the air and threw them. He caught their legs underwater and pulled them under. They both tried to climb him and fell off him laughing, into the water.

Way off on the other side of the bay, Danny Dalton saw white smoke coming from the refinery stacks. A tanker was anchored offshore, a metallic lozenge against the sky, waiting to dock. He dug his toes into the firm, rippled sand and thought of all the clean water around them, and the layers of shale and thick oil that lay below. He had a moment when he could feel the past, heavy and solid beneath his feet. It sounded hushed and fluttering, like the wings of a bat, or of a bird in a closed room. These were the noises he heard in his house.

He marveled at how he had found his wife. At how she had seemed immediately interested in him, big Danny Dalton, as he stood in an art gallery looking at paintings, checking them off on the inventory list in front of him. He still had a mental image of himself, bulky, paint flecked, mumbling. And Marion, so long necked and beautiful, wearing her body so comfortably, with a small opal glowing green and misty blue on a thin gold chain around her neck. She had liked the incongruity, the roughness, and the things he knew about painting. When she touched his hand, it was like being touched by something from another world. They were born to be together, she said. She glowed next to him, seemed to suck up his energy and bulk and radiate it as light. When she started her medical training she was already pregnant, but he had kept them running, with his odd hours and his devotion to routines. He thought of himself as a dog, as something faithful and steady to the end. But his devotion had not been enough.

He still thought they looked right in the photographs. Just the four of them, faces pointed upward, whipping hair and glinting cheeks. He thought that even after she had left and gone.

He remembered the night that Tom was conceived. It had been a certain thing and they knew what had happened even before the test results were back. The night was warm but licked with a strong wind that blew the tops off the waves and filled their ears with sand. They came down onto the beach at midnight, under the black silhouette of the cliffs and the calls of seagulls nesting on the ledges above. The sand was cool and they could barely hear each other speak due to the constant blast of wind. Red lights glinted on the refinery stacks around the coast. She had already stepped out of her shorts and T-shirt and was pulling him down to the surf. He saw the white of her teeth and then the tan line at the top of her legs as she ran in front of him.

He threw his clothes off, and they plunged straight in, kicking through the shallows, flopping down when they were in knee-high water. Specks of phosphorescence floated in the dark water and when he held her by the waist there were green sparks running along his forearms and down between her legs. He felt washed by invisible showers of phytoplankton, drifting into him in thick curtains. They clung to each other and she arched back against him and he felt as if he was pushing into her with the power of something from the deep water. They drifted out to where they could barely feel the bottom with their toes. Wavelets broke against their mouths and he tasted salt on his tongue.

"What will I do when you die?" she said into his ear.

"I've got a while yet."

"I know, but what will I do when it does happen?"

"It won't happen."

"When we go, we go together," she said and then laughed and swam to shore with high overhand strokes. He stood alone balancing on his toes on the sandy bottom, feeling that this olive-skinned woman, who seemed like a dream to him, was right. They would have to die together, because he couldn't imagine it any other way.

They packed up and loaded everything into the truck. The two children sat outside on the flatbed to dry off. They leaned their backs against the cabin, and sat among piles of wood, loose tools, snub-head nails, carpenters' pencils, tattered blueprints, and tubes of wood glue. The truck rattled loosely when they went over bumps and they beat their hands on the top of the roof every time he stopped too quickly. Katie put on her purple cat's-eye sunglasses and stared down the cars behind them in rush-hour traffic. His children seemed special and invincible in the back of his work truck. Danny Dalton went up the hill from the beach, past the expensive split-level houses with steep driveways and tinted windows, across the railway line, and out onto the plain. He drove with one arm hanging out of the open window. The afternoon sun cast their shadow long and flat in front of them as they eased along the coast.

The old man — Willis Dalton — did not recognize him now. It seemed almost incredible that he had been such a force, such a personality, and so dominant over his life. Willis Dalton had grown up a farm boy in Gippsland, the third son of Protestant farmers who prayed as hard as they worked. He spent his youth rounding and shearing Merinos, repairing bore pumps, and sleeping in the open. He was given his first watercolor paint set when he was ten years old. By the time he was twenty, he was painting in oils and hailed as the best landscape artist of his generation. He cultivated his roughness, reveled in being devoid of social graces and pretensions, and had no time for critics. His paintings were praised despite him. He wore farmers' work boots all his life, swore openly and freely, and called a spade a spade. His paintings sold enough to allow him to buy a large house in the city and to marry the daughter of an American gold speculator. He had been an alcoholic for twenty years before anyone would admit it, by which time Danny Dalton was a carpenter, not an artist.

Now Willis Dalton's short-term memory had gone, eaten away by the alcohol. He couldn't remember one moment from the next. It was as if he didn't exist in the present at all. But he could remember everything he did as a boy, and he could remember the time when his children were growing up. Danny Dalton could talk about the past with him, even though Willis Dalton didn't know who Danny was now.

It was Marion who had first diagnosed him. She was still an intern, full of new information and a frightening objectivity. They'd been married only a year when she spent an hour in the front room of his father's house doing mental-function tests. She'd called it something with a Russian name, explained that it was irreversible and that Willis Dalton was finished. Sometimes Danny Dalton felt as if Marion saw this as partly a reflection on him — as if the son was responsible for the father.

He wondered what Marion would have said about the noises he heard. He wasn't sure they were real. Perhaps they were auditory hallucinations or some type of posttraumatic stress disorder. Perhaps he had a phobia. It seemed possible that he was going mad. Marion would have worked it out. He could see her shifting into her clinical mode and questioning him with cold eyes — eyes as removed and analytical as you could get on a person. Diagnostic questions would fire out of her, straight from the pages of the DSM manual. When she was like this, her manner was so impersonal that she seemed to speak like a machine. He knew that after a few minutes she would have relaxed, let a tiny smile cross her lips, and told him it was nothing psychiatric, nothing pathological. Just noises. Noises for which there was a reasonable explanation. She spent her days working with maniacs and she liked coming home to his routines. Sometimes he wanted to be more interesting. But in truth, he was content with his house and children — she said he didn't have the imagination to be mad.

Danny Dalton loved painting, and thought he could have made a career in it, but his exacting father had told him he wasn't good enough. Willis Dalton had taken him out to farm country and they had painted together in the bush overlooking sheep runs, bent old blue gums, and burnt hills. He'd come up behind him, rip the paper off his easel, and tear it up in front of him. "Stop now," he'd say, "before any more of this rubbish comes out." Danny Dalton hadn't understood. The unsteady lurching, the long naps, and the smell of alcohol were so much a part of his father that he never thought about them. He thought the viciousness and the anger were there because of him. He stopped painting and started building things. A part of him was terrified of the flaw that he saw in his father — the fatal flaw. He wondered if he carried it with him, too, a single crack that would eventually bring everything down around him.

It was only later that he realized what his father's drinking had done to his mother. She had spent years hiding it from the world, living with it just under the surface, and avoiding his shouting and violent moods. She stayed until there was no money left. His father stopped painting and spent days sitting in the sun with bottles of whiskey. She collected the last ten canvases from the studio and walked out. She gave one of those canvases to Danny. He had hawked it around the galleries and sold it for a small fortune. It was the money that he had used to buy the land on the cliff and to build the house.

It was a warm night, and they drove home through the smell of burning leaves. In Tom's bedroom, he watched his son put the sea urchin shells that he had collected that day on a wooden shelf. When he found the shells on the beach, he blew the sand and water out through the holes at each end and carried them on a string around his neck. He had long rows of the domed shells arranged by size and color — little dry memories of the ocean, with sandy red-and-black markings.

The thin cotton curtains were blowing into the room and gum leaves rustled on the tree outside. Tom was quiet and intense and had never talked about his mother. Danny Dalton wanted to know what he was really thinking, but didn't want to force the issue. His son had Marion's obsessive tendencies. He liked to put objects in order and had his own organizational systems for everything from socks to basketball cards. Tom had taken all of Marion's textbooks and arranged them by size on a shelf in the corner of his room. Occasionally Danny Dalton would find him asleep over Kaplan and Sadcock's *Complete Textbook of Psychiatry*, his head nodding into descriptions of bipolar disorders or the organic brain syndromes. A slim volume on forensic psychiatry was among these books — it was full of descriptions of autoerotic misadventure and paranoid schizophrenics who had run amok with knives. Danny Dalton had slipped the book out of the shelf and hidden it in his own room, where he occasionally flipped through the pages with a kind of morbid fascination.

When the children were in bed, he went back out to the kitchen, popped a bottle of lager, and poured the frothing liquid into a glass. He sat looking at his own dim reflection in the window, his ear to the wall. The noises were soft and fluttering and seemed to envelop him. He ran his fingers over the smooth brown wood near his face.

He had looked up Hong Kong in the *Encyclopedia Britannica*. Some of the wealthiest real estate in the world with Chinese and British origins. All packed onto an island the size of a small suburb. No wonder they needed psychiatrists. He couldn't imagine living on such a small island — he needed wide horizons, emptiness, and air you could see through. When the University of Hong Kong had called and asked where Marion was, he told them she could not accept the doctoral position this year for personal reasons, and gave them a story about a death in the family that they seemed to accept. They had not called back. A part of him was surprised that she hadn't arrived to take up her position. She had simply chosen to disappear from their lives. He did not tell anyone that she was not in Hong Kong. He knew that her friends believed that there was another man involved. They accepted her disappearance as a legitimate act. As a bid for freedom.

The knock at the door was a surprise and he jumped to his feet when he heard it. Henry Gannet stood on the doorstep wearing a red-and-green batik shirt. He had wet, combed hair and held a plastic shopping bag in one hand.

"Evening. I've brought you some tomatoes. Fresh from the garden." He held the bag, bulging with heavy fruit, at arm's length.

"That's very kind." Danny Dalton stood, his big arms immobile by his side.

"Nothing like them when they're fresh. I eat them raw, like apples, with a little salt and pepper."

"Great."

"Wondered if you'd like to have a talk."

"Oh, fine." Danny Dalton stood back a step and Henry Gannet walked quickly inside, still holding the plastic bag of tomatoes out in front of him at arm's length.

"I wondered how things were going for you," Henry Gannet said. He had a stiffness of manner that he tried to hide with casual shirts and Indian sandals. He smelled of Italian aftershave and Lux soap. His cheeks were fleshy and pink.

"Everything's fine, Henry." He took the tomatoes and put the bag on the floor, then sank down in the low-set couch that had frayed arms, and stretched back in it. Henry Gannet remained standing, his hands in his pockets.

"I noticed that the exterminator was here."

"So you said on the beach."

"It looks serious then."

"What looks serious, Henry?"

"The infestation or whatever you have. With all this wood in the house, it was always a possibility. Bound to happen in my view, in this climate, and with the variety of vermin we have in this part of the world." He shrugged his shoulders. "I'm amazed it's been this long."

"Henry, the exterminator didn't find anything."

"So why was he spraying, Danny? You don't spray if you don't have a problem."

"Because I wanted to make sure. Because I think I can hear things."

"Hear things?"

"Yes. I think that I can hear something, but we can't find anything, so I think it's nothing."

"You shouldn't make light of this, Danny."

"I'm not making light of it."

"I have to say that Elsie and I are very concerned, as your neighbors."

"I can see that."

He knew that they thought of him as a slow, heavy simpleton. As a laborer. As a man who hadn't been able to keep his wife. He wondered if they knew more than they let on. Marion was their friend. She had volunteered to till and fertilize their vegetable plots a few times a year — they had a diesel tiller that she used to turn in compost and lime. When she had time, she helped with the seeding and maintained the compost mound. They were happy to have the help. Marion enjoyed the soil on her hands. Sometimes he would watch her working in the sun and imagine her as a stranger, as someone he had never met.

Henry Gannet said, "We have a lot to lose. Termites can walk across the space between two houses in a few moments. Before you know it, we'll have them in our woodwork. And then our house will be worthless. We'd be lucky to be able to sell. I've got a lot of my retirement money tied up in that house, Danny. A great deal of money."

"There's a lot of money in this house, too."

"I know that."

"What do you want from me, Henry?"

"I want you to assure me that you're taking it seriously. Don't cut corners. Don't let it lie, Danny. Do what has to be done to treat the problem."

He wondered what they really knew about Marion and what they were hiding. Marion didn't pack anything, left without any artifacts from her life, and he was numb when he thought about it. The Gannets did not have enough to do, he thought. They had too much time on their hands. It was possible that they had encouraged Marion to leave. Turned her against him. Elsie Gannet was a young woman who had married an elderly man — she had issues.

"I'm doing everything I can," Danny Dalton said.

"Look, let me arrange for another company to come and look at the house. I'll pay. Think of it as a second opinion."

"I don't think so, Henry."

"One of my colleagues lost his house. He didn't know a thing until he dropped through his own floor. It had been eaten away. The whole thing was honeycombed with ants. Rotten to the core, Danny."

"Henry, you'll have to leave it to me."

"Don't take it lightly. It's very serious, Danny."

"I know that."

"I've got my eye on you. You should know that. I'm concerned, that's all. As a neighbor. For your own good."

Danny Dalton stood up quickly and shook Henry Gannet's hand. He did not look at him as he led the way to the door. He felt a wild anger that he could not show. It went on inside his head, a pressure that blurred his vision. He felt as if all the anger was contained inside his skull. None of it reached below his neck. His shoulders and arms felt limp and heavy as he opened the door. The warm air outside was heavy with the scent of frangipani. Crickets sounded in the hedge. Henry Gannet walked across the front lawn and when he was a safe distance away, stopped and said, "I'll be in touch. I'll follow this up." He was still standing there when Danny Dalton shut the door.

The Gannets did not see the care that had gone into the building of his house. They saw only that he had done it himself — that he had needed to do it himself.

He built the house for her. He designed it, poured the foundations, and then built it from the ground up. He'd become a carpenter without trying. He'd been a natural with wood, and was careful and exacting with his hands. He'd gotten clean out of the city after his mother left his father and was settled with one of her friends. He'd worked at a sawmill for a while, and then hooked up with a carpenter who did seasonal work around country towns, doing anything from building wool sheds to replacing the oak in old homesteads. He'd learned how to do dovetail joints and how to get his angles and joins exact. He liked the feel of it, the raw solidness of the wood, and the crispness of something put together right. He liked the smell of sawdust and the feeling of smooth pine under his fingers.

He'd lived in a caravan for six months on the block while he did his house. Marion and the children stayed with his parents and he went down and spent nights and weekends with them. He'd done the frame in western red cedar, used double the usual square footage, and made sure it could withstand a good sea storm. He finished the interior with pine and did the trim with bits of reclaimed oak, and some antique teak that he'd salvaged from the shipyards.

He worked on the final touches for three years. It felt like something that was completely his, glowing with deep brown hues inside, and smelling of beeswax and varnish. It stood like a wooden ship anchored there above the cliffs. He knew that it was an expression of himself that belied his appearance. People looked at him, the big boxer with the squashed nose, differently after they had seen the house. And he knew that Marion had seen another side of him, too, and he wanted her to love him more for it. He wanted her to understand what it meant, and to see it as a symbol for the two of them. And now he was terrified that it was being eaten away.

He went back to the kitchen and sat down. The humming noise was clear and constant and his anger made it worse. He sensed that the noise was not real, that it was something inside him that needed to be repaired.

He had never understood Freud but he thought there was something to the unconscious. He was not an educated man, but he was not stupid and he picked things up quickly. Maybe the noises were a part of his fatal flaw. Provided he could stay with his children, he didn't care what happened to him. He would have to be bull mad before he let anyone take him away from his children.

He'd never complained about the sex. There was something about his roughness that appealed to her. It had all seemed very strange to him, a revelation when she brought out a suitcase full of steel handcuffs, a leather hood, and a stock whip of the type that he'd seen used to round up sheep. He didn't understand her need to be tied up and beaten, but she was excited by it in a way that he had never seen before — it was almost like a compulsion — and she was turned on by the violence. When he saw what being handcuffed did for her, he learned to go along with the routine, and to do what she asked. He was never too rough — although sometimes she begged for pain and he would feel his big forearms contracting as he brought the whip down onto the backs of her legs.

People go into psychiatry for the cure, some people said — psychiatrists were as screwed up as the people they purported to treat. He had thumbed through her psychiatric textbooks. She did not have a formal diagnosis, he realized, she was at one end of the normal spectrum of sexual behavior. He could not understand what drove her and wondered if something had happened at home when she was growing up. But he was not a narrow-minded man. And she was so upright and responsible in the rest of her life — a doctor with a cool clinical manner who worked with her hair pulled tightly back off her face — that what she did in the bedroom didn't seem to matter. If the truth be told, he was a little excited by her need to be tied up as well. "Abuse me," she would whisper to him, "tie me down and beat me up." The warm nights would be filled with the chink of steel handcuffs as he put them on. She liked to be lashed like a starfish, naked, to the four corners of the bed.

It was in this position that she asked him to use the vegetables, fresh vegetables from the garden, on her. The Gannets would have flinched if they had known what he was doing with their fresh produce. He had seen that cool clinical look come over her as she looked down at him while he held a squash or an ear of corn, and been frightened by her abandon, her disinhibition, when she was so vulnerable and unable to move her arms and legs. She'd wanted him to put the mask on her so she couldn't see what he was doing.

And she had wanted him to put his hands around her neck, too, and tighten the grip as she lunged under him, almost as if he was choking her. He read about this later in the textbook of forensic psychiatry — the intensity of the orgasm was heightened by the brain hypoxia induced by compression of the carotid arteries. She'd asked him to put his hands around her neck, whispered for him to press harder and harder, lost in a world of her own. Her thin pale neck looked so small in his large carpenter's hands. Sometimes he found himself looking at his hands as if they belonged to someone else.

Since she had been gone, he found himself pulling out her books — he had looked at *Psychopathology of Everyday Life* and *Sexuality and the Psychology of Love* by Freud — trying to get a handle on how sex could affect everything in your life. It was heavy going and he still wasn't sure whether everything came down to repressed urges. He couldn't make any sense of most of the ideas he read about. He flipped through the books by Carl Jung as well, Marion's favorite, and read every word of one of his essays, "Marriage as a Psychological Relationship." But he didn't feel as if it helped him get in touch with Marion or his own unconscious. He couldn't believe there were processes going on inside him that he didn't know about. He had packed all of the Freud and Jung books into a box and dumped them into the crawl space in the ceiling.

He finished the beer and walked outside on bare feet. It was high tide below and waves were breaking at the base of the cliff. The blades of thick grass felt rough and spongy against his toes. There was cigarette smoke in the air and he walked over to the fence and looked through the leaves of the lemon tree. Elsie Gannet was smoking in the vegetable garden next door. The tip of her cigarette glowed red in the dark and he heard her blowing smoke into the air. He waited and watched her walk back through her garden and go inside.

He listened to the wind in the ghost gums and smelled eucalyptus in the air.

Then he walked through the gate at the end of his garden and along the path to the cliff edge. This part of the garden was overgrown with nettles and Scotch thistle, and the plants swirled around him as he passed through. The nettle leaves were rough on his shins. He stopped still and listened carefully, but could hear nothing other than the crickets and the ocean. At the cliff edge, there was a high stone wall and he found his footholds and hauled himself up the side.

The top of the wall was still warm from the sun and he felt crumbly cement chips against his fingers. He had a sudden and dizzying view of the bay, black and thick in front of him. The water sparkled in the glow from the streetlights and he could make out fingers of white surf reaching up onto the sand. Red lights flashed on the stacks of the refinery in the distance, and the headlights of a few silent cars moved along the esplanade. He had never feared the sea, had always been calmed by it. He wanted his children to be the same. They were comfortable in the water and he was careful not to fill them with fears and superstitions that were not justified.

A faint breeze moved across his face. The cliff dropped straight down below him, a rough-and-tumble slurry of sandstone and clay. But he had sat there often and knew the angles and balance points by feel and felt safe on the wall. He imagined himself at the rudder of a large ship, plowing through the night, surrounded by long trains of Portuguese men-of-war.

On their honeymoon, they had gone to the island of Thassos, in Greece, and wandered between sun-white houses on steep, cobbled steps. In the scouring sun Marion's hair turned the color of whole meal flour, her olive skin baked deep gold. They sat and drank sharp thick coffee in small cups in the midafternoon and watched old men with scrawny legs return from fishing. The fishermen had white-bristled faces and black eyes. Marion took his hands in her hands. He remembered looking down and seeing his big burned fingers in her small palms. His knuckles were round and uneven. A boxer's hands. She traced a figure eight in his palm. When she held his hands, he felt powerless, weakened, calm. They walked together and he sucked in the colors — the brilliant blues and greens, the terra-cotta reds and bleached whites of the hills. In the evenings, they sat on the cut-stone dock facing the Aegean Sea, dangling their legs down into the warm water and feeling wisps of breeze float through their hair in the dark. They went swimming at night together, out through the thick warm water, and looked back at the white lights of houses above them on the hill. One night, Marion stood up on the stone dock and stripped off her shorts and T-shirt. She stood for a moment smiling at him, the pale light washing over her small breasts and the curve of her hips, and then dove down into the sea with a quiet splash. He watched the flash of her ankles as they disappeared below the surface.

A minute passed. A second minute passed. She did not reappear. He looked out into the darkness and felt a moment of crushing panic. He stood up and threw himself out into the water in the direction he had seen her go. He fell down through the water in the dark, attacking it with his hands and forearms, kicking madly with both legs. Waves of phosphorescence spun in front of him. He lunged down, seeing nothing and feeling out in front of him. His forehead rammed into the sandy bottom and he swam with his chest to the sand, grasping out in front with his hands, his lungs bursting. After a couple of minutes, he came up again and broke the surface with a gasp. He felt the quiet of the night around him, saw the lights glinting on the water. As he focused, he made out Marion sitting on the dock again, shaking water out of her hair with both hands. His arms trembled and saltwater stung his eyes.

"I thought I'd lost you for a moment there," he panted to her over the water.

"I'm a very good swimmer, " Marion called back to him.

"I thought you'd gone under."

"You worry too much."

"I came in to save you." He swam over to the heavy stone dock wall and pulled himself out of the water, next to her.

"I don't need saving," she said to him, taking one of his hands in both of hers. Drops of water slapped onto the dry stone. He heard the sound of his own breath running in and out between his teeth. He knew he could never let her go then, felt at her mercy, like a boat on the open sea, desperate to find land.

He pulled himself to his knees and then stood up on the wall. He felt alone and dwarfed by the geological forces under him. He wondered if he had always been mad. Perhaps he had been crazy to believe that Marion could ever be his wife. He was nothing but a carpenter who looked like a boxer. He looked out into the black sea and balanced on the balls of his feet. He brought his big fists and forearms up in front of his face and looked out toward the bay. He would find his wife on his own if he had to. He was alone but he could take it. The children were coping and that was all that really mattered.

He started throwing punches out into the air, one after the other, left arm, right arm. He jabbed with his fists into the empty air and felt blood running into his face. The punches flew out toward the refinery, the horizon, the world spread out in front of him. He felt the energy running out along the length of his arms, spinning off into the night. The children were coping. That's what mattered. He swung his arms and put his head down. He felt light on his feet on top of the wall and heard noises in his head. He punched, left arm, right arm. Later he would look through the textbook of psychiatry again to see if he could find out what was wrong with him.

7

BLUE

Simon reached the summit on the morning of his father's fiftieth birthday. He moved slowly over the final buttress onto a gentle slope that was covered in an unbroken layer of snow. He took short labored gasps. It required all of his effort to walk the last steps. His crampons made a squeaking sound as they broke through the thin crust of ice on the surface. All he could hear was the noise of his own breathing, rasping through his face mask, and the regular soft metallic click of the valve to the oxygen cylinder. He knew that Gilbert was close behind him. But he had not seen Brechner for over two hours. He could feel the muscles in his thighs twitching, and the back of his throat was raw. After several minutes of steady breathing, he allowed himself to turn off the oxygen. His mouth tasted of warm rubber. The air was thin and dry on his lips and he could feel its emptiness, its inadequacy. He checked his watch and the altimeter. He tightened his crampons, blew his nose wetly onto the snow, and cleaned condensation from his goggles.

A small cairn was sitting on the highest point: four river stones from the valley far below were stacked together and a Japanese flag from the expedition two weeks previously was wrapped around a thin metal pole that had fallen over the stones. It was as still as a forest clearing in winter. Absolutely soundless and clean. Simon allowed himself to listen to the empty wildness of it. There was a purity about the world at this altitude that he sought out. He pulled in twenty feet of slack rope on his safety line and knew that Gilbert would be with him soon. Brechner was roped to Gilbert and would be about fifty feet farther back. He looked at his watch for the second time, and then saw the clouds away near the horizon, still a long way off but hanging dark and heavy.

The cool, thin air and the fresh snow brought back the memory. He was ten years old and running over the field at the back of their house in Oxford. His father lay bleeding, next to the gun, in the woods behind him. His desert boots were soaking wet, with a layer of ice around the toes, as he clambered over the back fence into the field. He was wearing mittens and blowing pillows of his own breath in front of him as he ran. As he came through the field, the snow was deeper, and he plunged in up to his hips and fell forward onto outstretched hands. The blood from his mittens smeared red onto the white snow. He plunged and fell like that until he reached the cleared path at the end of the field, smearing the blood with each fall, wiping it in streaks in front of him, like Japanese letters onto rice paper.

Then he was running into the warm kitchen of the house, which smelled of sweet tea and bread, and shouting for his mother. She had gone to early Mass in town and the house was empty. He ran out of the front door and down to the neighbors' houses, the Strongs, the Newtons, the Barnabys, the Timmlers. There was a Sunday-morning stillness in the air. And as he ran from door to door, realizing that no one was at home, he felt his desperation give way to fear.

The ambulance would not arrive for another two hours. The bullet had shattered his father's second thoracic vertebra, shearing his spinal cord and lodging in his right lung. He was alive because the bullet had stopped before it reached the blood vessels of his chest. It had been called a hunting accident. There were three pheasant on the snow next to his father, mixing their blood with his. And his father, the best climber in Britain, would never walk or use his hands again.

Gilbert appeared after a few minutes, a lumbering bear taking slow, measured steps over the buttress. His rhythm was beat out into the rarefied air — breath, ice pick in, step, breath, ice pick in, step. He crunched onto the plateau and stood there, as he pulled oxygen down into his lungs, and worked out where he was. He was frozen like that, half bent over, his hands hanging by his sides for a full five minutes. Then he lurched forward again, heaving his boots out of the crust with each step, and advancing up toward Simon.

"Jesus." Gilbert pulled off his face mask and spat. His lips were scaled with dry skin and his nose was blistered and peeling. The tip of his chin was layered with frozen saliva.

"Where's Brechner?"

"He's coming. We unhitched the safety at the bottom of the last ridge. Told me to push on. Said he'd wait for us if he couldn't make it on his own."

"I'm not waiting for him."

"Let's give him a few minutes."

They stood together in silence looking at the view around them. Milky clouds hung in the valleys far below, and Simon imagined himself looking down at the backs of birds. Off to the south and west, the Himalayan chain stretched away as a series of craggy sentinels in the glinting light: Everest, the Lhotse Notse wall, Amadablam, and farther around, the Annapurnas and K-2. Bright sunlight made little refractive rainbows in his goggles. Simon was thinking immediately of getting down. Before their brain cells stopped working. Before they lost their capacity for judgment and perception. They were metabolizing calories faster than they could replace them, leaching their muscle mass out into the atmosphere. Simon could already see that something was gathering and knew that the weather killed climbers out here. They drank from their water bottles, and Simon allowed himself to slip off a glove and get into one of his jacket pockets for chocolate, nuts, and energy bars. They forced themselves to eat. The food was tasteless and frozen hard.

"Brechner was a mistake," Simon said.

"We needed Brechner."

"Not if he kills himself."

"He's a good climber."

"I'm not carrying him down, I'll tell you that."

"Look. We'll give him five minutes. If he's not here, we'll get off. Pick him up on the descent." Gilbert had untied his camera and a small tripod, which he began setting up on the snow for pictures. Simon raised his face to the sky and turned on the spot slowly. He felt a breeze, for the first time, from the southwest.

It was because of Brechner that they were on the mountain at all. He was providing more than half the financing for the expedition. Brechner was his father's identical twin. He had rarely visited after the accident. When he did, he sat with his back to Simon's father, talking to him, but not looking. It is very difficult for twins, his mother said, because they are joined in some special way, and what happens to one also happens to the other. His mother said that in one sense Brechner might have felt as if he was paralyzed, and that they had to understand that and respect it. Brechner had only one eye. His right eye had been knocked out with a golf club when he was eight years old. He had been playing with friends by the river. The flat end of the club had gone straight into his eye and crushed it like a grape. Simon's father said that he had felt the pain in his eye, too, back at the house, at the same instant. He had known what had happened, he said, although he had not been there. Brechner had gone on playing, despite a lot of discharge and pain. He had finally appeared, his sleeve smeared with vitreous humor, and they had removed the eye that night at the Radcliff Hospital. Simon's father had temporarily lost the vision in his own right eye, as if he had been struck, and he claimed that his sight was never the same after his brother's accident.

Simon walked carefully around the flat island of snow at the top and sat down to adjust his boots. Black rock and fluted ice falls towered around him. The deep valleys to the west were still in shadow.

"I think I hear Brechner." Gilbert was squinting into the lens of his camera. Simon heard the tapping of an ice pick over the edge of the buttress.

"It's him," Gilbert said.

"I don't know if that's a blessing or a curse."

"He's here now. Let's get on with it and get off."

"He'll need to rest."

"Fine. We'll give him a few minutes."

"We can't afford much time now." Simon allowed himself to sit back against the stones on the summit. He felt his breathing slow. The muscles in his legs had stopped twitching.

Simon had never really known Brechner, who was always the quiet, smart brother. While his father had been a natural optimist, socially gregarious and a gifted athlete, Brechner was given to sullen moods and had no interest in sports. He had been accepted to medical school at the University of London and had decided to go on to specialist training in ophthalmology, surgery of the eye. No one had ever heard of a one-eyed eye surgeon. Eye surgery is fine work done under high-powered microscopes, and it requires the facility of depth perception, which Brechner could not have with only one eye. Through hours of practice in the laboratory, on cadaver specimens, Brechner taught himself how to read depth using secondary cues such as light and shadow. He excelled as a microscopic surgeon through sheer force of will, Simon's mother had said. He had a bulldog quality. His family thought he was doing it to somehow give himself sight back: the more eyes he worked on, the more sight he resurrected, the less blind he felt.

And Brechner had proved himself in the mountains. Simon had been amazed by his confidence, the nut-brown strength of his calves, and the intensity with which he fixed you with his good eye. He had never slipped. On the four-week trek up to base camp, it had been Brechner who had led the way through the Arun River valley, past the teeming white glacial water, and across the wire swing bridges. It was Brechner who had managed the donkey and yak team. It was Brechner who had looked after them. He had negotiated passage through the difficult valleys, past short men with machetes and waist knives. He had known which villages were friendly, and had led them into smoky mud houses smelling of cow dung and corn to eat gritty rice and small nobbly potatoes. And

Brechner had walked across the fixed ladders in the ice fall, and taken their steep ice pitches without hesitation. It was Simon who had slipped, not Brechner.

It was Simon who had slipped. He felt a dull pain radiating though his left leg. His shoulders and neck were beginning to ache. He had been shaken more than he thought by the fall. He tried to put it out of his mind. In the calm stillness, to the slow tapping of Brechner coming up the final buttress, Simon calculated how much time they would need to descend. They had set off from the final camp, perched on a sheltered ice platform, at three o'clock that morning. It had been bitterly cold, dark and still when they lumbered out of their sleeping bags to collect snow for tea and to gear up for the long walk to the top. As the stove hissed in the tent, in a cocoon of lamplight, Simon had asked Brechner again whether he was sure that he wanted to make the final leg. Simon and Gilbert had wanted to do it alone because they had climbed together for years. They had established routines and could pace each other. They felt safer on their own.

"I'm coming. It's my birthday," Brechner had said with a leer, his false eye glinting in the hazy light.

"You don't need to prove anything, Brechner," Simon had said.

"How do you know what I need to do and what I don't need to do?"

"It can get dangerous for all of us."

"I'm coming to keep you honest."

"You don't need to."

"He was my brother."

"What's that got to do with anything?"

"It's more important to me."

"He was my father."

"If you try and stop me, I swear, I'll take this ice pick and run it through both of your heads." Brechner had lurched forward, unshaven and gray faced in the small tent.

"Calm down, Brechner. It's okay."

All of them were crusty and irritable from lack of sleep and oxygen. Simon and Gilbert both felt an obligation to Brechner, and had promised that they would do their best for him. Simon knew that this was no basis for any decision on the mountain. Today, the walk up had taken eight slow hours, the first three of them in darkness. The fall had slowed them down but they had pushed on. They had faced the huge mass of ice in front of them knowing that emptiness and death lay on either side. Simon knew how to shut out the world around him and to concentrate on the bubble of light from his headlamp. He had focused on the familiar rhythms of ice pick and crampon, and the slow lift and push with each step. Inside this ice-blue world, he could feel every part of himself moving, his diaphragm contracting and pulling in air, the cartilage of his knees turning over on itself, the small bones in his hands shifting against each other. Simon did his best to fashion hand- and footholds that would support Brechner, and to set guide ropes in difficult stretches.

Now, standing on the top, he calculated that it would take them another six hours to descend. It would be faster over the slopes, and a little slower over the ice climbs. If they were doing well, they would be back at camp by five that afternoon. But sitting there, as they waited for Brechner to appear, Simon knew that the storm would be on them before they got there. Dark clouds were boiling on the horizon and he felt a steady breeze against his cheeks.

"Angels' breath," Gilbert said.

"I feel it."

Simon shifted his weight off his left leg and looked again at the distant sky. Above the clouds, it was black. A deep black that hung like a bottomless, starless night.

Simon knew that his father's family somehow held his mother responsible for the accident. As if there was something that she could have done to prevent it. When they came to the house to visit his father, they ignored her. They never talked to her, never drank the tea or ate the sandwiches that she made. He could still see her standing in the living room, in the background, in her tweed skirts and cashmere cardigans, watching them come and go like strangers. There had been a hardening in her, he knew. The same hardening that had allowed her to get a secretarial job at an insurance office in Oxford. It was here where she found a new circle of young women friends who took her out of the house. And that was how she met other men. Men with lives and legs and arms.

Eventually they moved his father home. The iron lung was put in the living room against the windows so he could see outside. That was his enduring image of his father, a head protruding from an industrial metal tube. The regular click and clack of the respirator filled the house day and night. Small wooden steps were placed along one side so that Simon could climb up and talk to his father. He stood there for hours: feeding him mashed vegetables and drinks through a straw; lathering him up with a horsehair brush and shaving his face with a safety razor; combing his hair; wiping the crust from his eyes; and cleaning trails of dribble from his chin and neck. And Simon read to his father standing on the steps by the iron lung, *The Times, Life* magazine, and the cartoons from *Punch.* He watched his Adam's apple slide along his throat as he laughed. It was going up and down those steps that he had decided that he would become a climber.

"If you do climb," his father had said, "promise me you'll never fall."

"How can I promise that?"

"You can promise. Falling is in the mind. If you don't believe that you can fall, then you won't fall. You can't. Promise me that."

"I promise."

His father had been the best climber in Britain. He had done pioneering ascents of the Matterhorn, Mont Blanc, and the Eiger. The last month before his accident, he had been planning an expedition to the Himalayas. The house was filled with coils of rope, jangling bundles of pegs and cleats, piles of oiled leather boots. He had been the consistency of steel, all calf and thigh and forearm. With the visiting nurse, they carried him flapping and limp, like a rag doll, to the bath. Simon saw his hard father shrink. A withering and wasting that seemed to suggest that he was somehow slipping away. Gradually disappearing to nothing. When his father cried, there was nothing Simon could think of to say or do. When he saw the big tears welling over his father's red eyelids, all he could do was to cry himself. Hanging over him, his tears fell, in heavy drops, down onto his father's upturned face. There was a mingling of salty liquid that ran in clear rivers down into the clacking iron machine. "Look at the two of us," his father always said, "like two babies."

His father died of pneumonia a year after they moved him home. *Streptococcus pneumoniae* was responsible, the doctor said, as if this knowledge would help. The clacking of the iron lung got faster and faster, like a train on tracks, and his father filled up with water. He drowned on land. Brechner came to the funeral, but spoke to no one, and left immediately. The iron lung was sitting empty in the front room for six weeks before the hospital came to collect it, more lifeless and cold than ever. Sometimes, while it was there, Simon climbed up and looked into the metal container and thought of nothing, his mind as empty as the machine in front of him. "Looking in there isn't going to bring him back," his mother said.

Simon had never seen his mother cry over his father. She was working and trying to rebuild her life, he understood that. But when his father died, a closeness between them was lost. He began to find strange men, smelling of hair oil and talc, in the house. He often ate dinner on his own in the kitchen, listening to radio 1, stirring sugar into his tea with a noisy teaspoon.

Gilbert and Simon had to lift Brechner onto the summit. He was shaking uncontrollably and barely able to walk. His gloves were missing, and his down jacket was unzipped and hanging open. The tips of his ears were eggshell white. They dragged him over the buttress and onto the flat snow. The oxygen mask had slipped onto Brechner's left cheek and his lips were blue and covered in flecks of ice. Simon shifted the oxygen mask so that it covered his mouth and nose and they lay him on his back. They readjusted his outer jacket, pulled new gloves onto his hands, and secured the jacket hood over his head. Simon wondered if his ears were frostbitten.

"He's in trouble," Simon said.

"Looks like he's hypothermic."

"He's lost it. He doesn't know where he is."

"Let's heat him up and see where we are."

"I'll be damned if I'm carrying him off."

"I'll get out the stove and heat some water. We've still got time."

"Why the hell did he try and come up?"

"It was the fall that did this to him. He was fine before the fall."

Simon knew that the fall had been his fault. He knew that Gilbert was not judging him, he was simply stating a fact. Gilbert took off his small pack and began setting up the stove while Brechner lay, quite unresponsive, on the snow between them. His breath rasped hoarsely through the refitted oxygen mask. Looking down at him, Simon saw himself reflected in Brechner's goggles, against the blue ocean of the sky. He eased the goggles up over Brechner's eyes. His skin was a pale goggle-shaped wedge, and his eyelids, like two pale mollusks, were tightly shut. His eyelashes were sprinkled with tiny droplets of water. At that moment, the false right eye, a tear-shaped almond with a vibrant blue iris, popped out onto Brechner's cheek. Simon saw the glistening plastic object staring back at him. It was slippery, and he had to make several attempts with his gloves to pick it up. He held the eye in his upturned palm. The iris was the color of the sky, the white of the eye the color of the peaks around him. He laid it carefully in the snow, a shining sapphire, next to Brechner.

After Simon's father died, Brechner had disappeared. He had sold his flat, all his belongings, and gone traveling. His family heard from him occasionally through tattered postcards from Rabat, Tripoli, and Bombay. There were rumors that he was insane and that he was addicted to heroin. Many believed that the death of his twin had caused him to give up on life. When Brechner finally resurfaced three years later, he was living in Nepal and working as an eye surgeon again. He had a permanent post office box in Kathmandu and was doing cataract and trachoma surgery in the Himalayan foothills. Rarely in the capital city, he was unmarried, and spent most of his time up in the mountains, working in remote villages. He spoke Nepali and the Sherpa dialect. His family was grateful that he was alive and that he had found a purpose. When his parents went to visit him, he refused to meet them, remaining in the mountains until they had left.

Crouched down near the surface, Simon felt a steady breeze, and smelled water and dry earth in the air. Farther down the range, plumes of white rose from the higher peaks as blasts of loose powder snow kicked up into billowing clouds that shimmered and were gone instantly. The front was building on distant ridges and racing toward them in the freshening breeze. He was desperate to move, to escape, to get down. Gilbert had the small white-gas stove hissing in front of him and was melting snow. Simon stood up and hugged himself to keep warm. The ritual of boiling water comforted him. He picked the Japanese flag from the stones and cracked it open, shaking it into a red-and-white sheet, and planting it upright again. It was really Gilbert who calmed him, he knew that. It was Gilbert who was able to maintain focus, to see things clearly, to take measured steps. Simon found a string of prayer flags under the heaped snow around the stones and unfurled it. Faded pink and yellow wings fluttered against his hands.

Gilbert was Simon's best friend. His only real friend. The only person who understood the exclusionary nature of his obsession. They had become climbing partners ten years ago and were a matched set. Gilbert was square, heavily muscled, slow, and virtually speechless. Every act was carefully weighed, laboriously planned. He had a harnessed power that stopped people talking and made them watch. Simon was a talker, a dreamer, gifted and energetic, but without control. Simon would always have been the first up a mountain, using a route of his own, but he would have killed himself if it had not been for Gilbert. Simon felt no fear, while Gilbert lived with it. Simon never had a girlfriend, while Gilbert always did. Simon smoked unfiltered cigarettes, while Gilbert refused them.

At university they had begun with granite walls in Snowdonia and the Lake District. Holidays took them into the Alps. They spent three winters learning to ice climb, and working as lift operators, tour-bus drivers, and cleaners for chalets and pensions. They had climbed the Matterhorn five times, Mont Blanc twice, and the Eiger once. They had slept in the backs of vans, eaten from cans for weeks, and broken six fingers, eight toes, and a collarbone between them. Simon knew that Gilbert was the reason that he could continue climbing. Gilbert had saved Simon's life on three occasions. Because of Gilbert, Simon had never fallen. Last winter, Gilbert had caught Simon on a safety line after he had dropped off a ten-thousand-foot ice cliff. The downward snap of the rope had broken Gilbert's collarbone. On the way to the hospital in Berne, they had sat in a clean bus and eaten hunks of black sausage on pieces of bread pulled straight from the loaf.

"Your problem is that you're not afraid enough," Gilbert said to Simon.

"There's no time for fear," Simon said.

"There should be time for fear. I'm the one with the cracked shoulder."

"You have the fear. I'll take the risks. Someone has to."

"Do you know why you climb?"

"No, I don't know why I climb. Climbers are just climbers. There's no reason."

"It's got something to do with your father."

"No it hasn't."

"I think you're trying to prove something."

"I don't know. The day I feel afraid is the day I'll stop. That I can say for certain."

In the summers, they went their separate ways. Simon spent time with his mother in the small flat in Brighton to which she had retired. He sat in her kitchen among the blown-glass trinkets, cracked linoleum, and a fine dusting of beach sand, planning climbs for the following year. He got a regular seasonal job at a bakery, working the dawn shift, watching daylight emerge through the blue dawn sky as he threw crusty warm loaves into wire baskets. His mother was resigned to his lack of interest in real work, settled life, routines. When he sat hunched and concentrating over maps and supply inventories, his jaw slumped on his chest and his teeth set and grinding, she saw only her husband. He kept a packet of Camels in front of him on the Formica kitchen table, smoking without thinking, his legs crossed and jiggling. His irises were speckled with brown and his hands were square and gripped paper as if it were wood. He walked up and down sand hills in boots to strengthen his calves and thighs.

Simon and Gilbert knelt over Brechner and helped him to sit up while they poured hot water into his mouth. The oxygen had worked. He was breathing steadily, and was awake and looking around. The wind was rushing past them, tugging at their hoods and sleeves. Simon felt their vulnerability, as they huddled there, small figures on a crushing landscape. They were in and out of shadow now, as plump clouds began racing across the sun. They got Brechner to keep down five mugs of the warm liquid and drank one each themselves. In fifteen minutes, they were able to heave Brechner to his feet. He stood there, feet apart, stomping the circulation back into his legs.

"I'm okay," Brechner said.

"You sure?" Simon asked.

"I can walk."

"Whenever you're ready."

"Your eye came out." Simon crouched down, collected the plastic object from the snow, and held it on his palm, toward Brechner.

"I don't need the eye. I'm leaving it."

Brechner took his eye and placed it carefully onto one of the stones, working it down into the snow. Gilbert took three shots of them standing on the top and then packed everything away. Simon took a photograph from his inside pocket. He held it flapping in front of him. It was a black-and-white shot of his father in the year before his death. In the photograph, his father was sitting on a sunny rock ledge, eating lunch and waving at the camera. At the moment of the photograph, he had been distracted, and was looking out to one side, still waving, with a sandwich in his mouth. He was there, but not there. Bright sun made his hair seem white, and his forearms were brown against his white shirt. Simon pinned the photograph to the snow by the Japanese flag with an ice screw.

It had been Simon's idea to attempt what would have been his father's last climb. A Himalayan peak ten thousand feet below Everest, but more technically difficult. Since his father's death, five climbers had been killed attempting to climb it. Simon studied his father's original survey maps and route plans, read through his notes on strategy and camp placement, and abstracted his old supply lists. It was only later, when the logistics had been finalized, that he got the notion of timing the ascent for the anniversary of his father's fiftieth birthday.

He had called Brechner on a long shot. He had not seen him for twenty years, since he was a child, but he needed to raise more money. If Brechner was living in the Himalayas, he reasoned, maybe he would be sympathetic to the climb they were planning. Despite everything, Brechner was family, and his father's brother. Simon called a phone number in Kathmandu for the Sunshine Guest House and Dining Room and waited for fifteen minutes while the disembodied voice at the other end went off to find him. In the background, Simon heard food frying and the clucking of chickens. Brechner had answered the phone asking, "What's happened?" It took Simon ten minutes to explain the expedition, and there was complete silence at the other end of the line. When he finished, there was a long pause. Brechner said, "I'll think about it," and hung up. But Brechner agreed without question when Simon next called, on the understanding that he would be a part of the climbing team, would help them plan it, and that he would be on the summit bid. The money was transferred from an English bank the same week. "We're climbing with a one-eyed fifty-year-old man," he told Gilbert, "but we have the money." Neither of them believed that they would end up climbing with Brechner. They both imagined that he would give up early.

They flew into Kathmandu in early November, over hazy, terraced hillsides and valleys filled with rivers like silver ribbons. Half a ton of equipment and supplies came with them. Simon met Brechner in a dim coffee shop, surrounded by the fruity smells of apple pies, sewage, and wood smoke. The windowsills were flecked with the bodies of dry flies. A patent-medicine vendor stood in the street outside, and a legless beggar on a trolley was leaning his back against the counter. Brechner came in quickly, busily. He was a small, compact man, bald, with dry flat lips. He was wearing khaki pants and shirt, a faded blue parka, and mud-spattered trainers. They shook hands at the table and Brechner ordered in Nepali. Two glasses of hot, sweet, milky tea were brought to them.

"I know what you're thinking," Brechner said.

"What am I thinking?"

"You're thinking I'm an old man, possibly mad, with one eye."

"You said that, not me."

"I've lived in the mountains for ten years. I know them. I've pulled out more cataracts with these hands than most eye surgeons would do in a lifetime."

"I respect that."

"I'm used to the altitude, I'm acclimatized. It'll take you weeks to build yourselves up."

"Right."

"And another thing. I'm not mad. I'm here because I choose to be. I'm over your father. This is not some self-punishment trip."

"I didn't think it was. I didn't really think you'd be mad either."

"What I want to know is why you're doing this. This is not a simple climb. It's a dangerous place. I've met three of the people who never came back from up there. And all of them were top climbers. Top climbers. It's not like Europe. It's different."

"Climbing is what I do."

"Listen. You'll never be as good as your father. Never. He had a natural gift. If you think you can in some way compete with him, you're wrong." Brechner's fingers were like fat sausages. The back of each finger was capped with a dense tuft of black hair. Simon could smell alcohol on his breath.

"I'm not trying to compete."

"You've got to know when to walk away. You know there's not a Nepalese villager alive who would go up this mountain."

"Why?"

Brechner drained his tea in a single gulp. "Because it's not a mountain. It's a spirit. We're going to have trouble getting porters and Sherpas for the climb."

"Do you believe that?"

"This is what I believe. If your father were alive, and sitting in my place, he'd tell you to give this up. Spend time in the mountains, sure. But give this one up."

Outside, a flock of sheep was being driven past the dusty window of the coffee shop. The small steel bells around their necks were rattling in the thin air. The shepherd, a young boy, had a bright red scarf wrapped around his head. In his hand he held a long, polished wooden stick that he was tapping, gently, onto the backs of the sheep nearest him. Simon finished his tea and felt the thick residue of sugar at the bottom of the glass against his lips. He knew that he could not give up.

It was after dawn when Simon slipped. They had been climbing in the dark for more than three hours, and the sky had lightened to blue and then opened up around them into flourishes of pink and gold. Simon felt the warmth on his back and was grateful for the light. The slope in front of him flared brilliantly in the sun and he switched off his headlamp. He turned and waved to Brechner and Gilbert behind him.

They had been climbing in a diagonal line up a ridge that angled west toward the summit. Just after sunrise, they came to the first wall, a sheet of ice that led onto a terrace and the next ridge above them. It was a two-hundred-foot turret that had sheer drops into swirling valleys on either side. They gathered at the base before beginning the climb. They ate some chocolate. Brechner lifted his goggles onto his forehead and looked back down the mountain. "Although this is madness," he said, "I've got to admit that it is spectacular." Brechner's glass eye was never completely aligned in his head, so one side of him always seemed to be looking off somewhere else. When they were children, they had laughed at the glass eye, and Brechner had periodically pulled it, with a brief burrowing of his fingers, from its socket, held it at arm's length, and chased them around the house. There was a part of Simon that was disturbed by that face, the face of his father, so incomplete and inhuman without an eye on one side. "It'll be better from the top," Simon said, and began the lead pitch.

The ice was good and firm, and he moved quickly up the first hundred feet. He avoided looking at the airy bottomless valleys on either side, deeper and vaster than he had ever seen. He pounded deep holds into the wall with his pick, sending showers of ice like powdered sugar over his shoulder. He hammered screws every twenty feet and set a fixed rope through carabiners as he went. The metallic sound of the hammer against steel sounded empty and small against the mountain, as insubstantial as water and air. It took him an hour to get to the top. Thin rivulets of water glinted against the wall as the surface ice melted in the morning sun. Brechner and Gilbert were a hundred feet below him.

He had reached the top terrace, and was balancing too close to the edge when it happened. He heard a soft crack. He felt his feet shift slightly. And then the sheet of ice below him sheared away from the wall. His legs were flung outward. He plunged off the edge, toward Brechner and Gilbert. He felt the ice screws on the safety line pinging out of the wall as he dropped past them. He wasn't able to make a sound. He felt a strange peacefulness as he rushed past the blue wall, saw his own ax scraping a narrow trench down the ice as he fell, and heard all of the breath forced through his mouth and ears as he was caught at the end of the rope. He heard the rope crack as it took his fall. Simon was slammed violently into the wall. Brechner, one hundred feet above him, anchored on a fixed line and with two axes buried to the hilt, was immobile and silent as he caught his full weight. Simon hung in the air below, held by Brechner on the safety line. The rope was taut and shuddering. He swung in wide arcs back and forth across the face. With kicking feet, he maneuvered over to the wall again and got purchase with his crampons and ice ax. He dug himself in. He was shaking and panting, sucking away oxygen from his cylinder. He clung unsteadily to the wall below Brechner and Gilbert and off to one side, near the edge. Snow and ice fluttered down from above them.

"Are you on?" Gilbert shouted.

"I'm on."

"Okay, forget it, forget it. Calm down now."

"I'll be all right."

"Okay. Now concentrate. Let's get back to the top."

Simon slowly began climbing again. He was climbing when he heard the next crack, and when he heard Brechner shout.

That summer Gilbert and Simon had spent two months in the Alps on training climbs. The world was so ordered and clear in Europe that anything had seemed possible. Simon had felt himself tightening, becoming brown and firm. In the mountains, he shaved every day because it made him feel quicker. Gilbert's girlfriend, Marie, was with them for the last three weeks. She joined them for cross-country hikes over passes dappled with purple wildflowers. Sitting cross-legged on cow-cropped grass they had laughed at nothing, talked about the Himalayas, and snapped hysterical group photographs. On their last week, they went for a celebratory meal in Chamonix. At an outdoor restaurant, sitting on pine decking dotted with tables and umbrellas and overlooking Mont Blanc, they had ordered salmon and Italian Chardonnay. The salmon, roasted whole, was surrounded by garlic and almonds. On the underbelly of the fish, the skin was a luminescent blue that sparkled and flashed in the sun. The flesh was white outside and soft pink inside.

"This is my last year climbing," Gilbert said over coffee.

"What do you mean?" Gilbert was holding Marie's hand on the table in front of her. She was rubbing the back of his hand with her thumb.

"Just what I said. I want to do other things. I can't do this all my life. I'll never be as good as I am now. I've applied for an engineering job in Sheffield."

"And if you get the job?"

"I'll take it, I guess."

"And give up no money, canned food, and me." They all laughed.

"Yes."

"Well, if that's what you've got to do."

"Simon, I think you should consider it, too. Doing something else for a while."

"How?"

"What do you mean? Just do something else. Make a change."

"Why? I mean, I'm not sure that I want to."

"Because there comes a time. That's all. We'll never be as good as we are now. We won't be lucky forever."

"I'll be lucky forever."

"I won't be."

Simon felt the hard, crumbly whiteness of the sugar cubes in a small silver bowl in front of him. He broke two of them down into the thick-rimmed coffee cup with a small blue crest monogrammed along its rim. He felt his toes, wet in his boots. Looking out over the mountains, reflected in the blue skin of the fish, he knew that he could never stop. And he knew that it was Gilbert who kept him climbing.

Simon felt the temperature dropping on the summit. For the first time, the sun disappeared completely, plunging them into a dusky gloom. Simon knew that they did not have any more time. He was not sure how fit Brechner was, but knew that they would have to go, and take a chance. He didn't have to speak to Gilbert. "Going. Going now," Gilbert said, lumbering over to the edge.

They shortened the safety lines to twenty feet. Gilbert was the lead and they put Brechner between him and Simon. Between them, he reasoned, they would be able to hold him if he slipped. "Happy birthday, Brechner," Simon said as they pulled on their oxygen masks again and stopped speaking. Simon knew that he had to find a rhythm and concentrate on the ground in front of him. He was thinking too much about Brechner. He was too anxious, too eager to get down. Climbers killed climbers, he knew. It was the thin air, the tiredness, and the cold that were doing it to him. He took long deep breaths of oxygen. He checked his gloves and jacket again and tried to relax his abdomen and calves. And then he lumbered around and eased himself back off the edge after Gilbert and Brechner. Simon heard the metallic rattle of pegs and clips around Gilbert's waist as he lowered himself down the slope ahead of him.

They descended down the buttress and were moving along the first ridge when the cold front hit them. The wind picked up to a steady fifteen knots and walls of cloud began blowing over the mountain. The air filled with curtains of gray fog. The cloud in front of Simon's face was wispy and glutinous. Ahead of him, he saw the dark form of Brechner, hunched forward, walking with wide swings of his arms. The safety line was limp between them and lay on the snow like a crack on a white cement wall. Simon could still just make out Gilbert up front, walking smoothly and with long high steps down the incline. Their footholds were still clearly visible in the snow, and Simon concentrated on placing his boots in the center of each to minimize his effort and to reduce the chance of slipping. He felt the muscles in his forehead clenching. His eyes were dry and gritty. Simon knew that they would need about an hour to traverse this top ridge, which angled to the south. It was the most vulnerable they would be on the descent. He imagined the three of them in his mind as bobbing specks, like currants swirling in milk.

In another fifteen minutes, it began snowing. Heavy flakes began angling into them from the south and the air became opaque. Brechner was reduced to a smudge and then disappeared. They were in a whiteout. By stooping, Simon could continue to follow the indentations in front of him. He estimated that they had about ten or twenty feet on either side of them on the ridge. He knew that they had to reach the end of the ridge before the snow obliterated the previous path. Without this to guide them, they would walk off the edge. Simon concentrated on maintaining his rhythm, focusing on each step, and on the regular pulls of his breathing.

Simon couldn't see anything around him when he heard the voice of his father. "Over here," it said, "over here." It was Brechner, calling to him from up ahead, shouting over his shoulder, trying to keep him on track. Brechner was looking after him again. Taking responsibility for him. Simon eased his face mask to one side, and called back, but his voice was weak and was carried off instantly by the wind.

Simon felt the weight of the shotgun, black and oiled, in his small hands. It looked like one of the dark tree limbs, outlined starkly against the snow. His father was out in front hiking vigorously into the brambles, the high thicket, attempting to flush pheasant into the air. He was lifting his arms above his head and then flapping them down onto the sides of his legs as he walked. "Hey," he was calling, "hey, hey." Simon followed behind, his fingers delicate and small on the barrel. As he walked, the barrel tilted and dug into the snow. He had to keep lifting it up to his shoulders to move forward.

He concentrated on walking with his head down. The footholds were beginning to fill up with fresh snow. He could see the hard, compressed ice, blue in the base of each footprint, disappearing. His knees were aching. He felt hundreds of little icy flutters against his cheeks. There was sweat coursing down the inside of his goggles.

The gun was cocked and ready. He had shot it five times before with his father. He had never hit a pheasant, but he understood the balance and pull of the gun, and how to rest it on his shoulder and aim into the sky. He felt his toes, wet inside his desert boots. There was a warbling sound as the pheasant showered upward. "Over here," his father shouted, "over here." Simon ran two steps, hefted the gun onto his shoulders, and fell forward. He felt the thick metal pressure of the trigger against his second and third fingers. He pulled as he fell, pulled gently, and felt the gun lurch under him. He smelled cordite and wet grass under the snow. He saw his father pitch forward and drop like a stone.

Brechner was calling to him again. Simon had to bend almost double to see the footholds. He felt himself breathing and stepping. He felt his abdominal muscles contracting sharply each time he took a step. He knew that he was breaking his rhythm, speeding up against his will. The sound of the oxygen mask had gone and was replaced by the constant blast of wind in his face.

When Simon opened his eyes, he realized he had been asleep. He was propped against the stone cairn on the summit, slumped with his chin on his chest. He didn't know how long he had been there. The wind was cold against his face. Dark clouds raced above him, obscuring the sun. He took off a glove and felt the stickiness on his left shin, and the bone, poking up out of his leg. He couldn't feel any pain. He was alone. He called out, but he knew that Gilbert and Brechner had never reached the summit with him. Gilbert and Brechner had fallen. Simon had watched it happen just after his own fall. He had clung to the ice alongside them, as it cracked again, and sent them slipping downward. He saw Brechner flaying with his ice pick as they slipped. He saw Gilbert sliding away. Simon had shouted Gilbert's name. And then he had released his safety line. He had watched the rope flap down after them. They had vanished over the edge, into Tibet, into nothing. He had climbed alone to the top, blindly stumbling upward, toward the sky.

Simon sat and listened on the summit. He could not feel his fingers or toes. He saw his footprints disappearing in front of him, their icy blue bases smothered by new snow. He saw the mountains reflected in the blue skin of a fish. He saw bright sunlight in a blue sky as he tipped his head back, and felt the bitter taste of coffee grounds against his tongue. He felt wet feet and toes capped with ice and his own breathing against his lips. And then without moving, he shut his eyes and began walking, head down, toward his father, waiting for him in the snow.

8

ACTS OF MEMORY,
WISDOM OF MAN

"Fortune favors the prepared mind," my father told us when we were growing up. "You must train your mind to be a steel trap." He made us remember facts that he considered important. When we started high school, he had us memorize world geography: capital cities and their populations; the states of America; all the countries abutting Luxembourg, Hungary, the Ivory Coast. Then he began with human anatomy: the structure of the lung; the valves, chambers, in-flow and out-flow vessels of the heart; the muscles of the foot. Every week in the summer, he gave us a memory quiz, at Saturday lunch, sitting around our mahogany dining room table.

The summer of 1968, the summer that would change our lives, our father started us on the twelve human cranial nerves. I was fourteen years old, about to go into my first year of high school, and my brother, Alex, was nineteen, and had just received his high school diploma. At night, I sat with the heavy volumes of *Gray's Anatomy* and *Cunningham's Textbook of Anatomy*, my father's textbooks, looking into red-and-brown lithographs of the human system splayed open on the pages like meat in a butcher's window. After lunch on Saturdays, we would sit at the table while our father asked us questions and recorded our scores in one of his oilskin-bound notebooks.

Alex remembered facts with very little effort. "Here's the thing, little brother," he said to me, "I can remember the details without caring about any of them. You can't remember the details, but you care about all of them. This is not entirely fair, is it?" I was only fourteen years old and anatomy fascinated and overwhelmed me. I have a photographic memory, a blessing and a curse, perhaps, that has served me well in adult life, but when I was fourteen, my anxiety got in the way of my memory. The idea that I was in direct competition with my brother unsettled me. I never felt confident and spent hours looking at pages in the books, watching the anatomical drawings blur into each other. The more I concentrated, the more chaotic the information seemed to become.

That June we began learning the seventh facial nerve, a complicated tree of motor and sensory branches that fanned across the face. To me, the nerve was like a frenetic street map of boulevards, avenues, and alleys for which there was no clear beginning and no definite end, in which even the smallest of the branches seemed to have dazzling significance. I took it very seriously, staying up late at night to read the textbooks under the steel reading lamp on my desk. Big powder-winged moths flew in through the open bedroom window and flapped against the lightbulb. On hot nights, I would hear Alex outside shooting basketball at the hoop in the yard. Alex could remember anatomy after an hour or two of fevered effort on his bed. He approached the task with the intensity with which he approached ball games. He saw it as a contest.

On a Saturday afternoon in June, we were sitting at the mahogany table after lunch when my father took out the notebook in which he had written four questions about the facial nerve. It was a warm day with a strong cool breeze off the river. The French doors were open to the garden, and the wind blew the smell of cut grass and pollen inside. My mother sat at the table reading a newspaper. My father wore half-moon reading glasses with gold frames, and looked over the glasses with raised eyebrows.

"Tell me where the facial nerve exits the skull," my father said to Alex.

Alex sat forward in his chair with his elbows on the table and his chin in his hands. "The stylohyoid foramen," he said.

I knew my brother was right. My father wrote in the notebook with his fountain pen. My mother turned the pages of the newspaper loudly, smoothing the paper on the table with both hands.

My father turned to me. "Describe the sensory functions of the facial nerve, Harry."

I sat still and tried to remember. I had understood it when he read it, but could not make it real to myself. Alex grinned and winked at me, pointed at his own face, moved the muscles connected with his own facial nerve. I resigned myself, stayed silent, felt the moment slipping away, could not reach what I had read and seen in the textbook diagrams. The wooden tabletop was polished and smooth under my fingers, and shimmered a little with reflected sunlight, like the surface of a pool.

"Harry," my father said. "Let's have it, partner."

"He doesn't know," Alex said.

"Oh for God's sake," my mother said. "Stop this nonsense. Why should he know this? I don't give a damn about the nerves of the face. Harry should be outside. He should be using his facial nerves on a girlfriend."

"It is useful training," my father said.

"Training for what, Ishfaq Maroon? What, please tell me, is so important about knowing all this anatomical business? Let them be boys."

"I am training them to use their minds, Shabana."

"Pure nonsense. You are training them to be exactly like you. This is what you do, you direct. You are a controller."

"Shabana, I have never controlled. I am trying to prepare them for the harsh realities of modern life. How have I controlled, for God's sake?"

"I did not want to leave India. I was forced," my mother said.

"You were not forced," my father said.

"Yes, I was forced."

"The sensory part of the facial nerve supplies taste to the anterior two thirds of the tongue," Alex said.

"What are you talking about?" my father said.

"You know what I am talking about," my mother said.

"Harry," my father said. "The human brain is a lobulated, walnut-shaped organ weighing approximately three pounds. It can be whipped into shape like a flaccid muscle, with regular and vigorous use. Lift weights with your brain, Harry, and it will bloom into something worthy of Mr. Atlas himself."

"The sensory part of the facial nerve is in the chorda tympani branch, which also supplies vasodilator nerves to the submaxillary and sublingual glands," Alex said.

"We live under draconian rule," my mother said. "It is stifling."

"Without discipline, we are nothing," my father said. "All is lost."

"Mastery over the gallbladder, Ishfaq Maroon, is that what is important? A lifetime of punishment so that you can achieve mastery over a damned gallbladder?" my mother said.

My father stood up. "I have succeeded," he said quietly, "in my own way. Kindly do not mock." He took off his reading glasses, put them into the top pocket of his shirt, and stood for a moment with the tips of his fingers pressed together. Then he walked out the French doors and into the garden. My mother did not watch him go. She licked her thumb and forefinger, turned a page of the newspaper, and read with her hands on her lap. We sat there, the three of us, silent at the table, until Alex slid the notebook across the table and closed it with a thump. "I win," he said and a gust of wind blew in through the windows and lifted the pages of the newspaper gently, so that they fluttered for a moment, then fell back flat on the table, and I felt, for the first time, as if something silent and unfathomable had changed between my parents.

My father was a surgeon and an amateur collector of beetles. His love of beetles defined him, and gave him a place in the world. Fourteen years earlier, when we immigrated from India, he brought two thousand beetle specimens with him, packed in iron trunks, and he saw these insects as the key to some hidden and essential mystery. He was obsessed with the systematic classification of his specimens, and he could talk about beetle phenetics and phylogeny for hours.

He had been born into a family of Muslim merchants in New Delhi who made a fortune shipping indigo to England in the nineteenth century. He was the youngest of three brothers. His own father, a man I never met, became a collector of beetles who amassed a huge personal collection. He was visited by entomologists from England and America, and took his son on extended field trips to northern India. My father learned the systematic classification system for beetles when he was a boy, and imagined that an ability to order and rank the natural world made him more European than the people around him.

My father told us this without shame or hesitation. He grew up going to English schools in India, reading the Romantic poets. His imagination was fired, he told us, by the gold-plated palanquin abandoned by Siraj-ud-Daula on the battlefield of Plassey, the Boer War, and the formidable ball skills of W. G. Grace, the legendary cricketer. "I was a Muslim," he said to us, "but considered myself a gentleman first, a capitalist second, and a doctor third." He studied medicine and went to England to complete his training in gray stone and slate English hospitals under walls of drizzle. Some of his teachers were the sons of the army men and box wallahs who had been the backbone of the British Raj in India, and my father saw this as a type of weird symmetry, a coming home of sorts, the closure of a circle of connections and origins. He was instilled with the trappings of Englishness: a reverence for rules, an appreciation for white picket fences around green playing fields. He studied at Guy's Hospital in London and returned to India with English textbooks, subscriptions to *The Lancet* and the *British Medical Journal*, and a wardrobe befitting an English Gentleman.

He moved us to Iowa seven years after partition and wanted to believe he was free of India. He preserved his father's collection of beetles and began his own collection, calling himself an amateur coleopterist worthy of respect, and collecting jewel beetles from around the world. In winter, he wore plaid shirts and hunting jackets and deer caps with ear flaps. On spring days, we sometimes drove west to the Mississippi just to look into the sheer immensity of the stream.

Our life in the Victorian clapboard house on the banks of the Iowa River was orderly and predictable. My father noticed the quiet still-faced men and women who worked the farms and saw something worthwhile there that he wanted us to understand. He was embraced by the hospital community, and made a minor name for himself specializing in procedures involving the gallbladder. I realized when I was young that it was my father's Englishness that was admired and that made him acceptable: his manners and accent; his refinements and clothes; his stories of picnics at Oxford with friends from Christ Church, wearing a straw boater that he had made specially for such occasions.

We grew up without Bible or Koran. My father called organized religion an outrage, and proclaimed himself an agnostic, committed only to the principles of democracy and individual freedom. Hard work. Discipline. No festivals or ceremonies. No fanciful rituals, hocus-pocus, or mumbo-jumbo. Make yourself an Emperor Among Men, he told us, think for yourself and become an Emperor using your own wits. Understand the natural world. Read the works of Mr. Charles Darwin. *The Voyage of the Beagle*, he said, was more illustrative than religion of any kind, read chapter seventeen on the Galapagos Islands and understand the lessons contained there. My father worshiped Charles Darwin for his love of beetles and his connections to Josiah Wedgwood, the founder of the famous pottery, as well as for his contributions to biology. Darwin represented the best of the Victorian spirit of curiosity and self-discipline, conducted by gentlemen with private estates. My father clung to a nineteenth-century view of the world. "This is the curse of my generation of Indians," he said, "we are more English than the English themselves."

He did not seem to be a fallible man. He seemed to have mastered the world with his Darwinian theories and strict application of scientific principles. He taught me to examine facts, to reason arguments, to ground whatever I thought on solid evidence. When I look back, I realize that my father must have been as surprised as we were at my mother's outburst at the lunch table that Saturday in June.

It was the first time my parents had disagreed so strongly in front of us. I dwelled on what I had seen and could not sleep. That night I got up and went into my father's study. An old-fashioned oak desk faced the window overlooking the garden and I switched on the desk lamp. The plaster on the wall was cream colored and transected by a filigree of fine cracks. An articulated human skeleton hung on a thin metal stand by the window, and on the wall there were two framed pictures: Holman Hunt's *Our English Coasts, 1852*, and a photograph of Winston Churchill at the Yalta conference. All of these details, the smell, the dark shapes, and the pictures, made me feel better.

My father's folio notebooks were arranged along one shelf of the bookcase. He had cataloged his beetle collection in these notebooks and saw the creation of lists as a way of wresting order from chaos. The oilskinbound folio notebooks were sent to him from a stationery supplier in Oxford who had been producing them for more than one hundred and fifty years. The notebooks had been carried by explorers and gentlemen into the outposts of the empire and had been used to document such things as the botany of Amazonia and the skull phrenology of New Guinea Highlanders.

For the previous two years, I had helped to catalog the beetle collection. The beetles that my father brought from India had never been formally documented, although my grandfather had been able to give the biologic name of each specimen from memory. At first, they all looked alike to me. I learned how to examine the beetles systematically, to slow down when I felt like rushing, and to see all of them as different. I began to understand the beauty of subtle variation. I taught myself to use the reference texts; my father had copies of the beetle catalogs of Junk and Schenkling, listing over two hundred thousand species. He showed me a copy of the first edition of *Systema Naturae*, published in 1758 by Carolus Linnaeus, which established the first system for classifying all plants and animals on the basis of comparative anatomy. "This Linnaeus fellow," he said to me, "set out to describe all the organisms in the world, for God's sake, Harry. All of them. The sheer audacity of it is inspiring. Swedish chap. Organize. That is the key. Organize." He told me about Johann Fabricius, who had classified insects on the basis of their mouthparts, describing over four thousand new species of beetles between 1775 and 1801.

I was a diligent young man, unusual in one so young, I think, as I look back. I gave the pinned specimens a catalog number and logged each beetle by family name. I recorded descriptions of habitat, diet, and geographic distribution if I could find them. It was not an effort for me. I used my father's ink pens and wrote in a left-handed compact script that I am still rather proud of.

That night I remember getting up and running my fingers along the thin spines of the notebooks. I took one from the shelf. The cover was black and rough in my hands. I pulled the window open, sat down again at the desk, opened the book, and began reading the specimen names. I still remember clearly the list of stagbeetles recorded on the first page:

STAGBEETLES OF NORTHERN INDIA

Dorcus curvidens
Dorcus antaeus
Dorcus tityus
Dorcus nepalensis
Lucanus cantori
Lucanus lunifer
Rhaetus westwoodi

I had been reading for perhaps five minutes when I noticed another person sitting in the armchair in the dark corner of the room. I had a moment of panic and sat up quickly. It was my mother. She was a pale figure out beyond the island of lamplight, sitting absolutely still in the chair. Her feet were set squarely on the floor in front of her and she wore a pair of white cotton pajamas.

"I could not sleep either," she said.

"It's too hot," I said and put the notebook on the table.

"I am glad you read, Harry. There is a difference between understanding things and remembering them."

"I know."

"The cleverest people don't memorize things. They have ideas of their own."

"I don't feel like I have any ideas, really," I said.

"My father was like you, Harry. He was interested in things. He read a great deal. He had wonderful ideas."

I leaned back in the chair. I was wearing shorts and the leather of the chair was smooth against my legs. The breeze through the window felt cool on my skin.

"Did you mean what you said today? About being forced to leave. India, I mean," I said.

"I can never forgive myself for leaving home."

"You could go back."

"There are some things you cannot do, even when you want to, Harry. I know this is difficult to understand."

"I can see that," I said.

"The strangest things remind me of home, Harry," she said. "Today Mr. Elkhardt came with some pig manure for the garden. I asked him in for a cup of tea. And you know, the thing I noticed about that man Elkhardt was his hands. Farming hands. Rough hands through the work. They had that thickness of skin they get, Harry. Like a type of hard leather. He shook my hand and you know, the only thing I could think of was when I was a little girl. Because everyone had hands like that, Harry, back then. Hard skin. When you felt it, it didn't feel quite like a person. It took me back to those days."

"The pre-refrigerator days."

This was how my mother described her life growing up in India. She spoke of the pre-refrigerator days with a kind of nostalgia. The longer she was out of India, the more romance and importance the pre-refrigerator days assumed. They were a part of her formative years. They had given her a solid grounding in what life was about. I knew, even then, that there was no romance to be had in a world without electricity, water, or functional latrines. My mother had the selective memory of all immigrants.

"Elkhardt's hands, Harry. They reminded me of a boy I used to know in India. Years ago now. A tall boy who had to work with a plow from a very young age. He would come to our house selling things. Eggs, vegetables, that sort of thing. He had hands just like that. I remember going out to see him in the yard, and he never spoke. But sometimes my mother would give me the money, and I would put it in his hand. And I could feel his skin, Harry. Thick skin. He was only a boy, really. It amazed me because I had never felt skin like it. And I realized, I think, that people lived very differently from my family. I've never forgotten that."

"It's funny how you remember things. Things you haven't thought about in years," I said.

"It is reassuring to me, Harry. That memories do not disappear. Sometimes that is all we have, our memories. Acts of memory are the wisdom of man, Harry. What do we have if we do not have memories? Not a great deal."

My mother got up and walked over to the window. Her hair was long and fell around her shoulders. The light from the lamp shone on her forehead and eyes and I saw my mother for a moment as a young woman.

She stared into the dark window, watching my reflection in the glass. "We all make choices in our lives," she said. "You will have to make choices, too, Harry."

"I understand," I said.

"Be yourself, Harry," she said. "This is the best you can do."

She turned from the window, walked over to my chair, and kissed me on the forehead. "You will be absolutely fine," she whispered. Then she quietly opened the door and left the room.

I went back to the notebook and read the pages covered with neat handwriting. I thought about what my mother had said and fell asleep in the chair with the notebook in my hands. I did not hear my father come into the room early in the morning to switch off the lamp. When I woke up, there were cardinals in the trees outside and a few dry leaves on the windowsill. The book was pressed flat to my chest, like a Bible.

The day after the episode at the lunch table, I found my father in his beetle museum, standing at the window, looking out into the garden with a pair of binoculars. My father had devoted a room to his beetle collection, which he called his museum. It was filled with the two thousand specimens that he had brought from India as well as hundreds that he had gathered since. The most impressive and colorful beetles were arranged on glass-fronted display tables. Others were stored on flat wooden trays in tall vertical filing cabinets. My father turned quickly when he heard me walk into the room. He was a small man with delicate fingers, and his hands looked childlike on the heavy steel binoculars.

He gave the impression of being in the middle of a train of thought. "Harry," he said. "Here is a lesson." He led me to one of the display cases and pointed to a beetle mounted on corkboard. It had brilliant-green coppery wings. "There it is," he said. "The species *chrysochroa* from the Buprestid family. That fellow has been in the collection since the late nineteenth century, Harry. My father got him. He came from the forests of Arakan, in Burma, along the Bay of Bengal. There were several species of Buprestids in those forests that were considered to be articles of commerce, Harry, like jewelry. They were harvested in the rainy season, sent to Calcutta, and used in trade."

There was an original copy of the *Cyclopedia of India*, revised in 1885, on a shelf in the room, and my father went and got it. The book was dusty and leather bound. He flipped rapidly through the pages and after a few minutes he stopped and showed me a passage about beetles. I read out loud:

> Five thousand maunds of beetle wings are procurable during the rains, a maund being a measure of weight varying from twenty-five to eighty-two and one-eighth pounds, depending on the substance being weighed. In the Bengal bazaar, a maund equals eighty-two pounds and two ounces, and in Akyab, beetle wings fetch six to seven rupees per maund.

The pages of the book were yellow and smelled musty with age. Afternoon sun came in through the window and it was hot in the room. Beads of sweat appeared on my father's top lip. "What do you think of that?" he said, tapping the book with the back of his hand.

"Beetles were quite valuable," I said.

"Everything is arbitrary, Harry. That is what it tells me. These beetle wings are worth nothing today. Then, they could make you a fortune. Everything is arbitrary. All meaning, Harry, depends on a set of arbitrary rules and laws. Do you see, partner?"

"I see," I said.

"What is this collection of beetles, Harry, if it is not classified and ordered and put into a system? I'll tell you. Nothing. Nothing at all. Without a set of rules and laws, nothing means anything."

"Like money," I said.

"Merely colored paper and pieces of punched metal. The value comes from us, Harry, it is not inherent in the material."

"Religion."

"The same."

"Science?"

"There are no absolutes, Harry. I happen to believe in natural selection and the scientific method. We must all decide on our own set of guiding principles. The key is this: you must have principles."

Everything is arbitrary. I pondered my father's words. I went over to the window and looked out through the trees. My mother was kneeling in the vegetable garden between rows of seedlings, working with a trowel. She was wearing a straw sun hat with a chin strap. The hat shone white in the sun against the black soil in the beds. It occurred to me that my father had been watching my mother when I came into the room, studying her through the binoculars.

"Do you think Shabana would agree with us?" I said as I watched my mother.

My father shut the book with a firm slap. "I honestly do not know," he said.

I watched my mother in the garden for several minutes. It was so quiet that I thought my father had left the room, but when I turned around, he was still there, standing absolutely still with the book in one hand and the binoculars around his neck, caught for a moment in a shaft of sunlight. When I reflect back on this moment, I understand that marriage is based on arbitrary laws, too, ephemeral understandings that are as trifling as the line down the center of a highway that prevents cars from running into each other. At the time, all I saw was my father watching my mother, as if he were observing the behavior of one of his beetles in the wild.

On my father's desk was a photograph of my family taken at the New Delhi airport on the night in 1954 when we left India for good. I still have the photograph today, forty-five years later, on my own desk, and it has been there so long that I do not notice it. In the picture, my mother and father are leaning toward each other, looking surprised in the confusion and the heat. I am only one year old, cradled in my father's arms, my head twisted toward the camera, and Alex is down on the floor between my parents, looking up at my mother's face with both arms stretched above his head. My mother looks young and defiant with the heavy cardboard tickets in her left hand. The man with the camera, hunched and bent backward, is reflected in the glass window behind us.

I imagine us walking to the plane across the wet tarmac, heavy pools of monsoon water sparkling in the airport lights. I imagine my parents strapping themselves into the cloth seats in the silver-bodied plane. When I think of that moment, I can feel the terror and anticipation of going up into the rain-swept sky, thick with heavy clouds like black balls. Looking into the photograph, I can interpret it in two ways. For my father, there is excitement, frenetic energy, and the optimism of a new life. For my mother, there is anger, frustration, and a kind of despair born of the fact that she has no choice, no way to go back. Now I can see that, for her, it was a heartbreaking moment.

We flew to England and stayed two months in a one-room bedsit while waiting for our immigration papers to be completed. My father vowed never to return to India. He had been terrified at partition when he saw the wild crowds and the people lying dead in the streets. He cursed Hindus and Muslims alike, and claimed himself to be a disillusioned man. "We must go west," he had said, "seek a new frontier. Free system. Separation of church and state. Rights of the individual." It had taken him seven years to save enough money to get out of India, and to get the surgical position in an American hospital. He moved us to Iowa

City with the promise of a clinical job and vast open plains given over to corn and hogs, atop soil that was denser and blacker than any we had ever seen.

I have always thought of my mother as Indian. When she went out, she put on tweed skirts and cashmere sweaters with underwire bras, but at home she still wore her traditional saris and shawls. My father called her a vigorous woman. She kept busy, even when nothing needed to be done, walked quickly on short muscular legs. Relatives sent food and spices to her, wrapped tightly in cloth bundles. She kept a supply of cardamom and cumin, mustard oil and white poppy seeds and lentils in glass jars. Once a week, we ate Indian food, steaming bowls of hot dhal, potatoes dribbled with mustard oil, parathas, and oily slabs of flatbread. The smells made my mother nostalgic and she would drift off on Sunday afternoons and doze in sunny spots in the garden.

She tried to keep in touch with her family. The oldest were still in Bihar and New Delhi. Younger cousins had fled into Amritsar in 1947, crossed the new border into Pakistan at Wagah, and now lived in Lahore. She kept up a correspondence. Her own family told her that she was better off in America. She told me that she missed small things: the sounds and smells of markets, the bustle of people in and out of houses, the ripe mangoes, and the pedantic debates with men sitting barefoot in wicker chairs.

But my mother's memories of India did not mean anything to me. I know that it is now not fashionable to admit it, but in 1968, at the age of fourteen, I felt as if the swath of Iowa farming country on which I had grown up was my home. I went to school with the children of farmers but was not treated like an immigrant and felt that I belonged with them. My skin was a pale tan, not much darker than the summer faces of the children who helped with the harvest on the windswept plains of the grain bowl. I was not ashamed of my broad midwestern accent, and thought of India as my father did: a place of barbarism and religious extremism; brothers killing brothers; petty bureaucrats. A place where I did not belong.

.   .   .

Whatever was happening between my parents was never discussed. There was an unspoken rift, a hairline crack that was not easy to see. The previous year, my mother had learned to drive. The summer of 1968 my father bought her a secondhand Cadillac, a gigantic steel-framed car that made her seem absurdly tiny hunched behind the wheel. The freedom provided by the car allowed her to visit friends during the day, and go shopping on her own. I recognized how relaxed and talkative she was when she returned from these excursions, and felt that a part of her had left us. She talked about taking summer law classes at the university. "I need to be fortifying my mind," she said, "and obtaining skills. I need to be useful."

My mother's newfound independence was encouraged by her best friend, Gretchen Tappero, the wife of Peter Tappero, who was head of the entomology department at the university. My father often invited Peter over to the house to discuss his beetle collection. They would bring my father's specimens outside into the sunlight to examine their morphology with magnifying glasses. Gretchen came to the house with Peter and had struck up a close friendship with my mother. They liked to argue about books. Gretchen knew and loved everything by the expatriate writers in Paris after the First World War: Miller, Nin, Stein, Hemingway, Fitzgerald. My mother scorned anything written after the turn of the century, still read Swift, Walter Scott, and Dickens. But they enjoyed these arguments, and I saw even then that Gretchen fascinated my mother and represented a type of freedom that she sought for herself; Gretchen was a vegetarian, believed strongly in women's rights, was opinionated and independent.

Gretchen spoke loudly, in declarative sentences. "People in this part of the world are small minded," she said at the dinner table one day. "Small-minded farmers. If it does not involve the price of hogs, then it doesn't matter. This is what Iowa is like." She had discovered that there were no copies of *Tropic of Cancer* in the local library when she came to town, a book that had been banned for several years, and went on a semipublic crusade to get it on the shelves. "Sex," she said, "is nothing to be ashamed of. People here seem to entertain the idea that it doesn't happen at all. Certainly not in books. Censorship, that's what it is. People

want to impose their own small-mindedness on others. I'm not standing
for it." My father had smiled and looked uncomfortable and nodded
politely. Sex was not a subject ever discussed by my parents, and I felt
myself blushing when I heard this. But my mother had seemed pleased,
and had agreed with Gretchen.

Gretchen was in her early thirties, ten years younger than Peter. They
seemed very different. He was quiet and dry and pale, consumed by his
profession, and spoke infrequently and carefully. During the summer, he
went on field trips, and because he was often not there, this added to the
sense that he was a distant and reluctant figure. Gretchen, in contrast,
spoke her mind and did not seem to care what anyone else thought. She
was an anthropologist who had done her degree at Harvard, and now had
a position at the university. She had been on Mount McKinley, in Alaska,
and knew about maps and navigation, and how to climb using ropes.
"You know you're really alive when there's a chance that you'll die," was
the sort of thing she said about why she climbed, and, "When you're on a
mountain, you're closer to God." She had done her thesis work in Africa,
living for a year with villagers in southern Ethiopia where she observed
traditional health practices. While there, she contracted cholera and
malaria and ate concoctions of local herbs to get better. On the way to
Ethiopia, she had traveled through Egypt, and then had crossed the Red
Sea and spent time in the port cities of Assab and Massawa. Later she
traveled through Sudan and overland into the Central African Republic in a truck with German diamond smugglers. She was interested in
things that I had never thought about: languages and customs; the transmission of disease; the lost cities of Africa that had been the center of
the world. She seemed as exotic as the beetles in my father's collection
and I confess that I was as entranced by her as was my mother.

Gretchen often appeared at our house with no warning. She would
come in through the back door with a handful of flowers from her garden or jars of jam she had made herself. One afternoon, she let herself
in with a basket of groceries and made us dinner; when my mother came
home, Gretchen had several pots boiling on the stove, and had made
some Middle Eastern dishes. She wore long skirts made of brightly col-

ored material, muslin shirts, heavy silver earrings and bracelets. She often wore her hair, which was long and black, in thick braids. In Alex's last year of high school, she took out reference books from the university library that he needed for his classes, and brought them over after school. Sometimes I would find them sitting at the kitchen table together with the books spread out in front of them. She also brought books of Chinese poetry and Beat poetry, and could talk with some knowledge about these, and her ideas about social revolution. At the time, she seemed exciting and unconventional in a way that was beguiling to teenagers. Once I came home from school and found her sitting cross-legged with Alex on the roof outside his bedroom window. Both of them had their eyes shut. I stood at the window and watched them. After several minutes, Alex opened his eyes and saw me. "Meditation, little brother," he said, "is the pathway to enlightenment." He shut his eyes again. Gretchen remained motionless and silent, and I climbed out onto the roof and joined them. I sat and pretended to shut my eyes, too. I had no real idea what they were doing, but felt that I was on the threshold of a new kind of life, my life as an adult, sitting out on the roof of my parents' house.

I now see that my father saw Gretchen as a threat, a dangerous influence on his wife. My father had a very English sense of propriety, and a traditional view of what women should say and do. Gretchen did not want children and my father said that this was selfish and unreasonable. She was vehemently opposed to the Vietnam War, a cause that my father supported. "She is one of these hippies," my father said to us. "Very nice. No problem. But remember, this attitude did not give us the internal combustion engine or the miracle of antibiotics. These people with flowers in their hair shy away from progress utterly. Not a good thing. I am a reasonable man, but I will tell you this. When I want a neurosurgeon or a tax accountant, I will not be knocking on the door of a hippie, thank you very much."

Our house was on the top of a hill that sloped down to the Iowa River. My father kept a flat-bottomed aluminum boat in a small pine boat shed. He had been fishing on the Iowa River for years, although he had never been comfortable on the water. In India, he grew up with harrowing stories of an uncle and cousins who had gone down in a boat rounding the Cape of Good Hope on a night that was so black, you couldn't see your own hands in front of your face. He had been dropped into the municipal swimming baths in New Delhi a few times when he was young by overzealous relatives, and had emerged terrified and spluttering, with a dislike for swimming. Fishing on a boat represented America to him. By mastering his fear of water, he was overcoming his own childhood terrors. "I am a man," he liked to say, "who is best characterized by Mr. Darwin's description of the Chilean stag beetle, *Chaisognathus granti.* Bold and pugnacious."

That July I kept my bedroom windows open and lay in the heat unable to sleep. Every day was hot and the nights were still and silent at the top of the hill and filled with a strident chorus of cicadas in the reeds by the river. At night, I began hearing the thump of oars against the side of my father's boat. In the mornings, the boat and the oars would be wet and muddy. I began watching from my window at night, leaning out over the windowsill, looking onto the lawn until I saw the dim shape of my brother running down the hill. Then I pulled on shorts and went down to the river, hidden in the deep black under the trees, to watch Alex pull the boat into the water and row downstream. I lay on my chest on the damp cool ground with my ears pressed into the grass, alive with microscopic life. I waited there. Sometimes I went to sleep under the trees, waking with my cheeks hot and flushed and insects crawling on my bare legs. Three or four hours later, Alex would come back up the river, drag the boat out of the water, and run back up the hill.

I started waiting for Alex under the trees. I watched as he took the boat out a few nights a week, studied him as my father had shown me to observe the behavior of certain beetles in order to identify their feeding and mating habits. Even then, I had the patience of a naturalist. I liked the idea of being invisible, but a few days later Alex found me lying under the trees waiting for him. He came up behind me in the dark, sat on my chest and pinned my arms with his hands.

"What the hell are you doing here, Harry?" Alex whispered.

"Nothing," I said.

"You're following me, little shit."

"Where are you going with the boat?"

"None of your business, little brother." He put his knee into my chest and pressed down.

"I know."

"I'm training. That's what I'm doing. Training in the boat."

"I understand."

"If you tell anyone, I'll kill you, little shit. With my bare hands." He put one hand over my face and squeezed my cheeks hard. Then he got off me and ran down to the boat. I followed him and watched as he rowed out onto the river and slipped downstream. The end of his cigarette glowed red in the boat as it drifted away. I knew that Alex was meeting someone downriver, someone he wanted to keep secret. I had the urge to shout something important across the water, something to show that I knew, but could do nothing more than stand and listen to the insects in the grass around me, thousands of them, sending signals out into the night.

When I review that summer, I see clearly, with the benefit of distance and wisdom, that I wanted to be my brother. I was quiet and awkward, while Alex seemed confident and able to master with ease everything he attempted. He was a natural athlete, excelled at any sport he tried, had run the hundred-yard dash in under eleven seconds the year before. His schoolboy trophies for basketball and tennis, small gold-plated figurines on Bakelite plinths, were arranged on the mantelpiece. That summer he had begun going out with the varsity cyclists on weekends, riding with them in close formation across the rolling farmland for five or six hours at a time.

There was an assurance about Alex that I coveted. He was comfortable talking to girls. It was quite plausible that he would go out at night in a boat. My mother said that Alex was dangerous because he was so good looking. He had eyes like a girl, she said, like the daughter she never had.

I was not physical. I was a reader and noticed small things: insects and plants; where birds nested; when trains ran. I was shortsighted and wore heavy spectacles. My father told me, only half joking, that I looked like Mahatma Gandhi with hair. Round faced, small bodied, and stick legged. I often had a sense of how little I understood my brother, his confidence, the feeling that everything he did was certain. I thought of him as a complicated watch or an intricate machine with a hidden mechanism.

There was something contained about Alex that seemed to terrify my parents. They avoided him, didn't want to get in his way, knew he smoked cigarettes but never challenged him about it. The summer of 1968 he was more of a lodger than a brother. He came and went as he pleased, went to parties in Chicago for the weekend, had friends who would pull up the gravel drive in their own cars with loud music playing. He got up late and lay around smoking cigarettes outside in the afternoon, languid and contemplative. Girls sometimes came to the house, too, some of whom I recognized from high school, and others whom I had never seen. Alex was nonchalant with these girls, affected a sort of casual disdain with them that I was convinced made him more desirable. He would take them down to the river and go out in my father's aluminum boat, rowing slowly with a burning cigarette between his lips. If he wanted to impress them, he would start the outboard motor and speed up and down the river for a mile or two. When he was alone, he often went fishing on the river in the afternoon, with my father's tackle, and would spend hours floating slowly downstream in the boat.

Now Alex was going out at night for a secret rendezvous. I knew his secret and felt somehow closer to my brother as a consequence. In the afternoons, I watched him on the water from my bedroom window with a pair of my father's binoculars. I looked at myself in my bedroom mirror and tried to master the self-possession that I saw in Alex. But all I saw was what my father saw: Mahatma Gandhi with hair. I had seen footage of Gandhi on the Salt March, scrawny, thin boned, as busy and wound up as a sugar ant, but without much appeal to members of the opposite sex. My heavy spectacles did not help and I tried taking them off and navigating without them. That summer I pulled out my father's anatomy books and studied the sections on the female reproductive tract. I had a reasonable grasp of the surface anatomy, understood the blood supply and the basic mechanics, and felt as if this understanding would somehow help me learn to attract girls.

Perhaps this was the vanity of a bookish young man; I have always felt that by understanding something completely, I should be able to master it. I was reading *Gray's Anatomy* on the grass by the river one afternoon when Alex came up behind me and pulled the book out of my hands. He lay down next to me and shaded his face from the sun with the open book.

"Harry," Alex said, "you are approaching women the way our father approaches his beetles." His voice was muffled under the heavy leather-bound text.

I blushed and said, "I'm just reading."

"It's not what you know," Alex said. "It's what you do."

"You're Casanova, I suppose. The greatest lover the world has ever seen," I said.

"That's *Mr.* Casanova to you, little brother."

"I'm only five years younger than you, I should point out. Hardly little."

"You're not little. Although I am big. Enormous, in fact." Alex lifted the book from his eyes and squinted at me. "Just joking," he said.

I looked into the water. A line of ducks was paddling downstream.

"I'm just not like you," I said and got up. "I don't have secrets."

"What do you know about secrets?" Alex said, but I turned and walked away up the hill. I remember that moment quite vividly, because I felt for the first time that I had some important knowledge that gave me a certain power over Alex, and that made him take notice of me.

At the dinner table that night, the sense that I held some essential secret about Alex was reinforced. My father pulled out a letter from his eldest brother, Abdul, also a physician, who now lived in Bombay. He smoothed the handwritten letter flat on the table and put on his reading glasses.

"Let me tell you what Abdul says in this letter," he said and read: "'I have given up my private practice, because I can no longer countenance the conditions for people here. There are five or six hundred thousand people in this city who sleep on the pavements at night wrapped in blankets or shawls. I have decided that I will help them.'" He stopped reading and looked over his glasses. "What do you think of that?" he said. I had met my uncle Abdul on a handful of occasions when he came through the States for medical conferences. I remember a tall man with black eyes who rarely spoke.

"Abdul is acting on his conscience," my mother said. "Good for him."

But this was not about Abdul. My father sat back in his seat with both hands on the table in front of him. "You may recall," he said, "the words of the great American man of letters, Mr. Mark Twain. He was in Bombay in 1896. Driving through the streets at night he said, and I quote, 'Everywhere on the ground lay sleeping natives — hundreds and hundreds. They lay stretched at full length and tightly wrapped in blankets, head and all. Their attitude and rigidity counterfeited death.'"

"That was Mark Twain?" I said.

"Mr. Mark Twain, Harry. Did you hear? *'On the ground lay sleeping natives — hundreds and hundreds.'*" He sat forward and slapped the table with his open palm, then reached over and grabbed me by the elbow. "Don't you see, Harry? Don't you see?" He clasped my arm firmly and shook it. "Nothing has changed in seventy-two years. Do you see? Nothing, whatsoever, has changed in seventy-two years!"

"Things change slowly there," my mother said.

"Things never change there," my father said. "Life is less valuable there. Don't you see? What did independence mean? What is a person, there? What are ten people? Nothing at all."

"Does anyone want dessert?" my mother said. "I have ice cream with chocolate sauce."

My father let go of my arm and stared at my mother. "And where did that ice cream and chocolate sauce come from?" he said. "Why can we enjoy ice cream and chocolate sauce, while the people of Bombay sleep in the gutter?"

"We have a fridge?" Alex said.

"We have a constitution," my father said.

"The constitution of an ox," Alex said.

"Flippancy," my father said, "is cheap. I am talking about human rights. You have never had to think about it. It is too easy to take all of this for granted. You have nothing to be worrying about apart from your basketball and your girlfriend."

"Girlfriends," I said, too quickly. And then added, "He has more than one."

"I'm surprised you know what a girlfriend is, Harry," Alex said suddenly. He blushed, and I could see immediately that I had embarrassed him.

"The point is," my father went on, staring fixedly at his hands, "it is the system in India that needs to be changed. The entire system. I want you boys to understand that."

"Casanova," I said under my breath, but my father did not appear to hear me and continued staring at his hands.

"Samuel Clemens," my mother said as she got up from the table. "That was his real name, I believe."

A few days later, well after midnight, I awoke to find Alex in my bedroom. He was standing absolutely still with his arms folded, looking out of the window. It was a hot night and the window was open. I fumbled with my glasses and put them on.

"What are you doing?" I whispered.

"Thinking," Alex said.

"I understand," I said.

Alex climbed out of the window and sat on the sloping roof. I followed him out, crawling across the smooth warm shingles on all fours. The river sparkled at the bottom of the hill, below us. Alex took two cigarettes from the pocket of his sweatpants. He gave one to me, and I took it, and held it awkwardly in my palm. Alex lit the two cigarettes, pulling on his own until the end glowed bright red. He sucked the smoke deep into his lungs. I let the cigarette burn in my hand.

"Tell me what you know," Alex said through a mouthful of smoke.

"You're going to see someone in the boat," I said. "That's obvious."

"I'm going to see a girlfriend."

"Why do you have to go out and see her at night? Let her come over."

"She doesn't want to come over."

"Sounds weird to me," I said and felt ash from the cigarette drop onto the back of my hand.

Alex took a long drag on his cigarette. "I don't want you telling anyone."

"I won't tell anyone," I said.

"Stop watching me," Alex said and exhaled loudly. A freight train moved silently across the plain below us, throwing a thin beam of light into the dark.

"Why do you have to be so mysterious?"

"It's for your own good, little brother. Honestly."

"Are you doing it?" I let the cigarette drop onto the roof with a tiny explosion of red ash.

"Yes, we're doing it."

"I hope you're using protection."

Alex lit another cigarette. "You sound very sophisticated, little brother," he said, "but you don't know what you're talking about."

"Missionary. Doggy style. I know all that. The Kama Sutra was invented in India, for Christ's sake."

"Not by any of our relatives, I think, Harry. Not by a Maroon."

Alex coughed and looked up at the sky. "Every star is a wish made a million years ago. Do you remember that, little brother? You told me that. You used to know all the names of the constellations, too."

"I still know them."

"It doesn't mean anything, really. I don't think it does."

"The things I remember?"

"Sex, Harry. Don't get hung up about it."

I took off my glasses and wiped the lenses on my T-shirt. A thin breeze blew around us on the roof. "I'm not hung up," I said.

"You're different, Harry."

"What's that supposed to mean?"

"Don't try and be like me. I'm not like you."

Alex finished his second cigarette and crawled back inside. I lay on the roof and tried to imagine the woman that my brother was going to meet. Perhaps she came out onto the river in a boat to meet him. I had met some of Alex's girlfriends, but this girl was different. She was only available at night. She never came to see Alex. She was likely to be beautiful, it seemed certain to me, shy, inaccessible. Perhaps they took the boat down the river, away from the houses, and went into the uncleared forest down there. There was something wild about a girl who would meet only at night on the river and who didn't want to be seen. There was an element of abandon to it, a sense that nothing else mattered. I found myself imagining an Indian girl with long hair and black eyebrows who was fluent with the diagrams in the Kama Sutra.

I sat in the dark on the roof for a long time. Then I crawled inside, took a pair of heavy tailor's scissors from the worktable in the beetle museum, and walked down the hall to Alex's room. The door was slightly ajar and I put my ear to the crack and listened carefully and then gently pushed the door open and slid inside. I stood absolutely still for a moment and looked at Alex in bed. His face and arms were visible in the gray light through the window. I went slowly across the floor on my toes and kneeled down by the bed. The scissors were heavy in my hand. I breathed lightly through my mouth and examined my brother's face on the pillow, the round jaw, the high forehead and arched eyebrows visible in the dim light, his black hair flared around him on the pillow. When he was asleep, Alex looked like a child, preposterously young and innocent, something quite removed from his conscious self.

I listened to Alex breathing. I waited there for a long time and then shuffled forward carefully on my knees. When I was close enough, I extended one hand and very slowly took a strand of my brother's hair between my fingers, lifted it up from the pillow, and cut the hair with the scissors. I was sweating under my T-shirt. The hair felt sharp and dry in my palm. I eased back from the bed and moved slowly to the door. In my own room, I ran the thick square of black hair between my finger and thumb, felt the fine filaments in my fingers, and lay down with it in my hand. It was only as I drifted into sleep that I realized why I had gone into my brother's room. I had wanted him to wake up.

That's what I had wanted. I had wanted Alex to find me there, standing by his bed in the dark, watching him with the scissors in my hand.

When Alex was fifteen, it was clear that he was going to be a champion. That year he captained his high school basketball team and they won a state championship, in the last five seconds of play, with a long basket thrown by Alex from center court. I sat with my father to watch the final. We sat high on bleacher seats in the auditorium, surrounded by a cheering crowd. Alex was carried around the court on the shoulders of the team. When he walked off the court, he seemed to me to be taller and brighter than anyone else. We had to wait half an hour to get close to him. Other parents shook my father's hand. Watching Alex in the crowd, black haired, quite unselfconscious, I realized that my brother was beautiful. I saw him for a moment as an outsider, the way other people saw him, as an untarnished vision, and in that moment understood everything that I would never be able to be.

We drove home in the Oldsmobile and my father recounted every key play of the match. Alex sat in the front seat with his feet up on the glove compartment and his arms thrown over the back of the seat. His hands were light brown and broad, and he tapped the upholstery with his fingers. Watching him laughing with my father, I felt lighter than I had ever felt, as if I had been released from a terrible burden. I knew that afternoon that I would never be able to compete with my brother.

When we got home from the game, we pulled on shorts and ran down to the river. In the fading light, we jumped into the muddy brown water. Alex swam out into the middle of the stream with long slow strokes. I dove in, touched the bottom with my hands, and climbed back onto the dock. The wood was warm and dry and I lay on my back staring at the darkening sky. I shut my eyes for a moment and imagined my brother drowning. I visualized what I would need to do to save him: how I would dive from the dock, the number of strokes I would need to reach the middle of the river, how I would clasp him around the chest from behind to keep his head above water. I went through the actions in my mind, imagined pulling him back to the bank against the current, dragging him up onto the grass by the arms, and clearing his mouth with my finger, the way I had learned in swimming class. If needed, I would pinch my brother's nose, tilt his head backward, and blow air into his mouth from my own mouth. Growing up, I sometimes imagined that I was all that stood between Alex and disaster. When I was alone, I reviewed accident scenarios in my mind, felt better when I thought of my brother as a series of rehearsed actions, planned and choreographed in advance.

I stood up and balanced on the end of the dock. The water in front of me looked as solid and smooth as glass in the twilight. Alex was swimming toward me across the river. I listened to the sound of my brother breathing and the quiet splash of water as he swam.

Alex came up to the dock and said, "The way you stand there watching me, you'd think you were a lifeguard, little brother. Ready for action."

"I'm just watching."

"I like the idea, though. My own personal lifeguard. Would you jump in and save me, Harry?"

"You're a better swimmer than me. You're not going to need saving."

Alex pulled himself up onto the dock and blew water from his nose. He sat on the edge and grabbed me around one ankle.

"If you wanted me to stop playing basketball, Harry, you know I would."

"What's that supposed to mean?"

"People make a big deal of it, but it doesn't really mean anything to me. I don't *believe* in it, really, Harry. I don't think it makes me any different from you."

"I don't want you to stop playing."

"I know that. But you could, Harry, that's the point."

"You don't have to feel sorry for me. I'm all right."

"I know you're all right. I'm just saying that being brothers is more important than being able to throw a basketball."

"You're hurting my ankle," I said.

"You're smart, Harry. I know that. All I'm saying is, don't let yourself think for a minute that basketball is more important than having a brain. I don't think it is."

"If you're good at something, you should do it. You don't have to apologize," I said.

"I'll stop if you want me to." Alex held my ankle and smiled up at me. I tried to lift my leg but could not move it in my brother's grip. I stood there, anchored at the end of the dock, unable to pull away until my brother decided to release me. Sometimes I feel, even now, as if he never let go.

The next day, the day after the state basketball final, a journalist and a photographer from the local newspaper came to interview Alex at home. They took his picture in front of the trophies on the mantelpiece and then sat him down in the living room and asked him questions. I stood watching for a while, and then my father tapped me on the shoulder and led me up to his study. He went to the bookshelf and got down an original copy of Darwin's autobiography, written in 1876. Darwin, he told me, almost did not go on his famous voyage on the HMS *Beagle*, the voyage that would ultimately lead to his theory of natural selection, because Fitzroy, the captain of the boat, had not liked the shape of Darwin's nose. He sat back in his desk chair and read to me from the book.

> Afterwards on becoming intimate with Fitzroy, I heard that I had run a very narrow risk of being rejected, on account of the shape of my nose! He was an ardent disciple of Lavater, and was convinced that he could judge a man's character by the outline of his features; and he doubted whether anyone with my nose could possess sufficient energy and determination for the voyage. But I think he was afterwards well-satisfied that my nose had spoken falsely.

My father closed the book and sat back in the chair. "Something as superficial as a nose could have prevented us from having one of the greatest scientific endeavors of history," he said to me. "The absurdity of it is paralyzing." He sat silent for a moment. I stood and leaned against the desk. Finally my father sat forward on his seat and said quietly, "You and I have noses like that, partner," he said. "They may not be attractive. They may not be noticed in a crowd. But by God they will not get in our way." I see now that he was trying to make me feel better, to be charitable. But at the time it did nothing but reinforce my own sense of inadequacy. It confirmed in my own mind that I had no natural talent, that my ambitions needed to be smaller, that I was quite ordinary. I had none of my brother's abilities and would never be noticed the way he was. I was not attractive. My talent lay in my ability to understand things by studying them. If I examined facts closely enough, in sufficient detail, and with a modicum of application, then I could invariably work them out.

That summer I went into my brother's bedroom when he was not there. I walked around the room and itemized his scanty possessions: neatly organized piles of shoes and boots for basketball, soccer, cycling, and tennis; bats and rackets and gloves; lines of *National Geographic* and *Time* magazines; a purple lava lamp; stacks of Motown singles and rock albums; and several packets of condoms slipped into a sock and hidden at the back of his underwear draw. I regularly counted the condoms and then put them back carefully where I found them. Alex's bedspread had been used by my father as a child in Delhi, and I felt as if this piece of heavy cloth carried the weight of my family's past in India. I lay on the bed and imagined being my brother.

I was lying on Alex's bed one afternoon, listening to his Rolling Stones singles, when he came home early from cycling.

"What are you doing here, little brother?" he said, turning down the volume on the small mono record player. "This is my room."

"Free yourself from the shackles of materialism," I said and pretended to close my eyes. Alex sat on the floor, took off his shoes and shirt, and began doing sit-ups.

After a few minutes, he said, "Something's going on between Ishfaq and Shabana."

"Right," I said.

"That's cool," Alex said, exhaling loudly with each sit-up. "They need to sort it out. We need to keep out of it."

"Let them deal with it," I said.

"You got it."

"Ishfaq doesn't want to change, does he?" I said.

"He's the one who wanted to come to this country," Alex said. "So he should understand what that means."

"What does it mean?"

"Live and let live, Harry. Fulfill your potential or something like that. Shit or get off the pot. Everyone deserves an equal chance. Shabana does not get a very good deal, Harry. She can't get a credit card without Ishfaq's signature. She doesn't work either. It's still very traditional."

I sat up on the bed and said, "There are five rubbers in your drawer today. That's three less than last week."

Alex kept doing his exercises on the floor. "You should be an accountant, Harry, or a bookkeeper," he panted. "I admire your attention to detail."

"Someone has to keep an eye on things."

Alex stopped the sit-ups and let himself fall back flat with his hands under his head. "It's got nothing to do with you, Harry," he said.

"They're just rubbers. All I did was count them."

"Our parents, Harry. You're not the problem. It's between them. We have to let them work it out."

"They may not work it out," I said.

"That's possible," he said. I got off the bed, took Alex's hands in mine, and pulled him to his feet. "I didn't mean to upset you," Alex said as I turned and left the room. Tears were running down my cheeks, tears that I did not expect and that I could not stop, falling like summer rain from a cloudless sky.

In July, my father received a package of beetles from Africa. They came from Mr. Roland Hadjeebhoy, a coffee exporter who lived in Kenya. My father had been put in touch with him by members of his distant family, some of whom now lived in East Africa, and had been corresponding with him for years. Roland Hadjeebhoy claimed to be able to procure beetles from all over the African continent through an extended network of paid natives who worked on commission, and every year he sent my father new specimens for his collection.

This was an occasion of great excitement for my father, and I am sure that he saw the new beetles as something that would bring us together as a family. He refused to open the box until he could have Peter Tappero with him, and left it sitting on the dining room table for a week. Peter and Gretchen came to lunch on a hot Sunday afternoon. We ate outside under the Norway pine tree in our backyard. After lunch, I brought the box from the house and put it carefully in front of my father. He clapped his hands together, stood up to get a better angle of attack, and began cutting the cardboard with a fruit knife.

"These are illegal immigrants from Africa," my mother said.

"Not being alive, I am not entirely sure that they are immigrants at all," my father said, using the knife like a saw.

"Not strictly speaking, I suppose. Not like us. We are the real immigrants," my mother said.

"All of us are immigrants, aren't we?" Gretchen said. "It's just a question of how far you want to go back. Peter's family were Sicilians."

"Precisely," my father said. "We have been here for fourteen years, Shabana. The time will come when you're not an immigrant anymore. Look at Harry here. Harry is fully American. Is that not right, partner?"

"Yes, partner," I said.

"It's sad," Gretchen said.

"What is sad?" my mother said.

"That we are sitting here staring at these poor dead things."

My father stood with the knife raised in one hand. "Remember, they do not have a higher brain," my father said. "They cannot feel sad. They are also dead."

"But we can feel sad for them," Gretchen said. "Peter has heard me say this before. But, really, I can see no sense in collecting them."

"They represent," my father said, "a record of the species. Without a record, we cannot begin to understand them."

"There are so many important things to do, though," my mother said. "People are rioting in this country, for God's sake. Vietnam is a terrible mess. And here we are scrutinizing these insects that in my youth were considered to be household pests. It is silly."

"It is a science," my father said, concentrating on the box in front of him. "And forgive me, but it is not silly. There are a thousand interesting facts about beetles, each of which teaches us something important about the nature of life."

"Meanwhile the country burns around us," my mother said.

"Revolution!" Alex said and tapped his fork on the table.

My father got the box open and pulled wads of newspaper and cotton out of the top. There were four large beetles inside, pinned to a display board. He put the board in the middle of the table and looked down at it with his hands behind his back.

"A pair of African Goliath beetles if I am not mistaken," he said.

"Sap eaters," Peter said. "Magnificent specimens."

"Terrific," my father said. "They are big fellows. Super."

Each beetle was the size of my hand. They had black-and-white-striped thoraces and smooth, speckled elytra, with hairy middle and hind legs and small pointed mouthparts. The legs were long and black with sharp hooklike feet.

"You know that beetles have a long history of being used as decorative items," my father said. "Ladies in India and Sri Lanka, for example, kept the iridescent green beetles of the species *Chrysochroa ocellata* as pets. They wore them on festive occasions. They pinned them onto their clothes. At home they treasured them, you know. Bathed and fed them, and kept them in cages. They were not seen as repulsive."

"I wouldn't wear a beetle if you paid me," Alex said. "Would you, Harry?"

"I'd think about it."

"Yes, but would you *do* it. You can think about it for as long as you like. I don't think you would," Alex said.

"I might."

My mother stacked the plates. "Ridiculous," she said under her breath.

"Let me help you clear the table," Gretchen said. She stood up and began collecting plates. She had taken off her sandals and was barefoot. She came around the table to take the plates from us. The beetles looked otherworldly and grotesque on the white tablecloth and small flying insects hung over them in a cloud. Gretchen walked carefully on the mat of sharp brown pine needles under the tree and when she got to our side of the table, she put the plates down, picked up one of the beetles, and held it up to her neck.

"I think they could be very becoming," she said. "There's something powerful about them. Very primeval." She walked up and down in front of the table, holding the large beetle in front of her.

"I agree," my father said. "Look at the scarab in ancient Egypt. That little fellow was virtually a God."

Gretchen held up the large black insect. "And it could make a very serviceable hat," she said and laughed. She twirled around a few times and lifted the beetle up and down above her head. She had been drinking wine with the meal and I suddenly realized that she was drunk. She was slightly unsteady on her feet. She bowed extravagantly and then lost her balance and toppled sideways onto the ground.

"For God's sake," Peter said and got to his feet suddenly.

Gretchen lay on the ground laughing. She rolled over onto her back with the beetle in her outstretched hand. My father took it from her, held it gingerly in both hands, and put it carefully on the table.

"It is the heat, perhaps," my father said. "Help her up, Harry."

Gretchen pulled herself up onto her elbows. "I'm sorry," she said and shook her head. "I lost my balance for a moment there."

"Nothing to worry about," my father said. "Harry will take you inside for a while. Out of the sun." I could see that he was furious. He stood very still with both hands gripping the sides of the table.

"Are you sure you're all right?" Peter said to her.

"Yes," she said.

"Go inside and wash your face," my mother said. "You will feel better."

"I'm fine."

I helped her up and Peter came around the table and brushed the dry pine needles off the back of her dress. She pulled her hair away from her eyes and smiled at him. I led her across the lawn to the house. The lawn was spotted with daisies that shone bright yellow in the sun. Bees hung in the flowers and flew around our ankles. She walked carefully

through the grass, lifting her bare feet high, leaning on my elbow. Halfway
to the house, Gretchen laughed again, for no reason.

It was dark and cool inside and I took Gretchen into the kitchen. I
poured her a glass of water which she drank down without pausing.

"I'm feeling fine," Gretchen said. I stood with my back to the sink.
Gretchen seemed dangerous, reckless in a way that I imagined made her
independent and unpredictable. I wanted to impress her.

"Perhaps you would like to see my father's jewel beetles," I said.

"More beetles?" she said and laughed.

"They are much better than the ones outside. Very pretty. They're
worth seeing."

I took her upstairs to the beetle museum and showed her the colorful insects of the Buprestidae family behind the glass-topped display cases.
I recited some of the names: the brilliant-green *Sternocera aurosignata*
of Southeast Asia; the yellow-banded *Demochroa gratiosa* from Malaysia;
the green-and-gold-striped *Chalcophora japonica oshimana* from Japan.
Gretchen nodded and listened and I could see that she was swaying
slightly when she stood still. She smelled strongly of wine.

I took her into my father's study and got two of the classification texts
from the bookshelf. Then I sat down at the desk and told her that I would
find the names of the two new African beetles. Gretchen stood and looked
out the window. She was silent for a moment and then said, "You know,
of course, that your mother is a very intelligent woman."

I said, "Yes."

"She could do anything she put her mind to. Perhaps a doctor or a
lawyer. Certainly a profession."

"I know," I said.

"This is how it is for a lot of women. But they must go on regardless."

I turned the pages of the textbook and pretended to concentrate.

"I think you do understand, Harry. That things are changing. The next
generation will be different. It's up to you to give your mother permission."

"Permission to what?" I said, still looking down at the book in front
of me.

"Permission to be herself. To take her own path. To find herself, Harry."

"I get you," I said.

"Man is born free and everywhere he is in chains," she said. She walked over to the desk, bent over, and gave me a kiss on the cheek. Her lips were warm. "I've been drinking," she whispered confidentially, and then left the room.

I looked out of the window. My father and Peter Tappero stood at the table under the tree, bending over the beetles. Alex was lying flat on the grass in the shade of the tree. My mother had walked down the hill and was looking out at the river. As I watched her by the moving water, she seemed separate from the garden and the beetle collection and the hot afternoon in a way that was quite fundamental. For an instant, I understood what I often saw but did not notice — that she did not want to be there at all.

The desk was smooth under my fingertips and the leaves of the books were crisp and filled with fine print. Something indefinable in my life felt different and uncomfortable. I looked out into the bright sunlight and watched Gretchen join my mother by the river. They were still there talking when I decided the new beetles were *Goliathus goliatus* and *Goliathus meleagris*, named after the giant vanquished by David in the Old Testament, often found feeding on the sap exuded from the wounds in certain hardwood trees.

In 1968, it felt as if the world was coming apart. It was the year of the Tet offensive and the breakdown of the Vietnam peace talks in Paris. It was the year the Reverend Martin Luther King Jr. was assassinated, with rioting in a hundred cities. And it was the year Bobby Kennedy was shot moments after declaring victory in the California Democratic primary. We saw the war in Vietnam on the television every day. In May, we saw the antiwar peace march in Chicago broken up by police wielding clubs against civilians.

My mother began listening to the BBC World Service news, morning and evening, sitting at the kitchen table with a notepad. She took notes on every broadcast, writing long, numbered lists in purple ink with her fountain pen. She kept the notes in a drawer in the kitchen. "Information," she said to us, "is power. If you don't understand what is happening, then you can do nothing about it." She watched Walter Cronkite on television, staring into the flickering black-and-white images, shaking her head and making clucking noises with her tongue. She bought two maps, one of the continental United States, and one of Vietnam, Cambodia, and Laos. She hung the maps on the kitchen wall so she could follow reports of the war in Vietnam and of domestic unrest. My father rushed in and out to work. When the radio was on, he would ask my mother to write down the cricket scores from England.

At the bottom of the lawn was a large fig tree, planted in the 1850s by the original owners of the house, and my mother had claimed it as her own. The tree sat by the river and cast big heavy boughs out over the stream. In the summer, it was laden with figs and every morning and evening filled with hundreds of birds, fighting for the ripe fruit.

When I was young, my mother started climbing the tree and sitting in it. The broad boughs arched over the river and provided some safe flat places to sit, and there was a place about twenty feet up where the limbs made a kind of natural seat. High among the leaves, my mother could sit and be invisible. She sat in the tree for hours, suspended over the water, looking out over the river and off into the farming country. Eventually my father made a series of cut-wood steps up the trunk and along the limbs to make it easier to climb. My mother disappeared on summer afternoons and sometimes went up the tree at night, sitting in the swaying boughs, surrounded by the glossy green leaves and the fruity aroma of sticky figs. When I was twelve years old, I asked her what she was looking at when she sat in the tree and she told me that she saw the Arabian Sea. I am looking at the Arabian Sea, she said, the boats and the fish and the people on the Arabian Sea. She told me that she was thinking of home and that from the tree it was possible to see it, all of it. I had believed her absolutely, and gone up the tree myself to sit in the same place. In the gently rocking branches, smooth and gray under my fingers, all I saw, of course, was the river, and the marshy banks, and the silver grain silos in the distance. But I realized then that it was possible for things that could not be seen to be important.

That summer I found my mother sitting in the tree more often. The day Bobby Kennedy was shot she sat up in the tree half the night. I understand now that she was not hiding from us, that she was getting a different perspective, working things out. The world must have seemed to be in a state of violent flux. But when I was fourteen years old, the fig tree terrified me, and I imagined that one day my mother would simply not come down at all, that she would prefer being away from us altogether.

At the end of August, the Democratic National Convention took place in Chicago and we watched the antiwar rallies in Grant Park and Lincoln Park and then the pitched battles between the demonstrators and National Guardsmen. I felt as if we were watching a war action in another country entirely. There was a sense of impending doom. "All these people want," my mother said, "is to express their opinion in a peaceful way about the war. It is a scandal. Do these politicians want to pretend that nothing is happening over there? That no one is dying?" Hubert Humphrey was voted the Democratic presidential candidate, and on the last day of the convention, the peace plank proposed for the party platform was voted down. My mother was furious. My father told her that it would all blow over, and that she should not get upset. This prompted my mother, on the night of August 28, to run down to the river and fling her green card, the only symbol of America that she possessed, out into the water.

My father brought a flashlight from the house. We could still see the card floating on the surface a few feet from the end of the dock, and Alex swam out and got it. "She would not want to be losing that," my father said. "It would be most regrettable. Most regrettable indeed. In the morning, she will see reason."

I took the card, wiped it dry on my shorts, and climbed up into the fig tree. The wood was smooth and cool and smelled like rotting fruit. My mother was sitting up in a fork in the branches, looking out over the river.

"We found your green card," I said.

"Thank you, Harry."

"You're angry about the war, aren't you."

"We all should be. It is ridiculous."

"Free yourself from the yoke of convention," I said.

My mother was silent for a moment. "Where did you hear that?" she said.

"I can't remember," I said.

She put her hand on my shoulder. "You're right," she said.

Everything seemed altered after the Democratic convention. The next day I came home from my swimming class late in the afternoon and found Alex, Gretchen, and my mother sitting in the living room with a reefer, listening to music. Gretchen was sitting cross-legged on the floor with Alex. My mother was sitting on the sofa, wearing a bright green sari. Gretchen had lit several sticks of incense and put them in glasses on the coffee table. Fine tendrils of blue smoke rose toward the ceiling. I sat on the couch next to my mother and watched Alex take a deep draw from the reefer and hand it to Gretchen.

"Harry, we are trying something new," my mother said to me.

"Raising our consciousness," Alex said through a mouthful of smoke.

"Neat," I said.

The music from the stereo was quite loud. Gretchen had brought over the Beatles' *Magical Mystery Tour* album and "All You Need Is Love" was playing. Gretchen handed the reefer to my mother, who held it between her middle and index fingers like a cigarette and took three short puffs. "Very interesting," she said. She bent toward me and whispered, "Not for you, Harry. You're too young. Perhaps when you're older." I had, of course, seen people smoke dope at school, it was not uncommon, and I knew what they were doing. I dutifully handed the reefer back to Alex, who was tapping his knees in time to the music.

"They're English, you know," my mother said to me.

"The Beatles," Gretchen said. "Peter collects the insects. I collect the LPs."

"Very innovative," my mother said, "very free. This is what Mozart might have seemed like in the eighteenth century."

"Cool," Alex said, taking another long draw on the reefer.

"Things are so different for young people today," my mother said. "You know, I did not see your father before our wedding day. Our parents decided we were suited. They arranged the marriage. This seems so far-fetched, does it not? It seems like something that might have happened in the dark ages."

"I know," I said.

"We are a product of our past," Gretchen said. "But we make our own future." She took a mouthful of smoke and handed the reefer back to my mother, who had another puff and whispered to me, "I need to be start-ing dinner." I passed the reefer to Alex, who got up and put the needle back to the first song on side two. It was John Lennon singing "I Am the Walrus."

"Interesting lyrics," my mother said after a while. "Sharpened by the use of primal rhythms."

"It's a kind of musical montage," Gretchen said. "At the end of the piece, several lines from Shakespeare's *King Lear* have been super-imposed onto the recording. Act four, scene six, I believe. They use a full orchestra, too. Is this not a wonderful joining of the new with the classical?"

My mother smiled. Alex sat on the floor and laughed. "Of course he's not really a walrus," he said. "And he can't really sit on a cornflake. The lines are not supposed to be taken literally."

"And what on earth is an eggman?" my mother said as she stood up. "A person who has the responsibility for delivering eggs, I suppose. This is quite fascinating, too."

The song ended and Gretchen got up to turn the record over. My mother went into the kitchen and I went upstairs. It was dark and cool on the landing and I went into my parents' bedroom. Everything about my parents felt solid when I stood in their bedroom. The bed was large and oak framed. I noted the objects arranged along the top of my father's chest of drawers, and can still remember them: piles of coins and paper currency; a pocket otoscope; a ball of rubber bands; a gold tie clip in the shape of a serpent; a silver nail clipper with the nail file extended; a small pile of nail clippings; a blue plastic container of Metamucil; a small pair of scissors and a long black comb with fine plastic teeth; a packet of Q-tips (unopened) and another of corn pads (opened); and a shoehorn made of cream-colored ivory. When I saw these objects, carefully arranged, I saw myself more clearly and felt as if I was closer to my father.

I lay down on the bed and looked up at the ceiling. The pillow smelled vaguely of pomade and aftershave. A portable alarm clock ticked on the bedside table. The distant rumble of music came from downstairs. I felt drowsy and rolled onto my side, away from the door.

My father sat on a low stool on the other side of the bed watching me. He was wearing his pin-striped work suit.

"I got home early," he said. "I'm hiding."

I lay on the bed staring at him. "We're listening to the Beatles downstairs," I said.

My father nodded and stood up. He put his arms behind his back and looked out of the window. "Someone has to operate on the gallbladders of the world, Harry." He paused for a few seconds and then said, "Do you blame me?"

"Only if you blame me," I said.

"I have tried to do something useful," he said. "Do no harm. That is the code by which I have tried to conduct myself." He pushed open the window, put his head outside, and took a deep breath.

"A noble profession," I said.

My father laughed. "It is important to expose yourself to new things. I'm glad you do. I've never worried about you, partner. You understand the scientific method. You are perfectly sensible." He turned from the window, took off his tie, and undid the top button of his shirt.

"They're smoking an illegal substance."

My father walked to the closet, opened the door, and draped his tie carefully on the tie rack. "I am not a narrow-minded person," he said. "It seems as if things are changing, I know. But nothing ever really changes, partner. The most important things stay the same." He took off his jacket and hung it on a coat hanger. "The gallbladder, for example, will always sit in the right-upper quadrant of the abdomen. There will always be a common bile duct. Gallstones will always need to be removed." He took off his cuff links and dropped them onto the chest of drawers.

"Natural selection," I said and sat up on the edge of the bed.

"Fundamental," my father said. He sat on a chair, undid his shoelaces, and pulled off his shoes.

"The first law of thermodynamics."

"Indisputable."

"Gretchen thinks marriage is a yoke to keep women suppressed."

"Of course many rules are arbitrary. Of course they are. But that is what keeps us together. Shabana and I had an arranged marriage, yes. Our parents decided for us. But we trusted their judgment. We believed in it. It is all a question of belief. You see that, don't you, partner?"

My father stood in front of me in his socks. "I see that," I said.

"If you take away all the rules, then there is nothing left. It is like these trousers." He unbuckled his belt and tugged it off. "If we take away the anchor, there is nothing to hold the society together." The trousers fell to his ankles. "And what, then, are we left with, partner? What is the result?"

"Underwear," I said.

My father chuckled. "Anarchy," he said. "Chaos. Then you have bare hairy legs, partner. Apes is what you have. Primates fighting it out in the trees."

He changed into his casual slacks and a pair of sandals, then went over to a picture on the wall and tapped the glass with his fingernails. It was a photograph of himself, wearing a scarf and a white jacket, taken at Oxford in the nineteen thirties. He was standing in front of the Radcliffe Infirmary. "Look at that smile," he said to me, "that is the unabashed smile of a young man who believed that all he needed to know of the world was contained in the British Museum." In this frozen moment, there was a kind of youthful optimism and certainty. I found myself wishing that it was me in the photograph, bundled up against the cold on that day in England all those years ago, with a set of firm and unwavering beliefs.

"The Vietnam War is an immoral action that should be stopped," my mother said at lunch two days later. It was the Sunday following the Democratic National Convention and we were eating idlee sambaar outside, under the pine tree. Wasps with black legs came from the flowers and hovered over the bowls on the table. It was a very windy day and pine needles dropped onto the tablecloth.

"On the contrary," my father said, "I would not be standing in Alex's way if he wanted to join the army."

"A ridiculous notion," my mother said. "Pure nonsense. What Alex needs is an education."

"I'd have to consider enlisting," Alex said without looking up from his plate.

"How would you consider it? On the basis of what?" my mother said.

"Whether or not I believed in it," Alex said.

"There you are," my mother said. "There is nothing to believe in. Vietnam is a scandal."

"You would need to have your wits about you in the army," my father said to Alex, chewing vigorously and gesturing with knife and fork as he spoke. His gold watch slid up and down his arm as he reached for bowls on the table.

"Forget about it," my mother said. "The army is not for any rational person." Her fingernails clicked against the bowls of food. She pointed her fork at Alex as she spoke.

"And what does that mean?" my father said.

"It means what it means. You cannot think for yourself in the army. If they tell you to do something, then you must do it. Whether or not you think it is the right thing to do."

"But this is what the military is all about, Shabana. They give him orders and it is his business to follow them. Otherwise it is not the military. These things run on discipline."

"Nonsense. They run on blind stupidity, Ishfaq. I would advise that if the army tells you to do something that is likely to get you shot, then do not do it. You would be serving your country much better by remaining alive. Indeed, you would be serving your mother better by staying alive, darling." She smiled at Alex, and tapped his shoulder with the fork.

"He would have to follow his orders in the military, Shabana. Otherwise he is seen as coward. It is treason, my dear. Pure treason. They can court-martial him for it. It does not reflect well on the family. He is disgraced. No. It would be important to follow your orders, Alex, and pass me the water."

"What do you know about orders, Ishfaq? What orders have you ever followed? You have done as you pleased, as you well know, and now you are telling him about orders. You left home because of the fighting at partition. Now you are telling him that there is some merit in engaging in it in Vietnam. This is nonsense."

"What I saw in India was anarchy, Shabana. Loss of the rule of law. Absence of the democratic principles. The army here upholds these principles. There is a difference. They are fighting the red peril. Give me the chutney. Please."

"The red peril! What is the red peril? I'm not sure what this silly red-colored peril even is! What principles are being upheld by fighting this nonexistent thing, that has nothing whatsoever to do with America?" My mother spoke with her fork beating the air in front of her. "Tell me. Someone please tell me. It is not a childish game for goodness' sake. There are real guns and real bullets. It is our *real* son who would be going. There is no glory and it is not pretty. Go to college. Get an education. Alternatively, go to Canada. I know people there."

"Are you proposing that our son not do his bit for the country, Shabana? After everything this country has done for us? You see what is happening over there. The communists seek world domination. Give me that bowl." When he got angry, my father ate. He helped himself to thirds, filled his mouth with potato pancake and gulped water after every mouthful. Flecks of masticated food spun into the air in front of him when he spoke. He was sweating from the food.

My mother said, "Go to college. I advise it. He is only part American anyway. He is half Indian. He was raised as pacifist."

"He was raised to have some sense of right and wrong," my father said. "You have to be prepared to fight for what you believe in."

"You would let him go! This is ridiculous. Pure idiocy. Alex, you would regret it for the rest of your life." My mother stopped eating and gripped me firmly by the shoulder.

"Could you kill a man, Harry?" my mother asked me.

"Of course he could. If he had to, he could," my father said.

"Let Harry answer."

"I could kill a man," Alex said.

"Of course you could," my father said.

"It depends," I said and looked at my brother.

"Depends on what?" My mother stopped eating and looked at me with her elbows on the table and her chin resting on her hands.

"Well, if someone was going to kill me, then I suppose I'd have to think about it."

"'Think about it!'" My father spoke through a wad of pancake and chutney. "There is no time to think, Harry. Think and you are finished."

"I wouldn't think about it," Alex said.

"Of course not." My father sipped water and chewed loudly between sips.

"I told you he was pacifist. You see. He is pacifist!" my mother said.

"What I mean is, I'd think about it in advance. So I'd know what to do. Immediately," I said. "But I wouldn't choose to kill anyone."

"Harry, war is not kind. There is no time to think. You will have to shoot to kill. This is the rule when standing up for what you believe in," my father said.

"You sound like that John Wayne," my mother said. "You make it sound romantic, Ishfaq, like a Hollywood affair. It is not romantic. You should know better than all this John Wayneism. You have seen the consequences. In India. You have seen what it means."

"John Wayneism, nonsense. Killing in the heat of battle is a necessary thing," my father said. "We would have no peace unless there was war, Harry. He who hesitates is lost."

"Right," Alex said.

"Go to college!" my mother said, stacking the plates.

"Fight for your principles," my father said and then stood up from the table.

I followed my mother across the grass, into the house, carrying bowls. The grass was warm in the sun and then cold in the shadow cast by the house. Inside it was dark and the old floorboards creaked loudly as we walked into the kitchen. Yellow rubber gloves were draped on the sink. From the dark, cool kitchen, I watched my father and Alex walking down the hill in the sun. My father had his fishing gear.

My mother sat down at the table while I stacked the bowls and plates in the sink. Tears ran down her cheeks and dropped onto the table and fell onto the back of her hands.

"Harry," she said, "I am being stupid. Forgive me for these tears. I don't know. Ishfaq and I are having an argument. Forgive me for this."

"It's all right," I said and sat down next to her.

"I worry, Harry. Alex could be drafted. I feel it is worse because he is Indian in his blood. I don't think of myself as an American. Not really. And I don't think of Alex as an American either."

"He *is* American."

"I know. But I worry that we haven't given either of you enough to go on. Your father and I grew up Muslim, and we don't practice the religion, of course, but it gave us some sort of code for looking at the world. There are principles of decency in it that I think are very important. Even if you are not a religious person."

"You've been good parents."

"How will this help you in the army, Harry? You need something more if you are going to face being killed. This is what faith is for. I'm afraid that neither of you has any faith like this. It is terrible for me to think that you don't."

"Alex believes in the country. I believe in it, I guess."

"What has this got to do with the country? Learning how to run around with a gun? Look, I want to give you something." She got up and went over to a cupboard and reached up to the top shelf. She took out a fat book, bound in black leather, and handed it to me. "This is the Koran. It's my copy. This one is in English. I still read it, you know. From time to time. It gives me something. I'm not even sure what it gives me. But I grew up reading it and it makes a lot of sense."

I had never seen the Koran. I opened it and flicked through the pages, which were fine and crisp, densely packed with script.

"Don't let your father see it. Just take it. For my sake. Try reading it. You are not too young to begin."

I closed the book and held it on the palm of one hand. It was heavy, had a heft and weight that felt important. I had never seen this side of my mother. She never cried. She was a reader of newspapers, a listener to radio news. She had never seemed to need a faith, seemed self-contained and unassailable. I didn't know how to treat her when she was upset.

"All right," I said, and reached over and wiped the tears from her cheeks with the back of my hand. "I'll read it."

"Don't tell your father." My mother got up and went to the sink to do the dishes. I felt the weight of the book in my hands and looked at my mother's back and wondered whether I really understood her at all.

Upstairs, I concealed the teachings of the Prophet Muhammad in the back of my closet under a pile of *National Geographic* magazines. I shut the closet door and knew instinctively that I would not show the book to Alex, not because I was afraid that he would read it, but because I was afraid that he would not read it, reject it absolutely, attach no value to it at all.

I went into the beetle museum, selected several jewel beetles from a display case, and took them into my father's study. From the window, I saw my father and brother pushing the boat out onto the river. I switched on the lamp and took a pair of tweezers and a magnifying glass from a drawer. I examined the beetles carefully, confident that I could identify all the fine structural differences on my own.

BEETLES OF AFRICA

Eudicella gralli (Central Africa) — gray — 5 specimens
Fornasinus russus (Central Africa) — green and white — 5 specimens
Rhamphorrina splendens (Zimbabwe) — red — 10 specimens
Fornasinius russus (Central Africa) — dark green — 5 specimens

In the light thrown by the lamp, the small bright bodies of the beetles were smooth and perfect, each piece precise and interlocking, lengths and angles right, the colors impossibly vivid, each tiny hair or joint perfectly adapted to survival. But it was their color and beauty that struck me again. The iridescent, shimmering insects seemed so perfect that they appeared to have been molded and shaped by an artistic hand. Alone in the dark room, in the island of lamplight, with the river moving slowly at the bottom of the hill, I could understand how it had once been thought that something so perfect must have been created by a divine hand.

I knew that creation had been the predominant belief in the mid-nineteenth century when William Paley's *Natural Theology; or Evidences of the Existence and Attributes of the Deity* had been so influential, a book that my father kept and still read as evidence of man's innate gullibility. Darwin fought the church with his theory of natural selection, he told me, fought prevailing opinion with logic and reason. And this spirit was something my father took as a strategy for life. Think for yourself and do not be influenced by popular ideas or philosophies that have no basis in observable fact.

Now my mother had given me the Koran. I felt as if I had stumbled on an irreparable difference between my parents. It seemed impossible to describe blind faith to my father. How could he understand the need to believe in things that can never be seen? What to him were the distant past, dreams and miracles, all the unseen possibilities for the future?

I packed the beetles away and went down to the river. It was late in the afternoon and the sun was low in the sky. Fast-moving clouds cast shifting shadows across the surface of the river. I sat on the dock and watched the river and waited for my father and brother. They were still out in the boat when the sun went down. It was cool and damp in the twilight, and I walked back up the hill to the house.

My mother was working in the kitchen and I watched her through the window. She looked stern in the bright overhead light, held her head erect, and was stiff backed as she walked to and from the stove. I used to stand outside and watch her like this when I was growing up, and always thought she looked younger when she was alone, more like a girl. I walked around the house on the gravel path, under the heavy boughs of a row of maple trees, and went in through the front door. The house smelled like green curry and hot oil. Orderly piles of cut lime, tomatoes, spinach, and cauliflower were arranged on the kitchen table. My mother was sweating in the heat. The three silver bracelets on her wrist jangled as she cut vegetables at the table.

"Harry, you are late," she said. "I am in the thick of it. Things are under way."

"I see," I said.

"You look tired," she said, handing me a black-handled paring knife. "Chop something for me. The onions, please. "

She sat down at the table and ground cardamom and mustard seeds with a mortar and pestle. She leaned forward over the table as she ground the seeds and moved her arm as if she was tightening a screw. Her forearms were thin and muscular.

"Alex goes out in the boat at night," I said. "To see a girlfriend."

"I know, Harry. I was not born yesterday. This is what young men do."

"I don't mind," I said. The handle of the knife was slippery in my fingers.

"I'm sure she is a respectable girl," my mother said.

She kept grinding with the mortar and pestle. Her hair was pulled back from her face and held in a bun.

"I know you're angry," I said.

"I am frustrated, Harry. This is a testing time."

I cut the onion into heavy white chunks. The cooking and the cold metal of the pots and the smell of limes made me think of summer days, green leaves, hot glass in the windowpanes.

"I know you're different from Ishfaq," I said. "I know you don't like him very much."

My mother took a sip of tea from a china cup on the table and looked at me over the rim of the cup. I had never been able to argue with her. She had a way of achieving finality with a sentence, a tone of voice, an unconscious attitude. When she did not want to talk, she was impenetrable. She put the cup back onto the saucer with a clatter. The dimpled wood of the table was waxy and familiar under my fingers. She went to the stove and stirred the pots with a wooden spoon. "I think of my mother, Harry. She spent her life looking after people. Huddled over a hot fire, pounding flour, making bread, you name it. Killed herself. Hands like the hands of a laborer, she had. She died in that damn kitchen. But she kept the family together. Raised her children. That is what I will do, too."

The wooden spoon on the table was stained yellow with saffron. Two old iron *karhais* sat on the counter, ready for use on the stove. The windowsills were covered with rows of colored pebbles and stones, dried flowers, and perfectly preserved walnut shells. My mother saw beauty in everyday things. Dead things. There were lines of polished acorns in the bathroom, arranged along the side of the bath. She made wreaths from dried flowers and sticks and hung them on the backs of doors.

"I won't tell anyone," I said.

"Nothing is easy, Harry. I am making a reasonable effort. Life is never as simple as it seems when you are a child. You are not a child any longer, Harry. Neither is Alex." She stood at the stove with her back to me.

"Alex is like Ishfaq, isn't he?" I said. "He's sure about everything."

My mother nodded and continued stirring pots on the stove. When she turned, she was crying again. "We will all be together this evening," she said. "We will eat this food. Like a family."

"Right," I said. "Like a family."

That night it rained heavily, a solid downpour with no wind. After dinner, my mother put on a raincoat and went out to the fig tree, despite the protests of my father. Alex and I watched her walk out of the kitchen door and down the lawn. My father followed her with an umbrella open in his hands and tried to get her to come back inside. From the kitchen window, we watched our father's flashlight bobbing in the rain at the base of the tree. Eventually he trudged back up the hill alone, soaked, his shoes covered in mud, and told us to go to bed. That night I threw my window open and listened to rain hitting the river. I lay down and imagined my mother sitting up in the dripping leaves of the fig tree, clinging to the wet branches in the darkness, looking out into the Arabian Sea.

The Vietnam argument cast a pall over the house. The next day, Monday, my father left early to begin his morning operating list. Alex got up late and then went fishing in the boat. I ate lunch alone with my mother in the kitchen. We sat silently at the table with the World Service playing. I did not want to leave my mother alone, but I recognize now, with the benefit of hindsight, that she must have wanted to be alone.

After lunch, she packed up the leftover Indian food from the night before and asked me to drop it off at Peter and Gretchen Tappero's house. "They, at least, will appreciate it," she said and put bowls of food in a plastic carry bag that I slung over my shoulder. The Tapperos lived three miles down the river, and because it was a beautiful afternoon, my mother suggested I walk.

I used a path that went through a pine forest some of the way. The path was bone dry and sandy and under the trees I breathed in the warm summer smell of pine resin. Brief glimpses of the river were visible at the bottom of a steep hill. I came out of the trees and walked that last mile to the house along the main road. I was hot when I got there, and my glasses were fogging over.

The house was surrounded by forest. It was a mock Tudor cottage made of stone block, with a shingled roof and large bay windows at the front. It seemed strangely and inappropriately English in the grove of hot dry pines. Trees hung over the roof, making the house feel dark and slightly damp. The garden was unruly, with a long-untended piece of grass and several amorphous overgrown shrubs.

There was no doorbell. I knocked on the front door several times but no one answered, so I tried the door and found it open. I walked carefully inside and found myself in a dark hall. The house smelled of cooking food and some other perfume that I did not recognize. Drum music was playing loudly in the background, a heavy, pounding chorus that made me feel slightly disoriented.

It is surely revealing of my character that I did not simply leave the food and return home. But I was curious to see where Gretchen lived, so I walked carefully down the hall in front of me. One wall was lined with carved wooden masks that looked African. The masks depicted animals with long teeth and elongated ears, decorated with elaborately woven pieces of dry grass, beads, and animal hair. The living room wall was hung with thick rugs woven with intricate patterns, steel knives, clubs and sticks, and several carved plinths made of polished dark wood. There was an unruliness to the rooms, a lack of order and attention that I had never seen in a house before. Magazines, letters, and miscellaneous pieces of paper were piled onto chairs and covered the dining room table. Furniture took up all the available space: chests, high-backed chairs, and a long wooden bench that looked as if it had been cut from the single trunk of a tree. Three low couches sat in the living room, draped with pieces of bright frayed cloth. Pillows with embroidered covers lay on the floor. The rugs and pillows and the exotic clutter seemed quite original and bohemian to me, something that disregarded convention and suggested unspoken possibilities.

The drum music was coming from a reel-to-reel tape recorder sitting on the floor in one corner of the living room. The tape box was discolored and on the outside of the box "Drums of the Burundian Highlands" was written in pencil, and then a name, "Marceilline Ntkatikabora," and I decided that it was a home recording, made by someone who had gone and witnessed some kind of ceremony themselves.

There was no one in the room. A sliding glass door was open to the garden and I walked outside and stood on a stone patio. A row of carved wooden figures with dangling breasts and large round abdomens, and huge elephantine genitalia, stood along the patio. Then there was a piece of dry overgrown lawn, in which several rusty abstract iron figures had been placed, half obscured by the tall grass. Beyond the grass, the trees began, pressing in from all sides. A path led directly back into the trees. Tiny strips of colored cloth had been tied around the trunks of the trees along the path.

It was warm and still. The drum music through the open door and the strange statues made me feel as if I was standing at the outpost of a distant principality.

I went back inside and walked to the kitchen through a short hallway. The walls here were hung with framed photographs of people: a young boy holding a fish on a line; two girls wearing red and green head scarves, with babies on their backs; women laughing in front of straw mats piled with pyramids of oranges, potatoes, and peanuts for sale. There were three close portraits of men, unblinking and solemn, with brilliant white teeth and skin that was so black it was almost blue, looking into the camera as if it held the answer to something important. The men wore skullcaps, and had traditional scars in deep jagged rows on their foreheads and cheeks.

The kitchen was small and cramped. The sink was filled with pots and dishes and the counters were covered with vegetable peelings, paper bags, and bowls. Handwritten lists were taped to the side of the fridge — things to buy, things to do, birthdays. A small stainless-steel pot with a long spout sat on the stove and it was still hot. Through the window, I could see pine trees in the forest and a few fluffy white clouds blowing over a blue sky.

I went back into the living room and decided to wait. I admit to feeling a kind of forbidden pleasure in being in this strange house and I wanted to prolong the moment. I sat down on one of the large pillows on the floor by the sofas, still clutching the plastic bag of Indian food. I felt as if I was sitting inside a gaudy tent, surrounded by the spoils of war. It was a sensation that I recognized from my first camping trip, when I had slept away from home for the first time. On that trip, even the smallest of things, cooking and going to the toilet, and sleeping on the ground surrounded by nature, had seemed very different and interesting in unexpected ways. Just sitting on the floor seemed to change everything: how you saw a room, how you thought about things, what seemed important.

After a few minutes, I began to feel uncomfortable. I did not want Gretchen to find me sitting in her living room. The pounding music swirled around me. I got up again and went to the bottom of the stairs and called out. My voice was barely audible with the loud drum music playing. I walked up the stairs and onto a short landing covered in loose orange carpet. The door of the first room on the landing was open. It was an office room with a large desk and chairs, but it was empty. The next door was ajar and I knocked sharply with my knuckles. There was a kind of muffled answer, like someone calling out, and I imagined that it was Gretchen. I pushed open the door. Gretchen was sitting on the bed, quite naked, astride a man whose skin was very brown against the sheets. Her hair fell around her face and shoulders. She sat motionless, wide-eyed, staring at me. The sheets were very white in the sunlight through the windows. I recognized my brother immediately. I felt as if I was looking through a microscope, able to see a small and distant object very clearly for the first time. I clutched the bag of Indian food and stared at Alex, as foreign in that house as the African masks on the wall, lying under the pale, freckled body of my mother's best friend.

Now I am an ophthalmologist and specialize in disorders of the retina. I have given twenty years of my life to this mysterious and delicate profession and in that time have restored sight to many and watched blindness descend on some. My work is both an art and a science and is conducted under the microscope and in darkened rooms. My profession is a shelter and a retreat, I would be a blind man not to admit this fact, and acknowledge that I conceal myself within it. I have taken pleasure in the intricacies: the certainty of the anatomy, the fine precision of the surgery, the machine-tooled instruments.

I imagine that my life has turned on those seconds in 1968 when I stood at the threshold of that bedroom, looking in at my brother. The whole summer seemed to stop at that moment, and the chaos and disorder of my fourteenth year to be embodied in it. Everything dropped

away and I was left holding the only certainties that I had in my posses-
sion: a few principles of human anatomy; my father's collection of beetles
ordered by genus and species; and the heavy Koran, dormant and unread,
sitting under a pile of magazines in my closet.

My limited knowledge of the natural world seemed immediately
essential. It helped give substance to the disorder and laxity of the house
and garden around me, and I recognized, as I stood in the house that
day, how much I needed the untarnished certainty of these facts. Nothing made sense to me, least of all my brother, and I had an impulse to
impose order on my surroundings. This has stayed with me. It has led
me to look for firm truths in my own life. I have sought out boundaries
and parameters. I became an odd teenager. The world of my peers, a
world of popular music and television and fashion, and various fads,
seemed spurious to me. I did not notice women, and never had a girlfriend in high school. I spent my teenage years ordering my father's beetles and learning their biology. I went on field trips with my father to
collect new specimens. And I began reading the Koran, slowly at first, a
page or two a night, before I went to sleep.

What I did was this. I turned and went down the stairs and out into
the Tapperos' backyard, still clutching the bag of Indian food. The sky
was clear and deep blue and I walked down the path between the trees
at the back of the house. After five minutes or so, the path began to
slope downward. I followed it down, breathing deeply and beginning to
feel better away from the house. It became quite steep and I took long
strides down the hill and suddenly the path ended and opened into a
flat grassy area by the river. The river was brown and sluggish. A wooden
dock made of sunken wood piles and pine planks went out into the
water from the bank, and my father's boat was tied up there, bobbing
gently in the current.

I steadied myself against a tree and stood absolutely still. Pine resin
stuck to my fingers. The air was cool and I listened to the soft swish of
wind in the branches of the trees. The forest was alive with the sounds
of insects, invisible shiftings and movements that were just out of reach.
I had never been in the boat alone, but I climbed aboard, put the plas-

tic bag of food under the seat, and cast off. The boat rocked and bobbed under me. I secured the oars in their bolts and rowed upstream with clumsy, splashing strokes. As I rowed, I felt myself dwindling to nothing, becoming a pinpoint on the landscape, a part of a system that had an order and a forward movement, quite independent of anything I could say or do.

My father has been in the coronary-care unit of the Massachusetts General Hospital, my own hospital, for three days now and I sit with him as often as I can during the day, and most of the night as well. My parents were visiting me here in Boston when my father had the heart attack, sudden-onset left shoulder and jaw pain that came on when he was walking up the fire stairs to my apartment. He has been a very healthy man throughout his life, and has never had a problem with his heart. Now he tells me that he is quite ready to die. The attendings have shown me his EKGs and laboratory results, and I know that there is a chance that he will die. I managed to get him into the emergency room very quickly, but not quickly enough to prevent a great deal of muscle damage in the region of his left atrium and ventricle. Even as I write, his heart is throwing off volleys of abnormal beats and rhythms, and it is a run of these machine-gun beats that could carry him off.

He has become a moderately portly man, like many older Indian men, with a substantial girth and short thick legs. His chest is very brown in the hospital bed, tufted with gray hair and now adorned with a row of wire leads that run to the cardiac monitor that bleeps alongside him. The peaks and troughs of the tracing travel constantly across the dark screen, tiny mountains and valleys, day and night. I see myself in my father. I have the same small hands and feet, the same nose and mouth. And I recognize, too, that we share a certain unswerving commitment to principle and order. I have taken over his collection of beetles, now, and I file everything in my life according to strict systems. I have a room devoted entirely to filing cabinets. We have many similarities, and yet, at the same time, he is foreign to me. He comes from another time and another generation, from a pre-independence India that I never knew or understood. Sometimes when I see him in the light of day, wearing his Bermuda jackets and cravats and brogues, with pomade in his hair, he seems silly and out of place. I am amused when I see him deriving luxurious pleasure from a Havana cigar and a snifter of brandy, two of his regular indulgences.

He has a central venous line and they are giving him a pump infusion of morphine. On the night he came in, when he was moderately delirious from the morphine, he asked to see Alex. He said he wanted to tell Alex that he forgave him. He was persistent, and in the end I had to explain to him that Alex would not be coming to see him, but that I was sure he was thinking of him. This calmed my father for a while, and then later, when he came out of the morphine, he did not appear to remember this episode at all. The mention of my brother made me strangely nervous. It suggests to me that my father is sicker than he appears to be.

My mother has been quiet and busy. She is here during the day, and I have never seen her sitting down. I have insisted that she go and sleep in my apartment at night, while I sit with my father, and she has reluctantly agreed to this arrangement. At home, she has begun cooking Indian food in my small kitchen and then bringing in Tupperware containers of rice with chicken and vegetable curries for my father to eat. She has found an Indian store and buys supplies there. This morning she came in with large bags of *dalmoot* and *bhelpuri* as snacks, and this has made my father smile, although he will not eat any of it. I cannot tell what my mother is thinking. She always seems to be assured of his recovery, although I have explained to her the severity of my father's cardiac damage.

The nights are long and I cannot sleep sitting in the vinyl-covered chair in this hospital room. I listen to my father breathing and am filled with memories of my fourteenth year, and of Alex. In the darkest hours of the night, when all there is to see are the tossing trees outside the window, I understand why I am a Muslim. I have learned to have faith in a God that I will never see and cannot understand because I think this is what makes us human. Some things cannot be explained by reason alone.

Some things are quite beyond ordinary comprehension, I have resolved, birth and death, moral principles, right and wrong. I do not have any difficulties reconciling my belief in Islam with the principles of natural selection and basic biology. This is how I have learned to understand the differences between my father and mother.

I am far from a zealot and believe religion to be a private business. I still read the copy of the Koran that my mother gave me years ago, and this has become a worn and comfortable book, reassuring to the touch, much thumbed. I do pray, every day, in my own way, although not formally with a prayer mat, oriented toward Mecca. And I attend the mosque every week, too, for the company of others, and the pleasure of the ceremony, although I do not need a temple or a shrine for my belief.

But all of this was unknown to me that afternoon in August 1968 when I was fourteen years old, rowing my father's aluminum boat back up the river. I tied the boat up with difficulty, and then walked up the hill, toward the house.

My father had come home from work early and was sitting outside at the table under the pine tree. I told him quickly and precisely what I had seen. He sat with his palms flat on the table and stared out at the river. I sensed that he was holding some violent impulse inside him by sheer force of will. "Thank you, Harry," he said without looking at me, "for your honesty." I watched him in profile, the gentle hook of his nose, his long sloping forehead. Looking back, I can see that Alex's actions must have been somehow symbolic of everything that was wrong with the country at that time, of the lack of principles and discipline that he believed necessary.

He got up from the table and went inside to tell my mother. A few minutes later, they came outside together. My father had his arm around my mother's shoulders for the first time since I could remember. They were not talking to each other, and they did not say anything to me. We sat under the pine tree for about half an hour in silence, waiting for Alex to return. He finally arrived home and walked down toward us across the grass. He sat down with us under the tree and said, "I suppose Harry has told you," and I blushed and felt immediately guilty. My father nodded and then suggested that we go out on the boat. This was not something that we ever did as a family.

We went down to the river. My father held the boat steady while we all climbed into it from the dock. The breeze was strong and sharp and I shivered in my shorts and T-shirt. We sat down on the flat seats, and then my father got into the stern behind us. He pulled the cord of the outboard motor for five minutes before it kicked into life. We motored out onto the brown water, the surface rippled by the wind. In the open spaces between the trees on the bank, dense black clouds were visible on the horizon and sparks of lightning flashed on the flat country. A moist constant wind ran ahead of a storm front, and carried the scent of wet earth and hay toward us. Nothing was said, and Alex would not look at me. We went downstream for several miles along the bank. Then we came back up the river on the opposite side. My mother sat quite still and trailed her hand in the water, looking out toward the storm front. We repeated the process in the upstream direction, squinting into the wind, and I knew that my father was not looking at anything around us.

He stopped the boat in the middle of the river and turned off the engine. We rocked gently in the current. "Beautiful," my father said. "Quite beautiful. How lucky we are to live in this country." He was sitting behind us, talking to our backs. "I have worked hard to make this possible," he said, "and to give you boys a chance. This is what I have done. I have given you a chance." He shifted in his seat and the boat rocked violently for a moment. "I am not angry," he said. "But I will tell you this. There are certain principles that must be upheld for the sake of honor and decency. For the sake of this family." There was silence for a moment and then he said, "Alex must make amends. That is what he must do. He must do his duty."

We sat there for a few minutes more, silent on the brown water, and then rain began to fall. My father took us back to the dock. It was getting dark. Alex went to his room and I ate dinner alone with my parents at the kitchen table. When we were finished, I made my parents cups of strong black tea with milk and sugar. Then I put on a sweater and jacket and went outside and sat on the porch. Wind buffeted the maple trees along the side of the house. It was raining heavily now, a solid sheet of water that quickly filled the gutters and ran off the roof and splashed onto the porch. I looked out into the rain and imagined it the same way I imagined snow, each drop a perfect symmetry, a tiny perfection, shaped by physical forces that I could not completely understand. The water blew into my face and I suddenly understood what my father had meant when he had talked about duty. It was clear to me then, on that rain-swept porch, that Alex would be going to Vietnam.

When I was ten years old, my father took Alex and me running on the university football field on a cold day in October. He measured out one hundred meters with a tape measure and placed a piece of string along the finish line, strung between two garden stakes. The wind was freezing and I shivered as I knelt on the ground with Alex. We were barefoot and in shorts. My father stood by the finish line wearing a navy blue track-suit and heavy boots and a thick yellow scarf rolled up around his neck. He started us by waving a white handkerchief and shouting, "Run," then timed us with the Omega wristwatch that he had been given by his parents in India. He held his left wrist up in front of his face as we sprinted over the grass toward him.

Alex won every race. After four sprints, I was breathless and wheezing in the cold air, and my face felt numb. My father recorded our times in a palm-size notebook with tiny, cramped handwriting.

"Well done, well done," he said to Alex. "You are a natural athlete. You are faster than Harry. Very good." He clapped his hands together and blew steam in front of him and turned to me. "Harry, you are not try-ing. You have to want to win, partner. Quicker off the start, keep your eyes on the finish, keep your arms moving. Punch the air, Harry, punch the air. But you must want to win. It is very important, that."

I sat on the grass to get my breath and watched my father take off his boots and tracksuit pants. He was wearing white tennis shorts under-neath. His legs were short and fat, with heavy thighs, very brown in the pale light and dusted with tight black ringlets. He threw off the yellow scarf and jumped up and down a few times on the grass.

"Allow me to show you boys a thing or two," he said. "Let me show you how it is done, Harry. Let me limber up a little here." He did several squats with his arms raised above his head and then three vigorous push-ups. His feet were small and pale. When he jumped on the spot with his arms scissoring, his gut bounced under his shirt. "Warm-up is important, boys. And the mental attitude."

"Are you going to run?" Alex asked.

"Of course I am. I am going to be racing you."

He took off his wristwatch and gave it to me. "You time us, Harry. Watch the second hand carefully." I drew an extra column in the notebook and wrote "Ishfaq" at the top of it with the blue fountain pen. The ink smudged a little under my fingers and I blew on the page to dry the ink. When my brother and father were ready, I held the watch up and started them. My father heaved down the grass toward me with his forearms and fists swinging. His thighs shook and his thick hair blew high above his head. As he ran, he made a hissing sound through pursed lips. Alex looked tiny alongside him, his legs fragile and light. They raced up toward me against the wind and my father hit the string with his chest first. He won three times.

"Mental attitude, boys," he said. "I am an old fellow, but I have the attitude. Notice how I use my arms. This is the way to do it." He puffed and sweated in the cold air as we got dressed. My father's winning times were all five or ten seconds slower than those of Alex when he had been running against me a few minutes before. Alex had let him win. In the notebook, I made up my father's times to be faster than any Alex had managed: 10.3, 10.5, 10.3. I wrote the false times into the column under "Ishfaq" in small neat figures, and was careful that they did not smudge. I did not look at Alex as we pulled on trousers and shoes in the cold afternoon. We walked home under a gray sky and I understood that we had created a moment that would last forever, as clear and crisp as the blue numbers that I had written into the notebook with the fountain pen of my father. I knew that Alex had understood, too, and that we had shared something that we could never talk about.

My father did not let us go inside until my mother had taken a photograph of the three of us outside in our tracksuits. He got a comb from inside and pulled his hair back off his face, then stood between us with his arms around our shoulders. I shivered in the cold air and tried to smile. My mother's long hair spun in the wind as she held the camera up to her face. She took the photo with us standing against the side of the house. "The great legacy of the British, boys," my father said to us as we stood huddled on the grass, "is that they understood the importance of sport. Games are everything. Games teach us to play by the rules. Games give us order and discipline. This is what life is all about. Rules."

This photograph is on the bedside table in my father's hospital room. It is in a flat wooden frame, and it is the only picture that my father has with him. I have looked at the photograph in the light of day. Alex and I look young and happy. Our faces are pinched by the wind and my father is pulling us toward him. There is something euphoric about the picture and I understand that when we let my father win that day, we were letting him win for this moment, for the moment when we would see him filled with energy and light. Last night I took the wooden backing off the picture frame, and found the original page from the notebook in which I had recorded the false sprint times. The blue ink has faded and the page is yellowing. When I look at my own awkward childish handwriting, across the distance of forty years, I realize that an instant can change everything that comes after.

My father drove Alex to the recruiting station in Des Moines himself. I sat in the back of the car on the cool seat and watched the flat farming country slip past the windows. The war was not real to me, was not real to any of us, despite the television images and the casualty figures. It was only much later that we understood what it all meant, and learned about its particular horrors and futilities. My mother disappeared into the background. There was an unspoken understanding between her and my father, something that brought them together in a silent way that I sensed came from their past in India, and that they alone shared. I do not know what transpired between Gretchen Tappero and my mother, but I know that she never again came to the house. When

Peter came, he came alone, and never for dinner, and my mother avoided him.

Alex believed in what he was doing. He told me not to worry, and approached his military service the way he attacked sport; he had a sense of invulnerability like any nineteen-year-old, and imagined that because he was faster and stronger, he would stand above others. I knew even then that he took my father at his word, and believed that he had to make amends for his behavior. He was assigned to the Third Battalion of the Twenty-Sixth Marines and went into the field in late 1969. He was a regular and diligent correspondent and I have all of his letters filed.

The hospital room is white and sterile. My father reads the paper when he is awake and demands to see his own charts and test results. Doctors are notoriously bad patients. My mother chastises him, in her familiar way, and tells him to relax and concentrate on getting better. She has brought in her shortwave radio so my father can listen to the BBC, a habit that he acquired from her. Now he sits propped on pillows with the device held to his ear and the long silver antenna extended, cursing at the progress of the Kashmir peace talks between India and Pakistan.

At night, when my father is asleep, I take comfort in the knowledge that I have made my own way. I am an educated man and believe I do some good for people. I have a familiarity with the posterior segment of the eye that most men do not, and I can restore vision with this knowledge and my surgical skills. I have had several close women friends, some of whom I think entertained the possibility of marriage, but I have never been able to imagine it. It is not that I was not close to them, or that they did not like me, but rather that, ultimately, I do not need them in my life. I have my religion and my profession and my memories.

I imagine I am still with my brother by remembering him. Sometimes I dream about Alex with such vividness and clarity that I am absolutely certain, at the moment of waking, that he is there with me. I was already sixteen when the soldier in dress uniform came to give us the news of his death. The house was silent and empty. I sat with my parents and had the sensation that a part of myself was lost. I went and sat in Alex's bedroom and tried to hold on to the moment when I had last seen him. Later I corresponded with another boy who had been in his battalion and learned what had happened. They had been on patrol in eastern Quang Tri province and were ambushed late one afternoon. Alex had made a run for it into the jungle and managed to break away. He was sprinting down a jungle path when he stepped on an antipersonnel mine that blew his right leg away beneath the knee. They found him there, and got tourniquets around his leg, and then radioed for an airlift. He was taken to the evacuation hospital at Chulai and then on to Saigon. They got his leg stabilized but missed his ruptured spleen and he bled to death in a hospital bed, late one night, before they could do anything for him. He was alone then, as I am now.

Sitting with my dying father at night, what I see most clearly is that moment by the Iowa River all those years ago. I had just walked down from the Tapperos' house with the bag of Indian food in my hands. I heard the rustle of pines by the side of the river and smelled pine resin on my fingers. The wind in the trees was like a vague understanding, a whispered suggestion. I recognize that everything might have been different if I had not told my father about Alex. Perhaps my life would have followed a different path. Perhaps my brother would be alive today.

Now I listen to the breath in my father's lungs ebb and flow, and remember the feeling of triumph as I climbed aboard the boat and rowed upriver. It is the only time in my life that I have felt such triumph, and the last time. What manner of triumph was this? I saw instantly that what my brother was doing was wrong. But my sense of triumph came not from this, but from the sudden recognition that my father was right — right about Gretchen and the failings of a world without principles. It was an instant of belief in my father that I still carry — something so illuminating to me, so right, that I wanted my mother to share it, so that she, too, would see my father in a different light. I was only fourteen years old when I resolved that there were certain immutable laws that should never be broken, and that by telling my brother's secret I would be able to keep my parents together forever. I wanted to keep my parents together more than anything in the world, to unite them in a common cause, to hold them as they appeared in the old sepia-toned photographs from their youth.

I still believe that I took the only acceptable course. What is life without principles? What are we without strict codes of conduct? I am an old man, perhaps. Like many old men, I feel certain that we must accept the character we are born with. This is clear to me now, surprisingly so. It is as clear to me as this white hospital room. I must be accepting of my fate, my character. In the still hours of the night, when I am quite alone, I can see this. In the still hours of the night, I understand the truth about myself: that I am no different from my father, that after everything I have become him, that there is no escaping the destiny that each of us brings into the world.